John Mills

A Treatise on Cattle

John Mills

A Treatise on Cattle

ISBN/EAN: 9783337330583

Printed in Europe, USA, Canada, Australia, Japan

Cover: Foto ©Andreas Hilbeck / pixelio.de

More available books at **www.hansebooks.com**

A TREATISE ON CATTLE:

Shewing the most approved Methods of

BREEDING, REARING, AND FITTING FOR USE,

HORSES,	SHEEP,
ASSES,	GOATS,
MULES,	and
HORNED CATTLE,	SWINE;

With DIRECTIONS for

The proper Treatment of them in their several Disorders:

To which is added,

A DISSERTATION on their CONTAGIOUS DISEASES.

Carefully collected from the best AUTHORITIES, and interspersed with REMARKS,

By JOHN MILLS, Esq.

Fellow of the Royal Society of London, Honorary Member of the Dublin Society, of the Royal Societies of Agriculture at Paris and Rouen, of the Oeconomical Society of Berne, and of the Palatine Academy of Sciences and Belles-Lettres.

DUBLIN:

Printed for W. WHITESTONE, J. POTTS, J. HOEY, W. COLLES, W. WILSON, R. MONCRIEFFE, T. WALKER, C. JENKIN, and C. TALBOT.

MDCCLXXVI.

THE

PREFACE.

THIS Work was firſt written ſeveral years ago, and delivered to the Publiſher, in order to its being printed then as a Continuation of my Syſtem of Huſbandry: but, unhappily for Mr. Johnſon, a dreadful fire conſumed his houſe in Pater-noſter Row, together with his valuable Stock in Trade, and my comparatively inſignificant manuſcript. A rough Copy of it chancing, however, to remain among my other papers, for it is ſeldom that I can reſt ſatisfied with the firſt writing of any thing that is to be laid before the Public, at his requeſt I ſat about recompoſing it, as ſpeedily as an infirm ſtate of health, and ſome unavoidable avocations which intervened, would permit. The Treatiſe now offered to the Public is the reſult of that ſecond labour; in the proſecution of which, the moſt approved writers of different countries, and the practical experience of ſome judicious friends in this, have been my principal guides. To theſe laſt in particular, I owe an acceſſion of new materials, which were not in my former Copy, and by means of which this is conſiderably enlarged,—I hope, to the advantage of the Public. Happy ſhall I eſteem myſelf, if the execution of this part of my undertaking ſhould meet with the ſame approbation as my Five former Volumes have been honoured with.

Persuaded, as I am, that no people in the world excel, or perhaps even equal, the English in the whole of what relates to the management of Cattle in general; yet from a conviction that even the most experienced may gather at least useful hints from the different practices of other nations, I have occasionally shewn wherein any such differ from us in matters of importance, pointed out the grounds of that difference, and endeavoured to investigate the reasons on which it is founded. Likewise, wherever I have quoted, or borrowed from either ancient or modern writers, I have always mentioned the place referred to; and if, as hath not unfrequently been the case, I have seen cause to differ from them, I have assigned the reasons for my dissent.

It is chiefly, indeed, from what relates to the proper treatment of the various Accidents and Diseases to which all sorts of Cattle are liable, that I flatter myself the greatest utility may be derived from this work; and in that, besides the instructions I have been favoured with by a gentleman of great ability in the practice of Surgery, as well as deeply skilled in Medicine, I am confident, that neither of those excellent writers, Sir John Pringle, Bart. and Mr. Samuel Sharpe, will be offended at the liberty I have taken in applying to the brute Creation in similar cases, the plain and easy directions which they have given for the cure of the human species. They nobly aim at doing universal good; and will certainly agree with me, that, next to Man, Cattle are justly entitled to our tenderness and care, in return for the essential benefits we receive from them.

This naturally leads me to regret, that we have not in this Country some Institution like that of the Veterinarian School at Lyons, which is, by

Royal Authority, under the Inspection of a very able Surgeon and good Physician, M. Bourgelat, of whose superior intelligence the reader will find repeated proofs in this work. Humanity is shocked at the barbarity and ignorance of the generality of Farriers; and it were greatly to be wished, that men of education and skill would cease to think the healing of Cattle an object beneath their notice. Almost every nation in Europe now sends pupils to the Royal Veterinarian School at Lyons; and even supposing a pecuniary return to be the principal object aimed at by those who shall have completed their studies in that, or any similar Seminary, it cannot be doubted that their wishes would be amply gratified.

Having before mentioned the Five Volumes of my System of Husbandry, which were published some years ago, I gladly embrace this opportunity to inform the Public, that the impression being now disposed of, and numbers expressing a desire to see it reprinted, a new Edition of it is now on the point of being sent to the Press, in which all possible care has been taken to rectify the Errors that have been pointed out, and those which I have myself discovered, in the former Edition; to enrich it with the essential improvements that have since been made in the several branches of Agriculture, particularly the various new instruments invented for that purpose; to fit it more completely than before, for the use of the *Practical Husbandman*, and in a word, to render it more worthy of the Notice and Encouragement of the Public.

CON-

CONTENTS.

BOOK I.

Sect.

A TREA-

A

TREATISE

ON

CATTLE.

BOOK I.

Of Horses.

TO treat this ſubject with the greater clearneſs and preciſion, I ſhall divide it into three general parts, or chapters: The firſt will contain directions for judging of the qualities of Horſes, and conſequently for chooſing them, from their outward form and appearances; the ſecond will relate to the breeding, rearing, and fitting them for uſe; and the third, will be appropriated to their ſeveral diſeaſes, diſtinguiſhing, firſt, thoſe which proceed from internal cauſes; and, ſecondly, ſuch as are external; with the proper methods of cure in either caſe.

The epidemics, to which all ſorts of beaſts are expoſed, and the beſt means that experience has hitherto pointed out for guarding againſt, and curing the infection, will be carefully ſummed up in a ſubſequent part of this volume.

CHAP. I.

How to judge of Horſes.

IN order to judge of a Horſe from his outward appearance, it is neceſſary to examine attentively the conformation of his ſeveral parts, eſpecially his eyes, his mouth, his neck, his ſhoulders, and his legs, if it be a draught-horſe; and alſo his flanks and croup if it be a Saddle-horſe: likewiſe, to obſerve carefully his manner of ſtanding and of going, his appetite, his defects, and his age.

But as many of thoſe for whom this work is chiefly intended, I mean particularly Huſband-men, may not be acquainted with the various technical terms which muſt neceſſarily occur in the courſe of this ſubject; and as a horſe cannot be deſcribed in a manner ſatisfactory to ſuch readers, without previouſly explaining the ſenſe of thoſe terms, defining the ſeveral parts of his body, and noticing their perfections and defects; it will be proper, before I proceed farther, to give here an explanation of ſome of the leaſt generally known, though not leaſt important to be underſtood. To this end, I ſhall begin with the horſe's head, from thence proceed to his body, and, which ſeems to me the moſt natural way, though the generality of writers have not obſerved it, conclude with his extremities, which are the fore and hind trains.

The two parts of a horſe's head which anſwer to the *temples* in man, are called by the ſame name.

The cavities between the eyes and ears, above the eye-brows, are called the *eye-pits*.

In ſome caſes, two parts only are diſtinguiſhed in the *eye*, namely, the external and the internal. The former is the outward coat or tunicle, and the latter

thoſe

those parts which are seen by looking into the eye through the chrystalline humour, by the aperture of the pupil: but it surely is wrong to extend the meaning of the word pupil to the inside of the eye, as some have done; the pupil being, in fact, only an aperture of the uvea, communicating with the inward parts of the eye.

The parotid glands, which are situated between the ear and the locking of the under jaw, are called the *vives*.

The part which is contained between the eyes and the nostrils is called the *face*, and answers to the part called the nose in man.

The cartilage which forms the circular aperture of the nostrils, and terminates them above and below, is called the *rim of the nostrils*.

The tip of the horse's *nose* is the septem which divides his nostrils, and is formed by the lower parts of the face, terminating at the upper lip. M. de Solleysel indeed extends the name of nose to that part also of the upper lip which is under the nostrils.

The cavity formed by the two bones of the lower jaw, reaching from the throat to the beard, is called the *channel*; as is also that in which the tongue lies.

With regard to the teeth, which will be more particularly noticed when I come to speak of the age of horses; different names have been given to the six incisory ones in each jaw.

The two fore teeth are called *gatherers*; those adjoining to the gatherers are called *middle teeth*, and the last on each side are termed the *corner teeth*.

The two canine teeth in each jaw, one on each side, and at some distance from the incisories, are called *tushes*.

The vacant spaces in the two jaws, between the incisory and the maxillary teeth, are called *bars*.

The *crest* is that part of the neck which is terminated or bordered by the mane above, and the throat below.

The *withers* begin where the mane ends, and cover the upper parts of the two ſhoulders.

The capacity formed by the ribs is called the *cheſt*; but the lower part of the body is called the *belly*.

The *flanks* are at the extremity of the belly, at the end of the ribs, and under the kidneys: they reach to the beginning of the haunches.

The *haunch* is formed by the bone which, in a horſe, terminates the upper part of the flank, and extends to the rump, or croup,

The *rump* extends from the kidneys to the tail.

The *tail* is diſtinguiſhed into two parts, viz. the *hair* and the *dock*. The dock is the fleſhy part of the tail without it's hair.

The *buttocks* are ſituated under the rump and the origin of the tail, and extend to the place where the hind leg joins the body.

To explain the names given to the different parts of the fore legs, we muſt now return to the *ſhoulder*. This, among horſemen, includes the ſhoulder-blade, and the humerus; conſequently the parts which anſwer to the ſhoulder and arm of a man: for the real arm of a horſe ſeems blended or confounded by the ſhoulders being united with the body under the ſame ſkin.

The *elbow* is placed backward, as in man; but in a horſe it is ſituated oppoſite to the ribs, at the top of the fore leg, where that leg begins to ſeparate from the body. This is the firſt joint that appears prominent; for that of the arm, with the ſhoulder, is hidden by the ſkin of the animal.

The firſt part of a horſe's fore leg, ſeparated from the body, is called the *arm*, though it anſwers to what is called the fore-arm in man. The external part of a horſe's arm is called the thick part of the arm, and over it's internal ſurface runs a vein called the *plat vein*.

The joint called the *knee*, is ſituated at the extremity of the arm, and at the place of the wriſt in man; and, when the leg is bent, it forms an angle forwards.

The

The *shank* is the second part of the fore leg. It begins at the articulation of the knee, and answers to the metacarpus in man. Behind the shank is a tendon which reaches from one end of it to the other, and which is commonly called the *back sinew*.

The *fetlock joint* is the articulation at the lower extremity of the shank: the ankle-joint of a horse.

The *fetlock* is a tuft of hair which covers a kind of soft gristle behind the pastern joint.

The *pastern* is that part of the leg which reaches from the fetlock joint to the foot.

The *coronet* is an elevation at the lower extremity of the pastern, garnished with long hair, which falls round the foot.

The *hoof* is as it were the nail of the horse: the fore part of it is called the *toe*, and it's sides are termed the *quarters*. The hind part of the hoof is a little raised, and divided into two parts, both included under the name of *heel*. They extend to the middle of the under part of the foot, and, re-uniting under the sole, which is as it were the bottom of the foot, from what is called the *frog*. This is a horny substance like the rest of the foot, of which it is indeed a part; but the horn of the sole is harder than that of the frog, and softer than that of the hoof.

To explain the names of the several parts which compose the hind legs, we must return to the buttocks. Each of these contains what is called the thigh in man: therefore the buttock is properly the horse's thigh articulated to the body. It is terminated on the fore part by the *stiffle*, which is properly the articulation of the knee, and contains the *knee-pan*. Thus the stiffle is placed at the lower extremity of the haunch, at the beginning of the flank, and changes it's place as the horse moves.

The upper part of a horse's hind leg, when detached from the body, is called the *thigh*: it extends from the stiffle and extremity of the buttocks to the ham, and answers to the leg in man. Accordingly there is on the thigh of a horſe, a fleſhy part reſembling the calf of a human leg. On the inward ſurface of the thigh runs a vein called the *crural vein*.

The *ham*, or *hock*, is the joint which bends forward at the extremity of the thigh. This articulation correſponds with the tarſus in man. The hinder part of the joint called the *point of the hock*, is properly the heel. What is commonly called the *great ſinew*, which terminates at the point of the hock, is a tendon anſwering to the *tendo Achillis* inſerted in the human heel.

The *cheſnut* is a little bare knob in each of the legs of a horſe, of the conſiſtence of ſoft horn, about the bigneſs of a cheſnut, and nearly of the ſame figure; from whence it has it's name. In the fore legs, it's poſition is within the arm, a little above the knee, and on one ſide of it; but in the hind legs; a little below the ham, and on one ſide of it, alſo on the internal part. In ſome horſes it grows to the length of an inch, or an inch and a half, and then falls off, but ſoon after ſhoots out again.

Under that part of the hind leg which is called the hock, is the *ſhank*, then the *paſtern joint*, next the *paſtern*, and then the *foot*, as in the fore legs.

After this explanation, it is of little conſequence whether the horſe be divided into three principal parts, viz. the forehand, the body, or carcaſe, and the hind-hand; or into four, viz. the head, the body, the fore-train, and the hind train; * it being ſufficient to know what particular part is meant when it is

* In the former of theſe diviſions, the fore-hand includes the head, neck, withers, breaſt, and fore-legs; the body is compoſed of the back, kidneys, ribs, belly, and flanks; the hind-hand comprehends the rump, haunches, tail, buttocks, ſtiffle, thighs, hocks, and the other parts of the hind legs: and in the latter, where the head alone is conſidered as one of the four principal diviſions, the back, the kidneys, the belly, the ribs, and the flanks compoſe the body; the fore-train is formed of the neck, the ſhoulders, the breaſt, and fore-legs; and the hind-train, of the rump, the tail, the haunches, and the hind legs.

named,

named, and, which I ſhall next endeavour to point out, to be able to judge from the appearance of that part, whether it is, or is not, properly formed.

In a fine horſe, the head muſt be lean and ſlender, and not too long; the ears ſmall, erect, narrow, thin, ſteady, well placed on the top of the head, and at a proper diſtance from each other; the forehead narrow: the eye-pits filled; the eye-lids thin; the eyes clear, briſk, and full of fire, rather large than ſmall, and projecting to a level with the head; the eye-balls large; the under jaw bare of fleſh and not thick; the noſe a little arched; the noſtrils large and open; the partition between the two noſtrils ſmall; the lips thin, and the mouth of a middling ſize. The upper part of the creſt, where the mane iſſues, neareſt to the withers, ſhould at firſt riſe in a ſtrait line, and afterwards, as it approaches towards the head, form a curve nearly reſembling that of the ſwan's neck; but the under part of neck ſhould not form a curve, it's proper direction being in a ſtrait line from the cheſt to the lower jaw, with only a little bending forward; for a perpendicular direction would render the ſhape of the neck faulty. The upper part of the neck muſt alſo be ſlender, and thin of fleſh towards the mane, which ſhould be compoſed of fine long hair, but not too thick. The neck muſt be long and raiſed, but proportioned to the height of the animal; for if it be too long and ſlender, the horſe is apt to toſs his head; and when it is too ſhort and fleſhy, he is apt to bear heavy on the hand. The attitude of the head and neck contributes more than any other part of the body to give the horſe a noble carriage, and the moſt graceful poſition of the head is when the face is perpendicular to the horizon. The withers ſhould be raiſed and ſharp; the ſhoulders thin, flat, and not confined; the back equal and ſmooth, forming a ſmall convexity during it's whole length, by a riſing on each ſide of the back-bone: the flanks ſhould be full and ſhort; the croup round and full; the haunches plump; the dock, or fleſhy part of the tail, thick and firm; the arms and thighs thick and fleſhy; the fore part of the knee round; the ham large and rounded; the ſhank ſharp before, and large on the ſides; the ſinew well detached; the paſtern joint ſlender; the fetlock thinly garniſhed with hair; the paſtern large and of a middling length; the coronet a little raiſed; the hoof black, ſmooth, and ſhining; the inſtep high; the quarters round; the heels broad, and ſomewhat raiſed; the frog ſmall and thin; the ſole thick and concave.*

But as it is in very few horſes that all theſe external perfections are united, and in ſtill much fewer that goodneſs is joined with them; I ſhall proceed to what is by far moſt commonly the caſe, and accordingly give here, chiefly from M. de Buffon's Natural Hiſtory and Deſcription of the Horſe, with the addition of ſome very pertinent remarks in the *Maiſon ruſtique*, which ſeem to have eſcaped the notice of that juſtly celebrated writer, the reſult of the obſervations by which thoſe univerſally acknowledged excellent judges of horſes, M. de Solleyſel, M. de Garſault, and M. de la Guereniere, have pointed out the means of diſcovering the defects, and judging of the blemiſhes which disfigure moſt of theſe animals, eſpecially in their capacity of ſaddle-

* The curious, eſpecially the Germans, make an anatomical compariſon of the horſe with ſome parts of a woman, and of different animals; and that compariſon conſtitutes the deſcription of a perfect horſe. They ſay then, that a horſe, to be good, ought to have three parts of a woman, a wide cheſt, plump buttocks, and long hair; three of the lion, the ſtatelineſs, the boldneſs, and the fire; three of the bull, the eye, the noſtril, and the joint; three of the ſheep, the noſe, the mildneſs, and the patience; three of the mule, the ſtrength, the perſeverance in labour, and the foot; three of the ſtag, the head, the leg, and the ſhort hair; three of the wolf, the breaſt, the neck, and the hearing; three of the fox, the ear, the tail, and the trot; three of the ſnake, the memory, the ſight, the moulding; and three of the hare or cat, the running, the ſtep, and the ſuppleneſs. *Mais. Ruſt. Tom.* I, *Part* I, *Liv.* III, *Chap.* I.

horſes

horſes; for with regard to ſuch as are intended for the uſes of huſbandry, which are here my principal object, and by which I mean all ſuch common horſes as are employed in the country, for the cart, the plough, the ſaddle, and ſometimes the coach; it is ſufficient that they be ſound and ſtrong, that they draw well and freely, and that they be not vicious. The delicacy of ſhape which is required in the former, would render theſe laſt abſolutely incapable of performing the eſſential ſervices to which they are deſtined.

When a horſe has a large and ſquare *head*, in which caſe it is ſaid to be ill ſhaped, and commonly heavy on the hand, he cannot have an air of dignity or beauty; but he is, from that very circumſtance, the fitter for draught. If there be ſo much fat on it as that he may be claſſed with thoſe called fat heads, he will be ſubject to diſorders in his eyes. Another defect is, for the head to be too long. When the tip of the noſe is not in a perpendicular direction with the forehead, the horſe carries his head ill; and when the upper part of the head riſes above the curvature of the neck, the head is ſaid to be ill placed.

From the motion of a horſe's *ears* may be gathered a pretty ſure indication of his temper and preſent condition. When he travels, the tip of his ears ſhould be directed forward; for a tired horſe flags his ears, and ſuch as are vicious and ſpiteful, carry one ear forward and the other backward, alternately. All direct their ears towards the place where they hear any noiſe, and when ſtruck on the back or croup, they turn them backwards. Thick lapping ears are unſightly. When the diſtance between them is too great, eſpecially at the lower part, they are ill placed; and when they are not nearer to each other at the tip than at the root, the horſe's hearing is defective. Another fault is, for the horſe to be continually lowering his ears like a pig.

A low and hollow *front*, or *forehead*, is a great blemiſh in a ſaddle-horſe; but thoſe which are ſo made generally work well.

Many hold it to be a defect in a horse which is neither white nor gray, not to have a *star* in the forehead: but we shall soon shew, when we come to speak of the colours of horses, that the want of this mark, is not in reality any defect at all, and that it is easily made by art.

A horse with a large *eye*, projecting as it were out of his head, has a dull and stupid look; and small hallow eyes, besides giving him a melancholy aspect, never enable him to see well: but yet it would be wrong absolutely to reject a common horse for either of these imperfections, or for his having high eye-brows, which are looked upon as a mark of spitefulness; because those which are so made, commonly labour well and long.

Great accuracy is requisite in examining a horse's eyes, in order to be assured that his sight is good; for they are subject to several defects, which it is sometimes very difficult to discover. The person who examines them should stand near the light, but at the same time take care that he himself be shaded. The common practice of moving the hand before the eye, to observe whether the horse will shut it, is but a doubtful trial; as the impression of the air agitated by that motion, may make the horse close his eye without his perceiving any object: neither is the custom of looking at the eye, to see whether the cornea reflects objects like a mirror, much more to be depended on; because this effect will be produced if the cornea is bright, which it may be in a very bad eye, even without being transparent. It is therefore necessary to be sure of this transparency, or, in other words, to know whether the vitreous humour be turbid, or of a bad colour, instead of being clear and transparent; for in order to afford a distinct view of the pupil, it must be diaphanous. When the vitreous humour is turbid or suffused, it is an indication of the horse's being subject to fluxions. If this disease has vitiated the eye to a certain degree,

gree,

gree, it will be ſmaller than the other; which ſhews that it waſtes, and conſequently is abſolutely ſpoiled. An eye may indeed be good, though apparently ſmaller than the other, from the pupil's having been contracted by ſome accident; but then it is neither turbid nor brown. If a ſmall white ſpot, called by horſemen the *dragon*, be diſcerned at the hollow of the eye, the ſight of the eye is loſt beyond recovery; that ſpot encreaſing in time ſo as to affect the pupil. When the pupil appears of a greeniſh white, it is a defect, though not always attended with the loſs of ſight; and when there is more white in it than green, the horſe is ſaid to have a wall-eye. Sometimes, two or three ſoot-coloured ſpots appear above the ball, through the cornea of a ſound eye; but theſe ſpots cannot be diſcovered unleſs the cornea be clear, pure, and tranſparent. It's appearing double, or of a bad colour, is a ſure ſign that the eye is not good. Alſo if the ball of the eye be ſmall, long, and narrow, ſurrounded with a ring either white or of a greeniſh-blue colour, the eye may with certainty be deemed bad, and the ſight indifferent. The ſame judgment may likewiſe be paſſed, at leaſt generally, on ſuch as are ſunk in their ſockets, or one of whoſe balls is ſmaller than the other.

There are alſo temporary diſeaſes, which affect the ſight for a time only; ſuch as the ſtrangles, the coming of the foal-teeth, and of the tuſhes of the upper jaw.

When the two bones of the *under jaw* are too much loaded with fleſh, they are ſaid to be ſquare, and conſidered as a deformity: but if they are too near each other, and the *channel* between them not ſufficiently broad or hollow, it is a defect; becauſe the horſe, by not being able to bring together the bony ſepa of this channel on each ſide of his throat, which is called *brilding*, is prevented from carrying a fine head, unleſs the neck be thin in proportion to the contraction of the channel. If any tumor be perceived in this channel, it denotes a diſeaſe.

From a horſe's *mouth* being too large or too ſmall, ariſes an inconvenience with regard to placing the bit: in the former caſe, it comes too near the grinders or maxillary teeth; and in the latter, it either bears on the tuſhes, or cauſes humours in the lips. If the *lips* are too large and fleſhy, they cover the bars, and hinder the effect of the bit. When the *bars* of the palate are too fat and thick, the horſe feels the bit too ſenſibly: but it is to be obſerved, that the palate and gums are leſs fleſhy in old horſes than in young ones. The bars ſhould be raiſed, and the channel ſhould be ſufficient for containing the tongue within it, ſo high as to feel the bit. It is a fault for the bars to be too ſharp, their ſenſibility being then too great; and if, on the other hand, they are too low, round, and fleſhy, the ſenſibility is too little. The *tongue* ſhould be proportioned to the capacity of the channel in which it is placed: if it is ſo thick as to riſe above the bars, it is a fault, and hinders the impreſſion of the bit. Horſes whoſe mouths are dry, are not of ſo good a conſtitution as thoſe whoſe mouths are cool, and froth with the bit; neither do they feed ſo quickly, nor with ſo much appetite. A draught-horſe is not, however, to be rejected becauſe he is hard mouthed; it being often found that ſome draw the better for it.

The *beard* is alſo a part which contributes not a little to the goodneſs of the mouth. If the two bones which compoſe it are too diſtant from each other, and too little prominent, it will, from it's flatneſs, want ſenſibility; the curb then being only on one of it's ſides: but when, on the contrary, they are too near each other, and alſo project too much, it is too prominent, and conſequently too ſenſible; the curb bearing then only on the middle part. In ſhort, if the beard be either too hairy, or too fleſhy, or if it has any calloſities or knobs, theſe are faults, which indicate that the horſe has either too little ſenſibility; or that proper care has not been taken in riding him.

Ill

Ill ſhaped *necks* have been diſtinguiſhed into three kinds; the *reverted neck*, the *falſe neck*, and the *inclining neck*: the firſt is alſo called the ſtag-neck, being ſhaped like the neck of that animal, and forming a convexity forward, from the head to the breaſt: the falſe neck is ſtraight all along the throat; and behind, above the withers; is a cavity, from whence it is alſo called the hatchet neck: the inclining neck is that which ſeems to incline more to one ſide than the other, occaſioned by a ſuperabundance of fleſh on one ſide near the mane.

A draught-horſe is not at all the worſe for his neck being a little thick and fleſhy, and frequently he is the better for it's being rather low, and even inclining.

Mares are the more eſteemed for having a ſomewhat thick and fleſhy neck.

Stonehorſes have always larger necks than either mares or geldings.

Thick and buſhy *manes* which overload the neck, and ſometimes even make it incline, are very unſightly.

When the *withers* are too round and fleſhy, the ſhoulders want freedom, and the ſaddle is apt to rub them, ſo as frequently to cauſe very painful and dangerous ulcers: yet horſes which are employed in carrying heavy loads, ſhould not have the withers too high.

Horſes whoſe points of the *ſhoulders* are large and round, and the ſhoulders themſelves too large and fleſhy, are heavy, apt to ſtumble, and, unleſs their ſhoulders have an eaſy motion, are proper only for drawing. Thoſe which, beſides the above defects, have alſo the joints on each ſide of the breaſt large and prominent, are likewiſe fit for nothing but draught; for there the weight of their ſhoulders is of advantage, by enabling them to draw with the greater force; and their being fleſhy, helps to preſerve them from being galled by the harneſs ſo much as they would otherwiſe be. When they are ſo narrow and contracted about the ſhoulders, as that the fore legs almoſt touch each other at the top, the horſe is ſaid to be weak forward; and, in travelling he is apt to entangle his legs ſo as to fall. Pinned ſhoulders, by which is meant thoſe which ſeem ſtiff, bound, and motionleſs, give a heavy and uneaſy motion to a horſe, and expoſe him to ſtumble, and ſoon ſpoil his legs: moſt horſes which want fleſh on their ſhoulders are of this kind, and conſequently unable to bear any great fatigue; though ſome, even with ſuch ſhoulders, carry their feet well, the above motion proceeding only from the arm.

A broad and open *breaſt* gives a heavy look to large horſes; but would not be conſidered as a defect in thoſe that are ſlender, the breaſt in theſe laſt being generally too narrow.

Another defect in a ſaddle-horſe is, for the breaſt to project and hang over much beyond his legs; becauſe he then reſts heavily on the hand, eſpecially when he gallops, and is very apt to ſtumble and fall. But neither of the above is a defect of any conſequence in a draught-horſe: on the contrary, he perhaps draws the better for both; at leaſt his breaſt ſhould certainly be wide and open.

The ſhorter a horſe's *back* is, the better he gallops on his haunches, but he does not walk ſo well; and the rider ſuffers from the centre of motion being too near the ſaddle. If the back is long, the horſe walks with more eaſe, having a greater freedom with his legs; but galloping is more difficult to him. A low, or ſaddle-back; gives a horſe lightneſs, and is an advantage to a fine fore-hand; for his neck is raiſed, and he carries his head high; but he ſoon tires, and is unable to bear any conſiderable weight.

Horſes whoſe *ribs* have not a proper convexity, but ſeem to hang down, are called flat horſes. This defect hinders them from thriving; their belly flags, they are clumſy, ſhort-winded, and never have

have a handſome rump, though their baok may be good.

When the *belly* riſes towards the hind-legs, like that of a greyhound, the horſe is ſaid to want body, or to be narrow-bellied. Horſes of this kind generally eat little, but are ſeldom deficient in ſpirit and mettle.

If the belly hangs below the ribs, and at the ſame time is too full, the horſe is ſaid to be cow, or pot-bellied. If a horſe of this kind be young, eats much, and coughs often, it is to be feared that he will ſoon be broken winded.

Hollow *flanks* are another deformity; and if the laſt of the ſhort ribs be at too great a diſtance from the haunch-bone, or does not come low enough, the horſe both gets fleſh, and loſes it when gotten, with difficulty. Such a horſe is ſaid to be too ſhort, or open ribbed.

Horſes in general, when they feel a pain in any part of the hinder train, become thin flanked: when their flanks work more than uſual, without their having undergone any great fatigue, it is a ſign that they are diſordered; but if this happens only from a difficulty of reſpiration when in exerciſe, the horſe is called a *puffer*; or if the defect be leſs ſenſible, he is ſaid to be *thick winded*, and is eaſily diſtinguiſhed from one whoſe flank is affected; the throbbing of the flanks ceaſing in the puffer whenever he ſtands ſtill.

Rumps not properly rounded from the rines to the tail, and which, by falling too ſoon, appear ſhort, are diſtinguiſhed by the name of *plump-buttocks*. Thoſe which want prominence and extent behind, are called *gooſe-rumps*; and thoſe whoſe buttocks are flat, are called *mule-rumps*; but theſe are defects of no conſequence with regard to the goodneſs of a horſe.

When the bones of the upper part of the *haunches* are too prominent in a horſe which is not otherwiſe very lean, he is ſaid to have *high haunches*; but if he be very fat, he is then ſaid to be *cornered*. A flat ſide and

and low belly generally produce this defect, which always gives the appearance of leanneſs. If one of the haunches be lower than the other, the horſe is ſaid to be *hip-ſhot*. The conformity of the haunches may be judged of by the ſituation of the hock; for if this be too backward, the haunches are too long, and the horſe never has any remarkable degree of ſtrength: if the haunches fall perpendicular on the paſtern joint they are too ſhort, and hinder the flexibility of the ham.

When the *tail* is placed too high it renders the rump pointed; and when too low, it indicates a weakneſs in the reins. A horſe that cloſes his tail on one's endeavouring to take it up, may be ſafely looked upon as vigorous. Thoſe which have but little hair are called *rat-tales*, and looked upon as blemiſhed; as are alſo thoſe which have ſhort hairs, and whoſe tails, inſtead of forming a convexity at the rump, fall down almoſt perpendicular.

A horſe whoſe *elbow* is too much confined by the ribs, turns his leg and foot outward; and if it be too open, that is at too great a Diſtance from the ribs, he turns them inward: both are ſymptoms of weakneſs.

Long legs are the ſtrongeſt; and ſhort arms the beſt for motion, and the flexure of the leg. A ſmall arm, beſides being unſightly, is a ſure indication that the legs want ſtrength.

Large and puffed *knees* denote the leg to be affected; but when they are bare in the middle, they are a certain proof of it; eſpecially when there is good reaſon to conclude that it has been occaſioned by frequent falls, and that the hair has not been deſtroyed by any other cauſe. A large knee ſhews a horſe to be heavy. When it naturally bends a little forward, ſo that the ſhank is not perpendicular, the horſe is ſaid to be *ſhort-armed*; a defect which does not, however, leſſen the goodneſs of a horſe: but if this fault has proceeded from accident, or fatigue, he is ſaid to be *crook-legged*. Legs do not at firſt become

come crooked by ſatigue, but are ſtrait on the fore-part from the knee to the coronet, like thoſe of goats, and the horſe is then ſaid to be *goat-legged*; but if he be worked hard afterwards, the legs, not being able to ſtretch any farther, bend, and the horſe trembles when he makes a ſtep; though he may ſtill do good ſervice, eſpecially if he has large reins. Thoſe legs which bend a little backward at the knee, which is a fault quite oppoſite to the former, where they bend forward, are called *calves-legs*.

The length of the *legs* ſhould always be proportioned to the ſtature of the horſe; becauſe, when they are too long, he is not ſure-footed; and when they are too ſhort, he bears heavy on the hand.

The fore-hand of all mares is lower in proportion than that of horſes.

In cold and moiſt countries, too ſlender a *ſhank* is looked upon as a mark of weakneſs in the leg, and particular care ſhould be taken to examine whether there be not any ſwellings on it; becauſe theſe indicate diſeaſes of the bone, which are more or leſs dangerous, according to their ſituation.

When the *back ſinew* is ſlender, the horſe cannot endure much fatigue, but ſtumbles, and the leg grows round; that is, the ſinew no longer appears detached: which is a ſure indication of diſeaſe. It is therefore neceſſary to draw the hand along the ſinew, to ſee whether it be in it's natural ſtate, without tumour or obſtruction. If it be but a little diſtant from the bone, the defect is called a calf-leg; and in this caſe the ſinew is ſlender, and the leg will not long continue ſound. If the ſinew be too ſmall near the knee, it indicates weakneſs in that joint: but this is rarely the caſe.

When the *paſtern joints* are ſmall, they are too flexible, and therefore ſubject to ſwellings called *wind-galls*. Yet horſes of this kind go eaſier than others, and conſequently are fitter for the riding-ſchool and for parade, though good for little in carriages; nor can they eaſily be made to back in paſſing deſcents. When the paſtern joint is crowned, that is, when it projects all around beyond the hoof, without being made ſo to do by any wound or other accident, it indicates the leg to be in a decaying ſtate.

When the *paſterns* are either too ſmall, or too long, and at the ſame time ſo ill placed that the fetlock almoſt touches the ground, it is a ſure indication of weakneſs: but when this part, though long, ſupports itſelf in a good poſition, it is a mark of ſome ſtrength, eſpecially in the ſinew, which hinders the fetlock from yielding too much; but the horſe is fit only for parade: and in both the above caſes he is ſaid to be *long-jointed*; the paſterns being alſo denominated joints. Horſes with too ſhort paſterns are called *ſhort-jointed*. If the knee, the ſhank, and the coronet of theſe horſes, form one perpendicular line, the horſe is ſaid to be upright on his legs. Horſes of this kind are apt to ſtumble and fall, and to become fetlocked, eſpecially if the heel be too high. They are alſo more uneaſy to the rider than the long jointed. In ſome horſes, one ſide of the paſtern is higher than the other; but this is a ſlight fault, and eaſily rectified in the ſhoeing; as may alſo that which cauſes a horſe to be upright on his legs. The hair on the paſtern ſhould not be ſtiff or briſtly, eſpecially near the coronet; becauſe that may probably be owing to a farinaceous diſeaſe, called the *crown-ſcab*.

When the *coronet* projects beyond the foot, it indicates that the latter is withered, or the former ſwelled. This part of the horſe is very much exposed to accidents, particularly from the feet of one that follows, from his own hind-legs ſtriking againſt the fore, or from froſt nails put occaſionally in his ſhoes by unſkilful farriers.

A *foot*

A *foot* too ſmall in proportion to the body, is weak, often painful, and generally accompanied with *wire-heels*. If the heel be of a middling ſize, and the foot thin, it ſoon becomes hot on a hard road, and in a ſhort time the horſe goes lame. When a foot is too large, and the hoof and ſole thin, it is called a *fat-foot*: this alſo is weak; and horſes which have ſuch feet are dull and heavy.

White *hoofs* are more brittle than thoſe of any other colour, and frequently become very troubleſome: but it is eaſy to foreſee this danger, by obſerving whether they have been broken by the ſhoe-nails.

Circled feet are thoſe where the hoof is hollowed all around by a kind of tranſverſal gutters. This irregularity in the growth of the horny ſubſtance, proceeds from a heat and dryneſs in the foot, and often brings on lameneſs. When any part of the hoof has been cut off, it is called a *new quarter*. This is a deformity, becauſe the new hoof is more rugged, coarſer, and ſofter than the former.

When the quarters are ſo cloſe that the hoof, near the fiſſure of the frog, is too narrow, or when the heels terminate in a point, and are collapſed with each other, the horſe is ſaid to be *hoof-bound*: the heels and quarters thus ſhaped, preſs on one of the ſmall bones within the foot, and if they do not render the horſe lame, they at leaſt obſtruct his going. If the heels are long behind, the foot is too long, and ſubject to be hoof-bound, which may alſo produce *ſand cracks*, that is, fiſſures in one of the quarters, where they ſometimes extend from the coronet to the lower part of the hoof.

Weak heels yield under the preſſure of the body, low heels want thickneſs, and from either of them may proceed lameneſs; the heels in both theſe caſes not having ſufficient ſtrength, properly to reſiſt the incumbent weight.

When the *hoof* is too much ſpread at the bottom, and the quarters project, the horſe is ſaid to be *flat-*

footed, and he often limps, from the frog's bearing on the ground. It is ſubject to the ſame inconvenience, and owes it's origin to the ſame cauſe, as when the horn of the frog is too long. This is called a *fat frog*, and uſually attends low heels. A thin, pinched, and dried frog, are ſymptoms of the horſe's being hoof-bound.

When the *ſole* is too thin, it is eaſily injured; and when it is too thick, and projects above the hoof, that is, when the under part of the foot is not hollow, the horſe treads on the ſole, and conſequently muſt hurt himſelf, and halt; ſuch horſes are fit only for the plough.

What has been ſaid with regard to the ſhank, the fetlock-joint, the paſtern, the coronet, and the feet of the fore legs, being applicable to the ſame parts of the hind-legs; it remains only to conſider the thigh and the hock.

Lean *thighs*, in which the thickeſt part is not well marked, indicate a weakneſs in the hinder train; and when the internal parts of the thighs are too near each other, the horſe may be ſuſpected of weakneſs in thoſe parts.

Small *hocks* are weak: fat hocks is a name given to thoſe which are too fleſhy, and on that account ſubject to ſeveral diſorders which affect the legs. When the hocks are too near each other the hinder parts of the horſe are weak, though his back may be good. When they are turned too much outwards, he cannot reſt on his haunches, that is, he cannot bring his rump to be lower than his ſhoulders. Hocks which turn out when the horſe travels, always weaken his hinder parts.

If the *fetlock* projects in ſuch a manner that the horſe reſts only on his toes, it is a fault which increaſes with age, and is indifferent only when the horſe was ſo originally, and had it from nature.

The legs are to be conſidered relatively to each other, when the horſe ſtands ſtill; for from thence

is

is known whether his *position* be not defective. Thus, if the fore legs are too much confined at top, the horse cannot go well, and from their too often touching one another when in motion, he may trip and fall. If the hinder-feet are placed too forward under the belly, it indicates the horse to be weak or very much tired; because he endeavours to lessen the weight that bears on his fore-legs, by stretching the hinder as far under his body as he is able. When on the contrary, the hinder feet are placed backwards, so that the root of the tail is not perpendicularly above the hams, but more forward; this situation, though it offends the eye, does not indicate any defect; his haunches may indeed be too long, but this does not hinder his doing his paces well: the hinder train, however, is injured sooner in such a horse as this, than in one of a different make. If the hock is not placed so backward as it naturally should be, and the haunches, hocks, and legs follow the same direction in a right line, the horse moves with difficulty. Another bad position is, for the fetlock joint to project forward, as if it were dislocated. Horses which rest on their toes, instead of treading flat on the sole, stand in a bad posture; and if they turn their hind feet out, they want strength in the haunches to go well on a descent; nor can they back without difficulty.

Horses which, on being stopped, instead of remaining quiet, move their legs alternately, are suspected of being foundered, or worn out with labour; as are also those which place one of the hind legs on the toe; or those which put one of their fore-legs forward, and continue in that posture. These signs, however, are not always certain, being also customary in some horses which are turbulent and full of fire; and to others these motions and bad attitudes are natural: besides, they may proceed from lassitude; for this will make some horses hold up one of their fore-legs; it being no uncommon thing for these animals to rest on three legs: but if they rest one of their hind-legs upon the toe, and hold up one of the fore-legs, it is an infallible mark that their legs pain them.

The foregoing account of the different parts of the horse's body, will suffice to indicate, pretty nearly at least, from their external appearances, what may be expected from him when in motion, which is the point I shall next speak to; for there it is that this noble animal exerts all his abilities to serve us, and that the most certain judgment can be formed of him.

The most natural of all his paces is, perhaps, the trot; for the walk and the gallop, though much easier to the rider, are the motions which require most pains to render a horse perfect in.

When a horse lifts up his foot to walk, the motion must be equally bold and easy, and the knee properly bent; the leg which is lifted up must appear steady; and, when set on the ground, firm; bearing equally in all its parts; nor must the horse's head be at all affected with the motion; for if the leg falls to the ground suddenly, and at the same time the head sinks, there is room to apprehend that this is done, as in fact it most commonly is, to relieve the other leg, as not able alone to bear the whole weight of the body. This is a very great fault: as is likewise the horse's carrying his foot too much out or in; because it falls on the ground in the same manner. It is also to be observed, that bearing on the heel denotes weakness; and on the toe, a forced and tiresome attitude, which the horse cannot bear for any length of time.

The *walk*, though the slowest of all his paces, must be quick, neither too wide, nor too contracted, but perfectly easy, which greatly depends on the freedom of his shoulders, and is perceivable in the manner of carrying his head: if that be high and firm, it is an indication of strength and freedom. When the

motion

motion of the ſhoulders is not ſufficiently free, the leg is not lifted high enough, and the horſe is apt to ſtumble, and trip with his foot againſt the inequalities of the ground; and when the ſhoulders are ſtill more ſtraitened, ſo that the legs ſeem to have no connection with them, he ſoon tires, frequently falls, and is unfit for any ſervice. A horſe ſhould be firm on his haunches; that is, he ſhould raiſe the ſhoulder, and lower the haunch when he walks. He ſhould alſo ſupport his leg, and lift it to a proper height: but if he holds it up too long, or drops it too ſlowly, he loſes all the advantages of eaſe, becomes ſtiff, and is fit only for ſome oſtentatious parade.

The motions of a horſe ſhould not only be eaſy, but at the ſame time equal and uniform, both before and behind; for if the haunches ſtagger while the ſhoulders remain firm, the rider is incommoded by a jolting motion. The ſame thing happens when the horſe moves his hind-leg too far forward, and places it before the track of the fore-foot. Short bodied horſes are ſubject to this fault: thoſe which cut, or ſtrike their legs againſt each other, are not ſure-footed; and, in general, a long bodied horſe is moſt eaſy to the rider, becauſe, being at a greater diſtance from the two centers of motion, the ſhoulders and the haunches, he is conſequently leſs ſuſceptible of their jolts and impreſſions.

In the *walk*, the horſe lifts his legs to but a ſmall height, ſo that his feet nearly touch the ground. In a *trot*, they are raiſed higher, and the feet are entirely off the ground. In a *gallop*, they are raiſed ſtill higher, and the feet ſeem to rebound from the turf. In a walk, it is required that the motion be quick, free, eaſy, and ſteady. The *trot* muſt be firm, quick, and equal, the hinder impelling the fore parts, and at the ſame time, the horſe muſt carry his head up, and his body ſtrait; for if the haunches riſe and fall alternately at every motion of the trot, and the horſe vacillates, he trots ill from weakneſs: if he throws out his fore-legs, it is alſo a defect; for the fore-legs ſhould always be on a line with the hinder, and cover them. When one of the hind-legs throws itſelf forward, if the fore-leg of the ſame ſide remains a little too long in its place, the reſiſtance gives an uneaſineſs to the motions; and for this reaſon it is that the interval between the two beats in the trot ſhould be ſhort; but however ſhort it be, by this reſiſtance alone the trot becomes more uneaſy than the walk, or the gallop; in walking, the motion is more eaſy and pleaſing, becauſe the diſtance is leſs. In the gallop, there is ſcarce any horizontal reſiſtance, which alone is troubleſome to the rider; the re-action of the motion of the fore-legs being almoſt entirely upwards in a perpendicular direction. *

* Quadrupeds uſually walk by moving one of the fore, and one of the hind legs forward at the ſame time. The very inſtant that the fore off-leg is lifted up, the hind near-leg is alſo moved; and this ſtep being finiſhed, the near fore leg moves in conjunction with the off hind one; and ſo on alternately. As their bodies bear on four reſting points, forming an oblong ſquare, the moſt commodious manner of motion is a diagonal change of two of them at once; ſo that the centre of gravity of the animal's body may have but a ſmall motion, and always remain nearly in the line which connects the two reſting points that are not in motion in the three natural paces of the horſe; the walk, the trot, and the gallop: this rule of motion is always obſerved, but with the following differences.

In the *walk*, there are four beats in the motion; if the off fore leg moves firſt, the near hind leg follows inſtantly after; then the near fore leg moves in it's turn, to be immediately followed by the off hind leg. Thus the off fore foot touches the ground firſt, the near hind foot ſecond, the near fore foot third, and the off hind foot the laſt; which forms a movement of four beats, and three intervals, of which the firſt and laſt are ſhorter than the other.

In the *trot*, there are only two beats in the motion: if the off fore leg moves firſt, the near hind leg moves at the ſame time, without the leaſt interval between them; then the near fore, and the off hind leg, move alſo at the ſame time: ſo that this motion of the trot has but two beats, and one interval: the off fore, and the near hind feet, lighting together on the ground; the near fore foot and off hind foot are alſo on the ground at the ſame time.

In

The ſpring of the hocks has no leſs ſhare in the motion of the gallop than that of the loins: whilſt the loins exert themſelves in raiſing and impelling forward the anterior parts; the muſcle of the hocks, by it's ſpring, breaks the impetus, ſoftens the ſhock, and the gallop is eaſy in proportion as this ſpring of the hocks is eaſy and ſupple: it is alſo fleet and rapid in

In the *gallop*, there are uſually three beats: but as in this motion, which is a kind of leap, the fore parts do not immediately move of themſelves, but are driven by the force of the haunches and hinder parts; if the off fore foot is to ſtretch beyond the near, the near hind foot muſt be grounded firſt, to ſerve as a fulcrum to this ſpringing motion. Thus it is that the near hind foot makes the firſt beat of the motion, and alſo touches the ground firſt; then the off hind leg raiſes itſelf jointly with the near fore leg, and they both touch the ground again at the ſame time; and laſtly, the off fore leg, which moved an inſtant after the near fore and off hinder legs, touches the ground the laſt, which makes the third beat. In the gallop, there are therefore three beats and two intervals; and in the firſt of theſe intervals, when the motion is performed with rapidity, there is an inſtant when all the fore legs are off the ground, and the horſe's four ſhoes are ſeen at the ſame time. When a horſe has ſupple haunches and hocks, and moves them with ſwiftneſs and agility, the motion of the gallop is more complete, and the cadence made at four times. Firſt, he grounds the near hind foot, which denotes the firſt beat; next the off hind foot touches the ground and denotes the ſecond beat; the near fore foot grounding an inſtant after, denotes the third beat; and laſtly, the off fore foot, which touches the ground the laſt, denotes the fourth beat.

When horſes gallop, they generally lift the off fore foot up firſt, in the ſame manner as they uſe the ſame leg in the walk or trot. and by ſo doing they gain ground; the off fore leg advancing farther than the near, and being immediately followed by the off hind leg, which alſo advances beyond the near hind leg: but the reſult of this, conſtantly continued during a long gallop, is, that the near leg, ſupporting the whole weight, and puſhing forward the other, is the moſt fatigued. It would therefore, be right to accuſtom horſes to gallop alternately on the near and off leg; for by this means they would hold out the longer in this violent motion; and accordingly it is ſo practiſed in the beſt riding-ſchools, though perhaps for another reaſon, which is, that as the horſes are often made to ſhift hands, that is, to deſcribe a circle, the centre of which is ſometimes on the off, and ſometimes on the near ſide, they are accordingly taught to gallop ſometimes on the off, and ſometimes on the near leg.

proportion

proportion to the ſtrength of the muſcles of the hocks; and moſt equal when the horſe bears moſt on his haunches, and the ſhoulders are ſupported by the muſcles of the loins. Horſes which lift their fore-legs to an unuſual height when they gallop, are not the ſwifteſt goers; for they ſtrike ſhorter, and at the ſame time tire themſelves ſooner. This uſually proceeds from a want of freedom in the ſhoulders.

The walk, the trot, and the gallop, are the moſt common and natural paces: but ſome horſes have another, which is called the *amble*. It is very different from the three former; and at firſt ſight appears contrary to the laws of mechaniſm. The motion here is not ſo ſwift as the gallop, or even the trot. In this pace, the horſe's feet move ſtill nearer to the ground than in the walk, and are more extended: but what is moſt ſingular in it is, that the two legs of the ſame ſide, for inſtance, the off hind and fore leg, move at the ſame time; and then the two near legs, in making another ſtep, move at once; and in this alternate manner the motion is performed: ſo that the two ſides of the body are alternately without ſupport, or any equilibrium between the one and the other, which muſt neceſſarily prove very fatiguing to the horſe, who is obliged to ſupport himſelf in a forced oſcillation, by the rapidity of a motion in which his feet are ſcarcely off the ground. In this pace, the farther the hind leg extends beyond the place where the fore leg grounded, the better the horſe ambles, and the more rapid is the whole motion. Thus in the motion of the amble, as in the trot, there are only two beats: but this pace can never be performed but upon even ground, and is extremely fatiguing to the horſe, though very eaſy to the rider *. They who

* The amble has not the roughneſs of the trot, becauſe, in the amble, both the legs of the ſame ſide are lifted up together, ſo as to form but one motion; whereas in the trot, the fore-leg of the ſame ſide is at reſt, and reſiſts the impulſe during the whole time that the hinder leg is moved.

are

are ſkilled in horſemanſhip tell us, that horſes which amble naturally never trot; and that they are much weaker than others. Colts, indeed, very often perform this pace; eſpecially when they exert themſelves, and are not ſtrong enough to trot or gallop. Moſt good horſes which have been over-worked, and are on the decline, are alſo obſerved voluntarily to amble, when forced to a motion ſwifter than the walk. Upon the whole, the amble may be conſidered as a defective pace; not being common, and natural only to a very few horſes, which, in general, are weaker than others.

But there are ſtill two other paces, which weak or over-worked horſes take to of themſelves, and are much more faulty than the amble. Theſe, from their defects, have been called broken, diſunited, or compound paces. The firſt is between the walk and the amble; and the ſecond between the trot and the gallop: both are the effects of long fatigue, or great weakneſs in the loins. Horſes uſed to carry mails, by being frequently over loaded, take to the former, inſtead of the trot, when on their decline; and worn-out poſt horſes go into the latter when urged to the gallop.

Another circumſtance, and that one of the moſt eſſential, to be attended to in the choice of a horſe, is his age; to judge of which Mr. de Buffon has likewiſe ſummed up, from the beſt writers on this ſubject, the following conciſe but ſure rules.

The moſt certain knowledge of the age of a horſe is to be obtained from his *teeth*, of which he has forty, viz. twenty-four grinders, or double teeth, four tuſhes, and twelve fore teeth: mares have no tuſhes, at leaſt very ſhort ones. It is not from the grinders that the age is known: but it is diſcovered, as firſt by the fore-teeth, and afterwar by the tuſhes. The twelve fore-teeth begin to ſhoot within twelve days after the colt is foaled. Theſe firſt, or *foal teeth*, are round, ſhort, not very ſolid, and are ſhed at different times, to be replaced by others.

At

At the age of two years and a half, the four middle *fore-teeth* are ſhed, viz. two in the upper jaw, and two in the lower. In one year more, two others drop out, one on each ſide of the former, which have already been replaced. When he is about four years and a half old, he ſheds four others, always next to thoſe which have fallen out and been replaced. Theſe foal-teeth are replaced by four others; but theſe laſt are far from growing ſo faſt as thoſe which replaced the eight former, and are called the *corner teeth*: they replace the four laſt foal teeth, and by them it is that the age of a horſe is known. They are eaſily diſtinguiſhed, being the third, both above and below, counting from the midde of the jaw. They are hollow, and have a black mark in their cavity. When the horſe is four years and a half old, they are hardly viſible above the gum, and the cavity is very conſpicuous: at ſix and a half they begin to fill, and the mark continually diminiſhes and contracts till ſeven or eight years, when the cavity is quite filled up, and the black ſpot effaced. After eight years, theſe teeth ceaſing to afford any knowledge of the age, it is judged of by the *tuſhes*, which are four teeth, adjoining to thoſe laſt mentioned; and, like the grinders, are not preceded by any other teeth. The two in the lower jaw uſually begin to ſhoot at three years and a half, and thoſe of the upper jaw at four; continuing very ſharp pointed till ſix. At ten, the upper ſeem blunted, worn out, and long; the gum contracting as it's years increaſe. The barer therefore they are, the older is the horſe. From ten to thirteen or fourteen years, little can be ſeen to indicate the age; but at about this laſt period, ſome hairs of the eye-brows begin to turn grey. This mark, however, is equivocal, as is alſo that drawn from the depth of the eye-pits; horſes from old ſtallions, or old mares, frequently having grey hairs in their eye-brows when they are not above nine or ten years old,

old, and hollow eye-pits when they are quite young. In ſome horſes, the teeth are ſo hard as not to wear, and in ſuch the black ſpot ſubſiſts as long as they live: but the age of theſe horſes is eaſily known by the hollow of the tooth being filled up, and at the ſame time the tuſhes are very long. This is more common in mares than in horſes. The age of a horſe may alſo be known, though leſs exactly, by the *bars* of his mouth, which wear away as he advances in years.

Experience has fully proved, that no indication whatever of the qualities of a horſe can be drawn from the *colour* of his coat, as was formerly, for a long time, wrongly imagined: the beſt judges, and moſt accurate obſervers now ſmile at that antiquated prejudice, and unanimouſly agree that there are good horſes of all colours: ſo that, in fact, the whole attention due to the colour of a horſe, is only ſo far as relates to what is reputed beauty in him, and, conſequently to his price; ſome colours being highly valued for their ſingularity: for judgment has never yet been able to make real beauty be preferred to ſingularity. I ſhould therefore diſmiſs this ſubject without any farther notice, were it not that an explanation of the technical terms moſt commonly employed in deſcribing the different colours of a horſe, may not be unacceptable to ſuch readers as are not already acquainted with their meaning. To this end, I ſhall claſs them under three general heads, namely, ſimple colours, by which I mean ſuch as extend themſelves all over the horſe's body, without any mixture of others; compound colours, that is, thoſe mixed with others; and extraordinary colours, or in other words, ſuch as are of an uncommon mixture. The ſimple colours are the white, the dun, the ſorrel, the bay, and the black: the compound are the grey, the mouſe, and the roan; and the extraordinary comprehend the tyger, the pied, the ſtrawberry, and the flea-bitten. I ſhall begin with

with the moſt common and moſt natural, which is the bay. Indeed, if we reflect that the yellow, the bay, the brown, or the ſallow, are the moſt uſual, and therefore the moſt natural colours of wild animals; and that the bay, compoſed of tints of thoſe colours, is the moſt common to horſes, we may readily incline to think that if theſe creatures were alſo wild, they would all be bay, at leaſt in our climate. The other colours belong to them only as domeſtic animals.

The *bay* reſembles in colour a reddiſh cheſnut, with ſeveral gradations, diſtinguiſhed by the following terms; the bright bay, the light and dark cheſnut, the brown bay, the yellow bay, the blood bay, and the bright dappled bay. The brown bay is a very dark brown, almoſt black, except the flanks and the tip of the noſe, where the hair has a reddiſh caſt. The yellow bay needs no deſcription. The dappled bays are thoſe whoſe rumps are marked with a deeper bay than any other part. The term dappled is alſo applied to cheſnuts which are variegated with clearer ſpots of a brighter bay, or rather to thoſe whoſe rump is marked with ſpots of a darker bay. The manes and tails of all bay horſes are black. The bright bay uſed to be accounted phlegmatic, the yellow bay bilious, and the brown bay ſtill more bilious and ſpirited.

Black horſes are little leſs common than bay ones. They are of three different ſorts as to colour, *viz.* the ruſty, the common, and the jet. The firſt of theſe has a brown or ruſty caſt, and is perhaps more properly a ſpecies of brown bay. The flanks and extremities of theſe ruſty blacks are of a paler colour than that of the reſt of the body; and for this reaſon they uſed to be deemed inferior in point of quality to the other blacks. The jet, or bright black, is clear, ſleek, and very black. There is likewiſe a very ſhining black, which is, in ſome particulars, diſtinguiſhable from the jet.

The

The *dun* colour is of a yellowiſh hue. The manes and tails of ſome of the horſes of this colour are white; in others they are compoſed of dun and black; and in others again they are entirely black. Theſe laſt, in particular, have always all along the ſpine of the back to the tail a black liſt, generally called the mule's liſt. The dun has alſo ſeveral gradations: that in which the yellow is leaſt prevalent, is called *cream*, and is in fact a dull yellowiſh white. The bright dun has a little more yellow in it's mixture; the common dun has ſtill more; the golden dun is of a yet brighter yellow; and the dark dun is of a duller or deeper colour.

The *wolf-colour* is of two ſorts, clear and dark: both have tinges of dun, and ſometimes the mule's liſt. The dark coloured uſed to be reckoned the beſt horſes.

The *ſorrel* is a kind of ruſſet bay, or cinnamon colour. There are ſeveral gradations of it; namely, the bright ſorrel, reſembling the common colour of a cow; the common ſorrel, which is a medium between brown and light; the bay ſorrel, inclining to red or ruſſet; the dark and the duſt ſorrel, which is very deep and brown. In ſome of theſe horſes the mane and tail are white, and in others black. The common ſorrel uſed formerly to be held in ſo high eſtimation, that the Spaniards were wont to ſay, proverbially, "a ſorrel horſe is ſooner dead than tired." A lighter colour in it's extremities than in it's body, was looked upon as a mark of weakneſs. The lighter ſorrels were leſs eſteemed, though all reputed good upon the faith of their colour; and the dark or aduſt were ſuppoſed to be melancholic and docile.

The *roan* is a mixture of red and white, or of white, a dull grey, and a bay. It is diſtinguiſhed into three kinds, the common roan, the red roan, and the dark roan. The head and extremities of horſes of this colour are generally white, or, according to ſome authors, of a dull grey, and the body roan.

roan. It uſed to be taken for granted, that a roan horſe muſt be excellent if his extremities were black.

Grey horſes are divided into ſeveral ſorts, as dappled grey, ſilver grey, duſty grey, brown grey, &c. according as their coats are more or leſs intermixed with white and black, bay or brown. Dappled greys are diſtinguiſhed by ſeveral round ſpots, ſome blacker, and others whiter, pretty equally ſcattered over the rump and other parts of the body. The ſilver greys have very few black hairs, and thoſe thinly ſown on a ſleek white ground, ſhining almoſt like ſilver. In the duſty greys, there is a conſiderable mixture of brown and black with the white. White manes and tales are reckoned a great ornament to horſes of this colour. The iron grey have a great deal of black, and little white. The nutmeg grey is a mixture of bay, black, and white. The vinous grey is all over mixed with bay. The fronted grey has a white coat decorated with dark reddiſh ſpots pretty equally diſperſed over the head and body. The thruſh grey, ſo called from it's reſemblance to the colour of the bird of that name, has a dirty look, and is compoſed of a reddiſh coat thickly intermixed with black and white. The ſtarling grey, likewiſe ſo called from it's ſimilitude to the colours of the bird of that name, has a browner tinct than the dull grey; and the ſame appellation is ſtill given to it when it has a yet much larger mixture of black. Coal-grey horſes have a white or grey coat, with irregularly ſcattered black ſpots, as large as the palm of the hand. When theſe ſpots are larger than common, the horſes ſo marked are diſtinguiſhed by the name of *tygers*. Mouſe-grey horſes have generally black extremities, and the mule's liſt. White colts are rare; but the bay or black hairs of all grey horſes whiten as they advance in years. The antient opinion was, that neither the dappled greys, nor the tygers are ſo good as the coal-greys; that the ſilver-greys are dull and phlegmatic; that the thruſh-greys

are

are better than the dappled-greys; and that the vinous greys are the beſt of all greys.

The colour called *porcelain* is a grey mixed with ſpots of a blueiſh ſlate colour, not unlike blue and white china. Horſes of this colour are ſcarce, and uſed to be reckoned good, but capricious.

The *peach bloſſom* is a mixture of bay, white, and ſorrel, in ſuch proportion as to reſemble, in ſome degree, the colour of the bloſſoms of the peach tree. Horſes of this colour were thought to be apt to grow blind.

Pied horſes have a coat of white and other colours, irregularly mixed with large ſpots. The common pie is white and black; the bay pie, white and bay; and the ſorrel pie, white and ſorrel. All pied horſes were formerly deemed good, becauſe they were pies; and thoſe which had the leaſt white in them were reckoned beſt.

Now, whatever the colour of a horſe be, thoſe which have black manes and tails are moſt valued, chiefly indeed becauſe they are thought handſomeſt; and, on the contrary, thoſe whoſe flanks and extremities are of a colour leſs deep than that of the body, are leaſt eſteemed.

A white mark in the forehead of a horſe is called a *ſtar*, and is more or leſs large: but if it extends from the forehead to the noſe, it is called a blaze. This white mark is not pleaſing when it interferes with the eye-brows, nor when it reaches to the tip of the noſe. The ſtar, the blaze, and the white on the tip of the noſe are ſometimes found in the ſame animal. There are ſeveral methods of making ſtars by art, that is, of changing the natural colour of the hair into white; and in particular it may be done either by cutting off the ſkin, or by burning it; for the hair which grows again, after the wound is healed, will be white. There are alſo ſeveral ways of dying white eye-brows, or grey or white hairs, into bay or black: but this laſts no longer than till ſhedding time, that is to ſay, the ſeaſon when horſes change their coats; the new hair being always of it's natural colour.

When the lower part of a horſe's leg is white, he is ſaid to be *balzane*, or white-footed: when this white is fringed or irregularly dentilated at the top, it is called a *dentilated balzane*; and if it is ſpotted with black, it is termed an *ermined*, or *patched* balzane, or an ermined leg. If the white reaches too near the knee or hock, the horſe is ſaid to be too *high ſhod*: if the lower part of the hind and fore leg of the ſame ſide is white, he is ſaid to be but *indifferently marked*; but if the balzanes are on the off fore leg and near hind leg, or on the near fore leg and off hind leg, he is ſaid to be *traverſed* or *croſs marked*: and laſtly, if all the fore legs are white, he is ſaid to have four *white ſtockings*.

It is not poſſible to deſcribe all the tincts, mixtures, and gradations of the ſeveral colours of horſes; nor can the ſize or form of all the ſpots and marks obſerved on ſome of them be minutely defined: but with regard to thoſe in particular of which we have been ſpeaking, and the ſame is equally applicable to all others, M. de Buffon declares it to be his opinion, that the marks or ſpots which we ſee on the face of ſeveral horſes often deceive us by a falſe appearance, in that they change the aſpect of the animal, and, as it were, diſguiſe him: for inſtance, horſes with a white blaze have been thought capricious; and that for no other reaſon, than becauſe the contraſt of colours gives them a ſingular appearance, as ſcars on the face of a man give him a harſher look: and that of a ſtar in the forehead of a horſe is accounted a good ſign, it is only when it is in the middle, in which ſituation it is rather a beauty than a defect. As to the white ſtockings, he thinks that their being ſo much noticed is owing to their being ſituated on the legs, by the frequent motion of which they attract the ſight more than other ſpots; and that if they

have

have been generally taken for bad indications, it is only because their white feet, being more conspicuous, seem to pass closer together than those of other colours: hence the notion of these horses being more apt to stumble; whereas those which have stockings on all their four legs are not included in this suspicion, there not being the same apparent inequality in their going. But it would be needless to dwell any longer on this subject, and combat prejudices, which the most experienced horsemen have amply refuted. Their examples will be more powerful than reason, to undeceive others; and truth being once known, time alone will gradully extirpate error.

The *feather*, which is reckoned an ornament in a horse, and by some looked upon as a mark of goodness, is a point where the hairs part as from a centre, and revert so as to form a small conic cavity, nearly in the same manner as the petals, of a single flower, particularly a pink. The forehead, the breast, and the belly, are the places where these feathers most commonly are; though some horses have them likewise in other parts. Sometimes also two or three of them are seen together on the forehead, or on the hinder bend of the thigh.

The *Roman sword*, so called from it's resemblance to the sword used by the antient Romans, is in fact nothing more than a long feather, or a kind of furrow formed by the hair being inverted, running along the top of the neck, near the mane. This mark is very rare, and accounted a great beauty; for which reason those horses which have it are bought up at almost any rate by those who pique themselves on being uncommonly curious in a horse's coat. A Roman sword on each side of the mane makes a great addition to the price of a horse.

Three farther circumstances, the first highly proper at least, and the two last essentially necessary to be attended to in the choice of a horse, are, it's country and pedigree, if it be a fine horse that is

 wanted;

wanted; the uſes for which it is fit; and care to guard againſt the artifices by which the unſkilful are liable to be deceived.

The ſeveral breeds of horſes have been ſo much intermixed and the characters which would otherwiſe diſtinguiſh thoſe of each climate thereby ſo blended, that long practice, and very great experience, are requiſite now to know the horſes of different countries. All the information that we can have on this head, is drawn from travellers, and from the writings of the moſt expert horſemen, ſuch as the duke of Newcaſtle, Meſſrs. Garſaalt, de la Gueriniere, Solleyſel, &c. and ſome remarks, communicated by M. Pignerolles, equerry to the king of France, and director of the academy at Angers, to M. de Buffon, whom I ſtill continue to make my principal guide.

The fineſt horſes that we know of are the *Arabian*. They are larger and fuller than the Barbs, and not inferior to them in ſhape. But as few of them, eſpecially of the true mountain breed, are brought into this country, there have not yet been ſufficient opportunities for making circumſtantial obſervations on their perfections and defects.

The *Barbs* are more common than the Arabians in this part of the world. Their cheſt is long and ſlender, and riſes beautifully from the withers: they have little manes, the head well ſhaped, ſmall, and lean; the ears handſome and well placed; the ſhoulders flat and ſlender; the withers narrow and plump; the back ſtrait and ſhort; the flank and ſides round and not bulging out; the haunches firm and well ſhaped; the croup generally ſomewhat long, and the tail pretty high placed; the thigh well ſhaped, and ſeldom flat; the legs handſome, well ſhaped, and without hair at the paſtern joint; the foot well made, but the paſtern often too long. They are of all colours, but moſt commonly grey. The Barbs are ſomewhat negligent in their goings; but, when properly encouraged, they ſhew an amazing ſwiftneſs

ſwiftneſs and vigour; they are very light, and fit for running; and ſeem of all others the moſt proper to breed from. It might however be wiſhed that they were ſomewhat taller, the largeſt being but fourteen hands high; for fourteen hands and an inch is very extraordinary. Experience has ſhewn that in England, France, &c. they beget colts larger than themſelves. The mountain Barbs are accounted the beſt, and next to them are thoſe of the kingdom of Morocco. The horſes of the reſt of Mauritania are of an inferior quality, as are likewiſe thoſe of Turkey, Perſia, and Armenia.

The *Turkiſh* horſes are not ſo well proportioned as the Barbs: their neck is ſlender, their body long, and their feet are too thin; but yet, notwithſtanding theſe diſadvantages, they will endure great fatigue, and are long-winded: nor indeed is this to be wondered at, if we conſider, that the bones of all animals are harder in hot climates than in cold ones, and that, therefore, though their ſhank bones are ſmaller than thoſe of the horſes of this country, their legs are ſtronger. It is alſo worth noticing, that the coats of all hairy animals are ſhorter and ſmoother in hot countries than in cold ones.

The *Spaniſh* horſes, which are ranked next to the Barbs, have a long thick neck, with a large mane; the head full big, and ſometimes the fore-top large; the ears long, but well placed; the eyes full of fire, and the air noble and ſpirited: the ſhoulders thick, and the cheſt broad; the back frequently ſomewhat low; the ribs round, but the belly often too large; the croup generally round and large, though in ſome longiſh; the legs beautiful and void of hair; the ſinew well detached; the paſtern ſometimes longiſh like that of the Barbs, the foot a little lengthened like that of a mule; and the heel often too high. The fine-bred Spaniſh horſes are plump, nicely ſet, and place their legs well on the ground; they have alſo a great deal of motion in their paces, with much agility, fire, and

 ſtatelineſs.

ſtatelineſs. They are generally black, or of a light cheſnut; though there are ſome of all the uſual colours of horſes; but it is very rare to ſee any of them with white legs or white noſes; the Spaniards having ſuch a diſlike to theſe marks, that they never breed from horſes which have them. A ſtar in the forehead is all that they require; but they eſteem horſes of one entire dark colour as much as we diſregard them. Both theſe prejudices, though oppoſite, are perhaps equally ill founded, there being very good horſes with all kind of marks; and ſome excellent among thoſe which are all of one colour. The Spaniſh horſes are all marked on the off thigh with the mark of the ſtud where they were bred. They are, in general, under-ſized; though ſome riſe to fourteen hands and one or two inches. Thoſe of upper Andaluſia are reckoned the beſt of all, though they are apt to have too long a head: but this blemiſh is overlooked in conſideration of their excellent qualities, ſuch as courage, gracefulneſs, obedience, and ambition; and in activity they excel even the Barbs. Theſe advantages recommend them above all other horſes in the world, whether for war, for ſtate, or for the riding-ſchool.

The *Italian* horſes were formerly much finer than they now are, the ſtuds in Italy having been neglected for ſome time paſt. The kingdom of Naples, indeed, ſtill affords fine horſes, eſpecially for carriages; but they have, in general, large heads and thick necks: they are alſo indocile, and conſequently difficult to be trained. Theſe defects are, however, in ſome degree, compenſated by the largeneſs of their ſize, their ſpirit, and the beauty of their motions. They affect great ſtatelineſs, and are therefore excellent for parade.

The *Daniſh* horſes are ſo large, and ſo well ſet, that they are preferred to all others for coach-horſes. Some of them are perfectly well moulded, but, in general, they have a thick neck, broad

broad shoulders, the back somewhat too long and low, and the croup too contracted for the breath of the chest: however, they all move well, and are in general excellent for war and state. They are of all colours, even the most uncommon; particularly the pye and the spotted.

Germany affords some fine horses; but the generality of them are heavy and thick-winded, though most of them come from Turkish and Barbary horses, of which the Germans have several studs; as they also have of Spanish and Italian horses. They make no figure in hunting or racing; whereas the horses of *Hungary*, *Transylvania*, and some other adjacent countries, are very light and fleet *.

The *Dutch* horses are very good for coaches. The best of them come from Friezland. The countries of Bergue and Juliers also breed very good ones.

The *Flemish* horses are greatly inferior to those of Holland; they have generally large heads, broad feet, and their legs are subject to dropsical swellings. The two last are capital faults in coach horses.

France produces horses of all kinds, though not many fine ones. The best French saddle-horses come from the Limousin, are somewhat like the Barbs, and excellent hunters, but of slow growth. They must not be broke young, nor put to any service before they are eight years old. Auvergne, Poitou, and the territory of Morvant in Burgundy also produce very good ponies. But Normandy af-

* The Hussars and Hungarians slit the nostrils of their horses in order, as is said, to mend their wind, and prevent their neighing in the field; it being asserted, that horses whose nostrils have been slit cannot neigh. Whether this operation has in reality that effect, is more than I can pretend to determine. M. de Buffon, who likewise never had an opportunity of examining the fact, thinks it most natural to suppose that the slitting of their nostrils can only weaken their neighing — The Hungarian, Croatian, and Polish horses are noted for having what is called the mark in all their fore teeth, where it continues till they are very old.

fords the finest horses, next after those of the Limousin; and if they are not so good for hunting, they are preferable to the rest for war, are better set, and sooner trained. Lower Normandy and the Cotentin are famous for very fine coach-horses; they are lighter, and more sprightly than the Dutch horses, though these last are by much the most generally used for carriages in France. Franche-Comté and the Boulonois furnish likewise very good draught-horses: but a general fault in the French horses is, the too great width of their shoulders; whereas those of the Barbs are too narrow.

The finest *English* horses are very like to the Arabians and Barbs in shape: indeed they owe their origin to them: but the head of the English is much larger, though well made, and has a finer fore-top; and their ears are longer, but properly placed. The ears alone would indeed suffice to distinguish an English horse from a Barb: but the greatest difference between them is in their size, English horses being by much the largest and best set. The common height of our horses is about fourteen hands two inches; but even fifteen hands are not a very extraordinary size. They are of all colours and all marks; generally strong, mettlesome, bold, capable of bearing great fatigue, excellent for hunting and racing, especially those of Yorkshire, with which most of the princes in Europe are plentifully supplied: but they want air and agility, and are too stiff, owing to their not having sufficient freedom in their shoulders.

The above enumerated are the kinds of horses with which we are best acquainted: but as some may perhaps be curious to know what travellers have said concerning those of more distant countries, I shall here borrow from M. de Buffon a summary of their accounts.

" All the islands of the Archipelago* produce very good horses. Those of the isle of Crete

* See *Dapper's Description of the Islands of the Archipelago.*

were

were highly renowned among the ancients for agility and swiftness; but they are at present very little used in that country itself, on account of the roughness of the ground, and the mountains and precipices with which it almost every where abounds: the fine horses of these islands, and even those of Barbary, are of Arabian extraction. The native horses of the kingdom of Morocco are much smaller than those of Arabia, but very light and vigorous †. Dr. Shaw tells us, in his travels, that the Ægyptian and Tingitanian studs are now superior to all those of the neighbouring countries; whereas about a century ago, as good horses were found in every other part of Barbary. The excellence of these Barbs consists, he says, in never making a false step, and in remaining still when the rider alights or drops the bridle: they have a long pace, and gallop with rapidity, but are not suffered either to trot or to amble, the inhabitants of the country accounting those goings aukward, and even mean. He adds, that the Ægyptian horses are superior to all others for size and beauty: but these, and indeed most of the Barbary horses, owe their origin to the Arabian coursers, which are incontestably the most beautiful and stately animals in the world.

"According to Marmol*; or rather according to Leo Africanus‡, for Marmol has here copied him almost word for word, the Arabian horses are descended from the wild horses of the desarts of Arabia, of which there were studs in very antient times, whereby they have been multiplied to such a degree, that all Asia and Africa are full of them. They are so very swift, that some of them will overtake the ostrich. The people of Arabia Deserta, and those of Lybia, breed a great number of these horses for hunting, but

† See *l'Afrique de Marmol, Paris*, 1667, *Tom. II. p.* 124.
* *Ibid. Tom. I. p.* 50.
‡ *Africæ Descriptio, Tom. II. p.* 750, 751.

never

never uſe them either for travelling or for war. They keep them in paſtures when there is graſs; and when there is not, they feed them with dates and camel's milk, which renders them vigorous, ſwift, and thin of fleſh. They lay toils for the wild horſes, which they eat, and ſay that the fleſh of the young ones is very palatable: theſe wild horſes are ſmaller than the others, and commonly of an aſh colour; though ſome are white, with the main and tail very briſtly. Other travellers have given us ſome curious accounts relative to the Arabian horſes, from which I ſhall here extract only the principal parts ‡.

"No Arabian, howſoever poor and indigent, is without horſes. They generally ride mares; experience having taught them that they endure fatigue, hunger, and thirſt, better than horſes: they are alſo leſs vicious, more tractable, and not ſo much given to neighing as horſes. They accuſtom them ſo much to be together, that great numbers of them are frequently left to themſelves, ſometimes for whole days, without their kicking one another, or doing themſelves the leaſt hurt. The Turks, on the contrary, are not fond of mares; and the Arabians ſell them the horſes which they do not intend to keep for ſtallions. It is a very long time ſince the Arabians began to preſerve the breeds of their horſes with great care; to which end they keep exact accounts of their generations, alliances, and whole genealogy. They diſtinguiſh their breeds by different names, and divide them into three claſſes: the firſt is, that of the noble horſes deſcended from a pure and antient breed on both ſides: the ſecond is, where the horſe is of an antient breed, but not the mare; and the third is

‡ Particularly M. de la Roque, in his *Voyage fait par ordre de Louis XIV.* printed at *Paris* in 1714, *p.* 174, *et ſeq.* and alſo *l'Hiſtoire généraledes Voyages. Paris* 1746, *Tom. II. p.* 626.

that

that of common horſes. Theſe laſt ſell for little; but thoſe of the firſt claſs, and even of the ſecond; among which are ſome not at all inferior to thoſe of the firſt, bear an exceſſively high price. The mares of the firſt, or noble claſs, are never covered but by ſtallions of the ſame rank. They know, by long experience, all the breeds of their own horſes, and likewiſe thoſe of their neighbours; even to the name, ſurname, coat, marks, &c. of each. When they have not noble ſtallions of their own to cover their mares, they hire them of their neighbours, and the covering is performed in the preſence of witneſſes, who ſign and ſeal an atteſtation of it, before the Emir's ſecretary, or ſome other perſon in office: in this certificate they mention the name of the horſe and mare, and enumerate their whole pedigree. Witneſſes are alſo called at the foaling of the mare, and theſe ſubſcribe another certificate, containing a deſcription of the young colt, with the day of it's being foaled. The value of the horſe depends upon theſe certificates, which are delivered to the purchaſer. No mares of this firſt claſs are ſold under five hundred crowns (upwards of ſixty guineas) and many ſell for a thouſand, fifteen hundred, and even two thouſand crowns.

" As the Arabians have only a tent for their dwelling, that tent ſerves them alſo for a ſtable. The mare, the foal, the huſband, the wife, and children, lie all intermixed in a confuſed manner; the little children often on the body or the neck of the mare or foal, without experiencing the leaſt inconvenience therefrom; for theſe creatures remain ſtill and quiet, as if afraid of hurting them; and ſo accuſtomed are theſe mares to this familiarity, that they will bear all manner of play. The Arabians do not beat them, they treat them gently, talk and diſcourſe with them,

take

take a great deal of care of them; they let them always go their own pace, except in cafes of neceffity; but then, when once they feel their flanks tickled with the ftirrup, they inftantly fet off, and fly with an incredible velocity, leaping like hinds over hedges and ditches; and if the rider happens to fall, they are fo well trained, that they ftop inftantly, even in the midft of the moft rapid gallop.

"All the horfes of the Arabians are of a middle fize, genteely fhaped, and rather lean than fat. They drefs them very regularly every morning and evening, with fo much care, as not to leave the leaft filth upon their fkin: they wafh their legs, together with their manes and tails, which they leave at their full length, and feldom comb for fear of breaking the hairs: they give them nothing to eat in the courfe of the day, but only make them drink then two or three times, and at fun-fet they tie to their head a bag with about half a bufhel of well-cleanfed barley: thus thefe horfes eat only in the night, and the bag is not taken from them till the next morning, when it is found empty. In the month of March, when there is a fufficiency of herbage, they are turned out to grafs. At this feafon alfo the mares are covered; and it is the conftant practice of the Arabians to throw cold water upon the croup of the mare immediately after the action. When the fpring feafon is over, the horfes are taken from the pafture; and during all the reft of the year they have neither grafs nor hay, and even ftraw but very rarely; barley is their only food. The manes of the foals are cut at the age of a year, or eighteen months, that they may grow the clofer and longer: they are backed at the age of two years, or two years and a half at fartheft; but before that time, neither bridle nor faddle is put upon them. Every day, from morning to evening, all the horfes of the Arabians ftand bridled and faddled at the door of the tent.

"The

" The breed of these horses has extended itself in Barbary, among the Moors, and has even reached the negroes who inhabit the banks of the rivers Gambia and Senegal, where the lords of the country have some exceedingly beautiful. Instead of barley or oats, they are fed with maize, pounded or reduced to meal, and mixed with milk when it is intended to fatten them : but even in this hot climate they are permitted to drink but seldom *. On another side, the Arabian horses have stocked Ægypt, Turkey, and perhaps Persia, where there were formerly very considerable studs; one of which Marco Paulo speaks of, † as containing ten thousand white mares; to which he adds, that there were in the province of Balascia great numbers of large and swift horses, whose hoofs were so hard that it was needless to shoe them.

" All the horses of the Levant, like those of Persia and Arabia, have a very hard hoof; yet they are constantly shoed, but with thin and light shoes, which may be nailed on in every part. In Turkey, Persia, and Arabia, the manner of tending and feeding horses is the same, and in each of those countries their dung is made to serve for litter, after having been dried in the sun to take off it's smell; when it is pulverized; and spread about four or five inches thick on the floor of the stable or tent. This litter lasts a long time; for when it becomes again offensive, it is dried a second time in the sun, which entirely takes away its bad smell.

" There are in Turkey Arabian horses, Tartar horses, and horses of the native breed of the country : these last are handsome, and very slender ‡; full of vivacity, remarkably swift, and even grace-

* See *Histoire générale de Voyages. Tom. III. p.* 297.

† *Description géographique de l' Inde, par Març Paul, Venitien. Paris*, 1566, *Tom. I. p.* 41. and *Liv. I. p.* 21.

‡ See *Les Voyages de M. Dumont. La Haye*, 1699, *Tom. III. p.* 253. *et seq.*

ful;

ſul; but too tender to bear much fatigue: they eat little, are ſoon heated, and their ſkin is ſo ſenſible that they cannot bear a curry-comb; for which reaſon they are only rubbed with a cloth, and waſhed. Theſe horſes, though handſome, are, as we ſee, greatly inferior to the Arabians: they are even inferior to the Perſian horſes, which are, next to thoſe of Arabia*, the beſt and moſt beautiful of any in the Eaſt. The paſtures in the plains of Media, Perſepolis, Ardebil, and Derbent, are admirably fine, and a prodigious number of horſes are reared there, by order of government, moſt of which are very beautiful, and almoſt all of them excellent. Pietro della Valle † prefers the common horſes of Perſia to thoſe of Italy, and even to the moſt valuable horſes of the kingdom of Naples. They are generally of a middle ſize ‡, and ſome even very ſmall ‖, which are not for that the leſs good and ſtrong: but there are alſo many of a good ſize, and even larger than the Engliſh ſaddle-horſes §. They have all a ſlender head, a fine neck, and a narrow cheſt; the ears well ſhaped and well placed, the legs ſlender, the rump well turned, and a hard hoof: they are docile, ſprightly, agile, ſpirited, courageous, and capable of enduring great fatigue. They run extremely ſwift, without ever falling or ſtumbling; they are robuſt and very eaſily fed, barley mixed with fine chopped ſtraw being their only food, which is given them in bags tied to their heads; and ſix weeks in ſpring is all the time they are out at graſs. Their tales are never cut; geldings are not known among them; clothes are

* See *Voyages de Thevenot, Paris,* 1664, *Tom. II. p.* 220. *Chardin, Tom. II.* p. 25. *Amſt.* 1711. and *Adam Olearius, Paris,* 1950, *Tom. I. p.* 560. *et ſeq.*

† *Voyages de Pietro della Valle, Rouen,* 1745, 12*mo. Tom. V. p.* 560. *et ſeq.*

‡ See *Voyages de Tavernier, Rouen,* 1715, *Tom. II. p.* 424.

‖ *Id. ibid. p.* 220.

§ *Chardin, Tom. II. p.* 25.

laid

laid over them to prevent their receiving any injury from the air; they are rode only with a ſnaffle bridle and no ſpur; and great numbers of them are tranſported into Turkey, and ſtill more into the Indies. Travellers, who all ſpeak highly of the Perſian horſes, agree however in ſaying, that thoſe of Arabia are ſuperior to them in agility, courage, ſtrength, and even beauty; and that the Perſians themſelves ſet a much higher value on them, than on the fineſt horſes of their own country.

" The native horſes of India are not good *. Thoſe made uſe of by the great men of the country, have been carried thither from Perſia and Arabia. In the day-time a little hay is given them, and in the evening boiled peaſe, mixed with ſugar and butter, inſtead of oats or barley. This food ſupports them, and gives them ſome ſtrength; for otherwiſe they would ſoon waſte away, the climate being contrary to their nature. The native horſes of the country are, in general, very ſmall; ſome of them even ſo little, that, if Tavernier may be credited, the young Mogul Prince, who was between ſeven and eight years of age, uſually rode a horſe very well ſhaped, but not bigger than a large greyhound †.

" Exceſſively hot climates ſeem not to agree with horſes; as a proof of which, thoſe of the Gold Coaſt, of Indus, of Guinea, &c. are, like the Indian horſes, very bad. They carry their head and neck remarkably low, and totter ſo greatly in their goings, that one thinks them always ready to fall; they will not ſtir without continual beating, and moſt of them are ſo very low, that the rider's feet almoſt touch the ground ‡: they are beſides very untractable, and indeed fit only to feed negroes, who like their fleſh

* See *Le Voyage de la Boullaye-le-Gonz, Paris*, 1657, *p.* 256, and *le Receuil des Voyages qui ont ſervi à l' etabliſſement de la Campagnie des Indes, Amſt.* 1702. *Tom. IV. p.* 424.

† *Voyage de Tavernier, Tom. III. p.* 334.

‡ *Hiſt. génèrale des Voyages, Tom. IV. p.* 228.

as well as they do that of dogs *. Thus we ſee that the love of horſe-fleſh is common to the negroes and Arabians: it is likewiſe ſo in Tartary, and even in China †.

" The Chineſe horſes are not better than thoſe of the Indies ‡: they are weak, ſpiritleſs, ill-ſhaped, and very ſmall: thoſe of Corea are but three feet high. The Chineſe caſtrate moſt of their horſes; and they are ſo timid, that they cannot be uſed in war: accordingly it may be ſaid, that it was the Tartarian horſes that conquered China. Theſe laſt are indeed very fit for war; for though they are generally but of the middle ſize, they are ſtrong, vigorous, ſpirited, bold, light, and great runners: their hoof is hard, but too narrow; the head very airy, but too ſmall; the neck long and ſtiff, and the legs too high: yet with all theſe defects, they may be accounted very good horſes; being indefatigable, and exceeding ſwift. The Tartars live with their horſes nearly in the ſame manner as the Arabians. When they are ſeven or eight months old, they put boys on their backs, to walk them about, and gallop them at ſhort intervals. They train them up thus by little and little, and inure them to very ſhort diet; but never mount them for an expedition till they are ſix or ſeven years old, and then they are made to endure incredible fatigues, ſuch as marching two or three days without halting, being four or five without any other nouriſhment than a handful of graſs, and at the ſame time twenty-four hours without drinking, &c. But theſe horſes, which ſeem, and which are in fact, ſo robuſt in their own country, ſoon fall away to nothing when carried to China or

* *H. Tom. IV. p.* 353.

† *Voyages de M. Gentil, Paris,* 1725, *Tom. II. p.* 24.

‡ See *Les ancinnes relations des Indes et de la Chine, traduite de l'Arabe. Paris,* 1718, *p.* 204. *L'Hiſt. gen des Voy. Tom. VI. p.* 492, and 505. *L'Hiſt. de la conquête de la Chine, par Palafox, Paris,* 1673, *p.* 426.

the

the Indies; though they thrive pretty well in Persia and Turkey.

"The Inhabitants of Little Tartary have also a small breed of horses, which they value so greatly that they never suffer them to be sold to strangers. These horses have all the good and bad qualities of those of Great Tartary; which proves how far the same usage, and the same manner of bringing up these animals, impart to them the same dispositions and temper. There are likewise in Circassia and Mingrelia numbers of horses which are even handsomer than those of Tartary; and tolerably fine horses are also found in the Ukraine, Walachia, Poland, and Sweden; but particular observations have not yet been made on their good qualities and defects.

"Now, if we consult the antients with regard to the nature and qualities of horses of different countries, we shall find *, that the Grecian horses, and especially those of Thessaly and Epirus, were in repute, and very good for war; that those of Achaia were the largest then known; that the handsomest of all were those of Ægypt, where they were very numerous, and where Solomon purchased great numbers at very high prices; that horses throve badly in Ethiopia, on account of the too great heat of the climate; that Arabia and Africa furnished the best made horses, and especially the swiftest and fittest for the saddle or the race; that those of Italy, and particularly of Apulia, were also very good; that in Sicily, Cappadocia, Syria, Armenia, Media, and Persia, there were excellent horses, estimable for their agility and swiftness; that those of Sardinia and Corsica were small, but spirited and bold; that those of Spain resembled the Parthian horses, and were excellent for war; that the Transylvanian and Walachian horses had small well-shaped heads, manes reaching down to the ground, bushy tails,

* See *Aldrovand, Hist. Nat. de Soliped.* p. 48—63.

and were very fleet; that the Danish horses were well made, and good leapers: that those of Scandinavia were small, but well moulded, and very nimble; that the Flemish horses were strong; that the Gauls furnished the Romans with good horses for the saddle, and for carrying burthens; that the German horses were ill-shaped; and so bad as to be of no use; that the Swiss had great numbers of horses, and of very good ones for war; that the Hungarian horses were also very good; and lastly, that the Indian horses were very small and very weak.

"It results from all these facts, that the Arabian horses have ever been, and that they still are, the first in the world, as well for beauty as for goodness; that it is from them, either immediately, or mediately by the means of Barbs, that the finest horses in Europe, Africa, and Asia, are procured; that the climate of Arabia is, perhaps, the true climate for horses, and the best of all climates for them; since instead of crossing there the native breeds by foreign breeds, great care is taken to preserve them entirely pure; that if that climate is not in itself the best for horses, the Arabians have rendered it such by their particular attention in all times to ennoble the breed, by putting together only such individuals as were the best shaped, and of the first rank; that by an unremitted continuance of this care for several ages, they may have brought the species to a degree of perfection beyond what nature would have done in the best climate. We may also conclude from the above, that those climates which are rather hot than cold, and especially where the soil is dry, are the best suited to the nature of these animals; that, in general, small horses are better than large; that care is not less necessary to them all than food; that with familiarity and caresses one may obtain much more of them than by force and punishment; that in horses of hot countries, the bones, the hoofs, and the muscles are much harder than in those of our climates;

climates; that though heat agrees with these animals better than cold, yet excessive heat does not suit them; that great cold is likewise hurtful to them; in fine, that their constitution and temper depend almost entirely on the climate, the food, the care taken of them, and the manner of bringing them up."

I now return to the horses of this country, a short sketch of the history of which may not be unacceptable to some readers.

How, or when this island became provided with the various sorts of animals which we now see in it, is of little importance to the design of this work, or indeed to ourselves. Leaving therefore all the useful kinds, such as bullocks, sheep, hogs, horses, &c. to encrease and multiply under the care of the first inhabitants of this country, who, we are told, were careful to bring such with them; and letting pole-cats, snakes, and toads, with the numerous tribe of other vermin, find their way hither as they can; we shall at once descend to a less obscure period.

When Julius Cæsar invaded this island, he found its inhabitants abundantly provided with horses so well disciplined as to strike the Romans with admiration, and even terror *; and it is highly probable that these conquerors themselves, during their stay here, brought over foreign horses, as well as troops, to maintain the several posts of cavalry which they had formed in different parts, especially on the coasts. The Saxons also kept great numbers of horses in this island, and so likewise did the Danes †: but after

* *Cæsar, de Bello Gallico. Lib. IV. c.* 24, 29. *Lib. V. c.* 8, 11, 15.

† We read in Bromton, that in the reign of king Athelstan, or Ethelstan, a law was made to prevent sending horses abroad for sale; which shews that our horses were in request even at that time. In the year 1000, when Ethelred reigned, it was enacted, that the compensation for a horse that was lost should be thirty shillings, for a mare or colt of a year old twenty shillings, for a mule or young ass twelve shillings, for an ox thirty pence, for

ter the Norman conqueſt, both the value and the breed of our horſes ſeem to have declined. Henry VII, ever vigilant to promote the welfare of his dominions, and amongſt other things to raiſe at home a good breed of horſes, ordered that no ſtallions ſhould be ſent abroad without licence, but permitted the free exportation of low-priced mares when more than two years of age; and his ſon and ſucceſſor Henry VIII, made ſeveral ſevere laws againſt allowing ſtallions in ſome places under fourteen, in others fifteen hands high, and about two years old, to run in any foreſt, moor, or common, where there were mares: commanding magiſtrates to drive thoſe places about Michaelmas, and impowering and requiring them to put to death all ſuch mares as they ſhould find therein not likely to bear foals of a good ſize, and all ſuch geldings or foals as they ſhould judge would not prove ſerviceable. The northern counties were excepted from this order; which ſhews that they had not at that time any remarkable breed of horſes *. It was enacted that a certain number of breeding mares, at leaſt thirteen hands high, ſhould be kept in every park where there were deer. Theſe coercive ſtatutes were however ſo far from anſwering the purpoſe for which they were intended, that when we were threatened with the famous Spaniſh invaſion, in the reign of queen Elizabeth, there could not upon the ſtricteſt enquiry be found above three thouſand horſes fit for ſervice in the whole of Eng-

for a cow twenty-four pence, for a ſheep one ſhilling, for a goat eleven pence, for a ſwine eight pence, and for a man one pound. All this was in Saxon money, of which forty-eight ſhillings made a pound, and five pence a ſhilling: and ſhews us what then was the relative value of things.

* The caſe is greatly altered ſince, particularly with regard to Yorkſhire; and to a repeal of this law ſo far as related to Cornwall, by Stat. 21 Jac. 1. c. 28. §. 12. we owe the preſervation of that valuable race of ſmall horſes which the people of that country call Gunhillies, moſt admirably ſuited to their roads and labours.

land.

land*. By the defeat and dispersion of the Armada, the horses on board of that fleet were cast, some upon the shore of Galloway, and other parts of Scotland, by which the native breed of that country was much improved, and from whence it is not at all improbable that some of the Spanish horses were carried into the northern counties of England, where their coming had also the same good effect. The civil wars shewed the use of a superior race of horses, and at length it was perceived, that the true remedy consisted in following the custom of other nations, and that bringing over foreign stallions, attending to the breed, allowing all ranks of men entire liberty in this respect, and encouraging a love for and a pride in good horses, were the only means. The peaceable times which followed, afforded the means of compleating this plan. A little before the restoration, the exportation of our horses was permitted, but under very high duties, and plates were instituted to encourage races. In consequence of these measures, our horses soon became both numerous and valuable; and in the year 1670, the duty on exportation was reduced to a mere register-fee, of only five shillings a head, as it still continues to be. This alteration was speedily attended with all the good effects that could be wished for: fine studs were established in most parts of the kingdom, and supplied plenty of bred-horses for the course, our cavalry, and the saddle; and the spirit of emulation, natural to the inhabitants of this island, extended itself from persons of superior rank and fortune, by whom this work was begun, to the middling class of people, soon procured us other inferior sorts of horses proportionably improved. The notice of all our neighbours was speedily attracted, the reputation of our horses

* It cannot indeed be doubted, that one of the principal motives which instigated the Spaniards to that attempt, was the knowledge they had obtained of our weakness in respect to cavalry.

was juſtly raiſed, and the advantages reſulting from this general regard to theſe animals became manifeſt. Whether we have not gone too far in this pleaſing road, by over-ſtocking ourſelves with horſes, and employing them in works which might be better done by oxen; and whether the object of gain to individuals, by breeding of horſes for exportation, may not, all things conſidered, be a detriment to the nation, are points which have been of late pretty warmly, but, in my humble opinion, not yet ſatisfactorily diſcuſſed. Every one knows, that private benefits may eaſily ariſe from public loſſes.

A mixture of horſes of different breeds produces, in our ſtuds, colts which may all be ſaid to differ in ſize, proportion, temper, inſtinct, &c. From among this great variety it is that horſes are choſen for that purpoſe to which they ſeem beſt adapted. Thus very different horſes are uſed for travelling, hunting, war, the harneſs, the pack-ſaddle, &c.

Saddle-horſes for travelling ſhould be in the prime of their age, and of a good ſize, that they may be the better able to bear the fatigues to which they are deſtined. They ſhould be ſure-footed, their feet well made, their hoofs firm, their mouths ſenſible, and their motions eaſy; not too fiery, but quiet without ſluggiſhneſs. The fearful, and thoſe which are too nice in their food, ſhould be rejected.

All the horſes that are trained up for war ſhould be well ſhaped, vigorous, alert, and lively: their mouths cannot be too good, nor their motions too eaſy. Their trot and gallop ſhould be ſhort and briſk, and their thighs and backs ſtrong. The horſes uſed by officers ſhould be good-natured, gentle, dexterous, bold, and active: the fearful, or ſuch as are too delicate, or too fiery, are not fit for this ſervice. With regard to troop-horſes, it is ſufficient that they be ſtrong, hardy, and good trotters; that they have a good ſhare of foot, and a firm mouth.

In

In ſtate-horſes, the only thing attended to is a fine exterior; and accordingly the qualities which chiefly recommend them, are the beauty of their ſhape, coat, mane, and tail: though it is equally neceſſary that they ſhould be proud and ſpirited, their mouth good and frothing, and that they be continually champing the bit. Such as have a proud carriage, have a fine effect in this kind of pomp, where appearances are ſufficient.

Stone-horſes are reckoned fitteſt for riding poſt, becauſe they are beſt able to endure fatigue. They ſhould be ſhort punch horſes, ſtrong, ſure-footed, and ſo eaſy in the gallop that their reins be hardly felt. The greateſt danger in them is their growing reſtiff or wanton; but the ſoftneſs of their mouth, and the elegance of their ſhape, are of very little conſequence.

Hunters ſhould be fleet, active, vigorous, and long-winded, with a good mouth; though too quick a ſenſation would prove inconvenient on account of the branches of trees which ſometimes check the bridle. They ſhould alſo be cool; for if they were carried away by the noiſe of the horn and the dogs, it might prove dangerous to the rider. The horſes for the whippers-in may be more clumſy and leſs valuable, but they muſt be ſwift and vigorous.

Horſes for ſetting and ſhooting muſt be trained up to the ſport, and not terrified at the firing of a gun. They are generally of the galloway ſize, for the more eaſily mounting them. They muſt be quiet, without any kind of vice. If they walk well, it is ſufficient.

A horſe for taking the air is generally choſen of a middle ſize, rather ſmall than large; the paces of the former being leſs fatiguing than thoſe of the latter. He ſhould be gentle, and do his paces very well. No remarkable vigour is required: but a ſure foot and good mouth are eſſential.

Coach-horſes ſhould trot well, have low haunches, ſtrait backs, and an erect head, with a good mouth, nervous legs, and round feet.

For poſt-chaiſes, the ſhaft-horſe ſhould be of a good ſize, well ſet and long, and he ſhould trot faſt and eaſy; the other, on which the driver rides, may be more ſlender, but his gallop ſhould be ſhort and eaſy.

For carts, waggons, drays, the plough, &c. ſtone-horſes of a common breed, and ſtrongly made, are generally preferred. As they draw with a collar, there is a neceſſity for their being well ſet; their cheſt ſhould be large, and their ſhoulders thick.

Horſes for carrying burthens ſhould be well ſet, with large ribs and firm backs; but the driver's horſe ſhould be leſs clumſy, lighter and more ſwift, as he often trots. The mouths of theſe horſes ſhould be as hard as the hand that guides them is rough.

The above are the general uſes of horſes, and the principal qualities required in their reſpective ſervices. Thoſe of a common breed are not leſs neceſſary than the moſt beautiful, or thoſe remarkable for their ſwiftneſs: on the contrary, they are, in fact, more neceſſary in the eſſential concerns of life, ſuch as tillage and draught, the labour of which the others are not able to undergo.

CHAP.

CHAP. II.

Of breeding, rearing, and fitting them for use.

TO form a ſtud properly requires great care and expence. In the eſtabliſhment of a good one, five things are particularly neceſſary to be obſerved: 1, it's ſituation; 2, the choice of the ſtallions; 3, the aſſortment of mares; 4, the covering or copulation of theſe animals; and 5, the rearing of the colts, and fitting them for uſe.

The beſt places for fixing ſtuds in are thoſe which lie open to the eaſt or ſouth, on a dry ſoil, and are interſperſed with hills and dales, and here and there a few clumps of trees. Such are, in general, the whole province of Andaluſia in Spain, and moſt of the countries inhabited by the Arabians, remarkable for producing the fineſt and beſt horſes. The ſoil muſt be good and fertile in graſs, and it's extent proportioned to the number of mares and ſtallions intended to be uſed. The place thus choſen muſt be divided into ſeveral parts, and each of theſe muſt be well fenced with rails and ditches. The part where the paſture is richeſt ſhould be appropriated to the mares that are in foal, and thoſe with colts by their ſides. Thoſe which are not pregnant, or have not yet been covered, ſhould be kept apart with the fillies in another cloſe, where the paſture is leſs rich, that they may not grow too fat, becauſe this would be a hindrance to their breeding: and laſtly, the young ſtone-colts, or geldings, ſhould be kept in the

the drieſt part of the fields, and where the ground is moſt unequal; in order that, by running over the uneven ſurface, they may acquire a freedom in the motion of their legs and ſhoulders. This cloſe, where the ſtone-colts are kept, muſt be very carefully fenced off from the others, leſt thoſe young horſes ſhould break their bounds, and enervate themſelves with the mares. If the ſpace be large enough to admit of dividing each of theſe cloſes into two parts, ſo that horſes and oxen may be put into them alternately, the paſture will laſt much longer than if it be conſtantly fed on by horſes only; the ox improving it's fertility, whereas the horſe leſſens it.

In each of theſe cloſes there ſhould be a pond; ſtanding-water being better for horſes than running, which laſt is apt to gripe them, and probably often is the cauſe of that dreadful diſeaſe, the glanders *. They generally prefer water that is a little muddy. If there are ſome trees on the ground, they ſhould be let ſtand, their ſhade being both agreeable and ſerviceable to the horſes in great heats; but all ſtumps ſhould be grubbed up, and all holes levelled, to prevent accidents. Alſo it will be right to erect in different

* It is worth obſerving here, that thoſe travellers who ſpeak of the diſeaſes of horſes in hot countries, do not ſay a word of the glanders being ſo common there as it is in cold climates: from whence there is reaſon to think, that the coldneſs of the water may be one of the natural cauſes of this diſorder; theſe animals being, from the ſmallneſs of their mouth, the thickneſs and ſhortneſs of their tongue, and their great eagerneſs to drink, obliged to dip their noſe and noſtrils into the water, and to keep them there ſome conſiderable time if they would take a plentiful draught; and conſequently that this diſeaſe might, in ſome meaſure at leaſt, be guarded againſt, by never giving them quite cold water, and always wiping their noſtrils, after they have done drinking.—Aſſes are far leſs ſubject to the glanders than horſes; probably for no other reaſon than becauſe they drink in a different manner; for the aſs, inſtead of thruſting down his mouth and noſtrils into the water, only juſt touches it with his lips. What would ſeem to confirm this conjecture is, that the internal ſtructure of both theſe animals is very nearly alike.

ferent commodious parts of the ſtud a few ſpacious ſheds, for the horſes to ſhelter themſelves under in rainy or other bad weather. In theſe paſtures, the horſes ſhould feed during the ſummer; but in winter the mares ſhould be kept in the ſtable, and fed with hay. Likewiſe, the colts muſt be houſed, and never ſuffered to feed abroad in winter, except in very fine weather. Stallions which ſtand in the ſtable ſhould be fed more with ſtraw than hay; and be moderately exerciſed till the ſeaſon for covering, during which they ſhould have no other exerciſe, and be plentifully fed; but only with their uſual food.

This animal, and eſpecially the female, is capable of engendering at the age of two years, or two years and a half: but the foals begot by ſuch young horſes are faulty, either in their ſhape or in their conſtitution. A draught, or common horſe, ſhould be at leaſt four years or four years and a half old before he is ſuffered to approach a mare; but thoſe of a more ſlender and delicate nature ſhould not be admitted to copulation, till they are at leaſt ſix years old, and the fine Spaniſh or Arabian ſtallions not till ſeven. Mares may be a year younger. Their uſual time of heat is from the end of March to the end of June: but the moſt violent heat ſeldom laſts above a fort-night or three weeks, and this is the time when they ſhould be led to the horſe.

The ſtallion ſhould be handſome, well-limbed, with a ſtately cheſt, vigorous, ſound in every part, of a good race and country, and of a proper ſize, that is, fourteen hands and one or two inches high, for ſaddle-horſes; and, at leaſt, fifteen hands for coach-horſes; for without fine ſtallions, we cannot expect well-ſhaped horſes. He ſhould alſo be of a good colour, as a jet black, a fine grey, a bay, a ſorrel, a bright cheſnut, with the mule's liſt, the mane and extremities black; for all horſes of a dull or faint colour, together with thoſe whoſe extremities are white, ſhould be excluded from ſtuds. To every

ry

ry external beauty, a good ſtallion ſhould likewiſe join all the valuable qualities of a horſe, ſuch as courage, docility, mettle, ſpirit, agility, a ſenſible mouth, freedom in the ſhoulders, a ſure foot, ſupleneſs in his haunches, a facility of motion in all parts of his body, and eſpecially in the hams. It is alſo proper that he ſhould have gone through ſome of the diſcipline of the riding-ſchool: for it is obſerved of the horſe, which has been more attended to than any other animal, that he communicates, in generation, almoſt every good quality, whether natural or acquired, as well as, too often, every bad one. For this reaſon, particular care ſhould be taken to exclude from the ſtud every defective horſe, whether ill ſhaped, moon-eyed, glandered, paralytic, &c.

The Arabian, Turkiſh, Barb, and Andaluſian ſtallions are generally preferred; and next to theſe the fine Engliſh, who owe their origin to one or other of them, and do not ſoon degenerate, by reaſon of the excellency of their provender. The ſtallions of Italy, eſpecially the Neapolitan, are alſo very good; getting fine-limbed ſaddle horſes, when coupled with mares of that make; and excellent coach-horſes with ſtrong well-ſet mares. It is ſaid, that the Arabian and Barb ſtallions uſually beget horſes larger than themſelves in England, France, &c. whereas the foals of Spaniſh horſes, in the ſame countries, are always ſmaller. The fineſt coach-horſes are bred from the ſtallions of Naples, Denmark, or ſome parts of Germany and Holland, as, in particular, Holſtein and Friezland.

In theſe climates, at leaſt, if not in all others, the mare contributes leſs than the ſtallion to the beauty of the foal; but, perhaps more to it's diſpoſition and ſhape. She ſhould have a large carcaſe, be pretty full bellied, and a good nurſe. The Spaniſh and Italian mares are generally preferred for breeding of Saddle horſes, and the Engliſh, Flemiſh, Daniſh,

Danish, and Norman, for coach-horses. However, with fine stallions, fine horses may be expected from mares of all countries, provided they are well shaped, and of a good breed; for if they were got by a bad horse, their foals will often turn out very indifferent. In these animals, as in the human species, the offspring often resemble the progenitors; but in horses the female does not appear to contribute so much to generation as in the human species. A son is much oftener like his mother, than a foal is like it's dam: and when a resemblance happens between the foal and the mare, it is generally in the forehead, the head, and the neck.

It has been observed, that horses fed in dry and light grounds beget temperate, swift, and vigorous foals, with muscular legs and hard hoofs; while the same breed in marshes, and moist pastures, have produced foals with a large heavy head, a thick carcase, clumsy legs, bad hoofs, and broad feet. These differences proceed from the air and food; and so far are easily understood; but what is more difficult to be accounted for, and far more essential in the breeding of horses, is the necessity of continually crossing the breed, to prevent a degeneracy.

To form to ourselves an idea of the expediency of this mixture of breeds, commonly termed *crossing the breed*, let us consider, that nature has, in every species, a general prototype, after which each individual of that species is formed; and that this, in the realization, degenerates or improves from circumstances: so that, with regard to certain qualities, there is apparently a capricious variation in the succession of individuals; and, at the same time, a remarkable stability in the whole species. The original form subsists entire in each individual: but though there are millions of these individuals, not two of them are exactly alike in every particular; nor consequently any one of them the same as the model from

from which it received it's form. This difference, which at once demonstrates how far nature is from fixing any thing absolutely, and the infinite variations which she spreads throughout her works, is manifest in the human race, in every species of animals and vegetables, and, in a word, in every series of beings. But what deserves particular attention is, that the model of beauty and goodness seems distributed throughout the whole earth, every climate affording only a portion of it; and that continually degenerating, unless re-united with another portion from some distant country: so that to have good grain, beautiful flowers, &c. the seeds must be changed, and, as hath been repeatedly observed in various parts of my System of Husbandry *, never be sown a second time in the soil that produced them. In the same manner, to have fine horses, &c. foreign stallions must be given to native mares, or foreign mares to native stallions: for otherwise, grains, flowers, animals, will degenerate, or rather imbibe so strong a tincture from the climate, that the mother will so powerfully influence the form, as to cause an apparent degeneracy: the form remains, but disfigured by many dissimilar lineaments. Whereas, let the breed be mixed, and constantly renewed by foreign species, the form will advance towards perfection, and recruited nature display her choicest productions †.

The

* See in particular *Vol. I. p.* 359, 424.

† Though it may not strictly belong to a work of this kind to discuss the general reason for these effects, yet I am persuaded the reader will not be displeased at seeing here the judicious M. de Buffon's conjectures on this head.

" Experience," says that learned Naturalist, " shews that animals, or vegetables, transported from a remote climate often degenerate, and sometimes greatly improve in a small time; I mean, within a very few generations. That this is the effect of a difference of climate and aliment, is easy to conceive: and, in

The influences of the climate and aliment are remarkable, not only in the make of animals, but also in the colour of their coats; for, in the same climate, the wild and the tame are of the same, or nearly the same colour; whereas those which live in different climates

in length of time, the influence of these two causes must render such animals exempt from, or susceptible of, certain affections and diseases. Their temperament must gradually alter; the formation, which partly depends on the aliment, and partly on the quality of the juices, must also undergo a change in the succession of a few generations. This change in the first generation is scarcely perceptible; as the two animals, the male and the female, which we suppose to be the progenitors of the species, had obtained their full shape and constitution before they were brought from their native country; and that however a new climate and food may change their temperament, these cannot act on the solid and organical parts, so as to alter their shape; especially if they had attained their full growth: consequently, in the first generation there will be no disadvantageous change; no degeneracy in the first production of these animals; the impression of the model will be exact. At the instant of their birth there will be no radical defect; but the young animal, during its weak and tender state, will feel the influences of the climate. They will make different impressions on him, from what they did on his full-grown sire and dam. Those proceeding from the aliment will also be much greater, and act on the organical parts during the time of their growth, so as to vitiate a little of the organical form, and produce germs of imperfections, which will appear very sensibly in a second generation, when the parent, besides it's own defects, I mean those it derives from it's growth, has also the defects of the second generation, which will be then more strongly marked: and at the third generation, the defects of the second and third stock, caused by the influence of the climate and aliment, being again combined with those of the present influence on the growth, will become so palpable, as to obliterate the marks of the original stock; so that these animals of foreign extraction, will have nothing foreign in them, but be exactly similar to the natives. Hence arises the necessity of crossing the breed of horses, and renewing it at every generation, by importing foreign stallions for the use of native mares. And it is very remarkable, that this manner of renewing the breed, which is only in part, and as it were, by halves, has a much better effect than if the renovation was total. A horse and a mare of Spain, for example, will not here produce such fine horses as a Spanish stallion with an English mare. This, however,

climates are of different colours. The effects of the climate and aliment being always the same, they produce in wild animals this uniformity; and the variety of colour in domestic animals is owing to the

ever, will be easily comprehended, if we consider, that when a stallion and a mare of different countries are put together, the defects of both are compensated. Every climate, by it's own influences, and those of the food, imparts a certain confirmation, which is faulty through some excess or defect. Thus, in a hot climate there will be an excess of fire, and in a cold one there will be the contrary defect: so that by joining animals of these opposite climates, the excess of the one supplies the defects of the other: and as that reaches nearest to perfection in nature, which has the fewest faults, and the most perfect forms being only such as have the fewest deformities, the produce of two animals whose defects are exactly balanced, will be the most perfect production of that kind. This equality is also the more accuratley adjusted, the more distant the countries are, or rather the more opposite the climates natural to the two animals are to each other. The compound result is the more perfect, as the excesses or defects of the stallion's constitution are more opposite to the excesses and defects of the mare.

"To give foreign horses to native mares will therefore always produce a certain advantage; whereas an increase of horses of the same breed in a stud, will always cause a certain loss, as they will, in a very little time, infallibly degenerate.

"It may, perhaps, have been upon this very principle, and in consequence of long-since forgotten experience of the disadvantages resulting from alliances between persons of the same blood, that men, in general, first agreed to prohibit marriage between such as are very near of kin: for among all nations, even the least civilized, a brother was very rearly permitted to marry his sister. This custom, introduced among us by divine prohibition, but among other nations, founded on political views only, is, perhaps, owing to observation. Polity does not extend it's prescriptions in so general and absolute a manner, unless connected with nature: but if men once discovered from experience that a desire of preserving a race, without mixture, in one and the same family, would produce a degeneracy, they would consider inter-marriages with foreign families as a law of nature: they would all agree in a prohibition of marriages among their own children. And, indeed, it may be presumed from analogy, that in most climates, men, like animals, would degenerate after a certain number of generations." *Hist. Naturelle du Cheval.*

care

care of man, to ſhelter, to diverſity of foot, and to a mixture of foreign breeds. When the colour of the male is different from that of the female, the latter ſometimes gives riſe to beautiful peculiarities, as in pyed-horſes, where the white and black are ſo ſtrongly marked, and form ſuch a glaring contraſt, that it ſeems rather the performance of a whimſical painter, than the work of nature.

For the above reaſons then, among many others which experience might furniſh, the ſtallion and the mare ſhould be ſuited to each other in colour and ſize, their ſhapes ſhould be contraſted, and the breed ſhould be croſſed by an oppoſition of climates: but horſes and mares foaled in the ſame ſtud ſhould never be joined. It is by gradations that we muſt indeavour to arrive at natural beauty; for example, to give to a mare a little too clumſy, a horſe well made and finely ſhaped; and to a ſmall mare a horſe a little higher; to a mare that is faulty in her fore-hand, an horſe with a fine head, and noble cheſt, &c. But at the ſame time care ſhould be taken not to make any evidently diſproportionate copulations, as of a very ſmall horſe with a large mare, or a very large horſe with a ſmall mare: for the produce of ſuch copulation would be ſmall, or badly proportioned; and conſequently that is not the way to correct the faults of the one by the perfections of the other. Some allowance ſhould indeed be made for a mare that has never had a colt, becauſe her firſt foal is never ſo ſtrongly formed as the ſucceeding: for this reaſon it may be right to give her for the firſt birth, a larger ſtallion than it might be proper for her to have afterwards, in order that the defect of the growth may be compenſated by the largeneſs of the ſize. Theſe precautions are eſſential; but there are likewiſe other circumſtances which ſhould by no means be neglected; ſuch as, that no ſhort-docked mares be ſuffered in a ſtud, becauſe from their not being able to keep off the flies, they are much more tormented by them than others which have a long ſweeping tail; and their continual agitations from the ſtings of theſe inſects occaſion a diminution in the quantity of their milk, and has a great influence on the conſtitution and ſize of the colt, which will be vigorous in proportion as it's dam is a good nurſe. Care ſhould alſo be taken, that the ſtud-mares be ſuch as have always been brought up in paſtures, and never over-worked. Mares which have been brought up in the ſtable on dry food, and afterwards turned to graſs, do not breed at firſt: ſome time is required to accuſtom them to this new aliment.

When the ſtallion is choſen, and all the mares intended for him are collected together, another ſtone-horſe ſhould be produced, in order to diſcover which of the mares are in heat, and, at the ſame time, contribute to inflame them. All the mares ſhould be brought ſucceſſively to this laſt ſtone-horſe, which ſhould alſo be inflamed, and ſuffered frequently to neigh. He will want to leap every one; but ſuch as are not in heat will keep him off, whilſt thoſe which are ſo ſuffer him to approach them. But inſtead of being allowed to proceed ſo far as to ſatisfy his deſire, he muſt be led away, and the real ſtallion be ſubſtituted in his ſtead. This trial is neceſſary in order to aſcertain the true time of the mare's heat, eſpecially of thoſe which have not yet had a colt; for with regard to ſuch as have recently foaled, the heat uſually begins nine days after their delivery, and on that very day they may be led to the ſtallion to be covered; and nine days after, by the foregoing experiment, it may be known whether they are ſtill in heat. If they are, they muſt, in this way of proceeding, be covered a ſecond time, and ſo on ſucceſſively every ninth day while their heat continues: for when they are impregnated, their heat abates, and in a few days ceaſes entirely. Not but that mares will admit of copulation after they are pregnant; though it never is attended with any ſuperfetation.

Another,

Another, and moſt certain ſign of a mare's being in heat, is her ejecting a viſcid whitiſh liquor, called the heats, which likewiſe ceaſe on conception. It is alſo known by the inflation of the lower part of the *vulva*, by her frequent neighings, and by her endeavouring to get to horſes.

Before the ſtallion is brought to the mare, he ſhould be well dreſſed, becauſe that will greatly increaſe his ardour. The mare muſt alſo be curried, and have no ſhoes on her hind feet, ſome of them being ticklish, and apt to kick the ſtallion. A perſon holds the mare by a halter, and two others lead the ſtallion by long reins, till he is in a proper ſituation, when another aſſiſtant carefully directs the yard, pulling aſide the mare's tail; for a ſingle hair might hurt him dangerouſly. After the mare has been covered, nothing more remains but to lead her away to the field. It ſometimes happens that the ſtallion does not compleat the work of generation, but comes from the mare without making any injection. It ſhould therefore be attentively obſerved, whether in the laſt moments of the copulation, the dock of the ſtallion's tail has a vibrating motion; for ſuch a motion always accompanies the emiſſion of the ſeminal lymph. If he has performed the act, he muſt not on any account be ſuffered to repeat it, but be led away directly to the ſtable, and there kept two days: for however able a good ſtallion may be to cover every day during the three months that mares are in heat, it is much better to let him be led to a mare only every other day; his produce will be the greater, and he himſelf leſs exhauſted. During the firſt ſeven days, let four different mares be ſucceſſively brought to him, and on the ninth day let the firſt be again brought, and ſo ſucceſſively whilſt they continue in heat; but as ſoon as the heat of any one is over, a freſh mare is to be put in her place, and covered in her turn every ninth day; and as ſeveral retain even at the firſt, ſecond, or third time,

 it

it is computed that a ſtallion, by ſuch management, may, during the three months, cover fifteen or eighteen mares, and beget ten or twelve colts.

Many, inſtead of bringing the ſtallion to the mare, turn him looſe into the cloſe, where all the mares are brought together, and there leave him to chooſe ſuch as will ſtand to him. This is a very advantageous method for the mares: they will always take horſe more certainly than in the other; but the ſtallion, in ſix weeks, will do himſelf more damage than in ſeveral years by moderate exerciſe, conducted in the manner above-mentioned.

Though the uſual ſeaſon for the heat of mares be from the beginning of April to the end of June, yet it is not uncommon to find, amongſt a large number, ſome which are in heat before that time: but it is adviſeable to let this heat paſs off without giving them a ſtallion, becauſe they would foal in winter; and in that caſe, the colts, beſides the inclemency of the ſeaſon, would have bad milk for their nouriſhment. On the contrary, if the mares are not in heat till after the end of June, they ſhould not be covered that ſeaſon, becauſe the colts which are foaled in ſummer have not time to acquire ſufficient ſtrength to reſiſt the injuries of the following winter *.

When the mares are pregnant, and their belly begins to ſwell, they muſt be ſeparated from thoſe that are not ſo, leſt theſe laſt ſhould hurt them. They uſually go eleven months and ſome days, and foal ſtanding; whereas moſt other quadrupeds lie down. Thoſe which cannot foal without difficulty, muſt be aſſiſted; the foal muſt be placed in a proper ſituati-

* The Memoirs of the Royal Society of Agriculture at Rouen, publiſhed in 1767, ſeem here to differ from M. de Buffon: They ſay, that the beſt time for the ſtallion's covering of mares, is from the 15th or 20th of May to the 1ſt of Auguſt; becauſe, as mares go eleven months, there is the more graſs for them when they foal, they eat better, and have greater ſtore of milk. *Tom. II. Mémoire ſur les Haras de Normandie.*

on;

ten; and ſometimes, if dead, be drawn out with cords. The head of the foal uſually preſents itſelf firſt, as in all other animals *.

The general cuſtom of cauſing a mare to be covered ſo ſoon as the ninth day after ſhe has foaled, is certainly wrong; becauſe, in that caſe, having both her preſent and her future foal to nouriſh, her ability is divided, and ſhe cannot ſupply both ſo largely as ſhe might one only. It would therefore be better, in order to have excellent horſes, to let the mares be covered only every other year: they would laſt the longer, and bring foals more certainly: for, in common ſtuds, it is ſo far from being true, that all mares which have been covered bring colts every year, that it is looked upon as a fortunate circumſtance if half, or at moſt two thirds of them, foal.

The foal ſhould be ſeparated from it's dam when it is five, ſix, or at fartheſt ſeven months old; experience having ſhewn, that ſuch as are ſuffered to ſuck ten or eleven months, though uſually larger and fuller of fleſh, are not equal in other reſpects to thoſe which are weaned ſooner. The way to wean them, and to accuſtom them by degrees to a more ſolid nouriſhment than milk, is to give them bran twice a day, with a ſmall quantity of hay; increaſing this laſt as they advance in age. In this manner they ſhould be kept in the ſtable as long as they expreſs any deſire of returning to their dam: but when this un-

* At it's coming out of the matrix, it breaks the ſecundines, or integuments that incloſe it, which is accompanied with a great flux of the lymph contained in them; and at the ſame time one or more ſolid lumps, formed by the ſediment of the inſpiſſated liquor of the *allantoides*. This lump, which the antients called the *hippomenes* of the colt, is ſo far from being, as they imagined, a maſs of fleſh adhering to the head of the colt, that it is ſeparated from it by a membrace called *amnios*. As ſoon as the colt is fallen, the mare licks it, but without touching the *hippomenes*; which points out an error of the ancients, who affirmed that ſhe inſtantly devours it.

eaſineſs is over, they ſhould be turned into the fields; taking care, however, that they be not then faſting. An hour before they are turned to graſs, the bran muſt be given them, and alſo ſome water; nor ſhould they be expoſed either to ſevere cold or rain. In this manner they ſhould paſs their firſt winter. In the month of May following, they ſhould not only be turned into the field every day, but may lie in the open air till the end of October, taking care that they do not feed on the rowings or after-math; for by accuſtoming themſelves to this remarkably delicate and ſucculent graſs, they would contract a diſlike to hay, which, together with barley and oats ground, is to be their principal food during the ſecond winter. In this manner they are to be kept till their fourth year; ſpending the days only in the paſtures during the winter, but both day and night in the ſummer. When they reach that age, they are taken from the paſtures, and fed with dry meat: but one precaution at leaſt neceſſary to be obſerved in this change of diet, is, to feed them only with ſtraw during the firſt week, and to give them proper medicines againſt worms, which often trouble them, from bad digeſtions and too rank graſs. Every one knows that the firſt foal of a mare, and indeed the firſt-born of every animal, never is ſo ſtrong and vigorous, at leaſt in it's youth, as the ſubſequent productions of the ſame mother.

Whilſt the colts are weaning, they ſhould be kept in a clean ſtable, but not over-warm, becauſe too much heat would render them tender, and too ſenſible of the impreſſions of the air. They muſt frequently have freſh litter, and be rubbed often with ſtraw; but they ſhould not be tied or curried till they are three, or at leaſt two years and a half old; becauſe the roughneſs of this friction would give them pain; and their ſkin being too tender to endure it, inſtead of thriving, they would fall away. The rack and manger ſhould not be too high, leſt the neceſſity of lifting up their heads to reach the food ſhould accuſtom them to carry their heads in that manner, which would ſpoil their cheſts. When they are a year, or a year and a half old, the hair on their tails ſhould be cut, becauſe the ſucceeding growth will be ſtronger and thicker than the former: ſome cut it two or three times for this very reaſon. When they are two years old, they ſhould be ſeparated, the ſtone-colts to be kept with the horſes, and the fillies with the mares; otherwiſe the former would fruitleſſly weaken themſelves with the latter.

At the age of three years, or three years and a half, they ſhould be broke and rendered docile. To this end, a light eaſy ſaddle ſhould be put on their back, and continued there two or three hours every day. They ſhould alſo be uſed to receive the bit of a ſnaffle bridle into their mouths, and to ſuffer their feet to be taken up, and ſome ſtrokes given on the ſoals, as if ſhoeing them. If they are deſigned for draught-horſes, a harneſs ſhould be put on their bodies, together with a ſnaffle bridle: but at firſt no bridle ſhould be uſed. Afterwards, they ſhould be trotted on the level ground, with a caviſſon on the noſe, but without a rider, the groom only holding the rein, and either the ſaddle or harneſs on their backs. When a horſe intended for the ſaddle turns eaſily, and comes freely up to him who holds the rein, he ſhould mount on his back, and immediately diſmount, without riding him till he is four years old; as before that time his weight would be too much for him: but at four years old he may be ridden, and trotted at ſmall intervals.

When a coach-horſe is to be accuſtomed to the harneſs, he ſhould be put into the carriage with a trained horſe, and be led by a long rein till he begins to draw properly; then the coachman ſhould begin to teach him to back, being aſſiſted by a man who, ſtanding directly before him, is to puſh him gently backward, and even give him a few ſtripes, that he may attain it the ſooner, and with more eaſe. All this is to be done before the young horſes have changed their food to oats and ſtraw; for they grow more headſtrong and difficult to break, in proportion as they increaſe in vigour.

The bit and the ſpur are two methods contrived for obliging horſes to comply with their rider's intention; the former for rendering their motions exact, and the latter for increaſing their ſwiftneſs. But as the proper management of both of theſe belongs to the riding-maſter, and neither to the huſbandman nor to the bare breeder of horſes, it of courſe does not appertain to the intention of this work, and I therefore cannot do better than refer the curious in theſe matters to M. de la Gueriniere's *Eléments de la Cavallerie*, and Mr. Berenger's lately publiſhed excellent work on horſemanſhip.

I cannot, however, diſmiſs this ſubject without adding the following methods of taming a wild horſe, and a wild colt; the former from the author of the Lives of the Buccaneers, and the latter from M. de Garſault.

Wild horſes are very numerous in ſeveral parts of North America, and ſtill more ſo in the iſland of Domingo in particular, where troops of above five hundred of them have often been ſeen together. They are taken in toils laid for them in places where they frequent, and are eaſily entangled; but if it happens to be by the neck, they ſtrangle themſelves, unleſs ſome perſon is ready at hand to aſſiſt them. When taken, they are faſtened round the body and legs to trees, and there left two days without either meat or drink. This renders them tame, and in time they become as tractable as if they had never been wild.

M. de Garſault's method is thus. "Colts," ſays he *, "which have not been broke whilſt very

* *Nouveau parfait Mareſhal.*

young

young, are often ſo fearful of the approach and touch of a man, that they bite and kick in ſuch a manner as renders it almoſt impoſſible to bleed or ſhoe them. But if they are not to be managed by patience and mildneſs, recourſe muſt be had to the method uſed in falconry, for taming a bird newly taken, and intended to be fitted for flight; and this is, by not ſuffering him to ſleep till he falls down with weakneſs. So likwiſe a wild horſe muſt be faſtened with his hind parts to the manger, and a man ſtand day and night at his head, to give him from time to time a handful of hay, and hinder him from lying down. It is ſurprizing to ſee how ſoon the generality of horſes will be tamed by this method; though the obſtinacy of ſome is ſuch, that they muſt be watched in this manner for a week or more."

Mares uſually breed till they are fourteen or fifteen years old; and the moſt vigorous, till they are above eighteen. Stallions, when they are well managed, will engender till the age of twenty, and even longer: but it is to be obſerved, that thoſe horſes which are ſooneſt made ſtallions, are alſo the ſooneſt incapable of generating: thus the large horſes which acquire ſtrength ſooner than the ſlender, and are therefore often uſed as ſtallions, as ſoon as they are four years old, become incapable of generating before they are ſixteen.

The horſe ſleeps much leſs than man. When in health, he ſeldom lies down above two or three hours at a time, riſing up afterwards to feed; and when he has been over-worked, he lies down a ſecond time, after feeding; but in the whole twenty-four hours, he ſeldom ſleeps above three or four. Some horſes never lie down at all, but always ſleep ſtanding; and thoſe which do lie down, ſometimes alſo ſleep reſting on their hind legs. It has been obſerved, that geldings ſleep oftener and longer than Stone-horſes.

All

All horſes, like moſt other hairy animals, ſhed their coats once a year; generally in the ſpring, but ſometimes in autumn. They are then weaker than at other times, and ſhould therefore be more tenderly uſed, have ſome ſmall addition made to their food, and be more regularly looked after. Some horſes alſo ſhed their hoofs: a misfortune which too frequently attend thoſe that have been brought up in marſhy countries.

The duration of the life of horſes is, as in every other ſpecies of animals, proportioned to the term of their growth. Man, who is fourteen years in growing, may live ſix or ſeven times that ſpace; that is, ninety or an hundred years. The horſe, whoſe growth is ended in four years, may live ſix or ſeven times as long; that is twenty-five or thirty years: and the inſtances which might be produced in oppoſition to this rule are ſo rare, that they cannot be conſidered as an exception from whence any conſequences might be drawn *: for if large horſes are full grown ſooner than thoſe that are ſlender, their lives are accordingly ſhorter, and they become old at fifteen.

The horſe, after ſpending his life in the ſervice of man, is ſtill uſeful to him after death, though not in ſo great a degree as ſome other creatures. Of the hair of the mane and tail are made bottoms of ſieves, ſeats for chairs, ſettees, &c. waiſtcoats, womens hats, hair-cloths, hair-lines, and a variety of other things in the weaving and upholſtery buſineſs. Muſical inſtrument-makers employ it in the bows for fiddles: in the toy-ſhops we meet with it in comb-bruſhes and many other things, and, after being

* What Pliny ſays of the horſe that, after quitting the circus, ſerved as a ſtallion to thirty-three, and was then diſmiſſed; and Dr. Plot's finding in Oxfordſhire three horſes of forty years old, or upwards; can be looked upon only as extraordinary inſtances of longevity, and as ſuch it plainly is that both the above authors mention them.

prepared,

prepared, it comes into the hands of the peruke-makers. It is likewiſe made into fiſhing-lines, ſpringes, ſnares, &c. The other hair, when taken from the ſkin, is mixed with that of cows, and uſed for the ſame purpoſes. The ſkin itſelf is tanned and dreſſed, chiefly for the uſe of ſaddlers. Spectacle-rings and other trifles of that kind are ſometimes made out of the hoofs; and in France the enamellers uſe an oil made from the fat of horſes which affords a clear ſtrong light with very little ſmoke.

CHAP. III.

OF THE DISEASES OF HORSES.

PART I.

Of the internal Diſeaſes of Horſes.

INTRODUCTION:

Containing ſome general Rules for preſerving the Health of Horſes.

IT is better to preſerve the health of cattle by diligence and care, than to rely on the uſe of medicines; and as it is ſaid that the maſter's eye makes the horſe fat, ſo no leſs true is it that his inſpection will keep the horſe in health.

Let it be made a general rule, to give horſes as few medicines as poſſible; and on no account to imitate the abſurd practice of thoſe who are perpetually bleeding, purging, and forcing down balls, though their horſes are perfectly well, and ſhew not the leaſt ſymptom that requires ſuch treatment. Proper management in their feeding, exerciſe, and dreſſing, will alone cure many diſorders, and prevent moſt; for, as Mr.

Bartlet

Bartlet justly observes, * The simplicity of a horse's diet, which chiefly consists of grain and herbage, when good in kind, and dispensed with judgment, secures him from those complicated disorders, which are the effect of intemperance in the human body.

Care should be taken that the pavement of the stable be raised highest where the horses stand, and that their urine be carried off readily, so that it may not remain and hurt their feet, by softening them. The Romans † preferred hard solid oak to any other substance, for their horses to stand on, particularly as best calculated to harden their hoofs. The manger should be kept free from all kind of filth, lest it hurt the horses; and it should be divided into separate partitions, that so each horse may be secured in his share of corn; for there are some which swallow it much faster than others: and the situation of the rack should be suited to the stature of the horse, neither too high, lest the throat be hurt by extending it too much, nor too low, lest the hay or other food should fall into his eyes and injure them. A considerable quantity of light should be admitted into the stable, lest by the horse's being accustomed to darkness his eye-sight should be impaired when he is brought out into open day; and it should be rather cool than hot in the winter, because the sudden change from thence into an unusual cold will hurt the horse. If the weather is very severe, his body may be cloathed. In summer the stable should be well aired by night as well as by day.

The food of horses should be sweet and free from all impurities, especially the dung and feathers of fowls: hay is so essential an article in their diet, that no pains should be spared to procure the best; and when it is not extraordinary, the dust should be well shuck out before it is put into the rack; for such hay

* *Gentleman's Farriery, p. 1.*

† *Vegetius. Lib. I. c. xvi.*

is

is apt to breed vermin. The allowance of hay ſhould be proportioned to the conſtitution of the horſe, and a lean horſe ſhould have more than a fat one: but too much is hurtful, eſpecially to fine horſes.

Their oats ſhould be well ſifted, and cleared of duſt; and particular care ſhould be taken that they be neither muſty nor ſmell of rats; for theſe are very diſguſting to horſes. Well ripened oats are a more hearty and durable food than barley, and better ſuited to the conſtitutions of Engliſh horſes, as has been proved by experience; and a proper quantity of cut ſtraw and hay mixed with them, is ſometimes very beneficial to horſes troubled with worms, indigeſtion, &c.

Beans afford the ſtrongeſt nouriſhment of all grain, but are, in general, fitteſt for hard-labouring horſes. In ſome ſeaſons they breed a kind of vermin called the red-bug, which is thought to be dangerous. The beſt method of uſing them, is dried and ſplit, then mixed with bran, and given to the horſe before his oats.

The bran will keep his body open, and the beans prevent its ſcouring, which horſes of weak bowels are ſubject to, eſpecially on a journey. Too frequent a uſe of bran alone, either dry or ſcalded, is bad becauſe it relaxes too much. However, it ſhould always be ſweet and new.

The method which ſome practiſe of giving to young horſes oats, or peaſe, &c. in the ſtraw, is attended with, at leaſt, this inconvenience, that by pulling out the ſtraw, in order to find the corn, they contract a bad habit, which they never after forget, of pulling moſt of their hay out of the rack into the manger, or on the floor, with the ſame expectation.

Moſt of the diſorders of horſes proceed from their drinking bad water; ſuch as is too ſharp, too raw, chilling, or marſhy. Clear river water is the beſt; and accordingly, where it is near enough, the beſt

way

way is to take the horſe to the river to drink in the ſummer, but as ſeldom as poſſible in the winter, if there be a well at home; becauſe water freſh drawn from a well in the winter is warm, and conſequently good for horſes. If there be a neceſſity for uſing well-water in ſummer for the drink of horſes, it ſhould be drawn a long time before it is given them, and expoſed to the ſun in tubs, or clean ſtone troughs, to correct the too great crudity of the water, which would be very hurtful to them. Pond-water is good for them, but all marſhy waters are full of bad qualities, and therefore ſhould be avoided.

A Gentleman in Suſſex, with reaſon highly eſteemed for the great military ſervices he has done his country, as well as for his judicious improvements in agriculture, has, in his ſtables there, a ſtone baſon fixed in the wall before every horſe, with water in it, of which the horſe ſips as his mouth becomes dry; and another ſimilar baſon for his corn and cut ſtraw, inſtead of a manger.

Horſes ſhould have their quantity of corn portioned out to them at different times, becauſe when they receive it by little and little, they chew and digeſt it better; whereas, when they eat too greedily, it is ſwallowed without chewing, and thereby voided entire and undigeſted, with their dung. To prevent this, and to oblige them to chew it the more perfectly, many add to it chopt ſtraw. I would here recommend the uſe of the rollers mentioned in vol. v. p. 128, of my ſyſtem of huſbandry, becauſe the mealy part of the corn which has been paſſed through them will be ſo thoroughly bruiſed, that it will diſſolve entirely in the ſtomach; and, as was obſerved in the place here referred to, a leſs quantity thus bruiſed will be as nouriſhing as the more plentiful uſual allowance.

The vaſt improvements lately made in huſbandry have afforded a great variety of wholeſome food for horſes, which our forefathers were not acquainted

with.

with. In the winter, we now have not only hay of the best qualities, but also succulent plants which horses are fond of, and which are found to agree perfectly with them. Such are particularly carrots, potatoes, cabbage, turnips. These render the salt marshes much less necessary than when horses have lived long upon dry food; though they still are beneficial, especially after horses have been hurt by long-continued, or hard labour. Where salt marshes are not at hand, sea-salt should be mixed with the food of horses, for it has been found highly beneficial in many countries.

All kinds of cattle are observed to be fonder of salt, the farther they are distant from the sea. Thus, in America, horses which are bred up near the sea shew no extraordinary liking to salt whilst they remain near that element; but after being carried to a distance from it, they become fonder of salt than of corn. The case is the same in Switzerland, and doubtless in other mountainous countries. Is it, that there arises from the sea an exhalation so impregnated with saline particles as to render the use of salt there less necessary for cattle? In some parts of America there are spots naturally abounding in salt, to which even the wild creatures there resort at certain seasons, and lick up the earth with which it is mixed; whence those places are called salt-licks.

To those who have not a sufficiency of the abovementioned succulent plants, the improved husbandry offers lucerne, which rises early in the spring, and affords both food and physick: for, as Columella observes *, it is a remedy for sick cattle, and emaciated cattle grow fat with it. What is more, it continues during the whole summer so nourishing a food, that horses can go through all their usual labours without any corn, when fed with this plant †. How-

* *Lib. II. c. xi.*

† For proofs of this, see *Mills's System of Husbandry, vol. III. p.* 266, 271.

ever,

ever, though it is ſo well ſuited to ſoil and feed horſes, yet fields of graſs in which they may go at large, are alſo neceſſary, and eſpecially when their limbs have been any way diſeaſed.

A ſummer's graſs is likewiſe often neceſſary to horſes that have been glutted with food, and not ſufficiently exerciſed; and indeed, where it can be done with convenience, a month or two's running is proper for moſt horſes. May and June are in general the beſt time for this, becauſe the juices of vegetables are then in their higheſt perfection, the heat of the weather is not ſo overpowering as in July and Auguſt, and the flies, thoſe unmerciful plagues to all cattle, are far leſs troubleſome. Some even think that moſt horſes would be the better for being kept abroad all the year, where they have a proper ſtable, or ſhed, to ſhelter them from the weather, and hay at all times to go to. Thus treated ſay they, they are ſeldom ſick, their limbs are always clean and dry, and, with the allowance of corn, they will do more buſineſs than horſes kept conſtantly at home. At the ſame time it is to be obſerved, that the graſs of high-dunged fields, ſuch as thoſe near great towns are apt to be, is reckoned very injurious to horſes, eſpecially if they feed thereon all the ſummer.

If horſes grow hot and coſtive upon their being taken up from graſs, it will be right to mix bran and chopt ſtraw with their corn, and to give them now and then, for a fortnight, or longer, a feed of ſcalded bran. Their exerciſe and diet ſhould be moderate for ſome time, and both be encreaſed by degrees.

When horſes are *ſoiled* in the ſtable, care ſhould be taken that the herbage, of whatever kind it be, whether graſs, green barley, tares, clover, or any other proper vegetable that the ſeaſon affords, be young, tender, and full of ſap, and that it be cut freſh once every day at leaſt, if not oftener; for when plants are grown old and fibrous, they have loſt

loſt their fine ſap, have a tendency to putrefaction, and frequently cauſe obſtructions in the bowels; which are ſometimes attended with bad conſequences, unleſs an evacuation is procured; a proof of which is, that the excrement evacuated when the body is in that condittion often appears like dung that has laid long to rot on a dunghill.

When horſes loſe their fleſh much in ſoiling, they ſhould be taken up in time, and returned to a more ſolid diet; for it is not in ſoiling as in grazing, in which laſt, though a horſe loſes his fleſh at firſt, yet after the graſs has purged him, he ſoon grows fat.

The only general rule that can be given for the feeding of horſes is, that all horſes which work hard, and conſtantly, ſhould be fed well and plentifully: others ſhould be fed in proportion to their exerciſe, and not kept to certain regular ſtated feeds, whether they work or not.

Good feeding is not alone ſufficient for horſes; they muſt alſo be well dreſſed, that is to ſay, curried every day, to keep their ſkin free from filth and impurities, which might otherwiſe breed the mange, and occaſion numbers of inconveniencies that would make them fall away viſibly: beſides the motion of the curry-comb helps perſpiration; and it is a known fact, that a horſe well dreſſed, curried, duſted, and rubbed down, will preſerve his good appearance, and grow fat, with leſs food than one that is not taken equal care of in thoſe reſpects, though allowed a larger quantity to eat. The horſe's head ſhould be rubbed hard with a ſtrong bruſh, and particular care ſhould be taken to clean his eyes and eye-brows with a rubber, which generally is a piece of ſerge, as alſo his ears, channel, and other parts where the curry-comb could not be uſed. The bruſh is then paſſed all over the body, to lay the hair ſmooth, clearing it and the curry-comb alternately one with the other during the whole of this operation. To complete the buſineſs, after the horſe has been duſted he ſhould be rubbed heartily every way with a good thick wisp of ſtraw ſoaked in water, all over his body, and moſt eſpecially about the legs and joints, where it is proper to dwell longeſt: this rubbing opens the pores, diſpels the humours, enlivens and ſtrengthens the horſe. The mane and tail ſhould then be combed, but gently, beginning at the bottom and proceeding gradually towards the roots, not to tear off the hair. The horſe ſhould afterwards be taken to drink, cheering and enlivening him all the way. It is, however, to be obſerved, that all this trouble is not abſolutely requiſite every day for common draught-horſes in the country: they would indeed do better with it; but as the huſbandman cannot well afford ſo much time to be beſtowed upon them, I would only recommend the doing of it as often as can conveniently be.

The Romans, who were much accuſtomed to rubbing their own bodies, were particularly careful that their horſes ſhould be curried twice a day, and, as Columella obſerves *, found it of more benefit to them, than a large allowance of corn; and beſides, the frequent handling them renders them tame and gentle. Not contented with rubbing, they alſo had † near the ſtable, either a lawn, or a place covered with ſoft ſtraw, where the horſes might tumble or roll themſelves, which exerciſe is beneficial to their health; as their neglecting or avoiding ſo to do indicates the beginning of ſome indiſpoſition.

Frequent and moderate exerciſe conduces much to the horſe's health; but, in riding, eſpecial care ſhould be taken that the perſon who mounts him do not hurt his gait by being too impatient, nor with whip and ſpur wantonly force him to a full gallop, as is too often done: neither ſhould he be put on any ſtrong exerciſe whilſt his belly is full of meat or wa-

* *Lib. VI. c. xxx.*

† *Vegetius, lib. I. c. lvi.*

ter.

ter. The Roman writers all agree, that when a horſe is jaded, or has been over-worked, a mixture of wine and oil ſhould be poured down his throat, or, at leaſt, his mouth be rinced with it; and if by preventing their piſſing in due ſeaſon, a ſtoppage enſues, they order their loins to be well rubbed with the ſame mixture. Every one knows, that a horſe ſhould not be ſuffered to cool too faſt after he has been heated by violent exerciſe, and that his drinking cold water then will generally gripe him, and always endanger his wind.

After a journey, or other exerciſe, great care ſhould be taken that the horſe's feet be well waſhed and examined, in order that no hard ſubſtance may be left adhering to them. The heat ſhould alſo be taken off by the uſe of ſome cooling ointment, or poultice.

It is of eſſential importance for the health of horſes, that their ſtables be kept clean, and their litter renewed as often as can be; for the dung that is left there to rot becomes ſo hot, and the urine and other impurities that remain become ſo acid, that the feet of the horſes are heated and ſpoiled in a ſhort time. From thence proceed moſt of the diſorders in the feet, which often render them incapable of ſervice, without either the maſter or ſervants knowing the true cauſe. Beſides this, freſh litter never fails to make the horſe ſtale, when he returns from work and finds it in the ſtable, which he would not do if there was only old litter; and his retaining his urine when heated by hard labour would frequently bring on inflammations, obſtructions in the neck of the bladder, or in the urinary paſſage, and ſeveral other diſtempers, of which horſes often die, if not ſpeedily remedied.

A horſe ſhould not be worked hard while he is ſhedding his coat, as generally is the caſe in ſpring; and he ſhould alſo then be fed better than uſual. Some ſhed their coats in autumn; and others again, eſpecially the Dutch horſes, ſometimes caſt their hoofs.

We are apt to be too buſy in endeavouring to correct the works of nature. Upon this principle is founded the too common practice of cutting off all the hair from the joints and neck of a horſe, where it really is an ornament when kept clean and in order, and undoubtedly uſeful. The groom gladly clips the heels, to ſave himſelf trouble in waſhing them; but of all the abſurdities that man ever dreamt of, none ſurely can be more ridiculous, certainly none can be more irrational, than the barbarous cuſtom of *docking*, as it is called. What could poſſibly poſſeſs any one to think of robbing this fine, this noble creature, of ſo very neceſſary a defence againſt flies and other inſects, and at the ſame time, ſo great an addition to its beauty! Our gentry of the army are now become ſo ſenſible of the diſadvantages a horſe labours under from the loſs of his tail, eſpecially when tied to the ſtake in a camp, that it is ſaid, all their young horſes are to have their tails.

Nicking is equally abſurd, and as little neceſſary.

SECT.

SECT. I.

Of Bleeding, Purging, and Glyſters.

BY premiſing here ſome general obſervations concerning theſe matters, there will be the leſs need of repetition when they come to be directed in particular diſeaſes.

It was an early cuſtom to bleed horſes and other cattle at certain ſtated periods, eſpecially in the ſpring; and from the frequent repetition of this practiſe aroſe a neceſſity of continuing it, becauſe the want of an habitual evacuation occaſioned diſeaſes, as we find in the human ſpecies: but the more prudent among the antients condemned it. An opening and cooling diet may anſwer all the ends of bleeding, and frequently to better purpoſe, without making ſo great a change in the quantity of the animal juices.

When a horſe is to be bled, the operator cannot do better than obſerve Vegetius's following judicious directions*. Gird the horſe's neck with a leather thong, or a cord, ſo that the vein may be ſeen diſtinctly; then waſh the vein with a ſpunge dipped in water, that it may ſtand out the higher; preſs upon the vein with the thumb of the left hand, above the place in which the inciſion is to be made, that ſo the vein may be more tumid, and leſs apt to eſcape under the fleam, which is then ſtruck into it: or, inſtead of a fleam, a lancet may be uſed, reſting the hand on the middle finger, that the lancet may not pierce too deep. Having ſtruck the vein, give the animal ſome food to eat, in order that, by the moti-

* *Vegetius Renatus, de Morbis Equorum, &c. Lib. I. c. xxii.*

on of the jaw-bones, the blood may break out with the greater force. The blood at firſt is dark coloured, and ſo ſoon as it appears of a livelier red, the vein ſhould be cloſed; few authors mentioning the preciſe quantity that ſhould be taken away. Mr. Bartlet * adviſes rightly to bleed horſes by meaſure, from two to three quarts being in general a ſufficient quantity.

The Romans, who were very fond of rubbing the bodies of animals, ordered the blood to be mixed with vinegar, and the whole body to be then anointed therewith; or eſpecially the part where any particular complaint obtained: in a few days after, the animal was waſhed in the ſea, if near, or otherwiſe in common water.

Before the circulation of the blood was known, bleeding uſed to be ordered in different parts of the body, according to the ſituation of the complaint; it being then held eſſential that the blood ſhould be taken as near the part affected as poſſible: but now that it is known that bleeding in any part leſſens the quantity equally, the neck is generally preferred, as yielding a fairer vein. However it may ſtill be of uſe to bleed near the affected part, if there is a fair vein.

Many are afraid to purge their horſes, on account of the inconveniencies which have frequently been obſerved to ariſe from this operation. Here M. Bourgelat, Inſpector General of the Veterinarian School at Lyons, judiciouſly aſks †, Whether the precautions indiſpenſably neceſſary in the adminiſtration of purges have been obſerved? Has blood been taken away when needful; have mild and ſoftening drinks been given; have the hard excrements been diſcharged by means of glyſters, and has the action of the medicine been by this means directed to ope-

* *Gentleman's Farriery, p.* 11.

† *Matière Médicale raiſonnée, à l'uſage de l'Ecole Royale Vétérinaire, p.* 50.

rate

rate this way? Has care been taken that the stomach was not loaded with food, neglecting the precaution of keeping the animal fasting for six or eight hours before and after taking the purge? Have not strong purges been preferred to mild ones in disorders of the lungs, and where nature endeavoured to throw the sharp humours upon the skin? Have cooling purges been preferred in feverish disorders? Have the purges been adapted to the various purposes for which they were intended? In short, did not the animals labour under disorders which were in themselves incurable?

Now that we have mild purges which may be adapted to different cases, let us not be deprived of the only means of clearing the bowels: for after repeated trials on horses, mules, and sheep, it appears that these creatures cannot vomit; nor indeed does the structure of their stomachs admit of it.

When the intention is to cool and bring about the discharge of sharp humours, M. Bourgelat proposes the following forms. From four ounces to half a pound of Epsom salt, or Glauber salt, or the bitter cathartic salt, may be dissolved in a quart of water and given in the morning. Or two ounces of senna, with an ounce of any of the above salts, may be boiled in three pints of water for half an hour, and the strained liquor given in the morning.

When the intention is to stimulate to a greater degree, more powerful purgatives may be given; and as they do not readily mix with water, it is most convenient to make them into balls. Jalap in powder may be given, to anounce and a half; Scammony, to half an ounce; Aloes, to an ounce and a half, or two ounces. The medicines act much more mildly, if they are well rubbed in a marble mortar with some salt, such as cream of tartar, or nitre, till reduced to a fine powder; and they also dissolve more readily in the bowels. These may be made into balls, with honey, or any syrup. More costly gums are much harder of digeſtion, and perhaps not of an efficacy anſwerable to the expence: but if they are thought neceſſary, they may be added to the above, in the quantity of two or three drams. The chemical oils which uſed formerly to be added to balls, are in themſelves very heating, and by no means anſwer the intention of leſſening the griping. For this reaſon, phyſicians have now laid them aſide in their preſcriptions for man; as I think they ſhould likewiſe be for other animals.

The operation of a purge is much ſlower in horſes than in men; for it is from fifteen to twenty-four hours before it begins to work in the former; probably owing to the great length of their inteſtines: and if they do not purge at all, no bad effect need be feared from them, becauſe they then paſs off by urine, or become alteratives. Their operation is alſo more or leſs ſlow, according to the quality of the food of the cattle, whether green or dry; for in the firſt caſe, very mild medicines operate, eſpecially in horſes which are eaſily purged. Some may be purged with a pound of honey in a draught of bran and water, and this has very good effects in coughs, a loſs of fleſh from too hard labour, &c. when the medicine is continued for ſome days; intermitting it as occaſion may require. Purges given in a liquid form work more ſpeedily than in a more ſolid ſtate.

The caſes in which purging is neceſſary, will be pointed out when we come to ſpeak of particular diſeaſes: therefore we ſhall only mention here, as a general rule, that a purging medicine ſhould be given in the morning, before the animal has broken his faſt, and that he ſhould be kept from ſolid food for ſome hours after; though, in the mean time, it will be proper to give him warm maſhes. If he refuſes to take warm drinks freely, let him have them cold; for it is abſolutely neceſſary that he ſhould drink plentifully. A little hay may be given at

times;

times; and walking him about gently, will forward his purging.

As was before obferved of bleeding, fo in phyficking, many people think it is neceffary to purge their horfes at ftated times, and here again, by fo doing, they at laft render it neceffary: but on due reflection it will appear, that good health wants no mending, and that he who purges either himfelf or his horfe without fufficient caufe, rather impairs than betters the conftitution. They have a favourite feafon too for purging, which is the fpring; the very time when it is, of all others, the leaft neceffary: for nature then affords the beft phyfic that can be given. Every fucculent plant that grows contains a juice, not only purgative, but alfo highly falutary in it's faponaceous and deobftruent quality. Boerhaave, in order to enforce the practice of foilling cattle early in the fpring, mentions an obfervation made by butchers, purporting, that though they feldom kill ftall-fed cattle which have not concretions in the gall-bladder, yet fuch are never found in thofe that have been fed on grafs whilft growing.—If there was no other advantage arifing from the ufe of lucern, than the early opportunity it affords of foiling horfes, as well as other cattle, it would be well worth the hufbandman's while to cultivate it. In fo high efteem was it held by the antients on this very account, that the Romans gave it the name of *medica*, for its great medicinal virtues.

Purges fhould at firft be given in moderate dofes, left they prove too ftrong for fome horfes, and purge them too much. This, indeed, generally proceeds from the purging fubftances being of too ftimulating and acrid a nature, whence they force off the mucus which naturally lines the inteftinal canals, and thereby occafion moft fevere griping. In this cafe, mild fubftances, fuch as may line the inteftines, are proper; and of this nature are all mealy mafhes, efpecially if boiled up with gum Arabic, or the gums

which

which diſtil from our own fruit-trees. Sometimes a purge may bring into the inteſtines an acrid matter, which, by its irritation, continues the purging. When this happens, it muſt be diſcharged; and for this purpoſe the cooling ſalts anſwer beſt: from a gill to half a pint of oil may be mixed with the ſolution of the ſalt, becauſe, by adhering to the inteſtines it ſuplies the place of the abraded mucus. Warm ſtomachic liquors, ſuch as the bitter decoction of the ſhops, may alſo be given. Diaſcordium, to the quantity of an ounce, being diſſolved in the decoction, adds to its efficacy; and opium may take off the irritation, when given to the quantity of an hundred drops of the tincture. Agreeable to the above, Mr. Oſmer *(a)* orders gruel made of rice, and gum Arabic diſſolved in it, with Philonium Romanum at proper intervals.

As the purges in a liquid form muſt be given with a horn, it cannot be improper here to caution the unſkilled againſt the too-general want of due care in the uſe of that inſtrument. The creature is often held too long in the uneaſy ſituation which it is neceſſary then to put him in, and that no part of the liquor may be loſt, it is poured down his throat with ſo long-continued a ſtream, that he is in danger of being ſuffocated. Theſe inconveniencies might eaſily be prevented, by having a cover to the horn, and a valve which may be opened or ſhut by means of a ſpring near the ſmall end; for thus no part will be loſt, and the ſtream may be interrupted ſo as to give the animal opportunities of drawing his breath at times.

Glyſters are alſo given to horſes with great ſucceſs: but previous to their being adminiſtred, the hard excrements lodged in the great gut ſhould be taken out, by introducing the hand well anointed with oil. This not only makes room for the glyſter,

(a) *Treatiſe on the Diſeaſes and Lameneſs of Horſes*, p. 163.

but,

but, when a purge is given, removes those impediments, which otherwise, through the largeness of that gut, form a considerable resistance to the evacuation of the contents of the higher intestines, and thereby often bring on those severe colics and distension of the belly, which are sometimes the consequences of purges. The glysters not only contribute greatly to the removal of this obstruction, but also, when they are of a stimulating nature, by cooperating with the purge, render it much easier, speedier, and more affectual.

I join in opinion with Mr. Bartlet *(b)*, that a bag and pipe of a proper form is preferable to a syringe, with which last it is impossible for the operator to accommodate himself to the horse's motions, because of the length of the syringe; nor has he so much at command the force with which the glyster should be thrown up: for, as that gentleman observes, if it is thrown up with much force, it often surprizes the horse, and makes him reject it as fast as it goes in; whereas the operator having the bag entirely at command, can press the liquor up gently, or with what degree of force he finds necessary.

I shall hereafter have occasion to point out cases in which glysters are necessary; and shall then mention their proper compositions according to the end for which they are intended.

(*b*) *Page* 22.

SECT. II.

SECT. II.

Of a Cold.

IN other animals, as in man, the trachea arteria, or wind-pipe, and all its branches, are moiſtened with a fluid which accompanies the breath in expiration. This fluid may acquire a degree of acrimony, which, by the irritation it occaſions, creates a Cough, or an endeavour of nature to throw it off with the air in expiration. This acrid defluxion is generally communicated to the membrane which lines the noſe, palate and eyes, and is then called a Cold. The diſeaſe continuing for ſome days, this humour becomes thicker, ſo as ſometimes to aſſume a purulent appearance. If the diſeaſe is neglected at firſt, the glands which ſeparate this fluid become diſeaſed, and the lungs are from that time loaded with a tough glutinous matter, ſuch as we ſee thrown up in coughing. This diſeaſe is always attended with ſome degree of fever, ſometimes to a very conſiderable height. If it is accompanied with an inflammation of the lungs or pleura, a ſuppuration, and conſequent pthyſis or conſumption, follows. The utmoſt diligence ſhould therefore be exerted in endeavours to cure ſo dangerous an evil.

The ſigns of it are as follow: the eyes become heavy, and ſometimes watery; the noſe runs; the horſe rattles in his breathing, and coughs; the glands in the mouth and under-jaws ſometimes ſwell. If the fever is conſiderable, the flanks will work, and he will loath his meat; and if the glands about the palate ſwell, he will refuſe his water, becauſe deglutition is then attended with pain: his mouth too will appear

appear ſlimy and foul. If he coughs freely and ſtrong, is but little off his ſtomach, dungs and ſtales readily, and if his ſkin and coat feel kindly, the danger is not great.

This diſorder is generally occaſioned by ſome alteration in the horſe's manner of life, ſuch as his being ſuffered to ſtand in a cold place after having been heated with ſtrong exerciſe, his drinking too much cold water when over-hot, his ſtanding in a colder ſtable than uſual, or a neglect of due care in the management of him. Vegetius *(a)* obſerves, that a horſe thus diſeaſed frequently hangs his head down to the very ground, and, when he drinks, the water runs through his noſtrils; to remedy which, he directs that a gagg be put into the horſe's mouth, and that the hand of a man be then thruſted into it flat, in order to break with the nail a little bliſter, which will be found in it's upper part. He alſo remarks, that whatever irritates or injures the jaws or throat, ſuch as a beard of corn, a bit of bone, duſt, or ſtone, or any other ſubſtance that may ſtick in the throat, will occaſion a violent cough, and that unleſs ſpeedy relief be given, the intolerable pain thereby occaſioned may make the horſe run mad. In this caſe it is neceſſary to examine the mouth carefully in the ſun, that ſuch things may be the more eaſily diſcerned and pulled out; after which the part ſhould be waſhed with warm water wherein nitre hath been diſſolved. Likewiſe, in another place *(b)*, he ſpeaks of an almoſt incurable cough which ariſes from ailments in more internal parts, and is known thus: ſtop the horſe's noſtrils ſo that he cannot breath, and then obſerve his flanks; if they beat very faſt, the cough proceeds from a diſorder in his bowels: and if they beat ſlowly, it ariſes from a tenſion or ſtraining of the parts, which have been hurt by hard riding, or leaping over too broad a

(a) *Lib. III. c. lxiii.*

(b) *Lib. III. c. lxv.*

place.

place. Wounds alſo, from any cauſe, may after they are healed, by the cicatrice's contracting into a narrower compaſs, leave a roughneſs, which, by the irritation it gives, occaſions a continual cough.

On the attack of a cold, it will in general be adviſeable to bleed the horſe; and if the cold is attended with any degree of fever, the bleeding ſhould be repeated. After the firſt bleeding, it will be proper to procure looſe ſtools, at firſt by means of a ſtimulating glyſter. To this end, make a decoction of a large handful of mallow leaves and of chamomile flowers in a gallon of water, ſo that there may be about three quarts of the ſtrained liquor: add to this four ounces of any purging ſalt, and half a pint of oil. Or, if ſuch a decoction is not eaſily come at, milk, whey, or thin broth of any kind, may be given with ſome ſea-ſalt and oil. This, with maſhes in which honey and nitre have been diſſolved, will keep the body open.

M. Bourgelat *(c)* judiciouſly diſtinguiſhes the medicines proper for a cough into two kinds, namely, the mild cooling kind, and the ſtimulating, whoſe effects being different, they are given in different periods of the diſeaſe. He obſerves, that it is not ſo eaſy to judge of the ſtate of the diſeaſe in horſes, as in men, in which laſt the colour and conſiſtence of what is coughed up affords a means of judging; whereas in horſes, the cough brings the matter diſcharged from the wind-pipe only into the back part of the mouth, from whence it probably ſlips down into the ſtomach; unleſs it is brought up in ſuch quantity as to flow out by the noſe: and then very properly adds, "we may eaſily judge what ſkill is "requiſite to uſe judiciouſly arms which are ſo dif-"ferent in their effects; what inconveniencies "might ariſe on one hand, if the ſtimulating were "adminiſtered whilſt an acrid thin fluid is diſcharg-

(c) *L'Ecole Veterinaire, p.* 82.

"ed;

" ed; and on the other, after this humour has, by
" a due concoction, been brought to a kind of ma-
" turated purulent ſtate, how great the danger that
" the lungs might be too much weakened by a con-
" tinuation of the cooling relaxing medicines be-
" fore ſo neceſſary."

It is moſt adviſeable after evacuations to begin with maſhes and drinks, made of the mild and cooling ſubſtances, ſuch as the roots of liquorice, marſh mallows, the leaves of common mallow, linſeed, bran, the mealy ſubſtances, or ſliced figs. This decoction ſhould be ſweetened with honey, and t oit may be added ſweet oil, firſt mixed with honey. A quart, or three pints, of this drink may be given three or four times a day, with a horn; and either in the decoction, or with the horſe's other food: it will be right likewiſe to give about four ounces of nitre in the courſe of the day. Mr. Oſmer *(d)* directs for this purpoſe, two ounces of cold-drawn linſeed oil, one ounce of ſalt-petre, two drams of volatile ſalt of hartſhorn, to be mixed together, and given daily in ſome linſeed tea, barley-water, or any ſuch vehicle.

This cooling regimen is much ſafer than the warm drenches generally given by farriers: and even if it ſhould be continued ſo long as to bring the horſe very low, it is much eaſier to give a ſpur to nature when the creature ſeems languid, than it is to repreſs the diſorders which ariſe from too much heat, or too quick a circulation of the blood. Nitre is here of ſingular advantage as a cooler, as it cauſes a ſecretion by urine, which may carry off a great deal of the humour that might otherwiſe fall on the lungs.

If the cough ſtill continues, though the fever and other complaints abate, then pectorals of a ſtimulating nature may be given. Such are elicampane, hyſop, garlic, ſquils, gum ammoniac, &c. which may

(d) Page 255.

be

be made into balls, with honey, of an oblong ſhape, and never ſo large as to be difficult to ſwallow. Columella (*e*) recommends four ounces of the juice of leeks, with as much oil; in which he is ſeconded by Vegetius (*f*) who generally mixes wine with his drenches, by way of cordial. This laſt alſo ſays (*g*) that an obſtinate cough may be cured with half a pint of wine, three ounces of oil, and a raw egg, given with a horn for three days. He likewiſe recommends the (*h*) following as a cheap drench: Take powder of beans, fenugreek, and elicampane, of each ſix ounces; of comfrey three ounces, and of butter ſix ounces; beat them together with three pints of good wine, and a pint and a half of water, and give the horſe two hornfuls of it faſting, till he has drank up the whole. As in moſt other diſorders, ſo in this, he adviſes that the back, loins, cheſt, neck, and jaws, be rubbed with wine, oil, and ſalt. He alſo adds opium to his balls, which is found to be of great efficacy where the cough ariſes from ſome irritating cauſe, and is likewiſe farther beneficial, in that, by the calm it gives, it helps to reſtore a more equal circulation of the juices, and thereby to promote the perſpiration, which in a cold is generally interrupted.

The authors of the *Maiſon Ruſtique* (*i*) recommend the following powder, as a cure for either old or newly-contracted coughs. "Take roots of eli-
"campane, or marſh mallow, gentian, and galan-
"ga, of each eight ounces, ſtick-liquorice a pound,
"and as much leaves of tameriſk; moth mullein,
"and carduus benedictus, of each four ounces,
"fenugreek ſix ounces, and as much flour of ſul-
"phur; Spaniſh aniſeed, and cinnamon, of each
"two ounces; dry the whole in the ſhade, and
"pound it to about the bigneſs of coarſe rapee-
"ſnuff; mix the whole well together, and keep it

(*e*) *Lib. VI c. xxxi.* (*f*) *Lib. III. c. lviii.*
(*g*) *Lib. V. c. ix.* (*h*) *Ibid.* (*i*) *Tom. I. p.* 258.

in

" in a dry place, in a bottle closely stopped. The " dose is a good table-spoonful, mixed with moistened bran or oats, and it is to be given for several days running. If the horse dislikes it at first, " the quantity may be lessened then; but after he is " once accustomed to it, he will grow very fond of " it.—The use of this powder does not prevent a " horse's working: on the contrary, it will have " the greater effect for his so doing.—This powder " is likewise excellent to cool the flanks of horses " that are over-heated, and in the beginning of a " pursiness. It fattens the leanest, and kills their " worms."

Some have thought, and perhaps not without reason, that the cough which attends a cold is infectious. Whether it be absolutely so, or not, the wisest course certainly is to err on the safest side; and on that account to remove every horse into a stable, or pasture, separate from those that are affected with this disease, or indeed with any other internal disorder. If put into a stable, it should be well aired, and the manger and stand made very clean. The warm steam that arises from his mashes undoubtedly loosens the matter which flows from the nose, and has probably the same effect on the lungs; to the great present relief of the horse, and hastening of his cure. What food he now eats should be given in small quantity at a time, that it may not be tainted by his breath, which is loaded with some of the morbid matter.

In all modern writers, some chemical oils are favourite remedies; but if we attend to their heat, and how difficultly they are assimilated with the other fluids, I hope that the husbandman, for whom this work is principally intended, will belive my omission of them really meant for the benefit of his horses. Indeed, I have all along chosen the least heating stimulants. What probably gave rise to the opinion that carminatives, of which oil of aniseed is one of the principal, difpel wind, is, that after they are taken, the wind brought up fmells of them: a circumftance, which on reflection, will be found to afford the ftrongeft proof how very difficult thefe fubftances are to digeft, and that it is owing to their continuing to retain their priftine form, that the wind which is expelled is fcented with them. If any ftimulant is wanted, camphire feems the moft proper, as being of a diaphoretic quality, and greatly refifting putrefactions, as well as taking off fpafms. M. Bourgelat recommends it much in the contagious and inflammatory difeafes of cattle, given in the quantity of two drams or more in a day, either diffolved in a little fpirit of wine, and added to any other draught, or given in a ball. Nitre, in like quantity, makes it a ftill better medicine.

SECT. III.

Of a Fever.

A FEVER is a cold greatly increafed, but generally without a cough. When a horfe is ill of a fever, he droops his head, his eyes look ftaring, and are fometimes red and inflamed, his mouth and tongue are hot and dry, his lips hang down, he appears dejected, and feems to have a wearinefs all over his body: his limbs burn with heat, his pulfe beats ftrong and quick, at the rate of about fifty times in a minute: he fetches his breath fhort and quick, ftaggers in his gait, loaths his food, wants often to drink, ftales with difficulty, his urine is high coloured, he is reftlefs, feldom lies down, and if he does, he foon rifes again. Vegetius obferves (*a*), that if the favour proceeds from his having been worked

(*a*) *Lib. I. c. xxx.*

worked beyond his ſtrength, his eyes will be bloodſhot, and he will appear to ſupport himſelf beſt on his hind legs; for he will ſet down his fore feet as if they were bruiſed or foundered.

The cure ſhould here begin with plentiful bleeding, which ſhould be repeated, if neceſſary, on the ſame, or the ſucceeding day or days, leſſening the quantity at each time, from about three pints or two quarts to a pint: and as in all fevers the excrements are generally hard, they ſhould be taken out by the hand as much as poſſible, and the body ſhould then be opened with a ſtimulating glyſter, ſuch as a decoction of four ounces of ſenna added to a common decoction; or ſix or eight ounces of antimonial wine added in like manner.

Internally, the ſame mild medicines may be given as are directed in the foregoing article, Nitre, to the quantity of an ounce a day, either mixed with honey and made up into a ball, or put into the horſe's drink, is of great uſe. He ſhould be tempted to drink plentifully, by giving him ſuch maſhes as are pleaſing to him; and therefore whatever is diſagreeable ſhould be adminiſtered with a horn, leſt the fear of that diſagreeableneſs ſhould deter him from drinking.

When the firſt violence of the diſeaſe is abated, or when the ſtrength of the ſick creature ſinks, medicines of a more ſtimulating nature may be given. If the *Spiritus Mindereri* ſhould be thought too expenſive for horſes, the following mixture, recommended by Mr. Barlet *(b)*, may anſwer the ſame purpoſe. "Take of Ruſſia pearl-aſhes one ounce, of "diſtilled or common vinegar as much as ſhall perfectly ſaturate the ſalt, or ſo much, that when "more vinegar is poured upon the mixture no effervеſcence will ariſe, a quart of water, and four

(b) *Page* 33.

" ounces of honey. Mix these well together, and
" give a pint of this drink three or four times a day."

Sir John Pringle, Bart. acquaints us *(c)*, that in Dr. Clerk's opinion, of all the neutral salts, the crude sal ammoniac comes the nearest to the *Spiritus Mindereri*; and therefore it may be used here with great propriety, to the quantity of an ounce a day.

Instead of opening the body with purges, in fevers, it is more adviseable to repeat the glysters, so as to obtain that end; being less stimulating than the first. Whey, water gruel, pot-liquor, with salt and oil, may be sufficient.

Vegetius, in his usual way, recommends *(d)*, especially in the winter, to rub the diseased horse with oil and vinegar long against the hair, and then to cover him, and carry him to a warm place. He also advises other particular modes of treatment peculiar to each season: but all his prescriptions are so loaded with a multitude of ingredients, that it would be very difficult to ascertain the virtues of any one of them in particular.

In summer, the best food for a feverish horse is green succulent plants; and in winter, a little hay moistened with water; but no corn. He will eat but little at first; but if the disease does not last above three days, he will soon come to his appetite. If it exceeds that time, give him a masticatory made of assa-fœtida and savine, of each half an ounce, an ounce of liqourice rasped, and an equal quantity of sugar. This will cause a discharge of any matter that may load the glands, about the mouth and gullet, and so quicken in him a desire to eat. His drink should be given him rather often than much at a time, and he should be kept moderately warm; the extremes on both sides being equally hurtful, and perhaps most so on the side of heat.

(c) *Observations on the Diseases of the Army*, part III. c. i.
(d) *Lib.* I. c. xxx.

The

The horſe's returning appetite, and the cooler temper of his body, ſhew a recovery of health; and then ſome mild purgatives ſhould be given, ſuch as the purging ſalts before directed, or cream of tartar with a dram or two of jalap in powder to quicken it. Frequent rubbing contributes much to reſtore health.

Mr. Barlet *(e)* gives the following ſigns of a fever which he has obſerved to ſeize horſes. This fever is ſlow, with languiſhing and great depreſſion; the horſe is ſometimes hot in the mouth, though he is outwardly cold; at other times hot all over, but not to any extreme; his eyes look moiſt and languid; he has a continual moiſture in the mouth, which is the reaſon why he ſeldom cares to drink, and when he does, it is but little at a time; he feeds but little, and leaves off as ſoon as he has eaten a mouthful or two: he moves his jaws in a feeble looſe manner, with an unpleaſant grating of his teeth; his body is commonly open; his dung ſoft and moiſt, but ſeldom greaſy: his ſtaling is often irregular, ſometimes little, at other times profuſe; ſeldom high-coloured, but rather pale, with little or no ſediment. A horſe in this ſort of fever always runs at the noſe, but not the kindly white diſcharge, as in the breaking of a cold; but of a reddiſh or greeniſh duſky colour, and of a conſiſtence like glue, and ſticks like turpentine to the hair on the inſide of the noſtrils.

When, in this ſtate, a horſe's appetite declines daily till he refuſes his meat, it is a bad ſign. When the fever does not diminiſh, or keep at a ſtand, but increaſes, the caſe is then dangerous: but when it ſenſibly abates, and the mouth grows drier, when the grating of his teeth ceaſes, when his appetite mends, and when he takes to lying down, which perhaps he has not done for a fortnight; theſe are promiſing ſigns. If the running at the noſe turns to

(e) *Page* 37.

a gleet of clear thin water, if the horſe's hide keeps open, and if he mends in his appetite; theſe are ſigns of recovery.

The various and irregular ſymptoms which attend this ſlow fever require great caution and ſkill to direct the cure. In general, a moderate quantity of blood may be taken, proportioned to the horſe's ſtrength and other ſymptoms. In order to determine this quantity, the pulſe in the neck, where it is very apparent, ſhould be examined, and it's frequency and ſtrength ſhould determine the quantity; for it's hardneſs, more than it's frequency, is what indicates the neceſſity of bleeding. The bran and water with nitre, and an ounce of ſnake-root in it, may then be given, as before directed. As the ſtools in this caſe are frequent and looſe, there appears not any need of a glyſter; but a ſomewhat that will purge ſmartly ſeems to be wanted. An ounce of jalap, with a dram of calomel, made into a ball, will give that degree of ſtimulus which ſhall expel either ſlime, or worms, that may become an additional cauſe of this fever. If, after this, the fever ſtill wears the ſame aſpect, a dram of camphire diſſolved in ſpirit of wine, and a pint of ſtrong vinegar, may be added to the former mixture. Sweet hay ſhould be given frequently, and by little at a time, becauſe the horſe's breath may taint it if it ſtands long before him.

If the looſeneſs is too great, proper remedies ſhould be given to reſtrain it, ſuch as water in which a good deal of chalk is mixed, or diaſcordium to the quantity of half an ounce; and every thing that may excite a purging ſhould be avoided. If the horſe ſtales in too great quantity, the nitre muſt be diſcontinued; but if he does not make water enough, it will be right to give him a decoction of juniper-berries, with ſome Venice turpentine, firſt diſſolved in the yolk of an egg.

When

When the horſe begins to put on a more lively look, when his hair appears ſmooth and gloſſy, when his noſe grows clean and dry, when his urine ſhews ſigns of concoction, when his appetite mends, and when he lays down well, and both ſtales and dungs regularly, health is returning. Particular care ſhould then be taken, that his diet at firſt be light, and in ſmall quantities, and that it be encreaſed only by degrees as he gets ſtrength; for by over-feeding on recovery from a long illneſs, there is great danger of a relapſe, or ſurfeit, which are always difficult of cure.

If the fever ſhould prove of the intermitting kind, immediately after the fit is over, give an ounce of Jeſuits bark, and repeat it every ſix hours, if the fever is diſcontinuing, till the horſe has taken ſix ounces. Eruptions, or ſwellings of any kind, are to be encouraged in the decline of a fever, becauſe they denote a termination of the diſeaſe.

Here I would beg to eſtabliſh as a general rule in all diſeaſes, and on this occaſion apply it particularly to the horſe, that the atmoſphere be continually changed by the admiſſion of freſh air, without it's blowing upon the diſeaſed animal: and this may eaſily be done by having an opening in the cieling of the ſtable, to carry off the foul air.

The putrid fever is moſt apt to ſeize young horſes, eſpecially in hot weather, and in hot countries. It is diſtinguiſhed by the tongue and palate, which become black, dry, and hard; the whole body is hot, the head hangs down, the eyes are red, the breath is hot, and the heart beats much.

The cure conſiſts chiefly in bleeding, and a very cool diluting diet; to which end we find an ounce of crude ſal-ammoniac diſſolved in the horſe's drink, and ſtimulating glyſters recommended. For the farther treatment of this diſeaſe, and alſo what is neceſſary to be done in contagious or peſtilential diſorders, the reader is referred to the latter end of this volume,

volume, where thoſe matters will be profeſſedly treated of. In the mean time I ſhall add here, as pertinent to my preſent ſubject, the ſubſtance of Mr. Oſmer's account of a contagious diſeaſe in horſes which fell under his own eye.

"In the year 1750, I think it was, ſays Mr. Oſmer (*f*), that the diſtemper among the horſes was more univerſal than at any other time. Various were the ſymptoms, and different the degrees of illneſs among different horſes. Some had a diſcharge of matter from their eyes, noſe, and mouth; others had none: but in all there were great tokens of inflammation, attended with a fever and a violent cough.

"Moſt of the horſes which had a diſcharge from the noſe, &c. lived; and where ſuch diſcharges did not happen, nor a critical abſceſs fall on ſome part, moſt of them died.

"I made ſeveral inciſions in the ſkin on various parts of the body of dead horſes which had not any diſcharge from the noſe, and found in all of them a quantity of extravaſated ſerum lodged between the ſkin and the membranes. This indicated the propriety of ſeveral rowels, which ſome were of opinion would ſoon mortify: but in about thirty hours their good effects appeared; for the horſe thus treated began to look chearful, and to eat his meat, and in another day became as apparently well as ever he was in his life. Rowels had the ſame good effect on horſes which had a diſcharge at the noſe: for they got over it much ſooner than thoſe which had no ſuch aſſiſtance.

"If a horſe has a violent fever, with a dry cough, and there be no concomitant diſcharge at the noſe, he ſhould be bled largely. If a diſcharge at the noſe appears, bleeding will be found to do harm; being contrary to the attempt of nature in ſuch diſ-

(*f*) *Treatiſe on the Diſeaſes of Horſes*, p. 108, *et ſeq.*

charge.

charge. In both theſe circumſtances, he ſhould take cooling ſalts every ſix hours, the excrements being raked from him if he is coſtive; cooling glyſters ſhould be given, and three or four rowels ſhould be put into various parts where the ſkin is looſe.

"The danger of a mortification has been objected to theſe rowels: but if any ſuch ſymptom as a gangrane ſhould appear, on this or any other occaſion, warm fomentations, with ſome ſpirit of wine added at the time of uſing them, and a poultice made of oatmeal, cummin ſeeds, and the grounds of ſtrong beer, and kept applied to the part, are the proper remedies.

"A ſtud of mares and colts of various ages were attacked with this diſtemper in various forms. Some had a diſcharge from the eyes, noſe, and mouth; ſome had critical ſwellings, which fell on the udder; ſome were on the ſhoulder, others on the ſide of the jaw, under the jaw, and on the other parts.

"As they fell ill, they were taken to a houſe, and bled or roweled according to their different ages and ſymptoms, and ſaltpetre was given them: by theſe means they all became well, except the ſucking foals.

"When critical ſwellings appeared, I made large inciſions on the part, and let out large quantities of matter. So much was the blood vitiated, that after the firſt wound was well, many of them had other critical ſwellings fall on other parts, again and again; theſe were all opened, when ripe, and by this means they all at length became well. Some had ſeveral ſetons put in the ſkin, ſome in the depending part of the ſwelling, thinking by theſe evacuations to divert the febrile matter, and effect a cure: but after a trial of many days, I found this method of no uſe, the ſwelling all this time neither advancing nor receding. Upon which the ſetons were taken out, the ſaltpetre left off, and in a few days the ſwelling came

to

to good matter, by the discharge of which the animal got well in due course of time.

"But for the sucking foals, no remedy availed; the disease baffling all the attempts of art and nature. If you bled them, a swelling perhaps came on the part, and would remain indurated for several months, which was neither to be dissipated, nor brought to matter. The same kind of indurations would also fall on other parts. If the matter was formed and let out, fresh swellings succeeded each other; or some other symptoms of the disease remained for several months, even till they were weaned, the cause of this I think is evident. The mare that gives suck is never, at least that I could perceive, affected with this disease; which in all probability proceeds from the constant secretion of her milk, by means of which her vessels are still kept emptied, and herself free from any symptoms of a fever, and yet her blood may be much vitiated and corrupted.

"I have seen several foals at the mare's foot, whose blood has been so poor, as to occasion their legs to swell, even when they have been running about in the field, and must inevitably have died, if they had continued to suck much longer: yet, when taken from the mare and weaned, have been soon recovered, by the very means that before were found ineffectual. From which instances I am ready to conclude, that this long-continued illness of the foal is entirely owing to the depravity of the mare's milk.

"In order to remedy both mare and foal, the mare should be bled two or three times, and take some cooling salts every day; and the same should be given to the foal once a day or oftener, if there be occasion, with the use of setons. The milk of the mare should be drawn from her, unless it is intended to wean the foal: otherwise, such foal should be supported with cow's milk mixed with flour, till his health is reinſtated, by which time the habit of body in the mare will alſo be amended.

" When a critical ſwelling appears on any part, all means uſed to divert it are wrong, and ineffectual: but a poultice of bread and milk ſhould be applied to the part, to forward the matter, which, when ripe, and not before, is to be let out by a proper incision; and to prevent any future ſwellings on the ſame, or other parts, ſome diſcharge ſhould be continued for a time by an artificial drain, with the daily uſe of ſome cooling ſalts to correct the vitiated blood.

" I have of late followed a method ſomewhat different from rowels or ſetons, though analogous thereto, and think it much better than either of them, becauſe it ſooner brings on a diſcharge, and that in greater abundance, is attended with leſs inflammation, and may be continued as long as one pleaſes. It is, to make a number of inciſions into the ſkin on any part where it is looſe, to dilate or ſeparate the ſame with the finger all round as far as it will reach, and moderately to fill ſuch part every day with lint or tow dipt in a proper digeſtive for wounds; firſt taking out the former dreſſing.

" By theſe methods, all the ſymptoms attending this diſeaſe, in every age, will be removed, and it's deſtructive conſequences prevented.

" The uſe of cooling ſalts, with proper bleeding and glyſters, will generally be ſufficient to remove moſt common fevers: yet if the caſe appear urgent and dangerous, then, by way of ſecurity, inciſions of the ſkin, as drains, ſhould be uſed alſo. For want of ſuch ſecretions and evacuations, the horſe, though he may chance to recover from his fever, is liable to, and often is ruined by conſequential diſorders, ſuch as the farcy, a broken wind, tubercles of the lungs, conſumption, glanders, and œdematous local ſwellings, that are never removed.

" In

" In this diſeaſe, which I own is new to me, the horſes are ſeized with a variety of ſymptoms that require a different treatment. On this account, particular regard is to be had to the ſymptoms attending it, as the proper indications how to act; and with ſuch attention, the methods here directed will ſeldom fail to anſwer the deſired end.

" This diſeaſe begins, in general, with great debility of the limbs; and many horſes are ſo much weakened, as to reel and ſtagger about when led along, and that almoſt as ſoon as they are taken ill. It is attended too, in general, with loſs of appetite, a dry cough, their eyes become ſuddenly dim, glazed and lifeleſs, and they have no ſort of inclination to drink.

" But there being, I think, five different claſſes or degrees of this diſeaſe, I ſhall endeavour to diſtinguiſh them as clearly and conciſely as I can, for the information of the reader.

" *Firſt.* Beſides the ſymptoms already mentioned, ſome horſes are taken with a coldneſs of the external parts: theſe are chiefly affected with a weakneſs behind; they have no fever, nor tokens of inflammation, and there ſeems to be a tendency towards a general ſtagnation of the fluids.

" *Secondly.* Among other ſymptoms, are great tokens of inflammation, the fever is high, and the external parts are hot and burning. Theſe horſes are moſt affected in their head and ſight.

" *Thirdly.* In others, the diſeaſe falls on the throat, with manifeſt tokens of great ſoreneſs. Theſe ſeldom have any feveriſh heat, are not ſo much affected in their limbs, or ſight, as ſome are, and their appetite, both for eating and drinking, ſeems better than in thoſe of the firſt and ſecond claſs. They are, in general, miſerably reduced before this ſoreneſs goes off; though their falling away ought not to be imputed ſolely to their faſting, becauſe all horſes that have this diſeaſe to any conſiderable degree, are reduced in a very few days to the leanneſs of a dog-horſe.

" *Fourth-*

" *Fourthly*. Others are ſeized at firſt with a cough only, and ſhew little or no ſymptoms of illneſs, nor of any unuſual heat or cold. Theſe, in general, ſoon have a diſcharge of a ſerous fluid, from the noſtrils, as in the inflammatory fever. They are leaſt affected, and recover ſooneſt of any, and frequently too without any aſſiſtance at all.

" *Fifthly*. In others again, the phlegmon, or boil, appears ſoon after the cough, in ſome part of the head and body: and in ſome of theſe the vital heat is ſufficient ſpeedily to bring on a critical impoſthumation, without any art or aſſiſtance. In others, the vital heat is ſo little, that their lives are manifeſtly endangered before an impoſthumation can be obtained, even with the aſſiſtance of art.

" But when we talk about vital heat, it may perhaps be more proper to ſay, that the different progreſs of the critical boil in different horſes, is owing to the difference of their fluids, and the more briſk or languid circulation thereof, as they happen to be more or leſs viſcid. If this be not the true cauſe, from whence, I pray you, ariſe the two extreme ſenſations of cold and heat in different horſes, affected with the ſame epidemical diſeaſe? It may be obſerved too, that thoſe horſes are moſt affected with cold and ſhivering, in whoſe blood is found the leaſt ſerum.

" Having now deſcribed the different ſymptoms of this diſeaſe, I ſhall ſubjoin the different methods of treatment.

" To thoſe of the firſt claſs, bleeding is particularly found to do harm; and if it be done in any great quantity, the horſe ſoon drops, a violent palpitation of the heart ſucceeds, and death moſt probably follows ſpeedily. The blood of theſe, when taken away, and expoſed to the air for twenty-four hours, has not a drop of ſerum in it, but remains a coagulated ſizy maſs: nor do theſe, when coſtive, bear the evacuations by glyſters with advantage, but rather

ther with the contrary effect; and rowels also seem to do harm to horses under the circumstances here described. For these, the following medicine will generally produce, in a few days, the desired effect.

" Take of crude sal ammoniac and nitre, each one ounce; of Castile soap half an ounce; of camphire rubbed with a little cold-drawn linseed oil, two drams; and of mucilage of gum arabic enough to make these up into a ball or two, for one dose. Give it three times a day.

" But if, on the use of these medicines for a few days, the urinary secretions appear not to be enlarged, or the symptoms do not abate, then the quantity of nitre and sal ammoniac ought to be increased, according to the size, strength, and habit of body of the horse. His proper food at the beginning is hay and scalded bran, if he will eat it: his drink should be moderately warm, of whatever he likes best, and as much as he chooses.

" By the continuance of this medicine for a few days, as the stagnated fluids become thinner, the bodily warmth and strength encrease; and soon after, as the urinary secretions appear to be augmented, he begins to drink freely; upon which he generally becomes on a sudden well, recovers his limbs and his appetite at once, and is free from all complaints but his cough, which perhaps leaves him not entirely, till he recovers flesh.

" When these symptoms appear, and the horse's appetite is good, leave off those medicines, lest the fluids should become too much attenuated, and so a dropsy ensue. Avoid likewise the use of all other medicines at this time; for nature now will, in general, best do her own work, without art. Bran and oats scalded together are now his proper food. During his whole illness, he should not be taken out of the stable on any account; nor afterwards, till he has recovered his flesh, and been purged, which probably he will not be able to bear for a considerable time;

time; and as in the inflammatory fever, keeping the horse cool is very beneficial, so in this disease, keeping him moderately warm, with good rubbing, if he is inclined to be cold, and stiff in his motions, is very necessary.

" For those of the second class, bleeding in a moderate quantity is very beneficial, especially at the beginning of the disease. Here too evacuations by glysters will be of use, and the medicines before directed should be given in like manner. If the heat and fever continue twelve hours, and the vessels on the membranes about the eye appear inflamed and distended, a second bleeding in a moderate quantity may be necessary, and will generally be sufficient: but in this, or future bleedings, the direction for so doing is to be taken solely from the tokens of inflammation; remembering, that in this disease the horse can bear the loss only of a small quantity at one time; and having likewise some regard to his size and strength.

" The blood in horses labouring under these symptoms is very sizy, of a buff colour, and has but little serum, when it has stood for a time. In this case, therefore, rowels will be improper, because they promote a discharge of the lymph and finer fluids, of which there appears to be already a deficiency, or rather some degree of stagnation in the circulation thereof.

" For such as are affected with a soreness of the throat, bleeding, glysters, and rowels are all improper, unless there be manifest tokens of fever and inflammation: in either case, the medicine before directed is proper. These horses will eat bread and water-gruel together, if made thin.

" For those which have a discharge at the nostrils, bleeding is highly prejudicial, because this is an effort of nature, and a kind of crisis to get rid of the disease. Glysters too are seldom wanted here, because the horse in these circumstances generally has appe-

tite

tite enough to eat a quantity of ſcalded bran, ſufficient to keep his body open: but rowels, with the medicine before directed, help here to aſſiſt nature in unloading the over-charged veſſels, and getting rid of the extravaſated fluids; for though many horſes do well in this ſituation by the help of nature alone, without any aſſiſtance, yet I have ſeen many inſtances, both in this fever, as well as in the inflammatory, where, for want of theſe artificial helps, the extravaſated fluids diſcharged at the noſtrils have been of ſo ſharp a nature, as to corrode the ſoft membrane which lines the internal cavity of the noſe, and there produce ulcers, which, lying out of the reach of topical applications, often turn to the real glanders.

" For the fifth claſs, a poultice of bread and milk with lard ſhould be applied twice a day to the boil; and it might reaſonably be deemed very proper, where the pulſe is low, the circulation languid, and the external parts cold, to give the horſe ſome warm alexipharmic medicines, to enable nature to bring on the work of ſuppuration; but I have found in ſeveral inſtances, that ſuch medicines are on this occaſion of no account at all; for where I have perceived the blood to ſtand ſtill for many days, without advancing in the leaſt towards maturation, and the horſe has been in manifeſt danger, I have left off the uſe of warm medicines, and have given the medicine before directed, with camphire, thinking by this means to thin the fluids, and ſo to carry off the diſeaſe by the other common ſecretory ducts; and this has ſucceeded: but what is remarkable, and, I believe, contrary to ſpeculative reaſoning, the phlegmon or boil, which before ſtood ſtill, and would not advance at all, has ſoon after, when the urinary ſecretions have been enlarged, come to ſuppuration; and though this may appear ſomewhat ſtrange to the learned, yet it ought to be remembered, that bleeding has ſometimes brought the phlegmon in men to ſuppuration, which before made no advances thereunto.

" By

"By these different methods I have saved the lives of many horses, having lost a few only out of a great number; though I am ready to acknowledge, that, when this disease first made its appearance, I endangered the lives of many."

Vegetius *(g)* describes a contagious fever similar to the above, only he divides it into two classes, namely, that with the running at the nose, and that with the tumours in the skin. Speaking of the former, he says, "there flows from the horse's nose, instead of snot, a stinking and thick humour, of a pale colour: the horse has a great heaviness in his head, and hangs it down: tears fall from his eyes, and there is a wheezing noise in his breast: he becomes thin and meagre, with his hair standing on end, and of a sad aspect. The antients called this disease the Attican flux. When a bloody or a saffron-coloured humour begins to flow from his nostrils, he is incurable." And of the second he says, "there arises in the body of the horse ulcers, out of which flows a liquid greenish humour, without any discharge from his nose."

He *(h)* makes the cure consist chiefly in mild oily injections into the nose, anointing the head with warm oil, keeping the head warm, and giving *Diapente* made in this manner. Take myrrh, gentian, long birthwort, bay-berries, and shavings of ivory, of each an equal weight, made into a fine powder. Of this mixture, give the first day a spoonful heaped in a pint of old wine; the second day a spoonful and a half, and the third day two spoonfuls. In another place *(i)* he tells us, that, when the pestiferous humour passes between the skin and the bowels, it is to be cured, by making an incision in the skin, or applying a cautery, in the usual place, between the shoulder and the belly, by which a cor-

(g) *Lib. I. c. iii. et v.*
(h) *Lib. I. c. x.*
(i) *Ibid. c. xii.*

 rupted

rupted yellow humour will be discharged. If it flows in small quantity, he advises inserting into the wound the root of tithymal or spurge, which will bring out the remainder of the venom. A cautery may be applied to the breast of the horse, and when the eschar is cut, the root is to be inserted, and will remain there till the slough falls off, whereby the humour is drawn out of the whole body; the horse taking the *diapente* in the mean time.

SECT. IV.

Of Fevers attended with Inflammations in particular parts.

SO long as the signs of an inflammatory state of the blood appear over the whole body uniformly, the Fever is called simply an inflammatory Fever; but when the disease falls on some other part, the Fever then takes a denomination from the part affected. I shall begin with the head, and from thence proceed downwards.

Vegetius (*a*) observes, that when, by reason of excessive heat or cold, the vessels of the brain are distended, wholesome sleep is excluded; from whence a head-ach, sadness, and weakness, necessarily follow. These are the signs of the lightest indisposition of this kind: but when the vessels are greatly over-charged, and on one side only, the animal is affected with the staggers, his sight is weakened, tears frequently run down from his eyes, his head is heavy, and he leans it against the manger; his ears are motionless. As his disorder increases (*b*), he is

(*a*) *Lib. II. c. i.* (*b*) *Id. ibid. c. viii.*

seized

ſeized with a phrenzy, leaps ſuddenly, as if he wanted to make his eſcape, daſhes himſelf againſt the wall, and cannot be kept in by any method whatever. When the pulſe and quick-breathing indicate theſe ſymptoms to be attended with a proportionate degree of fever, we may judge that the brain is inflamed.

Plentiful bleeding, to the quantity of four or five quarts, is here the only immediate relief, and ſhould be repeated in ſuch proportion as the ſtrength of the horſe can bear. The body ſhould be opened by a glyſter, and, as before directed, the animal ſhould be put under the moſt cooling regimen. Vegetius recommends the addition of muſtard-bliſters. I do not know that the experiment has been made; but I can ſee no reaſon why the practice on the human body, of ſhaving the hair on the hind part of the head, and applying a mixture of the flour of muſtard and Spaniſh flies made into an adheſive paſte, ſhould not be followed here. It ſeems at leaſt not to be attended with any danger. He directs alſo *(c)*, that the head be well rubbed with oil, and that a cataplaſm compoſed of bay-berries, rice, nitre, vinegar, and oil of roſes, be applied warm, in the winter, wrapping up the head in a ſkin with the wool on it.

He *(d)* diſtinguiſhes this diſeaſe from real madneſs, in which the horſe will neigh as if he were in perfect health, fall upon either horſe or man and bite them, bite or gnaw the manger, and even his own flanks. In this laſt caſe, he adviſes to give him green food, and chiefly as much green parſley as he will eat, ſix ſpoonfuls of the juice of hemlock in half a pint of water, with other due evacuations *(e)*. If the hydrophobia is come on *(f)*, with a trembling, grinding and gnaſhing of the teeth, he muſt be put in a dark place, and water ſhould be ſet by him in

(c) *Lib. I. c. xvi.* (d) *Lib. II. c. xi.* (e) *Lib. III. c. xliii.* (f) *Ibid. c. xxxi.*

 a bucket,

a bucket, in ſuch manner that he may not hear the ſound of it. He muſt be well ſecured, that he may not hurt the perſon who attends him. In all diſeaſes of the head, which continue obſtinate, he adviſes the uſe of the actual cautery, in ſuch places as it ſhall make the leaſt blemiſh in. If the hydrophobia does come on, it is not worth while to riſk his biting any attendant. A ball ſhould then be the cure.

Vegetius (g) obſerves, that though the horſe may be cured of this diſorder, yet his brain is ſometimes ſo much affected or injured, that he remains heavy, ſtupid, and unfit for buſineſs. It is with difficulty he can turn himſelf to the ſide on which the inflammation was: he will lean on that ſide againſt a wall, and, not feeling the whip, go ſlowly, and hanging down his head; he loſes all gracefulneſs of gait.

Columella (h) ſpeaks of a ſpecies of madneſs which ſometimes ſeizes mares, though ſeldom. The ſigns of this are, that they run up and down their paſture, as if they were put to the ſpur, after looking round them as if they were ſeeking for ſomething. He adds, that this phrenzy is cured by leading them to a water where they may behold themſelves at full length, and from thence preſumes that it takes its riſe from their love of themſelves, and their having before ſeen only their head in the water.

The authors of the *Maiſon Ruſtique* mention (i) a diſorder which the eyes of horſes are ſubject to on the decreaſe of the moon, and is therefore called *lunatic*. The method of cure which they preſcribe is very proper for any diſorder of that kind, come when it will; namely, putting a ſeton in the nape of the neck. They propoſe, that the cord be compoſed of half hair and half hemp: this cord is anointed with any ointment, and drawn through the inciſion, as is uſually done in men.

(g) *Lib. II. c. v.*

(h) *Lib. VI. c. xxxv.*

(i) *Tom. I. p. 242, of the 7th edit. 4to.*

Though

Though the following do not properly belong to inflammatory diforders, I fhall however comply with common cuftom fo far as to mention here Apoplexy, Epilepfy, Convulfions for which no apparent caufe can be affigned, Palfy, and Lethargy; all thefe being fuppofed to proceed from the Brain.

SECT. V.

Of Apoplexy, Epilepfy, Convulfions, Palfy, and Lethargy.

AN *Apoplexy* feldom gives any previous fign of it's attack, unlefs when it becomes itfelf only a fymptom of Inflammation and Fever. The horfe is fometimes obferved to have watery eyes, or inflamed, to be drowfy, and to ftagger in his gait. If, after fuch fymptoms, he falls down fuddenly, without any other fenfe of motion than a working in his flanks, there may be hopes of his recovery by very plentiful bleeding. The bleeding fhould be continued till there appear fome figns of his recovering his fenfibility. If he drops fuddenly, without any previous appearance of indifpofition, he affords but little room indeed for hope; though bleeding as above fhould be tried, keeping his head raifed a little above the level of his body. If he recovers from the fit, glyfters made of a decoction of fenna and falts fhould be adminiftred immediately, as well as the body opened by powerful purgatives given internally: externally, a feton, rowels, and friction, fhould be ufed; and affarabacca blown up the nofe is thought to draw off the humour by the glands of the nofe.— The *Staggers*, when not proceeding from fome apparent

rent cause, is an apoplexy in a less degree, and should be treated in the same manner,

In the *Epilepsy*, or *Falling-sickness (a)*, the horse's eyes are fixed in his head, he stales and dungs insensibly, he reels, and falls suddenly. He has generally very strong involuntary or convulsive motions; at other times he is immovable, with his legs stretched out as if he was dead, excepting the motion in his flanks and breast, and after he has continued thus for some time, even to some hours, he recovers on a sudden, and at the gowing off of the fit foams at the mouth. Vegetius says *(b)*, that according as the cartilage in the nose is more or less cold to the touch, the returns of the epilepsy, or convulsions, will be more or less frequent.

No cure having yet been found for the epilepsy in mankind, there is the less reason to expect one for horses. Some writers have an opinion of the gums, for the epilepsy and convulsions; and accordingly advise the giving of assafœtida, galbanum, &c. to the quantity of two drams, or half an ounce; or two drams of Russian castor made into a ball, with one ounce of wild valerian root powdered, and honey: but the chief dependance is to be made upon antimony and it's preparations, given as an alterative, to restore the impaired state of the viscera, and of perspiration.

That universal cramp or convulsion, called by some the *Stag-evil*, which seizes all the muscles of the body at once, and locks up the jaws, so that it is almost impossible to force them open, is thus affectingly described by Mr. Gibson. "As soon as the horse is seized, his head is raised with his nose towards the rack, his ears pricked up, and his tail cocked, looking with eagerness as an hungry horse when hay is put down to him, or like a high-spirit-

(a) *Bartlet's Gentleman's Farriery*, p. 82.
(b) *Lib. III. c. xxxiii.*

ed

ed horſe when he is put upon his mettle; inſomuch that thoſe who are ſtrangers to ſuch things, when they ſee a horſe ſtand in this manner, will ſcarce believe any thing of conſequence ails him; but they are ſoon convinced when they ſee other ſymptoms come on apace, and that his neck grows ſtiff, cramped, and almoſt immovable; and if a horſe in this condition lives a few days, ſeveral knots will ariſe on the tendinous parts thereof, and all the muſcles, both before and behind, will be ſo much pulled and cramped, and ſo ſtretched, that he looks as if he was nailed to the pavement, with his legs ſtiff, wide, and ſtraggling; his ſkin is drawn ſo tight on all parts of the body, that it is almoſt impoſſible to move it; and if trial be made to make him walk, he is ready to fall at every ſtep, unleſs he be carefully ſupported: his eyes are ſo fixed through the inaction of the muſcles, as gives him a deadneſs in his looks: he ſnorts and ſneezes often, pants continually with ſhortneſs of breath; and this ſymptom increaſes till he drops down dead; which generally happens in a few days, unleſs ſome ſudden and very effectual turn can be given to the diſtemper."

Vegetius *(c)* divides this illneſs into ſeveral ſtates. The firſt, in which the creature is bereaved of his ſenſes, has his eys open, but is not ſenſible of what approaches him, and his lips ſwell as if he was poiſoned or infected, is a moſt malignant, and, as he ſays, infectious diſeaſe. In it's next ſtate, the whole body is bound faſt, the noſtrils are extended, the ears are ſtiff, the neck is immovable the mouth is ſhut faſt, the head is extended, the ſhoulders and legs are pinioned, and the joints ſo ſtiff that they cannot be moved; his ſpine is exceeding ſtiff, his tail is raiſed, and ſo ſtiff that it can neither be bent nor moved; his flanks are hard and pulled in, and he is unable to lie down: he refuſes to walk, though force be uſed, and then he frequently falls under his

(c) Lib. III. c. xxiii.

hinder parts; he fetches his breath with difficulty, ſighs often, ſnorts, draws up his flanks, and coughs when he attempts to eat, and his ſkin is ſtretched and tight.

"This diſorder, ſays he *(d)*, ariſes from the following cauſes, in the ſummer: the horſe's being ſtruck with a burning-hot ſun, or his becoming lame upon a journey; and being forced to run on till, from exerciſe and pain, he falls into a great ſweat; and in the winter, from his being ſuffered to ſtand in the cold air, or in a damp or new-built ſtable, when he has been heated, or when his jaw-bones in particular have been benumbed with cold." He tells us, that this diſorder may be cured in the ſummer, but not without great difficulty in the winter. To this end, he begins with plentiful bleeding, and then anoints the whole body with oils made very warm. He then orders the horſe to be covered all over, and buried in his own warm litter and dung, ſo that the diſtemper may exſude by the ſkin. As the horſe begins to mend, he ſhould be covered with cloths, and exerciſed by a rider in the warm ſun till he ſweats; he is then to be well rubbed, and again anointed and clothed.

The treatment of the human ſpecies in the locked jaw, and in ſimilar complaints, has taught a more effectual cure for horſes. Mr. Gibſon therefore wiſely adviſes an ounce of opium diſſolved in a glyſter, and then to add to it an ounce of aſſa-fœtida. The uſe of theſe muſt be continued daily, till the ſymptoms abate, and the horſe is able to ſwallow food: and as he may remain for ſeveral days in this condition, it is neceſſary to give him from time to time nouriſhing glyſters, compoſed of the moſt nutritive vegetable decoctions, in ſuch quantities as not to endanger their being thrown out again by their too great load, or over-potent ſtimulus. Camphire

(d) *Lib. III. c. xlvii.*

ſhould

ſhould be added to the ingredients they are anointed with: for example, if diſſolved in oil of olives and oil of turpentine, of each one ounce, and of the nervous ointment four ounces, it will form a mixture which may be kept for uſe, and will be found very ſerviceable. The head, neck, back, and loins, ſhould be anointed a long time. While the ſkin remains ſo tenſe, as it is in this diſeaſe, no digeſtion can be procured in any inciſions, and therefore rowels are not to be attempted, leſt they ſhould mortify, and thereby add to the violence of the ſymptoms.

Palſy and *Lethargy* are alſo imputed to faults in the brain, and therefore claſſed with the foregoing diſorders.

The laſt of theſe is thus deſcribed by Vegetius *(e)*. A horſe affected with a lethargy will conſtantly lie and ſleep, and has no appetite for either meat or drink: after he has been rouſed, he preſently becomes heavy again, and throws himſelf down; he grows lean; the tears run from his eyes as if he was blear-eyed; he ſometimes leans upon the manger and ſleeps; when he walks, he ſtaggers with his hind legs.

Bleeding is neceſſary here to empty the overcharged veſſels, with ſtimulating glyſters, and then purges, to clear the bowels of any matter impacted in the glands. In all other reſpects, this diſorder may be treated nearly in the ſame manner as the foregoing. The horſe ſhould be kept from ſleep by frequent exerciſe, and conſtantly rouſed with the whip or voice. If a well-digeſted diſcharge flow from his noſe, and the horſe be young, there may be hopes of a cure: but if an ill-coloured matter is diſcharged, and the horſe is old, and very ſleepy, there is little room to expect his recovery.

(e) *Lib. III. c. xli.*

SECT.

SECT. VI.

Of Inflammations and other Diſorders of the Eyes.

THE Eyes, like all other parts, are ſubject to Inflammations, which, if attended with any degree of fever, require immediate bleeding. If any vein appears turgid near the eye, that in particular ſhould be opened preferably; and the body too ſhould be opened with a glyſter and a cooling purge. Externally, mild applications are certainly moſt proper while the inflammation continues high, ſuch as, apples roaſted, turnips or carrots boiled, and maſhed with ſome oil upon them, and applied as a poultice. It is alſo proper to waſh the eye with warm milk and water. A cooling treatment of this kind may carry off the inflammation; whereas the ſharp warm applications commonly uſed, increaſe the pain and inflammation by their irritating quality. If the inflammation ends in a ſuppuration in the eye-lids, or on the external coats of the eye, honey mixed with the apple or other poultice becomes an excellent detergent and healing medicine.

Whether the inflammation proceed from an internal cauſe, ſuch as an inflammatory fever ſettling on that part, or from an external cauſe, ſuch as blows, duſt, &c. the applications ſhould be nearly the ſame. If any extraneous body reſts in the eye, that body ſhould certainly be got out, by waſhing the eye with milk or ſome other mild application. If a large ſwelling

ſwelling ariſes from a blow, and the ſkin is not broken, vinegar and water may aſſuage it, or a poultice made of them and flower may be applied; but if the ſkin is broken, neither vinegar nor any ſharp acrid ſubſtance ſhould be uſed, leſt they ſhould form upon the ſore a ſlough, which muſt be caſt off by a conſequent inflammation; whereas mild applications would bring on a kind digeſtion at firſt, and a ſpeedy cure.

A conſtant irritation, and conſequent inflammation, may ariſe from the eye-laſhes being turned in upon the eyes. In this caſe, it ſeldom is ſufficient to pull out the hairs, becauſe the young hairs that ſucceed them will probably take the ſame bend, and if they do, that part of the eye-lid muſt be cut off as deep as the roots of the hair reach. However, before we proceed to this extremity, Vegetius *(a)* adviſes to make an inciſion with a lancet on the inſide of the eye-lid, then to turn the lid outward, and by proper plaiſter and bandage keep it ſo, till the inciſion is cured, and by this means the growing of the hairs inward prevented.

When, by the continuance of any irritating cauſe, the veſſels have remained long turgid, and have by that means loſt their ſtrength, or tone, it is neceſſary to uſe applications which at the ſame time cool and ſtimulate. Such is the common and very proper application of the white of an egg beat up with ſome allum, ſpread on lint, and applied to the eye. A weak ſolution of white vitriol, or ointment of tutty, is likewiſe proper. Sugar of lead mixed with a cooling ointment is here very efficacious. Sir John Pringle *(b)* recommends the following form: Take of white ointment five drams, of ſugar of lead one ſcruple, to which add by degrees two ſcruples of the traumatic balſam, to be rubbed into, and laid on the eye. With this view Sir Hans Sloan's

(a) *Lib. II. c. xv.*
(b) *Obſervations on the Diſeaſes of the Army. Part III. c. ii.*

ointment

ointment is used, which is the tutty made into an ointment with viper's fat. Conserve of roses has long been a favourite application for this purpose. The eyes should be washed with the liquids three or four times a day, and a cloth dipped in them should be applied between whiles. The ointments are best administered with a feather, or rather a brush made of the softest hair, drawn through a quill. The eye-lids should be so far opened, that the medicine may penetrate between them and the ball of the eye, in order that there may not remain there any matter which, becoming acrid, would add to the irritation. Mr. Gibson *(c)* recommends the following wash: Take two drams of rose-buds, infuse them in half a pint of boiling water; when cold, pour off the infusion, and add to it twenty grains of sugar of lead. Vegetius *(d)* commends much the use of celadine in disorders of the eyes; and indeed, if we attend to it's efficacy in discussing swellings in the human body, I think not without foundation.

If a defluxion falls on the eyes from an internal disorder, or a vitiated state of the blood, the cure of the original complaint must be first set about, by giving such medicines as are necessary for that disorder. In strumous cases, a decoction of hemlock is found to be of great efficacy in men, and may therefore certainly be used in obstinate cases in horses: and so may likewise ground-ivy. In other respects, the external treatment may be the same as before directed.

From whatever cause the inflammation arose, if it continues, the external coats of the eye may be so much thickened as to become opake, and thereby impair the sight, or even totally destroy it. Sometimes an abscess is formed, which, by the cicatrice it leaves, destroys the sight. Excrescences may also

(c) *Farrier's Dispensary, p.* 148. (d) *Lib. II. c. xx.*

grow:

grow: these may be cut off, and if the film or cicatrice which is on the sight rises in the least prominent, it may be separated by a steady hand. If the veins on the ball of the eye appear all turgid, and do not give way to any of the applications already mentioned, the eye may be rasped, if I may use the expression, with a brush made of the awns of barley tied at the small ends, and used so that the awns touch the eye against their grain. This opens these superficial vessels, and so discharges their stagnant contents. The white vitriol, sugar of lead, &c. will then cool and heal up these superficial sores.

In a general opakeness without inflammation, the custom is, to blow into the eye such things as, by their roughness, or angular surfaces, shall wear down the opake skin, and by that means restore the sight; such are white vitriol, alum, fine sugar, sugar-candy, &c. in powder, and blown through a quill into the eye. The smart which they occasion excites a frequent motion in the eye-lids, and consequently a friction against the opake skin, which gradually wears it away. On this principle, substances are sometimes made use of which cannot dissolve, such as glass levigated, fish-bones, egg-shells in fine powder, &c. But if we reflect, that these substances remain real motts in the eye, exciting pain and inflammation, we shall surely reject them, and keep to such things only, as, when they have done their business, dissolve in the eye, and thus act a two-fold part, first of destroying the opake skin, and next of healing any remaining sores.

An obstruction from inflammation, or other cause, may happen in the passage by which the tears pass from the eye to the nose, and will occasion what is called a weeping nose. In this case, Vegetius (e) advises to examine the inner corner of the eye affected, and having found one of the small holes which receive the tears, to introduce into it a small pipe, and

(e) *Lib. II. c. xxi.*

blow

blow a mouthful of wine through this into the paſſage, thereby to clear it of any impacted, or obſtructing matter. If digeſted matter collects in the bag which receives the tears in their paſſage to the eye, the bag ſhould be opened, and the paſſage into the noſe cleared with a ſmall probe or ſilver wire, and the bag then be permitted to heal. If the bone is foul, every perſon who would do juſtice to himſelf and to his horſe, ſhould conſult a ſurgeon experienced in operations, and not truſt a matter of this delicacy to himſelf or a farrier.

A total blindneſs is often brought on by a cataract, which is a diſeaſe of the cryſtalline humour, rendering it ſo opake that the rays of light, which in it's natural tranſparent ſtate were tranſmitted to the back of the eye, become intercepted. But as great dexterity is neceſſary in couching, I would here again recommend the hand of a ſkilful ſurgeon; as well as to dilate the iris, or that ſubſtance which contracts and dilates, in proportion to the quantity of light, thereby to protect the back part of the eye from being hurt by too great a glare of light. Theſe being diſtempers in the internal part of the eye, very little can be done by external applications, unleſs it be by correcting the general habit of the body. As millipedes are obſerved to conduce much towards clearing the ſight in men, when the imperfection ariſes from an internal weakneſs, ſo the uſe of them may be recommended here, at leaſt, as a thing that can do no hurt; which is ſaying not a little of a medicine.

SECT. VII.

Of Disorders in the Nose.

THE *Glanders* is one of the Diseases most fatal to horses, because it has hitherto been found to be incurable; and what renders it still more to be feared is, that it is contagious; and that other chronical distempers, as those of the lungs, and the farcy, either bring it on, or end with it.

It is a chronical disease, in which horses may continue long to appearance in good health, discharging, sometimes from one, sometimes from both nostrils, a matter which in the beginning is slimy, but becomes afterwards thicker and white, then clotted and ropey, afterwards of a yellowish or greenish colour, and at last is reddish, and not uncommonly mixed with blood. The glands under the lower jaw, sometimes one, and sometimes more of them, are inflamed, painful, and adhere to the jaw-bone on the side on which the nose runs. If there is a discharge from both nostrils, the glands are then swelled on both sides. The discharge sometimes ceases on one side, and begins on the other; and then the glands on the side where the discharge ceases are partly dissolved; and on the side where it begins they become swelled, hard, painful, and adhering. When the disease has continued long, the matter discharged becomes so very sharp, that it corrodes the nose from which it flows, in time creates ulcers, and even penetrates into the bones, which, especially in the nose, are of so cellular a nature, that they are easily pervaded by it. The smell then becomes very fœtid, and the creature loses

loses his strength and good looks. He grows feeble, and so hideous to behold when ready to die of this lingering disorder, that humanity prompts us to cut short his miserable days by death.

It is but of late that some hopes of surmounting this disease have been entertained. I shall here lay before the reader a short account of the attempts made for this purpose.

In the year 1749, M. de la Fosse, Farrier to the King of France, presented to the Royal Academy of Sciences a Memoir (*a*), in which, after having examined by dissection the carcase of several glandered horses, and made a strict search into the state of their *viscera*, for ten years running, during which he was assisted by expert anatomists appointed for that purpose by the academy, he asserts this disease to be altogether local; and that the true seat of it is in the *pituitary membrane*, which lines the partition along the inside of the nose, the *maxillary sinuses* or cavities of the cheek-bones on each side of the nose, and the *frontal sinuses*, or cavities above the orbits of the eyes; that the liver, lungs, and other viscera of glandered horses are in general perfectly sound, and consequently that the seat of this disorder is not in those parts, as most authors have thought; "for how, says he, could such horses retain their appetite, good appearance, sleek and shining coat, with all other signs of health for many years together, as glandered horses are frequently known to do, with bowels so distempered?" But on a nice examination of the heads of the dissected horses here spoken of, he found the above-mentioned cavities more or less filled with a viscous slimy matter, the membrane which lines both these and the nostrils inflamed, thickened, and corroded with ulcers, which in some cases had eaten into the bones, and the glands under the tongue were hard and choaked up.

(*a*) *Traité sur le Siége de la Morve.*

In farther confirmation of his opinion, that the glanders is purely a local diſorder, he undertook to bring on the ſame ſymptoms in a horſe perfectly ſound; and ſucceeded therein, by ſyringing into the noſtrils a corroſive liquor calculated to inflame the pituitary membrane. The horſes on which he tried this experiment became glandered, that is, they had both a diſcharge from the noſe, and their glands were ſwelled, either on one ſide or on both, according as the injection was thrown up into one or both noſtrils. He adds, that repeated experience had taught him, that the glanders is often occaſioned by blows on the horſe's noſe.

M. de la Foſſe remarks, and the obſervation is really curious, that the ſublingual glands, or the kernels ſituated under the jaw-bone, which are always ſwelled in this diſtemper, do not diſcharge their lymph into the mouth, as in man, but into the noſtrils; and that he conſtantly found their obſtruction agreed with the diſcharge.

The method of cure propoſed by M. de la Foſſe was agreeable to this ſyſtem. He gave no internal medicine, and had only in view to cure the fault in the pituitary membrane, by injections fitted for that purpoſe; and in order to make an opening when neceſſary, he did not ſcruple to penetrate into the frontal and maxillary ſinuſes by means of a trepan, with which he made openings into the ſinuſes, one in the upper part of each ſinus, and one in the lower part, to give a freer vent to the matter diſcharged, as well as to the ingredients thrown in; and by ſeveral experiments of this kind, made in the preſence of the perſons appointed by the Academy, he ſhewed that theſe openings were neither mortal nor dangerous.

The cure of the milder kinds of glanders may firſt be attempted by injections and fumigations. Thus, if a horſe, after having taken cold, ſhould diſcharge for a fortnight or three weeks running, a limpid fluid, or whitiſh matter, from one or both noſtrils, and the glands under the jaw continue to ſwell and harden, rather than diminiſh, there is danger of this illneſs degenerating into a true glanders. To prevent this, after firſt bleeding, and treating him as before directed for a cold, let an emollient injection, compoſed of a decoction of linſeed, marſh mallows, elder flowers, chamomile flowers, and honey of roſes, or ſuch like, be thrown up as far as poſſible with a ſtrong ſyringe, and repeated thrice a day. If the running does not leſſen, or is not removed in a fortnight, by the uſe of this injection, a reſtringent one may then be given, made with tincture of roſes and lime water, and the noſtrils fumigated with powdered frankincenſe, maſtich, amber, and cinnabar, burnt on a hot iron, and the fume conveyed through a tube into the noſtrils.

This method has been found ſucceſsful when uſed in time; but the methods of cure depend on the ſtubbornneſs of the diſorder, and when it is inveterate, recourſe muſt be had to the trepan.

M. de la Foſſe performed the operation of the trepan on three horſes, two of which had the running from one noſtril only, and the third from both: he trepanned the two firſt on that ſide of the head which was affected, and the third on both ſides of the head. The wound and perforation filled up with good fleſh in twenty-ſix days, and the horſes felt no inconvenience from the operation; though, after the experiment, they were put to death.

The injections firſt made uſe of ſhould be of a deterſive nature, ſuch as, a decoction of birth-wort, gentian, and centuary, to a quart of which it will be right to add two ounces of Ægyptiacum, and tincture of myrrh diſſolved in honey of roſes, for otherwiſe this laſt will not mix with water; and when the diſcharge abates, and it's colour alters to a thick white matter, the injection may be changed for barley-water, honey of roſes, and tincture of myrrh: and finally, to dry up the humidities, and reſtore

restore the tone of the relaxed glands, Bates's alum-water, or a solution of colcothar, vitriol, lapis medicamentosus, or such like, in lime-water, may be used, and will most probably complete the cure.

The syringe used on this occasion should be large enough to contain half a pint of injection.

M. de la Fosse's above-related experiments would seem to prove that the Glanders is a merely local disease, situated in the head. And yet we find, upon as good authority, some other observations, which render it equally probable that it is a disease in the humours.

M. Malouin's office at the court of France having naturally thrown in his way the examination of several horses, belonging to the Royal Stables, that were attacked with this disease, he resolved to pursue the interesting inquiry; and the following is the result of his experiments communicated to the Royal Academy of Sciences.

He began with opening the bodies of several glandered horses. The brain in all of them was sound. The pituitary membrane was always red, thicker and looser than in its natural state, and more or less covered with a matter resembling that which ran from the nose. It was not equally affected in all: in some only a part of that membrane appeared to be diseased; in others, the whole was vitiated and ulcered. The *uvula*, or roof of the mouth, was most commonly affected; and it even appeared in many, that it was from this part chiefly that the matter flowed.

In almost all of them, the lungs were distempered, and more or less filled with tubercles and small abscesses full of matter resembling the glanderous discharge. The liver frequently had white spots upon it, especially on the convex side; and under these spots were almost constantly found abscesses like those in the lungs, and filled with the same kind of matter. Sometimes the mesentery, the kidneys, the pylorus, and the wind-pipe, were affected; but the æſophagus, ſtomach, inteſtines, and ſpleen, very ſeldom partook of it.

The longer the diſeaſe had continued, the more theſe parts were affected. When it had been but of ſhort duration, the pituitary membrane only was hurt; and the others were diſeaſed in proportion to the time the diſorder had laſted.

Thus informed, M. Malouin engaged M. Serviez, Farrier to the King of France's leſſer ſtables, to obtain leave for him to treat the glandered horſes in ſuch manner as he ſhould judge moſt proper. The requeſt was granted; and the horſe he firſt took in hand was examined by all the King's farriers, who agreed that he was glandered.—It was a grey horſe, aged about ten years, glandered on the right ſide, and diſcharging a very fœtid matter, which had ulcerated in the noſe.

The following is M. Malouin's own account of his proceedings, as delivered to the Royal Academy (*a*).

" I adviſed, that the horſe ſhould take once a day of my Æthiops Antimonial (*b*), and once a day of Periwincle (*c*); to give him to drink, in his water, leavened paſte, inſtead of the meal which is commonly uſed; to ſyringe his noſe with a decoction of birthwort (*d*), and afterwards with a vulnerary water; to apply to the ſwelled glands the emplaſtrum diachylon with the gums, with a digeſtive ointment and cantharides mixed together; and to purge him every

(*a*) *Hiſtoire de l' Academie Royale des Sciences, pour l' an* 1750. See alſo *La Chymie Medicinale de M. Malouïn, Tom. II. p.* 169.

(*b*) To make this medicine, Take crude Antimony and Quickſilver, of each half an ounce, and Flowers of Sulphur two drams; rub them together in a marble mortar till the Quickſilver diſappears.

(*c*) *Peruinca anguſtifolia, flore aut purpureo, aut albo, aut cæruleo*; the *Clematis Daphnoides* of the antients. *Vineapervinca Officinarum.*

(*d*) *Ariſtolochia longa vera.*

eighth

eighth day. I likewiſe adviſed that he ſhould be taken out every day, and walked with a longe as much as could be, in the ſun, and in dry weather; and to keep conſtantly rubbing him whilſt in the ſtable.

" This courſe was begun on the ſixth of June 1759. The farrier gave him twice a day the periwincle ſhred among his bran; he was purged every week; the plaiſter and digeſtive were applied to the gland: he gave up, from the beginning, ſyringing the vulnerary decoction into his noſe, becauſe, in order to do that, it was neceſſary each time to put him between the pillars: but he determined to make three openings with the trepan on the affected ſide, and paſſed through each hole a ſeton, the ends of which came out at the noſe, and by which a great deal of ſtinking matter was diſcharged. The vulnerary decoction was daily injected into the two upper holes; and when they were cloſed up, and there ceaſed to be a diſcharge from the noſe, ſpirit of vitriol was injected, to dry it up perfectly, ſaid the farrier.

" With regard to the gland, it leſſened and ſwelled at times, as is uſual in ſuch caſes; and as the plaiſter had no ſenſible effect on it, the farrier divided the ſkin over it, in order to lay upon the gland a mild cauſtic called *realgar*, which was kept on with compreſs and bandage. The gland was thus deſtroyed, and the ſore was perfectly healed in five weeks, without any other dreſſing.

" The horſe having been treated in this manner during four months, appeared perfectly ſound, and about the beginning of October was returned to his former diet.

" By the beginning of the enſuing year, he had recovered his good looks, the ſcars of his wounds ſcarce appeared, and no ſigns of the glanders remained. I was of opinion that they ſhould not have ceaſed purging him all at once, but rather have left it off by degrees. Being a ſaddle-horſe, he was returned to his uſual exerciſe, which he bore very well for three months more, and would probably have done ſo much longer, had it not been thought for the good of the ſervice to kill him, in order that, by opening his body, the effects of the cure might be ſeen. When opened, all the parts appeared ſound, excepting that the pituitary membrane on the diſeaſed ſide ſeemed a little ſwelled, and covered with the purulent matter of the glanders; which ſhewed that the purging ſhould have been continued. Though this matter may probably have been ſeparated conſtantly, yet it was not in ſufficient quantity to cauſe a ſenſible diſcharge; a circumſtance which ought to teach us, not to think that a glandered horſe is perfectly cured when the diſcharge ceaſes.

" The ſecond horſe that was put under cure was a bay, thirteen years old, eaſily purged, and naturally a great eater. He was ſhort-breathed, coughed ſometimes, worked much in the flanks, was exceeding lean and weak, and a white but very ſtinking matter ran from his noſe.

" On the firſt of March, 1760, he began his courſe. He took daily my antimonial Æthiops, and periwincle; he was purged every eighth day in the beginning of the cure, but afterwards at longer intervals. He was not trepanned, nor was any injection thrown up his noſe. The gland which was painful and fixed to the jaw, diſperſed without a cauſtic or any other application. The ſucceſs of this courſe was ſpeedy. The matter ceaſed to flow; the horſe breathed freely, without labouring in his loins, and he recovered his good looks. He was occaſionally purged, after being returned to his oats and common diet; and at the end of ſix months he was put to his uſual labour, as a coach-horſe.—In July 1762, (the time when this account was given,) he remained in perfect health, being occaſionally purged; and though he has the hardeſt taſk in the King's coach, that of carrying the poſtillion, he bears it well; and I have

I have obtained an order for his being continued on, that we may ſee what will become of him.

" The third horſe was in the laſt ſtage of the glanders. The very bones on the right ſide of his head were ſwelled, the glands were ſwelled, and he diſcharged from one ſide a very ſtinking reddiſh matter frequently ſtreaked with blood. The noſe had a a cancerous appearance, and even whilſt under cure he was ſeized with the farcy.

" Three openings were made with the trepan in 1760, and the vulnerary decoction was injected into the ſinuſes. The periwincle and birthwort in powder were given to him, with the antimonial æthiops, and he was purged as before directed.

" The farcy ſoon diſappeared by the uſe of theſe medicines; but the glanders kept it's hold, and never was entirely got the better of: yet the diſcharge leſſened, and became of a better quality. When the diſcharge leſſened on the right ſide, it began on the left, and then continued on both, without however increaſing in quantity. It at length diminiſhed ſo as not to appear for ſome days, and towards the cloſe was become white, without the bad ſmell. The gland on the right ſide was opened with a cauſtic, and a purulent matter, like ſoap-ſuds, was diſcharged from it. The gland on the left ſide ſubſided as the diſcharge from that ſide leſſened, and till it ceaſed entirely. The ſwelling on the bone was reduced to it's natural ſtate. The purging having been neglected for ſome time, a ſwelling aroſe in his left ham, but ſoon yielded to the purges that were then given, and the horſe recovered his good look. However, notwithſtanding theſe appearances, the glanders did not give way; and indeed, during the laſt year, it could ſcarcely be ſaid to mend, though the horſe had then been two years under his courſe; at the end of which time he was killed, in order to examine the condition the parts were in.

" The head appeared in it's natural ſtate, except on the right ſide, where the ſinuſes were ſtill bedewed with the matter diſcharged; and the tuberoſity of the cheek-bone was penetrated. Part of the gland remained adhering to the jaw-bone. The right lobe of the lungs was internally full of tubercles, and externally there appeared many ſpots of blemiſh. There was a ſmall abſceſs in the ſpleen. The reſt of the body was perfectly ſound.

" M. Serviez continues to treat glandered horſes, with various ſucceſs, in nearly the ſame manner, which conſiſts in giving to each of them every morning from half an ounce to an ounce and a half of my antimonial æthiops, and every evening a handful of periwincle ſhred among his bran. Great care ſhould be taken to keep their noſtrils clean, that they may not ſwallow the purulent matter. For this purpoſe, wine may be ſyringed up the noſe. They cannot be rubbed down too often. They ſhould be carried out into the ſun-ſhine every fair day; and the ſtable and litter ſhould be kept dry. Though purges often diſagree with horſes, yet it is indiſpenſibly neceſſary to continue uſing them here."

We are informed in the before-quoted Hiſtory of the Academy of Sciences, that notwithſtanding theſe experiments ſeem to prove the glanders to be a diſorder of the blood and other humours, yet M. de la Foſſe the ſon preſented a Memoir to the Academy of Sciences, in ſupport of his father's opinion; and that, in conſideration of the importance of this matter, the Academy appointed Commiſſaries to examine into it.

Four glandered horſes were opened in their preſence. The internal parts of all the four were perfectly ſound, except ſome white ſpots on the liver of one; and theſe were only ſuperficial. Not the ſmalleſt veſtige of the diſeaſe was ſeen any where, but in the frontal and maxillary ſinuſes, and in the gland under the lower jaw. The lungs eſpecially appeared to be in their natural ſtate. "How

" How, add the Editors of the foregoing accounts, ſhall we reconcile this difference of opinions? It can only be, by aſſigning two cauſes of the glanders, properly ſo called; the firſt external, which acts immediately on the pituitary membrane; and the other occaſioned by ſome preceding diſeaſe, which cauſing a flow of acrid matter through the noſe, irritates the pituitary membrane, and occaſions an inflammation of it. Among the external cauſes may be reckoned blows, too ſudden a cold, or too acrid a matter inſpired or injected. And this kind of glanders may be treated with injections, fumigations, &c.—Strangles, diſorders of the lungs, farcy, or many other diſeaſes, may become the cauſe of the ſecond kind of glanders; and it appears evident, that any topical application would be fruitleſs whilſt the original diſtemper remains, and that this muſt be cured at the ſame time that it's effects are carried off."

Horſes are peculiarly ſubject to this diſeaſe, becauſe, with them, whatever comes out of the windpipe muſt flow through the noſe; the uvula falling ſo low in them, that the paſſage by the mouth is interrupted; and hence it follows, that almoſt every diſtemper of the lungs muſt be communicated to the pituitary membrane. Horſes that are affected with the glanders from external cauſes, may long retain their good looks: but in the other caſes, their appearance muſt be proportioned to the degree of the original diſorder. If the firſt of theſe ſorts of glanders continues long, the whole maſs of blood may be affected, and thence produce internal diſeaſes; and by that means internal remedies may become as neceſſary here as in the other caſe.

The very ingenious Dr. Biſſet, in his Medical Eſſays (*e*), proves by ſeveral inſtances the efficacy of a ſeton under the jaw, in ſcrophulous inflammations of

(*e*) *Page* 119.

the

the eyes: and this confirms the propriety of opening the head or ſwelled glands in the glanders, becauſe, by the diſcharge it makes, that may conduce much to the cure; and ſhould therefore be one of the firſt things done.

M. Bourgelat, Inſpector of the Veterinarian School at Lyons, who publiſhed his work ſo late as the year 1765, ſpeaks thus of the Glanders *(f)*. "That formidable diſeaſe, the Glanders, baffles every means hitherto tried to cure it. The openings made by the trepan; all the injections thrown in to clear the mucous membrane, and reſtore it's tone; all the internal medicines that have been given, ſuch as mercury uſed in friction, or combined with antimony in the antimonial æthiops, periwincle, repeated purgations, hemlock, &c. have not abſolutely got the better of this deadly venom."

Horſes, as well as men, are ſometimes afflicted with a *Polypus*, which ſhould be extirpated when it hurts reſpiration. The method of extracting it *(g)* is by a pair of *forceps* with a ſlit at their extremities for the better hold, which muſt be introduced into the noſtril as far as poſſible, to make the more ſure of it towards the roots; then twiſting them a little from one ſide to the other, you muſt continue in that action, while you pull very gradually the body of the polypus. If it breaks, the extraction muſt be repeated as long as any part remains, unleſs it be attended with a violent hæmorrhage, which is an accident that ſometimes follows upon the operation, and indeed ſeldom fails to happen when the excreſcence is ſchirrous: however, the operator is not to be alarmed at the appearance of an immoderate effuſion after the ſeparation, for, generally ſpeaking, the veſſels collapſe very ſoon again: but if they do not, dry lint, or lint dipt in ſome ſtyptic will readily ſtop it.

(f) *Matiere Medicale raiſonnée, &c. p.* 135.
(g) *Sharpe's Surgery, ch. xxxiii.*

After

After the extirpation, the only proper uſe of eſcharotic powders is to deſtroy the remainder of the polypus which cannot be taken away, and to which acceſs cannot be had: and the eſcharotics may be better conveyed to the part by a long tent, than by any other way.

SECT. VIII.

Of the Diſeaſes of the Mouth and Throat.

VEGETIUS obſerves *(a)*, that when horſes are pained in their gums and teeth, it is known by the following ſigns: A great deal of ſaliva flows from the horſe's mouth, he will ſwallow his corn entire, and grows lean. Here, the mouth ſhould be examined, and if any defect appears, it ſhould be remedied, according to the nature of the caſe. Excreſcences, commonly called by the barbarous names of *lampas* and *barbs*, ſhould be cut off, whether on the roof of the mouth or about the tongue. Frequently too there are on the inſide of the lips and palate little ſwellings, or bladders, called *giggs*: theſe are cured by opening them with a knife or lancet, and waſhing them with vinegar; but if they ſpread into ulcers with white ſpecks, the beſt method will be to touch them with a ſmall flat cautery moderately hot till they ceaſe ſpreading; and when the ſloughs are caſt off, which nature will effect, the ſore may

(a) *Lib. II. c. xxxii.*

be

be dreſſed with a mixture of burnt alum and honey, one part of the former, and two of the latter. When the gums appear looſe and ſpongy, Vegetius adviſes rubbing them for a long while with powder of the bark of pomegranate and honey. This may alſo have a good effect when little ulcers are ſeen on the gums or tongue; as may likewiſe alum, if they do not give way to the former application. Rotten teeth, or ſuch as wound or hurt the horſe, ſhould be either pulled out, or filed down.

The chief diſorder in theſe parts is the Strangles, or what is analogous to a quinſy or inflammation of the tonſils in man; and, like it, is attended with fever, heat, and foulneſs in the mouth, a cough, an inclination to drink without being able to ſwallow, or to ſwallow but little, a loſs, of appetite, and from the ſame cauſe, an inability to eat. The ſwelling generally is internal; but ſometimes it appears externally, between the lower jaw-bones.

If this diſorder is obſerved ſoon after the horſe is ſeized with it, endeavours ſhould be uſed to carry it off by plentiful bleeding and a cooling regimen; but if it does not ſoon yield to this treatment, the intention muſt be to bring it to ſuppuration as ſpeedily as poſſible, becauſe of the creature's difficulty of taking ſufficient nouriſhment. Some authors, amongſt whom are the writers of the *Maiſon Ruſtique (b)*, look on this diſorder as ſo peculiar to young horſes that they ſeldom eſcape it, and therefore treat it as a critical diſcharge, in whatever part of the body the inflammation happens. Vegetius *(c)* adviſes a mixture to be made of two pints of oil and one of wine, added to water in which Syrian figs and leeks have been boiled and bruiſed with a ſufficient quantity of nitre, and ſome of this to be given frequently, becauſe, by it's oily mucilaginous quality, it ſoftens and lubricates the parts. He likewiſe adviſes, that the horſe be fed

(b) *Tom. I. p.* 225. (c) *Lib. II. c. xxvi, & c. xxviii.*

with

with green food sprinkled with nitre; or rather, that he be kept at pasture, if the weather will admit of it, because, by his hanging his head, whatever matter flows from the diseased parts, will fall out either by the nose or mouth. He directs also, that, to quicken the cure, several stones be made red hot, and that pieces of them be repeatedly put into a vessel full of urine held under the horse's head; his mouth being kept open by a piece of stick, the better to receive the fume both by nose and mouth, and the head covered so as to confine the steam: and after this, that the mouth, gums, and whole head be washed with warm water, in which as much salt has been dissolved as it will suspend, and a due proportion of the sharpest vinegar; and he finishes the cure with giving daily a powder composed of the roots of wild cucumbers and nitre, to keep the body open.

This disease bears so near a resemblance to the Quincy, that I cannot do better here than quote some directions given in the last-named disorder by the most judicious Sir John Pringle. This learned Physician recommends the following remedy, which he has sometimes found useful *(d)*. "Let a piece of "thick flannel, moistened with two parts of common sweet oil, and one part of spirit of hartshorn, "be applied to the throat, and renewed once in four "or five hours. By this means the neck, and "sometimes the whole body, is put into a sweat, "which, after bleeding, either carries off or lessens "the inflammation. The *formula* is new, but not "the intention; for the antients applied warm oil "with a spunge, and bags of warm salt: and some "later writers have recommended poultices made of "the dung of animals; which seems to be only a "coarse and offensive way of using the volatiles." I quote this passage with particular pleasure, because it confirms the rectitude of the practice of the Ro-

(d) *Observations on the Diseases of the Army*, p. 142. 4th Edit.

mans,

mans, to rub the bodies of their diſtempered horſes ſo much without as they did; a practice which ſeems to be entirely neglected by the moderns.

Sir John proceeds thus (e): "I obſerved little "benefit from common gargles; for at that time "I did not inject them with a ſyringe, which I "now conſtantly do. By this means the patient" (ſo will a horſe) "brings away a great deal of "tough phlegm, and generally finds ſome immedi-"ate relief; the glands of the fauces being cleared. "My compoſition is, thirteen ounces of barley-wa-"ter, or ſage-tea, with two ounces of mel-roſe, and "one ounce of vinegar: ſometimes I have added "a ſpoonful of muſtard for a greater ſtimulus. Even "in the ulcerous ſore throat, I lay the greateſt ſtreſs "of the cure upon gargling in this manner. I di-"rect as many ſyringefuls to be injected, one after "another, and as far into the throat, as the patient "can bear; and to repeat the medicine three times a "day."

If the ſwelling appears outwardly, a poultice will certainly be proper; as well as the addition of the warmer ingredients uſed for this purpoſe, ſuch as flour of fenugreek ſeed, onions roaſted or boiled, and added to flour and milk, with as much oil, or hog's lard, as ſhall keep it from growing dry. As ſoon as a fluctuation is felt in the external ſwelling, the tumour ſhould be opened, and treated in the manner that will be directed when I come to ſpeak of abſceſſes.

If the ſwelling breaks internally, the matter will be moſtly diſcharged from the noſe; ſo that to a perſon who has not attended to the preceding ſymptoms, the horſe ſhall appear to have the glanders. If the ſuppuration has proceeded kindly, as the matter diſcharged has no great degree of acrimony, nothing need be feared from it. The noſe ſhould however

(e) *Id. ibid.*

be

be kept clean by mild injections, and others of a more detergent nature should be syringed into the mouth. The infusion of sage, honey, and mustard, as recommended by Sir John Pringle, becomes here highly proper: and as borax is found to be very effectual in clearing the mouth and gullet in children of that troublesome complaint the Thrush, it might probably be added here to great advantage. If the discharge becomes sharp, fœtid, or ill-conditioned, then the use of the Jesuits bark, with warm aromatics, such as chamomile flowers, snake-root, &c. become necessary, together with keeping the parts warm.

Mr. Osmer (f) is clear that the strangles is only a critical swelling, and therefore should be brought to suppuration as soon as possible.

Farriers seem to have delighted in calling disorders by names which have no sort of affinity to either the complaint itself, or the part affected by it. Such as *lampas* and *barbs*, before noticed, and *Vives*, or *Ives*, a disease next to be treated of, chiefly on account of the propinquity of the part affected by it to the seat of the strangles: for as the strangles answers to an inflammation of the tonsils in men, so the *vives* is an inflammation or obstruction of the parotid glands, which often takes it's rise from a horse's being permitted to drink very cold water when he is hot, or suffering him to catch cold.

The symptoms of it are, that the horse loses at once his appetite, droops his head, his ears are cold, his mouth is hot and dry, he seems melancholy, rolls himself, lies down and rises often, and twists himself about exceedingly, on accout of the pains in his glands, and the gripings in his belly, which are accompanied with a retention of urine.

When this disorder happens to a young horse, it is deemed a critical discharge, the same as the stran-

(f) *Page* 122.

gles

gles is thought to be; and the opinion therefore is, that it ſhould be encouraged to come to ſuppuration, leſt the humour fall on ſome other part. This, however, need not be a general rule; for if it ariſes from any external cauſe, ſuch as the before-mentioned, bleeding, glyſters, and a cooling diet, ſhould be ordered. The embrocation with oil and ſpirit of hartſhorn ſhould be employed here, covering the neck with a lamb's ſkin, to keep it quite warm. If the ſwelling does not ſpeedily give way to ſuch applications, the intention ſhould be changed to that of bringing on a ſuppuration; and poultices ſhould be applied for that purpoſe. The method which ſome have propoſed, of bruiſing the tumour, is cruel and painful, and may be attended with bad conſequences: nor is the uſe of mercurials to be much more relied on; and at all events they certainly ſhould not be employed at all while the tumour is in an inflammatory ſtate. If the tumour is ſo large as to obſtruct the horſe's ſwallowing, or otherwiſe inconvenience him to any great degree, the beſt way is to cut it out.

The ears too may be affected with inflammations, which ſhould be treated in a manner ſimilar to the above directions; and in caſe of ſuppuration in the internal part of the ear, the matter ſhould be diſcharged, and the ear kept clean, by throwing in a mixture of milk and honey at firſt, and afterwards a decoction of birthwort, plantain, or ſuch herbs, with honey, in order to cure.

SECT.

SECT. IX.

Of the Pleurisy, and Inflammation of the Lungs.

MR. Gibſon pretends to deſcribe the ſeveral ſymptoms which diſtinguiſh theſe diſeaſes from one another: but at leaſt as good an authority, Sir John Pringle, declares, that " ſince he had read " the Diſſertations and Remarks of thoſe celebrated " authors de Haller and Morgagni relating to this " ſubject, he was convinced, that we ought to con- " ſider theſe two diſtempers as one; in which the " lungs are always inflamed, and often without the " pleura; but the pleura never without the lungs." The ſymptoms mentioned by Mr. Gibſon can therefore be taken only as to a greater or leſs degree of fever and inflammation.

In theſe diſorders, the fever riſes ſuddenly to a great height, the breathing is difficult, attended with a cough, the horſe ſhews great uneaſineſs, and ſhifts from place to place; in the beginning, he often ſtrives to lie down, but ſtarts up immediately. While the inflammation is moderate, a ropy ſlime runs out at the mouth, and a reddiſh or yellowiſh water gleets at the noſe, ſticking like glue to the inſide of the noſtrils. When the inflammation is great, the horſe's ears are burning hot, his mouth is parched and dry, his pulſe is hard and quick, and his flanks heave violently. Though, in the beginning, he makes many motions to lie down, yet afterwards he runs back as far as his halter will permit, and offers not in the leaſt to change his poſture, but ſtands panting with ſhort ſtops, and a diſpoſition to cough, till he has relief, or drops down. Mr. Gibſon makes the criterion of this diſtemper to be, the horſe's frequently turning his head towards the affected ſide, which, ſays he, has cauſed many to miſtake a pleuritic diſorder for the gripes, this ſign being common to both; though with this difference, that in the gripes the horſe frequently lies down and rolls; and when they are violent, he will alſo have convulſive twitches, his eyes being turned up, and his limbs ſtretched out, as if he was dying; his ears and feet ſometimes hot, and ſometimes as cold as ice; he falls into profuſe ſweats, and then into cold damps; ſtrives often to ſtale and dung, but with great pain and difficulty; which ſymptoms generally continue till he has ſome relief.

The cure of this diſorder muſt begin with large and repeated bleedings. A ſtrong horſe may loſe three quarts of blood, and if he is not relieved in twelve hours, he ſhould loſe two quarts more. Bleeding *(a)* in ſmaller quantities ſhould be continued till the ſymptoms abate, or weakneſs forbids it.

On this head Sir John Pringle moſt judiciouſly remarks, that "though we reject the critical days, we "muſt ſtill with the antients obſerve certain periods "of the inflammatory pleuriſy, diſtinguiſhable both "by the ſymptoms, and the indication of cure:— "for certain it is, that if the *ſputum*" [or in horſes a digeſted diſcharge by the noſe] "appears, we "are to conſider it as a means of cure, and therefore "not to divert it by continued bleeding or other eva- "cuations. Bleeding may be continued freely," ſays he, "for the firſt three or four days of the "diſtemper; but if in that time the ſpitting" [here, running at the noſe] "begins, the bleeding muſt "either be wholly omitted, or ſo moderated, as to "relieve the breaſt without imparing the ſtrength, or "checking the expectoration."

In horſes, we are deprived of one great means of curing this diſtemper, which Sir John ſeems chiefly to rely on, namely, bliſtering: but I think it might be renewed in this caſe, in the manner that Vegetius propoſes for another complaint, viz. by adding can-

(a) *Obſervations on the Diſeaſes of the Army, p.* 145.

tharides

tharides to ſtrong ſinapiſms. Might not the ſide of the horſe be ſhaved, and a quantity of the Spaniſh flies in powder be ſpread on the ſinapiſm, and applied to the part affected? In order to induce gentlemen to try this practice. I ſhall here ſubjoin what Sir John Pringle adds (*b*) concerning the effects of bliſters. " Bliſters not only ſhorten the cure, but " prevent the loſs of a great deal of blood. A pleu- " riſy taken in the beginning, will often be cured by " one large bleeding, and a bliſter laid on the ſide " affected. The objection to this practice is found- " ed on the ſtimulating quality of the epiſpaſtic: " but the relief is ſo certain, that theory ought only " to be employed in accounting for the reſolution of " an internal ſpaſm, or obſtruction, by ſuch a ſti- " mulus upon the ſkin.—The experience I have " had induces me to apply the epiſpaſtic in the be- " ginning of the diſorder: for in treating great num- " bers, I found no inconvenience from uſing the " bliſter immediately after the firſt bleeding; but, " on the contrary, a more ſudden and certain relief. " —Though the ſymptom may vaniſh upon bliſter- " ing, it will be more ſecure to bleed again; for if " the lungs are much inflamed, the cure cannot be " ſo ſpeedy; for though the firſt bleeding and bliſter- " ing ſhould give eaſe, yet repetitions of both will " be needful. Sometimes the ſtitch returns, and " fixes on the other ſide: but this being treated as " the firſt, will alſo give way."

The horſe ſhould be kept on a cool diluting regimen, giving him plenty to drink, rather often than much at a time. In his drink, figs, raiſins, barley, liquorice, and ſuch mild mucilaginous ſubſtances, ſhould be boiled; alſo nitre, to the quantity of two ounces; and oils diſſolved in honey and then mixed with water, ſhould be given; as likewiſe, ſpermacæti diſſolved in the yolk of an egg. When he be-

(*b*) *Ibid. p.* 146.

gins to run at the nofe, warmer things may be given to promote the expectoration; fuch as quills, or their oxymel, to the quantity of three or four ounces, or a folution of gum ammoniac. It has been faid, that the rattle-fnake root is peculiarly ufeful in this intention: but it has of late loft much of it's reputation in the opinion of phyficians. " I have likewife, " fays Sir John Pringle *(c)*, obferved fome good " effects from making the patient [the fame may be " applied to a horfe] breathe over the fteam of hot " water,—which is rendered more beneficial when " the phlegm is vifcid, as well as more grateful, by " adding a fmall proportion of vinegar." A mild glyfter fhould be given once a day; and if the creature is coftive, it may be quickened by the addition of three or four ounces of purging falt, or as much fyrop of buckthorn.

As pleuritic diforders are apt to leave a taint on the lungs, great care fhould be taken that the horfe have a light and eafy diet for two or three weeks, and that he be brought to his exercife gradually in an open air and fair weather; and as he recovers his ftrength, his body fhould be kept gently open.

If the inflammation, terminates in a gangrene or mortification, death enfues; or if it fuppurates, and the matter is confined, it foon brings death; or if it is ejected by the wind-pipe, the abfcefs fcarcely ever cures, and the acrid taint of the purulent matter difcharged by coughing is apt to infect found horfes. A prudent man will therefore not rifk an uncertain cure with the danger of his other horfes.

Vegetius *(d)*, in diforders of the lungs, probably in a confumptive ftate, recommends three eggs mixed with goat's milk and a fpoonful of honey, with other pectorals. He alfo directs *(e)* half a pint of

(c) *Ibid. p.* 148
(d) *Lib. III. c. xlv.*
(e) *Lib. IV. c. viii.*

raifin

raisin wine and three ounces of oil, with a raw egg, to be given for three successive days, having added to them beanflour and fenugreek seeds, elecampane, and comfrey. This mixture to be given to the horse fasting.

Likewise, with the same view of assisting the lungs, the *Maison Rustique* (*f*) recommends as an easy and excellent remedy, to put a dozen of eggs into so much strong vinegar as shall cover them to the depth of about half an inch, and when the shells are become soft by steeping in the vinegar, to make the horse swallow them all, whole, one by one, with a little of the vinegar, or, if it can be done, all the vinegar in which they were laid; then to walk him about gently for two hours, and afterwards give him scalded bran, but neither oats nor hay. Repeat this remedy, if necessary.

An inflammation sometimes seizes the muscles or their membranes between the ribs. This is known by a stiffness of the body, an inaptitude of motion in the shoulder and fore-leg of the side affected, attended with a shrinking when the part is handled, and a cough.

The means of cure are the same as in the former case; only that as the seat of this false pleurisy is external it may be more readily removed by external softening applications. Poultices here may be peculiarly useful, as likewise may oily embrocations. Indeed, the oil and spirit of hartshorn, before directed, might be rubbed all over the breast in the true pleurisy, as well as in this false one. This disorder frequently terminates in a suppuration, and the matter sometimes insinuates itself among the muscles of the shoulder or fore-leg, in which case an immediate outlet should be given to it.

(*f*) *Tome I. Part. I. Liv. III. chap. I. p.* 257.

SECT. X.

Of the Asthma and Broken-Wind.

AN Asthma is constantly attended with a cough, and may easily be distinguished from a consumption by the quality of the matter that is brought up, which, in an asthma, is not of the purulent and fœtid nature that is in a consumption, when the flesh and strength decay. An asthmatic horse has a difficulty of breathing, which can be easily distinguished from that shortness of breath which arises from inflammation, by the absence of fever, heat, &c. The cough is sometimes dry and husky, sometimes moist, throwing out by the nose and mouth quantities of tough white phlegm, especially after any action that has loosened the phlegm adhering to the fauces or wind-pipe, such as drinking, eating, or exercise, which, creating a discharge in the diseased glands, loosens the impacted or adhering matter. This discharge gives a temporary relief; and though a horse should be at the beginning of any exercise so short-breathed as scarcely to be able to stir, yet the exercise continuing to keep the wind-pipe clear of this tough matter, he may afterwards perform beyond expectation. As in man, so in horses, we often see that a true asthmatic cough does not greatly impair the flesh, nor the strength, if the exercise is gentle.

This disease is very hard to cure, and scarce ever curable where it has continued for some time. If the horse is full of flesh, he should be bled, but only in a moderate degree, because bleeding here is but a palliative when the disorder attacks with more than common force. During the violence of a fit of an asthma, the horse should be treated with a cooling regimen, giving him plenty of mealy drinks with nitre, and keeping the body open, first with glysters, and then by internal medicines.

As

As a radical cure can ſcarcely be expected, all that can be done is to render the diſorder as eaſy as poſſible. With this view, the uſe of gum ammoniac and aſſa-fœtida, of ſquills, garlic, elecampane, flower of ſulphur, and mercury, has long been practiſed. The quick-ſilver itſelf is here found more efficacious than any preparation of it. Balls of the following compoſition may be given: viz. Quick-ſilver half an ounce, freſh ſquils two drams, ſimple balſam of ſulphur twenty drops; rub them together till the quick-ſilver entirely diſappears; then add gum-ammoniac and aſſa-fœtida, of each half an ounce, and honey enough to make them into a maſs; to be given daily in ſuch quantity as ſhall keep the belly open. A ſolution of gum ammoniac may be given in a decoction of garlic, or pine tops. Theſe laſt may alſo be given with the corn. The antimonial æthiops is likewiſe here a good medicine; and a conſtant drain made by rowels may be of ſingular ſervice. What will alſo tend greatly to keep this diſorder under, is, early ſoiling in ſummer, with lucerne, or other ſucculent plants, while their juices are yet in a watery ſtate, and more purgative than when concocted by the ſummer's heat, which likewiſe renders them more nouriſhing; and in the autumn, the ſalt-marſhes afford no leſs relief, by their cooling and opening virtues.

M. Bourgelat ſays *(a)*, that ſulphur and lead, or ſulphur and ſteel, operate with ſuch certainty in an aſthma, as not to leave room to wiſh for any thing better: the writers of the *Maiſon Ruſtique (b)* had before recommended the following preparation: Take packets of Spaniſh ſteel, make them red hot in a new crucible put into a ſmith's forge; then rub them with rolls of ſulphur, which will make the ſteel melt like butter; after this, put them again into the

(a) *Matiere Médical raiſonnée, p.* 134. (b) *Tome I. p.* 252.

forge, that the ſteel and brimſtone may be thoroughly melted in the crucible: after this, pound the maſs in a mortar, and ſift it; there will remain a powder of ſteel, which is to be kept in a pot for uſe. Mix three pinches of this powder with the broken-winded horſe's corn, wetting the oats ſo that the powder may ſtick to them, and continue this for a month.

M. Bourgelat's preſcription (c) for a broken-winded horſe runs thus: Take equal parts of filings of lead, and flour of brimſtone, put them into a crucible layer upon layer, beginning with the brimſtone, till the crucible is full; then place the crucible upon burning coals till it becomes red hot, and, to quicken the operation, ſet fire to the matter. Take it off the coals as ſoon as it ceaſes to ſmoke. Pound the black matter which remains in the crucible: give two drams of it every morning to the animal, faſting; and continue ſo to do for ſome time.

A horſe's being broken-winded, ſeems rather a fault in the make and conſtitution, than a diſorder brought on. Thus, broken-winded horſes are generally narrow cheſted, ſo that the lungs have ſcarcely room to play. The lungs and pericardium are ſometimes obſerved in ſuch horſes, to be larger in proportion to the cavity, than they are in a ſound horſe. This enlargement of the viſcera is commonly attributed to their having been over-fed when young; but I am perſuaded, that if theſe parts had been of a due conformation at firſt, this diſproportion might not have taken place. Be that, however, as it may; this opinion leads to a rational method of cure, or at leaſt, to the only thing that can be done towards a cure; which is, an abſtemious cool diet, avoiding rich hay, and all other very nouriſhing plants. Keeping the horſe on green food in the field is of great ſervice; and the mixing of chopped ſtraw with his hay, as is uſually practiſed in this caſe, is perfectly right. This diſeaſe ſeldom affects horſes to any de-

(c) *Ubi ſupra; Formules Medicinales, p.* 57.

gree

gree before they have come to their full growth, when the cartilages at the ends of the ribs becoming ſtiffer, do not ſo eaſily give way to any ſtrong or ſudden expanſion of the lungs.

Some horſes are at times troubled with a dry cough, which impairs their health, and ſcarce admits of any medicines, except cooling evacutions now and then, and a ſpare cooling diet; keeping them well rubbed down, in order that the perſpiration may be free; becauſe an interruption of this is in all creatures apt chiefly to affect the lungs. For this purpoſe, antimony, or the antimonial æthiops, brimſtone, elecampane roots, and tops of broom, are proper.

The young of quadrupeds, as well as thoſe of the human ſpecies, are troubled with a cough when they are cutting their teeth; but it goes off as the teeth are cut. However, if it ſhould be very troubleſome, bleeding and a cooling regimen may keep it under; and if the gums are much inflamed, they may be cut wherever the prominence points out that a tooth is ready to pierce. Young horſes which are troubled with worms ſometimes cough: but this ceaſes when the worms are carried off.

It is obſerved of broken-winded horſes, that they draw in their breath ſlowly, their flanks filling up gradually and with a ſeeming difficulty, becauſe the lungs do not yield eaſily to the air drawn in; and that their flanks fall ſuddenly, and their breath burſts forth with violence; inſomuch that a man in the dark, by holding his hand on a horſe's mouth and noſe, may eaſily diſcover if he is broken-winded. Such horſes are alſo obſerved to loſe their delicacy in the flavour of their food, ſo as to eat even their litter; and to be very droughty.

To be certain that a horſe is broken-winded *(d)* ſqueeze his throat, near the channel, when his flanks beat, and make him cough, if the ſound of the

(*d*) *Maiſon Ruſtique, Tom. I. p.* 251.

cough

cough is dry, 'tis a bad ſign, and if it is dry and frequent, ſtill worſe; whereas little need be feared if it is attended with moiſture. A horſe that farts when he coughs is almoſt always broken-winded, and that ſort of broken-wind is thought the moſt difficult to cure. Horſes which have been broken-winded from their birth, or thoſe in which it has been long neglected, are incurable. Neither can broken-winded horſes that take in wind by the fundament, ever be cured.

In general, the great point in this diſorder is, to keep the horſe on a moderate diet, and give him moderate exerciſe; and it will be right to moiſten his dry food, ſuch as hay, corn, &c. with water, to prevent his drought, and conſequent too plentiful drinking.

SECT. XI.

Of the Colic, and Inflammation of the Bowels.

THE moſt frequent cauſes of colics in horſes are, inflammation in the bowels of the abdomen, and the ſwallowing of too much cold water when heated. When the complaint ariſes from this laſt cauſe, Mr. Oſmer *(a)* directs than an ounce of *Philonium Romanum* be given, and repeated if there be occaſion.

When the colic proceeds from inflammation, it is conſtantly attended with an extraordinary quickneſs of the pulſe; the horſe lies down often and ſuddenly riſes up again, he ſtrikes his belly with his hind feet and ſtamps with his fore-feet. When the pain is very violent, he may have convulſive twitches in his

(*a*) *P.* 156.

eyes,

eyes, and ſometimes ſtretch out his limbs as if he was dying; he falls into cold damps and profuſe ſweats, his ears and feet being alternately hot and cold. If the colic is attended with a ſtoppage of urine, he will often ſtrive to ſtale, turn his head to his flanks, and frequently turn on his back and roll about. If the inflammation proceeds towards a mortification, a little dung is ſometimes diſcharged with a fœtid blackiſh ichor.

This inflammatory colic may take it's riſe from any cauſe which excites an inflammation, and ſhould be treated as ſuch, with evacuations and a cooling regimen. The cure muſt begin with ſpeedy and plentiful bleeding. The ſtrait-gut ſhould then be emptied of all the hard dung that a well-anointed hand can take away. This will make room for a ſharp ſtimulating glyſter, in which four ounces of ſome purging ſalt, and as much oil, may be diſſolved; and it ſhould be repeated every four or ſix hours, till the horſe has a natural ſtool. If the pulſe continues hard and quick, with heat, a dry mouth, and thirſt, the bleeding ſhould be occaſionally repeated. Plenty of mild drink, ſuch as bran and water, ſhould be given; and inſtead of adminiſtering at once ſuch a quantity of a purgative medicine as might, by irritating, increaſe the diſorder, ſix or eight ounces of ſome purging ſalt may be diſſolved in a ſufficient quantity of water, and half an ounce of the ſalt ſo diſſolved be given every half hour, till the horſe has a ſtool.—The Romans always anointed the belly and back of horſes that were ill of any complaint in the bowels, with a mixture of oil and warm ingredients. The oil and ſpirit of hartſhorn before mentioned, may anſwer this purpoſe very properly; eſpecially if it be continued till the creature begins to ſweat, when he ſhould be covered up very warm. In ſimilar diſorders in the human body, Sir John Pringle lays very great ſtreſs on bliſters applied to the part affected.

ed. "As I have oftener than once," ſays he (*b*), "known the patient relieved in his bowels, as ſoon "as he felt the burning of his ſkin; and at the ſame "time have ſtools by a purge or glyſter, which had "not operated before; we have reaſon to believe "that the bliſter acts as an atiſpaſmodic, and not as "an evacuant."

If, by the uſe of theſe means, a natural ſtool is produced, and the horſe ceaſes to ſtart, tumble, and gather up his legs, there is room to hope his recovery: but if the ſymptoms grow worſe, and ſigns of a mortification appear, it is hardly to be expected that he ſhould get the better of a diſorder which has ſeized parts in themſelves ſo thin, and in which it makes ſo rapid a progreſs. The Jeſuit's bark being in many caſes found a powerful antiſeptic, ſome recommend here a ſtrong decoction of it, with the addition of a quantity of wine equal to that of the decoction: but this, I doubt, is ſaid more from theory than from any experience of its good effects; though indeed, no bad effect can attend it. Vegetius (*c*) adviſes that, in caſe a glyſter cannot be conveniently given, long and hard *ſuppoſitories* be made of honey and ſalt, and kept conſtantly in the anus, in order to excite ſtools. When the belly is very much diſtended, he (*d*) recommends tapping, after the following manner. "About four fingers breadth under the horſe's navel towards his yard, in the middle region of the belly, thruſt in a lancet, ſo as to pierce through the peritoneum, or membrane which lines the inſide of the belly, but with caution, leſt the inteſtines be likewiſe hurt; and after the lancet is taken out, introduce into the inciſion a pipe bored through with many holes, by which the water may be diſcharged."—It would ſeem more adviſeable to perform this operation with a trocar, as is now practiſed

(*b*) *Obſervations on the Diſeaſes of the Army*, p. 155.
(*c*) *Lib. I. c. xlii.* (*d*) *Lib. I. c. xliii.*

tised by surgeons in the dropsy, and to do it rather a little on one side, than in the middle of the belly, because the muscles there being more of a fleshy nature, will more easily heal, than when wounded in the middle, where they become tendonous.

After a free passage is obtained, it will be proper to give every night three or four grains of opium, and to continue it till there is no danger of a relapse: then the horse must have such food as shall be the least flatulent or irritating.

I beg leave here again to caution gentlemen against the many hot medicines commonly prescribed in this disorder, such as turpentine, oil of juniper, anise, pepper, &c. all which encrease the disease by their greater stimulus, and therefore are now entirely laid aside in similar disorders in mankind.

SECT. XII.

Of Worms and Bots.

HORSES, as well as men, are subject to two sorts of worms, the one round, resembling the earth-worm, and the other the ascarides, which lodge themselves chiefly in the strait-gut. The bots are a kind of large maggot, composed of circular rings, with little sharp prickly feet along the sides of their bellies, with which they fasten themselves to the lower orifice of the stomach, from the blood-vessels of which they draw their nourishment, and when many, create ulcers in it, and make such havock as quickly to destroy the horse. They adhere so strongly, that, even after the animal is dead, it requires a good pull to disengage them. The pain which they create occasions some degree of fever, the horse grows lean, and hide-bound. They some-

times

times give ſo much pain, as to bring on convulſions, eſpecially in the eyes. Though the belly is not ſwelled as in the colic, yet the horſes roll themſelves about, throw themſelves on their back, and put their head between their legs, to ſhew the place where the pain is. Vegetius obſerves (*a*), that if the ſtrait-gut is carefully examined by the hand, the bots will be found adhering to it in cluſters, that they ſtick ſo faſt as not to be pulled away without much difficulty, and when brought out, ſtick to the fingers.

We are told in the *Maiſon Ruſtique* (*b*), that there is a fly which finds the means of inſinuating itſelf into the fundament of horſes, and of laying its eggs there. As ſoon as it enters, the horſe is thrown into a kind of madneſs, jumping, running, toſſing his head, for a full quarter of an hour; but as theſe flies are only in the country, none but horſes which are fed in the field are in danger of them.

M. de Reaumur's account of this inſect, and of its manner of introducing itſelf into the fundament of the horſe, is ſo very curious, that I am confident my readers will readily pardon the length of the following quotation from that great and juſtly-admired Naturaliſt (*c*).

" Among the animals that are uſeful to mankind, " the horſe is certainly entitled to the firſt rank; " and yet this animal, conſiderable as it is, and con- " trived by it's figure and beautiful proportion to " afford us pleaſure, was not given to man only: " there is a ſpecies of fly, whoſe right in this crea- " ture may be looked upon as ſtill better founded " than ours.

" If the horſe be uſeful to us, he is abſolutely ne- " ceſſary to this fly; and the ſame Being that formed " the horſe, formed alſo this fly, which depends " wholly on the horſe for its preſervation and conti-

(*a*) *Lib. I. c. lii.* (*b*) *Tom. I. p.* 261.
(*c*) *Hiſtoire des Inſectes.*

" nuance.

" nuance. The flies we are ſpeaking of, like thoſe " of the other ſpecies, receive their firſt life and " growth in the form of worms: but theſe are worms " which can be produced and nouriſhed only in the " inteſtines of a horſe. It is there alone they can " enjoy the proper temperature of heat, and receive " the nouriſhment neceſſary for them.

" Beſides the long, and ſometimes very long, " worms which have been obſerved in the bodies of " horſes, there have been ſeen alſo in them ſhort " ones.——All authors, both antient and modern, " who have treated of the diſeaſes of horſes, have " taken notice of theſe ſhort worms; but M. Valiſ- " nieri is, I believe, the firſt who has traced them " to the laſt ſtage of their transformation, and ſeen " them change into a hairy kind of fly, like the " drone.

" The flies from which theſe bots are produced " inhabit the country, and do not come near houſes, " at leaſt not near thoſe of great towns; and there- " fore horſes are never liable to have theſe ſhort " worms in their bodies if they have been kept " within doors, eſpecially in a town, during the " ſummer and autumn. It is in the former of theſe " ſeaſons, and perhaps too in the beginning of the " latter, that the females of theſe flies apply them- " ſelves to the anus of horſes, and endeavour to " gain admittance, in order there to depoſit their " eggs, or perhaps their worms.

" The preciſe inſtant of their entrance will ſcarce " admit of an eye-witneſs, but by the meereſt " chance: yet M. Valiſnieri ſays, that Dr. Gaſpari " had beheld this very uncommon ſight.—The Doc- " tor was one day looking at his mares in a field, " and obſerved, that from being perfectly quiet, " they of a ſudden became very reſtleſs, and ran " about in great agitation, prancing, plunging, and " kicking, with violent motions of their tails. He " concluded, that theſe extraordinary effects were

" produced

" produced by ſome fly buzzing about them, and
" endeavouring to ſettle upon the anus of one of
" them; but the fly not being able to ſucceed, he
" obſerved it go off, with leſs noiſe than before, to-
" wards a mare that was feeding at a diſtance from
" the reſt; and now the fly taking a more effectual
" method to compaſs its deſign, paſſed under the
" tail of the mare, and ſo made its way to the
" anus.

" Here, at firſt, it occaſioned only an itching,
" by which the inteſtine was protruded with an in-
" creaſed aperture of the anus; the fly taking ad-
" vantage of this, penetrated farther, and lodged
" itſelf in the folds of the inteſtine; this done, it
" was in a ſituation proper for laying its eggs. Soon
" after this, the mare became very violent, running
" about, prancing, and kicking, and throwing her-
" ſelf on the ground; in ſhort, was not quiet, nor
" returned to feeding, till after a quarter of an
" hour.

" The fly then, we ſee, can find means of depo-
" ſiting its eggs, or perhaps its worms, in the fun-
" dament of the horſe; which once effected, it has
" done all that is neceſſary for them.

" If theſe worms are not already hatched when
" firſt depoſited in the horſe, but are then only eggs,
" it will not be long before they are hatched, from
" the nutritive heat they there receive.

" Theſe worms ſoon make their way into the in-
" teſtines of the horſe; they occupy ſuch parts of
" this region as are to them moſt convenient, and
" ſometimes, as we ſhall ſoon ſee, penetrate even
" to the ſtomach. All the hazard they appear to be
" expoſed to is, that of being carried away from
" the places they have fixed on by the excrement,
" which may ſeem likely to drive all before it. But
" nature has provided for all things; and when we
" ſhall have farther deſcribed theſe worms, it will be
" ſeen, that they are able to maintain their ſituati-

" on,

" on, and to remain in the body of the horſe as " long as they pleaſe.

" There is a time when theſe worms are of themſelves deſirous to leave this their habitation; it being no longer convenient to them after the purpoſes of their growth are anſwered. Their transformation to a fly muſt be performed out of the horſe's body; and accordingly, when the time of their transformation draws near, they approach towards the anus of the horſe, and then leave him of their own accord, or with the excrement, with which they ſuffer themſelves to be carried along.

" The figure of theſe worms affords at firſt ſight nothing remarkable, but they appear like many other worms of the claſs, that change into flies with two wings, and like the greateſt part of the worms of that claſs, they are provided with a ſort of ſcaly claws, with which they draw themſelves forward.

" A difference in colour may be obſerved between thoſe that are taken by force from the inteſtine of the horſe, and thoſe which come away of their own accord; ſome are greeniſh, ſome yellowiſh, and others nearly brown: theſe laſt are neareſt to, and the greeniſh ones the fartheſt from, the time of their transformation.

" If M. Valiſnieri and myſelf have rightly obſerved the poſition of their claws, ſome of them differ from others in this reſpect; but they are perfectly ſimilar in every other particular, and change into flies ſo nearly alike, that I am convinced they are of the ſame kind and origin.

" However this may be, the worms we now are ſpeaking of have two unequal claws; and ſince I have been acquainted with the nature and uſe of thoſe claws, it has ſeemed to me eaſy to conceive how they may remain in the inteſtines of a horſe, in oppoſition to all efforts of the excrements to

" force them out. One that I was handling and
" examining faſtened upon my finger in ſuch a man-
" ner that I found great difficulty to get it off. Theſe
" claws are a ſort of anchors, differently indeed diſ-
" poſed from the wings of common anchors, but
" contrived to produce the ſame effect.

" Beſides theſe two claws, nature hath given to
" each of theſe worms a very great number of tri-
" angular ſpikes, or briſtles, amply ſufficient to
" arm againſt the coats of the inteſtines, and to re-
" ſiſt the force employed to drive them towards the
" anus, provided the head be directed towards the
" ſtomach of the horſe.

" It will undoubtedly be aſked, whether theſe
" worms are not dangerous to horſes?—The mares
" which afforded me, for ſeveral years, thoſe on
" which I made my obſervations, did not appear to
" be leſs in health than thoſe which had none: but
" it may ſometimes happen, that they are in ſo
" great a quantity in the body of the horſe, as to
" prove fatal to him. M. Valiſnieri ſuppoſes theſe
" worms to have been the cauſe of an epidemical
" diſeaſe which deſtroyed a great many horſes about
" Verona and Mantua in the year 1713; and the
" obſervations communicated to him by Dr. Gaſpa-
" ri ſufficiently confirm his ſuppoſition.

" This gentleman, upon diſſecting ſome horſes
" that died of this diſtemper, found in their ſto-
" machs a ſurprizing quantity of ſhort worms; to
" give us ſome idea of which, he compares them to
" the kernels of a pomegranate opened: each of
" theſe worms, by gnawing on the coat of the ſto-
" mach, had made for itſelf a kind of cell therein,
" and each of theſe cavities would eaſily contain a
" grain of Indian wheat. One may readily imagine
" to how wretched a condition the ſtomach muſt be
" reduced by this means: the outer membranes were
" inflamed, and the inner ones ulcerated, and cor-
" rupted. A very ſmall quantity of theſe worms
" were

" were found in the ſmall inteſtines, and only a few
" in the larger, to which laſt they were found affix-
" ed, but had corroded them.

" It is, perhaps, only when theſe worms are in great numbers, and incommode each other in the inteſtines of the horſe, that they make their way towards the ſtomach; and indeed a very few flies muſt be ſufficient to overſtock the inſide of a horſe, provided they ſhould depoſite all their eggs, and theſe be animated; M. Valiſnieri having counted upwards of ſeven hundred eggs in the body of one ſingle fly.

" When one of theſe worms has quitted the anus of the horſe, it falls on the ground, and immediately ſeeks out for ſome place of ſafety to which it may retire, to prepare for the laſt ſtage of it's transformation, by which it is to become a fly.—Its ſkin now hardens and thickens by degrees, and at length forms a ſolid ſhell or cod, the ſhape of which ſcarcely differs from that of the worm. It is firſt of a pale red colour, which changes into cheſnut, and at length, by the addition of gradual and ſucceſſive ſhades of brown, the ſhell is rendered black. Before the worm paſſes into a nymph, it is of the form of an oblong ball; and it remains in this ſhape much longer than worms of the fleſh-fly kind. I have met with ſome that have not ſhewn the ſmalleſt traces of the legs, wings, and head of the nymph, even at the end of five or ſix days; and from thence I firſt learnt that theſe worms do not become nymphs immediately upon their firſt change, but that, in order to become flies, they muſt undergo one change more than caterpillars generally do to become butterflies."

Mr. Oſmer (*d*) rightly infers from M. de Reaumur's foregoing account of this inſect, firſt, that

(*d*) P. 183.

horſes may occaſionally die of ſpaſms and convulſions when theſe bots, for that is the name which our farriers give to theſe ſhort worms, lodge in the ſtomach and inteſtines, and corrode the ſame, inſtead of coming away by the anus; and ſecondly, that no medicines ought to be eſteemed a remedy for the bots, till we ſee them brought away dead by their effects; and therefore, that if they did not generally make their eſcape by ſome means unknown to us, horſes would die much oftener than they do of theſe inſects.

The cure which he (*e*) propoſes, is as follows: "Take of new milk one quart, honey half a pound; "give the horſe this in a morning: let him faſt af-"ter it an hour and a half: then give him a pint of "ſtrong brine, more or leſs, according to the ſize "and ſtrength of the horſe, and let him faſt ano-"ther hour. Repeat this three or four ſucceſſive "mornings." It deſtroys the worms, and leaves no appearance but of their ſkins, or ſhells, which are brought away with the excrement. Mr. Oſmer adds, that this method will likewiſe kill all ſorts of worms. Linnæus ſays, (*f*) that the bran of the flote feſcue graſs will cure horſes troubled with the bots, if they are kept from drinking for ſome hours.

The *aſcarides*, which are the other kind of worm I obſerved that horſes are ſubject to, are diſcovered by their being often protruded with the dung, together with a yellowiſh-coloured matter, like ſulphur; and the horſe troubled with them often rubs his breech againſt walls or poſts. A ſolution of ſublimate thrown up by a glyſter is here the proper cure.

Diſſections have ſhewn M. Bourgelat, that worms occupy almoſt all parts of the body. (*g*) He has found them not only in the æſophagus, ſtomach, and inteſtines, but even in the arteries and veins, eſpe-

(*e*) *P.* 184. (*f*) *Flora Suecica, Art.* 95.
(*g*) *Matiere médicale raiſonnée, p.* 129.

cially

cially in the *vena porta*; as alſo in the urinary and bilious ducts. Theſe parts, in aſſes, oxen, ſheep, and goats, are often full of leeches, ſlugs, or the *faſciola hepatica* of Linnæus. No part of the body eſcapes one kind or other of them.

M. Bourgelat obſerves, (*e*) that of all the purging medicines which carry off the worms and their eggs, or ſeed, bitters are the beſt, not only as being deteſted by them, but alſo as reſtoring the ſtrength and function of the bowels, and preventing their being bred again. Oils, which are found to lock up their pores, and thereby ſuffocate them, are alſo recommended here. In theſe opinions he is ſupported by Vegetius (*f*), who adviſes to boil wormwood, creſſes, and coriander ſeed, in a quart of oil, and to give half a pint of this, mixed with luke-warm water, in the morning, faſting, for ſeveral days together. He adviſes to add nitre to it, or to give it in the horſe's food; and after the ſtrait-gut is emptied of hard fæces, he directs a ſimilar oily glyſter to be thrown up, to deſtroy the aſcarides lodged there.

M. Bourgelat rightly adviſes (*g*), that the uſe of theſe medicines be followed by that of calomel, two drams, and as much jalap, in a ball with honey; becauſe this, by its ſtimulus, may break the coheſion of the worms to the parts, and expel them. He likewiſe thinks (*h*), that ſheep, eſpecially, ſhould frequently have ſalt given them for theſe worms, which are in the veſſels about the liver.

After the appearance of worms has ceaſed, it will be proper to continue the uſe of bitters every morning for ſome time, in order as was before obſerved, to recover the tone of the bowels, and to prevent a return of theſe troubleſome, though not always dangerous enemies. To this end, take wormwood and chamomile flowers, of each two handfuls; gentian

(*e*) *Ibid. p.* 131. (*f*) *Lib. I. c. xliv.*
(*g*) *Matiere medicale, p.* 131. (*h*) *Ibid. p.* 132.

root and Jesuits bark, of each two ounces; make a decoction of them in water till there remains two quarts, and give half a pint of this three times a day. Cinnabar and filings of iron, made into balls, may also be given for the same purpose, before the decoction.

SECT. XIII.

Of Purging, and of Molten Grease.

PURGING, in horses, as in men, is sometimes a salutary crisis, and in that case little need be done. We may guess it to be such when a healthy horse is seized with a purging preceded by a slight fever, or some other cause which we may not be able to assign. All that is necessary here is, by a mild opening diet to encourage the discharge, if it continues only a few days.

When the purging continues with a considerable degree of fever, signs of pain, or griping, loss of appetite, and a discharge of the mucus of the bowels, it is time to think of a remedy. If the horse is in flesh and strength, we should begin with bleeding, and then give mild purging medicines to discharge any acrid matter which may have fallen upon the bowels. Modern practice has taught physicians, that this is by much the safest and most efficacious method even in the dysentry, as we find on every occasion inculcated by Sir John Pringle, and by the ingenious and observant Dr. Monro in his very useful account of the diseases in military hospitals (*i*). "The purgative," says this last gentleman, "that "upon repeated trials we found to answer the best, "was sal catharticum amarum with manna and oil, "which operated without griping or disturbing the

(*i*) P. 70.

"patient,

"patient, procured a freer evacuation, and gave "greater relief, than any other purgative medicine "we tried. A great part of the cure depended on "the frequent use of gentle purges in the beginning, "to carry off the corrupted humours: the purgative "was repeated every second, third, or fourth day, "as the case required. It was surprizing with how "little loss of strength the sick bore the operations "of these purges; and I observed that the patients, "instead of being weakened, seemed stronger, and "more brisk and lively, after the operation of each, "from the relief it gave, by evacuating those pu- "trid corrupted humours which made them perpetu- "ally sick and uneasy while they remained in the "bowels."—For horses, three ounces of this salt may be mixed with four ounces of oil, and as much manna; the whole dissolved in a pint of water, and repeated occasionally. In order to take off the pain, and alleviate the excoriation frequently occasioned in the strait-gut by the acrimony of the matter discharg- ed, glysters of starch dissolved in milk, or mild oily mixtures, should be frequently thrown up. It is likewise of great consequence that the animal have plenty of mild drink and food, which may as it were sheath the sharp humour discharged into the bowels, as well as line them against its acrimony: such are, decoctions of farinaceous seeds; and ab- sorbents, such as chalk, and burnt hartshorn. If there are signs of much pain, from six to seven grains of opium may be given on the days free from purg- ing; and in order to encourage the perspiration, a dram of camphire, mixed with two drams of nitre, may be made into a ball with honey, and given with the opiate. With this view, it will be highly neces- sary to rub the horses well, and to keep the stable in which they are sweet and clean.

Vegetius, upon the same principle, advises (*k*) to

(*k*) *Lib. III. c. xvi.*

give the following compoſition. " Mix carefully " in a mortar two ounces of wax, one pound of " lard, half an ounce of tar, an ounce of caſſia, " and an ounce and a half of pepper, to be made " into balls, the horſe drinking with them an infuſi- " on of pomegranate-flowers in rough wine." Dr. Monroe (*l*) gives us the manner of rendering bees-wax miſcible with water, which is, by melting it with a third part of hard ſoap and water, and beating them well together, then adding gradually more water. Dr. Huck found this mixture to be very ſerviceable in North America after evacuations, where there was much pain in the bowels. The fat about a ſheep's kidney melted and mixed with milk, in the proportion of one fourth of the fat, is alſo found very proper in this view. This mild method anſwers much better than the uſe of aſtringents, and ſeems greatly confirmed by a horſe's being cured in a few days by eating green lucerne when it firſt came in, in ſpring, after his diſorder had baffled every other method before tried for ſeveral weeks.

In this purging diſorder, the extremity of the ſtrait-gut ſometimes comes out, in which caſe Vegetius (*m*) adviſes treating it in the following manner, if it is not readily got up when it firſt appears, before it is much ſwelled: ſcarify the gut with a lancet in the moſt prominent parts, and ſqueeze the ſcarifications ſo that the blood may be diſcharged; then foment it with warm water, and when it is ſoftened, return it. Continue daily to put up the hand ſmeared with ſome warm ointment, till the ailment is healed.

Somewhat allied to the foregoing diſorder is what is called *Molten Greaſe*, which is a fat or oily diſcharge with the dung, ariſing from the melting down of the fat of a horſe's body, generally occaſioned by violent exerciſe in hot weather. It is always attended

(*l*) *P.* 77. (*m*) *Lib. III. c. vi.*

with

with a feverish heat and restlessness, with startings, oppression, shortness of breath, and symptoms of internal pains. The horse soon loses flesh, and commonly becomes hide-bound, with a swelling in the legs. If not quickly remedied, it terminates in speedy death, or some obstinate disorder hard to be cured.

The cure should begin with plentiful bleeding, which should be repeated in proportion as the fever and oppression continue. The blood will appear replete with the dissolved fat, so as to feel greasy and slippery to the touch. Cooling nitrous drinks should be given, and at the same time such a purge as was before directed, to carry off the load fallen on the bowels, with mild glysters, to prevent pain and excoriation in the strait-gut. The horse should also be well rubbed, and cloathed warm, in order to encourage a discharge by the skin.

Though, in the beginning of a purging, as well as in the molten-grease, rhubarb, or othe warm medicines, do not answer, yet when the original cause seems to have been pretty well got the better of, they may then be occasionally substituted. Thus, rhubarb, or succotrine aloes, may be occasionally given to the quantity of from two drams to half an ounce, as shall be found necessary, and be occasionally continued until health is restored. M. Bourgelat *(n)* declares, that ipecacuanha is no less efficacious to horses than it is to men, given in the quantity of from two drams to half an ounce. This may be given instead of the rhubarb, or mixed with it, two drams of each. If the strength of the bowels is much impaired, warm bitters, such as a decoction of gentian, zedoary, orange-peel, Winter's bark, chamomile-flowers, may be given two or three times a day, and antimony mixed with bran or corn.

(*n*) *Ecole Vétérinaire; Formules, p.* 91.

SECT.

SECT. XIV.

Of the Jaundice.

THIS Diſeaſe is known by the duſky yellowneſs of the eyes, of the inſide of the mouth, and of the tongue and lips. The horſe is dull, loſes his appetite, and has a ſlow fever, which increaſes with the jaundice. He is often coſtive; his dung is of a light green, or pale yellow colour; his urine is high-coloured, and he ſtales with difficulty. The right ſide, or region of the liver, is hard and diſtended, and if the animal is much diſeaſed, the cure is ſcarcely practicable, but generally ends with a waſting diarrhæa.

The horſe ſhould be bled in proportion to the degree of fever. The ſtrait-gut ſhould be then emptied of the hard dung, and ſharp ſtimulating glyſters ſhould be given; and alſo at the ſame time a purging draught, to carry the bile downward. An infuſion of an ounce of ſenna with two ounces of a purging ſalt will anſwer this purpoſe, becauſe a ſtimulating medicine is firſt wanted. The belly may afterwards be kept open with balls compoſed of hard-ſoap an ounce, aloes half an ounce, as much millepedes, and honey; to be waſhed down with a decoction of madder, turmeric, and burdock. Antimony may be alſo given with the corn. If the diſorder does not yield to this courſe, recourſe muſt be had to calomel, two drams, with as much rhubarb, made into a ball; and the ſoap-balls and decoction be given between, and continued while the leaſt yellowneſs remains. It will be of advantage to rub the belly well, and anoint it with the volatile liniment, or oil and ſpirit of hartſhorn.

SECT. XV.

Of the Disorders of the Kidneys and Bladder.

INflammation of the kidneys is attended with the general ſymptoms of fever, together with a weakneſs, or a diſinclination to move the back and loins, and a difficulty of making water, which appears thick, and ſometimes bloody.

Copious bleeding is here neceſſary, and plenty of mild diluting drink, ſuch as a decoction of mallows, marſh mallow roots, linſeed, &c. Likewiſe, four ounces of oil rubbed in with the yolk of an egg, and two drams of nitre, may be given three or four times a day in a draught of the decoction. The ſtrait-gut ſhould be emptied by the hand of all the dung, which, by it's preſſure, may give pain to the kidneys, and by weighing on the neck of the bladder, prevent, the diſcharge of the urine. At the ſame time, mild glyſters with nitre and oil ſhould be injected. This will be a much ſafer way of treating this diſorder, than having recourſe to the more ſtimulating diuretics.

If a difficulty of making water comes on unattended with a fever, yet with ſigns of a pain, or inaptitude to motion, in the back, the complaint may be ſuppoſed to be in the ureters, or veſſels leading from the kidneys to the bladder. Here the intention of cure is much the ſame, namely, by diluents, and mucilaginous or oily medicines, to dilate and lubricate the paſſage, and thereby promote the diſcharge of the obſtructing matter. Here the plentiful uſe of honey becomes likewiſe proper; and alſo diuretics of a more ſtimulating quality, ſuch as, an ounce of balſam of capivi diſſolved in the yolks of two or three eggs, and mixed with half a pint of the decoction of mallows, &c. Spirit of nitre may be added

added to all the drink that is given, and garlic or onions may be added to the decoction of mallows. Glysters in which two ounces of turpentine and half an ounce of nitre have been dissolved, with four ounces of oil, are here thought to be of peculiar service. Opiates, as they take off the spasms or contractions occasioned by the pain, are also of great advantage; and may be given to the amount of five or six grains in substance, or of the tincture in proportion, mixed with the decoction of mallows.

If notwithstanding these means, a purulent matter is discharged along with the urine, it may be feared that suppuration has come on in the kidney, and that it will end in a consumption. In this case, the same medicines as above are to be continued, especially the honey and balsam of capivi. If the urine becomes coffee-coloured and fœtid, the inflammation is turning to a mortification, which is the fore-runner of a speedy death.

Vegetius (*a*) notes the following symptoms of a horse's having a stone in the bladder. "He is tortured, groans, extends himself, endeavouring to "stale, he cannot piss freely, but his urine comes "away by drops, a little at a time, and this he suffers daily. In order to ascertain it, put the hand, "well oiled, into the strait-gut, and at the neck of "the bladder, under the fundament, towards the "root of the yard, feel with your fingers, and you "will there perceive the stone. Too strong an effort sometimes bursts the bladder near the fundament, and lets the urine out by the fundament. "In this case, the stone may be taken out by introducing the fingers, or a proper instrument, by the "hole made in the bladder and rectum; and the "wound may be cured by the use of mild glutinating glysters; though this is seldom to be expected "on account of the violence which the parts had un-

(*a*) *Lib. I. c. xlvi.*

"dergone

" dergone before."—How far the ſoap-lee may be given with ſucceſs for the ſtone in horſes, I know not; or whether the ſtone may not be preſſed ſo low by the anus, as that it may be cut upon, is a point which I ſhall not pretend to determine. Vegetius likewiſe obſerves, *(b)* that the bladder may be ſo diſplaced, or ſo diſtended with urine, by hard running, that the horſe cannot ſtale; and in this caſe he adviſes, " to put the hand well oiled into the fundament, and preſs it downward towards the yard, " where will be found the bladder full of urine, " which ſhould then be drawn gently towards the " fundament, on the right and left ſide; and this " ſhould be continued till the horſe makes water."

He alſo remarks, *(c)* that " if, by hard labour or " exerciſe, a horſe be denied time to ſtale, an in- " flammation ariſes in the neck of the bladder, may " extend all along the urethra, and ſo ſtraighten " the paſſage that the creature feels great pain in " voiding it's urine. The ſame too may proceed " from ſeveral other cauſes, particularly hen's-dung, " or other noxious things or animals taken in with " the food, and may be known by the horſe's bend- " ing his legs and letting his belly down to the " ground. He here adviſes, to bleed in any vein " which appears neareſt the part; but if a ſufficient " quantity of blood is not obtained from that vein, " to bleed in the neck. The rectum ſhould then be " freed of dung, and after this ſix ſpoonfuls of " pounded ſalt mixed with a pound of oil, be thrown " warm into the horſes's fundament, his head being " placed downward, on a ſloping ground, in order " that the medicine may the more eaſily deſcend in- " to his inward parts. The ſtimulus given by this " will looſen his belly, and generally mitigate the " pain. If this remedy gives relief but ſlowly, " thruſt your hand as before directed into the funda-

(b) *Lib. I. c. li.* (c) *Lib. III. c. xv.*

" ment,

"ment, with great caution, towards the right ſide, "and reverſe or turn it towards the left, preſſing the "bladder gently; that ſo the urine may flow out: but "preſſing it hard would be hurtful."

He alſo propoſes *(d)* the following general remedies. "Reduce quick ſulphur into powder, mix it "with oil, and rub with it, as alſo with warm water, "the horſe's belly, yard, and loins." The Sarmatians wrapped their horſes in cloth from neck to feet, and fumigated them by ſtrewing caſtor upon live coals ſet under them, ſo that the ſmoke of the coals and caſtor warmed the whole body. When the coals were withdrawn, the horſe was walked a gentle pace, and ſtaled ſoon. Powdered ſalt made into a ſmall ſuppoſitory with oil and honey, and inſerted into the urethra, or hole in the yard, preſently provokes urine. Any crawling inſect put under the ſheath has the ſame effect. Standing near water that runs gently, provokes urine, as alſo does ſtanding in a place where otherhorſes have ſtaled. Figs boiled in water, and given with nitre, anſwer the ſame purpoſe; and ſo does garlic. If the ſeaſon of the year does not afford green food, give the horſe hay ſprinkled with honey and water, or barley boiled in water. Boil leeks, and ſqueeze out half a pint of their juice, which mix with ſix ſpoonfuls of oil and three ſpoonfuls of wine, and give it the horſe to drink, after which walk him up and down.—It is proper, ſays Vegetius *(e)*, to know the following travelling remedy, which is always at hand: after you have ſoftened clay with the urine of any horſe, mix it with wine, and after it is ſettled, pour the clear liquor through the noſtrils; it preſently provokes urine.

Horſes are likewiſe ſubject to diabetes, or making water in too profuſe a quantity, and this is ſeldom cured if they are weak or old. It is attended with a

(*d*) *Ibid.* (*e*) *Lib. I. c. lxi.*

loſs

loſs of appetite and ſtrength. For cure, a decoction may be made in lime-water, of comfrey-roots, tormentile, red roſes, pomegranate-rind, oak-bark, or ſuch like aſtringents, and a pint of this decoction given three times a day, with half an ounce of powdered Jeſuits bark added to each draught. Calomel, given as an alterative, has been found efficacious when the foregoing has failed. Horſes ſubject to a diabetes ſhould not be ſuffered to drink too freely, and lime-water ſhould be added to their common water.

When horſes have been much ſtrained by hard labour or violent exerciſe, they are liable to make bloody urine; but reſt and a cooling regimen will ſoon remove it. The aſtringents uſually preſcribed in this caſe have very little effect; and the only medicine of that kind proper to be given here, is the Jeſuits bark, to the quantity of half an ounce three times a day, or oftener if the caſe is very urgent.

PART

PART II.

OF THE EXTERNAL DISEASES OF HORSES.

INTRODUCTION.

I NOW proceed to treat of ſuch diſorders of Horſes as appear externally, and whoſe ſeat is within the reach of manual aſſiſtance. In doing this, I ſhall begin with thoſe of the ſimpleſt nature, and purſue the various appearances and changes that external injuries occaſion; tracing likewiſe to their origin ſuch external appearances as take their riſe from internal cauſes. By following this plain and eaſy method, there will be no occaſion to make uſe of many ſtrange hard names, too commonly uſed, which, far from conveying even the ſmalleſt idea of the diſorder itſelf, ſerve only to puzzle and confound thoſe who are but little acquainted with them; and at the ſame time their natures will be explained on more general principles.

I ſhall begin with a bruiſe, as being the ſlighteſt external injury; though when it proceeds from violent cauſes, it may be productive of great evils.

SECT. I.

Of Bruiſes.

A Bruiſe or Contuſion, is a hurt inflicted by a blunt inſtrument, which brings on a ſwelling, proceeding either from a ſtagnation of the circulating fluids in the bruiſed veſſels, or rather from a number of the capillary veſſels being broken.

If

If Bruiſes are not timely attended to, the obſtructions may bring on inflammation, ſuppuration, or even gangrenes, and all their conſequences. They may alſo be attended with inconveniencies ariſing from the part affected. On the joints, they bring on violent pains, inflammation, &c. on the breaſt, a difficulty of breathing, the intercoſtal muſcles being hurt: where the bones are ſlightly covered, the membrane next to the bones may be injured, as often happens in the head; whence great pain, &c. Internal parts may alſo be hurt; whence many bad ſymptoms, and even death.

I ſhall conſider Bruiſes in three lights; firſt, with a whole ſkin, and without any fluctuation of matter; next, as having a fluctuation of matter; and thirdly, as attended with a wound in the ſkin.

In the firſt of theſe caſes, the intention ſhould be to recover a free circulation in the obſtructed veſſels, and the abſorption of the extravaſated fluids. There are ſeveral methods ſucceſsfully uſed for the cure of ſlight bruiſes: thus, cold water mixed with ſalt, vinegar, ſpirit of wine ſimple or camphorated, anſwer the purpoſe.

Horſes are very ſubject to bruiſes on the withers, as it is called, or to be bruiſed by the ſaddle. In this caſe, the part ſhould be frequently bathed with warm vinegar, or verjuice; or a poultice may be applied, made with either of theſe and crumb of bread, or fine oatmeal, which laſt takes a better conſiſtence than the former. Which ever of them is to be uſed, the poultice ſhould be ſpread over with oil or hogslard, to prevent it's growing hard, or adhering too cloſely to the part. The following poultice, directed in the *Maiſon Ruſtique* (*a*), ſeems well adapted for this purpoſe. " Take a gallon of red wine, and boil it gently over a clear fire till it thickens; then add to it two pounds of wheaten flour, a pound of

(*a*) *Tom. I. p.* 206.

honey, and as much black ſoap; mix and lay it on the part affected. Where wine cannot be conveniently had, ſtrong beer may be ſucceſsfully uſed inſtead of it. On the third or fourth day, when all fear of inflammation is over, it will be adviſeable to rub the part with opodeldoc, or ſome ſuch warm ſpirituous application, which helps much to remove pain, as the friction does to force the obſtructing matter into the circulation. The acrid aſtringents have here no good effect.

Though, at firſt, when a bruiſe is received, a ſmall fluctuation ſeems to be felt, yet the extravaſated fluid may by the above means, or rather by nature, be again taken into the circulation: but if a conſiderable quantity of blood, or other fluid, is felt under the ſkin, vent muſt be given to it, leſt it putrify, and endanger the neighbouring parts. For this purpoſe, a ſtrong lancet is the beſt inſtrument; and the inciſion ſhould be made in the direction of the muſcles and fibres of the part affected, yet ſo as that the diſcharge ſhall be made in the moſt depending part. The extravaſated fluid being thus diſcharged, the inciſion may be dreſſed with any mild ointment, and covered with a-wine or beer poultice, in order to recover the tone of the bruiſed veſſels. The inciſion is to be treated afterwards in the manner that will be directed in the cure of an abſceſs.

If the bruiſe is attended with a wound in the ſkin, great care ſhould be taken not to let any very acid application touch the wounded part; for the conſequence would be, that all the wounded and contuſed fleſh would be turned to a hard dead ſlough, which muſt be digeſted off by means of inflammation and ſuppuration; whereas if mild applications are uſed, much of the bruiſed fleſh may again recover itſelf, and a kindly digeſtion will come on. Proper poultices may be applied over the dreſſings laid on the wounded part.

While these applications are used externally, bleeding must not be forgot, proportioned to the bruises and subsequent inflammation. The horse should have plenty of diluting warm drinks, in which nitre has been dissolved, in order to preserve the fluidity of the blood, and to carry off by urine the particles that may not be re-assumed into the circulation. This becomes particularly necessary in case the internal parts are hurt; and the body should be kept open by glysters and cooling purges.

SECT. II.

Of Strains and Luxations.

NEARLY a-kin to bruises are strains, in which the ligaments of the joints, and often the tendons which end at or near the joints, and their muscles, are over-stretched; by which means some of the smaller vessels may be broken, and the like pain and swelling, often too inflammation, may arise, as in the former case; and nearly the same method of cure is to be pursued.

Bleeding becomes necessary if the pain and swelling are considerable. Vinegar or verjuice are to be applied externally, or a poultice made with either of them and flower and hog's-lard, or oil; or such a poultice of wine or beer as before directed. As time is necessary here for the strained parts to recover from the injury they have received, an external application which shall, by being bound moderately tight round the joint, give it some degree of strength, is necessary. For this purpose, there is not perhaps any thing better than wine or beer, with some small quantity of a farinaceous substance and oil, boiled to the consistence of a jelly or plaister, spread on leather, applied to the part, and then covered with some ſmall binding to prevent it's being rubbed off; likewiſe taking care that this plaiſter do not quite ſurround the limb or joint to which it is applied, leſt the binding of it like a ligature ſhould ſtop the free circulation of the blood, and thereby cauſe the parts below it to ſwell. When there is no longer any danger of ſwelling and inflammation, and the joint begins to be ſtrengthened, perhaps moderate exerciſe and the ſoft treading of the field is the moſt eligible ſituation for a horſe.

Strains in particular parts may be diſtinguiſhed by the impaired motion of the ſtrained limb: for example, if the ſhoulder is ſtrained, the horſe ſtands with the fore-foot extended as if it were ſtiff, and when in motion he forms part of a circle with the lame leg. In this caſe, Vegetius *(a)* recommends the following application. "After the ſhoulder has been well embrocated with wine and oil in the ſun, take half a pound of bay-berries, a pint of wine, as much oil, and three ounces of nitre, boiled to the conſiſtence of an ointment. Let the ſhoulder be anointed with this ointment warm; let it be rubbed long at a time, and afterwards put the horſe to ſwim."

Mr. Oſmer *(b)*, after rightly obſerving that the cauſe of lameneſs in the fore-part of a horſe is not eaſily diſtinguiſhed by thoſe who are not attentive to it, becauſe lameneſs there may be occaſioned by ſtrains in the muſcular or tendinous part of the leg, from the ſhoulder to the foot of the horſe adviſes, when the muſcles and ligaments of the ſhoulder are ſtrained, to keep the horſe as free from motion as poſſible, and to apply vinegar and diſcutient fomentations, which will probably bring him to a ſound ſtate.

When the muſcles of the back and loins are ſtrained, as not unfrequently happens through the fatigue of a long journey, the ruggedneſs of the roads, over-

(a) *Lib. II. c. xliv.* (b) *Page* 63.

ſtretching

ſtretching in leaping, or carrying too great a burthen, the ſymptoms are, that the horſe drags his hinder legs, his loins ſtagger and ſhake, he cannot gather his limbs together, his tail falls down, and he ſometimes piſſes blood. Vegetius (*c*) here adviſes, that the horſe be bled, that the blood taken from him be mixed with oil and nitre, and that his loins be thoroughly rubbed therewith. Internally, he orders three ounces of nitre in powder, three ounces of honey, and three ounces of oil, mixed with three pints of old wine, to be poured down his throat in four days, an equal quantity each day; and that then a quantity of cypreſs-leaves and barley-flour be kneaded with ſharp vinegar, and laid upon the part affected.

The different kinds of lameneſs to which the hinder part of the horſe is liable, are moſt eaſily diſtinguiſhed from each other when he is put into motion. Thus, if the horſe be lame in any part belonging to the foot, he will endeavour to eaſe that foot, by not ſetting it fully on the ground: if the lameneſs be in the fetlock joint, or in the tendons of the leg, or in the hock, or if it proceeds from ſwellings ſurrounding the hock, ſuch cauſes will be manifeſt to the eye: if the lameneſs be in the ſtiffle, he cannot ſo well extend the limb, but will drag his toe upon the ground more or leſs, according to the degree of injury he has received, as in a lameneſs in the ſhoulder: and if it be in the ligaments belonging to the joint of the hip, or whirl-bone, he will reſt his foot indeed fully upon the ground, but will halt or ſtep ſhort in his trot, with that leg, though he may perhaps appear perfectly ſound in his walk.

Extenſion and counter-extenſion are the proper methods of reducing diſlocations. The part ſhould then be rubbed with vinegar, and a cataplaſm may be applied twice a day, compoſed of common ſalt and the white of eggs, mixed with a little vinegar

(*c*) *Lib. III. c. v.*

and oatmeal. During this application, reſt muſt be allowed.

A diſlocation of the hip-bone happens very ſeldom, and when it does, it proceeds from either a rupture or an elongation of the round ligament. Mr. Oſmer *(d)* mentions his having ſeen two inſtances of this kind, the one in a horſe and the other in a bullock; as well as a fracture of the thigh-bone, and of the *os ilium*.

" To diſtinguiſh, ſays he, with certainty the reality of theſe, it muſt be obſerved, that when the bone is broke in either of theſe caſes, the animal will in a few days begin to reſt upon that leg a little, and gradually more and more, till the bone conſolidates and becomes united; but when the round ligament is ruptured, or elongated to a certain degree, the head of the bone falls from the ſocket, the leg ſwings, the animal cannot reſt upon it at all; and, by continually bearing all the weight upon the other leg, he ſoon becomes lame of that alſo, and at laſt does not chuſe to ſtand at all.—Moreover, in the caſe of elongation or rupture of the round ligament, the whole limb becomes longer; and in caſe of a fraction of the thigh-bone, it becomes ſhorter; but in a fraction of the *os ilium*, this abbreviation may or may not happen, as depending wholly on the nature and manner of the fracture.—The common lameneſs attending this joint is occaſioned by the relaxed ſtate of ſome of the ligaments belonging to it, brought on by ſome ſtrain at firſt, and by exerciſe continued on ſuch weak part."

Vegetius *(e)* adviſes, in order to reduce a diſlocation of the hip, that the foot of the ſound ſide be ſhod with a ſandle, or ſhoe made of broom, carefully bound on, and ſo to raiſe that foot, that the animal may be able to ſet down the hoof of the lame limb flat and full upon the ground. In caſe of a lux-

(d) Page 57. *(e)* Lib. III. c. xviii.

ation

ation of the thigh, he advises that the horse be placed in the sun, that the hip be rubbed a very long while with warm wine and oil, till he sweats; that he be then pulled with a halter, and made to run by little and little, whilst another person, holding a thong or rope slack in his hand, follows him, and all of a sudden, in the midst of the animal's running, draws with violence the hip strait towards himself. If it gives a crack, the bone is returned to it's place, and he sets his feet down equally: but if the joint cannot be set right the first day, the hip should be pulled frequently on the second day in the same manner, till it return to it's place.—Strains in the lower joints are discovered by the lameness and swelling of the part.

Mr. Olmer *(f)* declares, that "the best remedy for a relaxation of the sinue, is to make a whey with some alum boiled in milk, to foment the part with this whey, and to bind on the curds by way of cataplasm; and after a few days, colcothar of vitriol finely powdered and mixed with white of eggs, is to be applied as a charge every twenty-four hours, and a smooth bandage kept on the part."—Here, I cannot help taking this opportunity to disapprove of the use of vitriol, or any such acrid application, in complaints of this kind; because it can scarcely be imagined that their particles can pierce the horse's skin so as to benefit the ligaments underneath; and if there is the least breach or sore in the skin, their effect must be the making of a slough, which must be cast off by means of inflammation and digestion, and thus occasion a new evil.

To remove inflammations, and to prevent induration and enlargement of the ligamentous parts and teguments of the fetlock joint, the consequence of repeated violence, it is a good custom to cause the joints of a horse, after a day's hard exercise, to be

(f) *Page* 81.

well fomented with flannels dipped in warm water. For want of this precaution, lameneſs often happens to this joint.

When the ſkin or ligaments are inflamed or enlarged by repeated violence, as aforeſaid, the horſe ſhould be bled plentifully, have cooling ſalts given him, and be turned looſe in ſome open building. The injured parts ſhould be fomented twice a day with a decoction of emollient herbs, ſuch as white lilly roots, mallows, elder leaves and flowers, bay-berries, or the like, boiled in water. The parts, when dry, are to be filled with ſome cooling ointment, and ſome of the fomentation ſhould be thickened with oatmeal, to the conſiſtence of a poultice, and kept thereon. When the tenſion and induration are gone off, more ſtrengthening applications may be made uſe of, and the horſe be turned to graſs, and indulged with proper reſt, in order that the diſeaſed parts may recover their former fineneſs, tone, and ſtrength. How much time and reſt are here neceſſary, will appear to any man that has ever ſtrained the tendons of his wriſt or ankle. Let him reflect on the pain he has ſuffered from the leaſt motion of the parts, and how long a time has been required before he could bear the extenſion of the joint, even when all appearances have been fair. Will not the caſe be the ſame with the horſe? And yet jockeys will prepoſterouſly exerciſe them daily, to keep them in wind, ſay they, or prepare them for the race.

To cure theſe ailments in the joints of horſes, the farrier bliſters and fires upon the joint; by either of which, applied whilſt the parts are inflamed, the inflammation thereof is certainly increaſed, and from thence a calloſity of thoſe parts is moſt likely to be intailed for ever. Such methods are as contradictory to the diſorder, as, to uſe Mr. Oſmer's words on this occaſion, (*g*) endeavouring to extinguiſh fire by

(*g*) *Page* 70.

pouring

pouring on it ſpirits of wine. If the fire reaches no farther than the ſkin, little advantage can accrue to the tendon; but the fibres of the ſkin will become contracted and leſs pliant: if the fire reaches the membrane or ſheath of the tendon, ſome of the glands, which ſerve to lubricate the tendon, are deſtroyed, and the tendon becomes more or leſs rigid: if the tendon be burnt, the conſequence will be ſtill worſe. Firing will then act as a bandage, that will be ſure to ſpoil the racer, and take away that pliancy which ſhould be in the joint. Bliſtering and firing do indeed, as Mr. Oſmer obſerves, (*h*) furniſh an advantage to the farrier, becauſe the leg is ſo much inflamed thereby, that it is impoſſible to ride the horſe for a conſiderable time after the operation; ſo that if he happens to get ſound, it is generally thought to be the effect of the bliſter and fire, but ought in reality to be imputed to the reſt he has had.

It is not improbable that the firſt uſe of this barbarous practice may have been owing to ſomewhat of the following nature; that when complaints of this kind had been neglected till a humour had fallen on this part, the bliſtering, or cautery, by giving it vent, reſtored the uſe of the joint; and the farrier, not attending to this circumſtance, erects this inhumanity into a general practice. I therefore moſt perfectly agree with Mr. Oſmer, (*i*) that firing ſeldom is of uſe in any kind of lameneſs, and that more horſes are undone than benefited by it.

A horſe's legs or hips may be broken; and in that caſe, if the bone ſtart out beyond the ſkin, the cure is difficult, becauſe the bandage muſt be undone every day to dreſs the wound: a fracture above the ham is incurable, becauſe it does not admit of a ligature. If the fracture be without a wound, in a place which can be bound up tight, the cure may be attempted. To this end the horſe muſt be ſuſpended in a ſling,

(*h*) *Page* 74. (*i*) *Page* 84.

ſo

ſo that his foot cannot reach the ground, leſt his bone be diſplaced by his ſtriking his hoof againſt the floor. The bone muſt then be ſet and bound round with a bandage, and ſplints on each ſide, with wool under them, to prevent their hurting the fleſh. If a ſwelling or inflammation comes on, the bandage muſt be taken off, and the part embrocated with oil and wine, or vinegar, and a poultice of the ſame tied round. As ſoon as the ſwelling ſubſides, the bandage muſt be again recurred to, and at times renewed for ſix weeks; in leſs time than which the horſe muſt not be permitted to ſtand upon the fractured limb.

SECT. III.

Of Wounds.

THE general conſtruction of the body being ſimilar in other animals as in man, the ſame reaſoning and treatment will nearly anſwer in both. I therefore ſhall certainly not be blamed if in this, and in ſome of the following diviſions of this chapter, I chooſe for my guide Mr. Sharp; a gentleman who has moſt highly diſtinguiſhed himſelf in his profeſſion.

"To conceive rightly," ſays he, in his truly excellent Treatiſe on the Operations of Surgery, (*a*) "the nature and treatment of wounds, under the variety of diſorders to which they are ſubject, it will be proper firſt to learn what are the appearances in the progreſs of healing a large wound, when it is made with a ſharp inſtrument, and the conſtitution is pure.

(*a*) *Introduction, chap.* 1.

"In

"In this circumſtance the blood-veſſels, immediately upon this diviſion, bleed freely, and continue bleeding till they are either ſtopped by art, or at length contracting and withdrawing themſelves into the wound, their extremities are ſhut up by the coagulated blood. The hæmorrhage being ſtopped, the next occurrence, in about twenty-four hours, is a thin ſerous diſcharge; and a day or two after an increaſe of it, though ſometimes thickened and ſtinking. In this ſtate it continues two or three days without any great alteration, from which time the matter grows thicker and leſs offenſive; and when the bottom of the wound fills up with little granulations of fleſh, it diminiſhes in its quantity, and continues doing ſo till the wound is quite ſkinned over.

"It is worth obſerving, that the loſs of any particular part of the body can only be repaired by the fluids of that diſtinct part: and, as in a broken bone, the *callus* is generated from the ends of the fracture, ſo, in a wound, is the *cicatrix* from the circumference of the ſkin only. Hence ariſes the neceſſity of keeping the ſurface even by preſſure or eating medicines, that the eminence of the fleſh may not reſiſt the fibres of the ſkin in their tendency to cover the wound. This eminence is compoſed of little points or granulations called *fungus*, or proud-fleſh, and is frequently eſteemed an evil, though, in truth, this ſpecies of it is the conſtant attendant on healing wounds; for when they are ſmooth, and have no diſpoſition to ſhoot out above their lips, there is a ſlackneſs to heal, and a cure is very difficultly effected. Since then proud-fleſh prevents healing only by its luxuriancy, and all wounds cicatriſe from their circumference, there will be no occaſion to deſtroy the whole *fungus* every time it riſes, but only the edges of it near the lips of the wound; which may be done with gentle eſcharotics, ſuch as lint dipped in a mild ſolution of vitriol; or for the moſt part only by dry lint, and a tight bandage, which will reduce it ſufficiently to a level, if applied before the *fungus* has acquired too much growth. In large wounds, the application of corroſive medicines to the whole ſurface is of no uſe; becauſe the *fungus* will attain to but a certain height when left to itſelf, which it will be frequently riſing up to, though it be often waſted: and as all the advantage to be gathered from it, is only from the evenneſs of its margin, the purpoſe will be as fully anſwered by keeping that under only, and an infinite deal of pain avoided, which muſt attend the continual repetition of eſcharotics.

" From this account of the progreſs of a wound made by a ſharp inſtrument, where there is no indiſpoſition of body, we ſee that the cure is performed without any interruption but from the fungus: a proper regard to this point is therefore here the principal object, with the uſe of ſuch applications as will leaſt interfere with the ordinary courſe of nature, which, in caſes of this kind, will be ſuch as act the leaſt upon the ſurface of the wound; and, agreeably to this, we find that dry lint only is generally the beſt remedy through the whole courſe of dreſſing: at firſt it ſtops the blood with leſs injury than any ſtyptic powders or waters; and afterwards, by abſorbing the matter, which in the beginning of ſuppuration is thin and acrimonious, it becomes in effect a digeſtive: during incarnation, it is the ſofteſt medium that can be applied between the roller and the tender granulations, and at the ſame time it is an eaſy compreſs upon the ſprouting fungus.

" Over the dry lint may be applied a pledget of ſome ſoft ointment ſpread upon tow, which muſt be renewed every day, and preſerved in its ſituation by a gentle bandage; though in all large wounds, the firſt dreſſing after that of the accident or operation ſhould not be applied in leſs than three days, when, the matter being formed, the lint ſeparates more eaſily from the part; for no force ſhould be uſed in the removal of it, nor ſhould any more of it

be

be taken away than what is loose and comes off without pain.

"Perhaps it may appear surprising," continues Mr. Sharp, "that I do not recommend other digestive or incarnative ointments, which have had such recommendation formerly for their efficacy in all species of wounds: but as the intent of medicines is to reduce the wound to a natural state, or a propensity to heal, which is what I have already supposed it to be in, the end of such applications is not wanted; in other respects dry lint is more advantageous. There are certainly many cases in which different applications will have their several uses, as will be shewn in the sequel.

"When a wound is recent (*b*), and the parts of it are divided by a sharp instrument, without any farther violence, and in such a manner that they may be made to approach each other by being returned with the hands, they will, if held in close contact for some time, unite by inosculation, and cement like one branch of a tree ingrafted on another. To maintain them in this situation sutures have been invented.

"From the description I have now given of the state of a wound proper to be sewed up, it may be readily conceived that wounds are not fit subjects for suture when there is either a contusion, laceration, loss of substance, great inflammation, difficulty of bringing the lips into apposition, or some extraneous body insinuated into them; though sometimes a lacerated wound may be assisted with one or two stitches.

"In stitching up a wound that has none of these obstacles, the needle is passed two, three, or four times, in proportion to the length of it, though there can seldom be occasion for more than three stitches. The method of doing it is this. The wound being

(*b*) *Treatise of the Operations of Surgery, chap.* 1.

emptied

emptied of the grumous blood, and an aſſiſtant having brought the lips of it together, ſo that they may lie quite even, the needle is puſhed from without inwards to the bottom, and on from within outwards, uſing the caution of making the puncture far enough from the edge of the wound, which will not only facilitate the paſſing of the ligature, but will alſo prevent it from eating through the ſkin and fleſh. As many more ſtitches as are made, will be only repetitions of the ſame proceſs. When the threads are all paſſed, thoſe in the middle of the wound ſhould be tied firſt. The moſt uſeful kind of knot in large wounds is a ſingle one firſt, and over this a little linen compreſs, on which is to be made another ſingle knot, and then a ſlip-knot, which may be looſened upon any inflammation. In ſmall wounds the compreſs is not neceſſary. One ſtitch is ſufficient for a wound two inches long; and in large wounds they ſhould be rather more than an inch diſtant. If a violent inflammation ſhould ſucceed, looſening the ligature only will not ſuffice; it muſt be cut through and drawn away, and the wound be treated afterwards without any future ſuture. When the wound is ſmall, the leſs it is diſturbed by dreſſing, the better; but in large ones there will ſometimes be a conſiderable diſcharge; and if the threads are not carried through to the bottom of it, abſceſſes will frequently enſue from the matter being pent up underneath, and not finding iſſue. If no accident happens, the ligatures muſt be taken away after the lips of the wound are firmly agglutinated, and the orifices left by them are to be dreſſed.

" It muſt be remembered that, during the cure, the ſuture muſt be always aſſiſted by the application of bandage, if poſſible; and this is of the greateſt importance in horſes, becauſe their muſcles eſpecially have a very ſtrong contracting power. The bandage, with two heads, and a ſlit in the middle, is by much the beſt, and will in many caſes be found practicable.

" If

"If a wound is attended with an hæmorrhage from a confiderable blood-veffel, it muft be ftopped, for which purpofe various means are ufed. If a veffel is entirely cut through, dry lint laid on it, and preffed upon it by proper bandage, is generally fufficient. If the hæmorrhage is too large to be ftopped by the application of dry lint, more powerful aftringents are recurred to. The *lycoperdon*, vulgarly called *lupi crepitus*, or puff-balls, has been highly extolled for this purpofe; the wound being filled with it's powder in the room of dry lint, with proper bandage; as is alfo the agaric of the oak duly prepared. Rectified fpirit of wine, or what is better, and of the fame nature, the fryar's balfam, applied cold to the wound, filling it with lint dipped in the balfam, and covering it with a large comprefs and bandage, is very efficacious. If thefe applications fhould fail, recourfe muft be had to the actual cautery: but the fafeft method is, to make a ligature round the veffel. This is performed by paffing a ftrong waxed thread into the flefh under the artery, by the help of a crooked needle, and the fides of the artery will coalefce.

"Inflammation, pain, and convulfions often attend wounds. If the horfe appears to be full of blood, bleeding is neceffary in thefe cafes, as are alfo fomentations, and the mildeft applications. If convulfions come on from a lofs of blood, opiates are the proper remedy."

SECT. IV.

Of Inflammations and Abfceffes.

I SHALL here again make Mr. Sharp (*a*) my guide, and would recommend an attentive perufal of the foregoing fection, of this, and of the following,

(*a*) *Introduction, chap. ii.*

lowing, to every one who would wiſh to reſcue his horſes from the ſavage and unſkilful practice of moſt farriers.

Inflammations, from all cauſes, have three ways of terminating; either by diſperſion, ſuppuration, or gangrene; and a probable conjecture which of theſe will take place may be gathered from the horſe's health, and other circúmſtances attending it. Thus, inflammations which happen in a ſlight degree of cold, and without any foregoing indiſpoſition, will moſt likely be diſperſed; thoſe which follow cloſe upon a fever, or happen to a horſe full of humours, will generally impoſthumate; and thoſe which befall horſes greatly weakened by other diſtempers, will have a ſtrong tendency to gangrene.

If the ſtate of an inflammation be ſuch as to make the diſperſion of it ſafely practicable, this end will be beſt brought about by evacuations; ſuch as plentiful bleeding, and repeated purges. The part itſelf muſt be fomented twice a day, and be embrocated with a mixture of three-fourths of oil of roſes, and one-fourth of common vinegar. Such a poultice may alſo be applied as was before recommended for bruiſes (*b*). The horſe ſhould be kept to a low diet and cooling drink, and the purge ſhould be continued till the ſwelling is quite ſubſided. When the inflammation is gone off, perhaps gentle friction may contribute to remove the remaining ſwelling more than any other application.

Here it is ſuppoſed that the inflammation had ſo great a tendency to diſcuſſion, as by the help of proper aſſiſtance to terminate in that manner: but when it happens that the diſpoſition of the tumour reſiſts all diſcutient means, it becomes neceſſary then to deſiſt from any farther evacuations, and, as much as can be, to aſſiſt nature in bringing on a ſuppuration.

(*b*) *See page* 194.

That matter will most probably be formed, we may judge by the increase of the symptomatic fever, and enlargement of the tumour, with more pain and pulsation on being touched. Inflammations after a fever, or other disease, almost always suppurate; but these soon discover their tendency, and should at first be treated gently, as if an imposthumation were expected. If the fever runs high, and the vessels seem clogged, experience has taught that bleeding quickens the formation of matter, though the practice should be followed with caution. If the horse is costive, his body may be kept gently open by glysters.

Of all the applications invented to promote suppuration, none are so easy as poultices; and of these there is not perhaps any one preferable to that made of bread and milk softened with oil. White lilly roots, linseed bruised, or, if greater warmth is necessary, fenugreek seed bruised, boiled onions, &c. may be added to the poultice. The tumour may be covered with the poultice twice a day, till it comes to that degree of ripeness as to require opening; which will be known by the eminence of the skin in some part of it, and a fluctuation of matter.

It appears to be but seldom that inflammations terminate in a gangrene in horses: but if the fever and other symptoms run so high, or the constitution of the animal is so far decayed, that a gangrene does come on, it generally proves fatal. If the tenseness of the skin goes off, and it feels flabby to the touch, if a thin ichor seems to be contained under the skin, and if the pulse quickens and sinks, and the animal grows cold, a gangrene is begun. In this case scarifying by several incisions through the skin is judiciously practised, because it discharges a pernicious ichor, and makes way for whatever efficacy there may be in topical applications. The common digestive ointments softened with oil of turpentine, seem as good a dressing as any for the scarifications; and upon them, all over the part, may be laid the *theriaca Londinenses* (London treacle), which ſhould always be uſed in the beginning of a gangrene; or what is equally good, if not preferable, a cataplaſm made with leye and bran, and applied warm; for this will retain its heat better than moſt other topicals. Some recommend the uſe of the grounds of ſtrong beer mixed with bread or oatmeal. Theſe dreſſings with ſpirituous fomentations, ſhould be repeated twice a day. Warm cordial medicines ſhould be given at the ſame time internally. Modern practice ſeems to eſtabliſh the bark as the chief medicine in this caſe. It may be given to the quantity of an ounce every two hours in a mixture, in which wine may make a conſiderable ſhare. After the ſeparation of the eſchar, the wound becomes a common ulcer, and muſt be treated as ſuch.

If we attend to the thickneſs and ſtrength of the ſkin of horſes, we ſhall find that all abſceſſes in them ſhould be opened. In ſmall abſceſſes there is ſeldom a neceſſity for a larger opening than what will give a free diſcharge to the matter; and in large ones, where the matter ſpreads a good way inder the ſkin, an inciſion ſhould be made to its utmoſt extent; or a circular or oval piece of the ſkin ſhould be cut away, which at once lays open a great ſpace of the abſceſs, ſo that it may be dreſſed down to the bottom, and the matter of it be freely diſcharged.

Notwithſtanding the depending part of an abſceſs is eſteemed the moſt eligible for an opening, yet it ſhould be always on the ſuppoſition that the teguments are as thin in that place as in any other part of it; otherwiſe it will be generally adviſeable to make the inciſion where nature indicates, that is, where the tumour is permanent, though it ſhould not be in a depending part.

It is generally taught that critical abſceſſes ſhould be opened before they come to an exact ſuppuration, in order to give vent the ſooner to the noxious matter of of the disease: but they who open before this period, miss the very design they aim at; since but little matter is deposited in the abscess before it arrives towards its ripeness, and besides, the ulcer afterwards grows foul, and is less disposed to heal.

When an abscess is already burst we are to be guided by the probe where to dilate; and as the horse's skin is strong, the knife is the best instrument for opening farther. The manner of opening with a knife is by sliding it on a director, the groove of which prevents its being misguided. If the orifice of the abscess is so small as not to admit the director, it must be enlarged by a piece of sponge-tent, which is made by dipping a dry bit of sponge in melted wax, and immediately squeezing as much out of it again as possible, between two pieces of tile or marble: the effect of this is, that the loose sponge being compressed into a small compass, if any of it is introduced into an abscess, the heat of the parts melts down the remaining wax that holds it together, and the sponge, sucking up the moisture of the abscess, expands, and in expanding opens the orifice wider, and by degrees, so as to give very little pain.

The usual method of dressing an abscess, the first time, is with dry lint only, or, if there be no flux of blood, with soft digestives spread on lint. If there be no danger of the upper part of the wound reuniting too soon, the dossils should be laid in loose; but if the abscess be deep, and the wound narrow, the lint should be crammed in pretty tightly, in order to have afterwards the advantage of dressing down to the bottom without the use of tents, which are now almost universally decried; though indeed still too much employed by the very people who would seem to explode them most; so difficult is it to be convinced of the true efficacy of nature in the healing of wounds. Formerly the virtues of tents were much insisted on, as it was then thought absolutely necessary to keep wounds open a considerable time, to give vent to the imaginary poiſon of the conſtitution; it was ſuppoſed too, that they were beneficial in conveying the proper ſuppurative or ſarcotick medicines down to the bottom of the abſceſs; and again, that, by abſorbing the matter, they preſerved the cleanlineſs of the wound, and diſpoſed it to heal. But this reaſoning is not now eſteemed of any force: ſurgeons at preſent know that a wound cannot heal too faſt, provided that it heals firmly from the bottom; they are well ſatisfied alſo, from what they ſee in wounds where no medicines are applied, that nature of herſelf ſhoots forth new fleſh, and is interrupted by any preſſure whatſoever; beſides, as to the conceit of tents ſucking up the matter, which is eſteemed noxious to healing, they are ſo far from being beneficial in the performance of it, that they are of great prejudice; for if the matter is offenſive in its nature, though they do abſorb it, they bring it into contact with every part of the ſinews; and if it be prejudicial by its quantity, they do miſchief in locking it up in the abſceſs, and preventing the diſcharge it would find if the dreſſings were only ſuperficial: but in fact, matter, when it is good, is of no diſſervice to wounds with regard to its quality; and ſurgeons ſhould therefore be leſs curious in wiping them clean when they are tender and painful. That tents are impediments to healing, rather than aſſiſtants, we may learn from conſidering the effect of a pea in an iſſue, which by preſſure keeps open the wound juſt as tents do; and if there are inſtances of wounds healing very well, notwithſtanding the uſe of tents, ſo there are alſo of iſſues healing up, in ſpite of any meaſures we can take to keep peas in their cavity. In ſhort, tents in wounds, by reſiſting the growth of the little granulations of the fleſh, in proceſs of time harden them, and in that manner produce a fiſtula; ſo that inſtead of being uſed for the cure of an abſceſs, they never ſhould be employed but where we mean to retard the healing of the external

external wound, except in ſome little narrow abſceſſes, where, if they be not crammed in too large, they become as doſſils, admitting of incarnation at the bottom; but in this caſe, care ſhould be taken not to inſinuate them deeper than the ſkin, and they ſhould be repeated twice a day, to give vent to the matter they confine. Tents do moſt good in little deep abſceſſes, whence any extraneous body is to be evacuated, ſuch as ſmall ſplinters of bone, &c. I have been the more particular in this quotation from Mr. Sharp, in order the better to explode the too frequent uſe of tents in farriery.

The uſe of vulnerary injections into abſceſſes has been thought to bear ſo near a reſemblance to the uſe of tents, that they both fell into diſrepute almoſt at the ſame time. It has been ſaid in their favour, that in deep abſceſſes, where no ointment can be applied, they digeſt, cleanſe, and correct the malignity of the *pus*; but the fact is, that they do ſo much miſchief by frequently diſtending the parts of the abſceſs, firſt when they are injected, and afterwards by their addition to the matter generated in the abſceſs, that they are hardly proper in any caſe: though one of the great miſchiefs of both injections and tents has been a miſtaken faith amongſt practitioners, that wherever their medicines were applied the part would heal; and, upon that preſumption, they have neglected to dilate abſceſſes, which have not only remained incurable after this treatment, but would often have done ſo for want of a diſcharge if they had been dreſſed more ſuperficially.

In dreſſing wounds it is common to apply the medicines warm or hot, upon the ſuppoſition that heated ointments have a ſtronger power of digeſting than cold: but as any medicine will ſoon arrive to the heat of the part it is laid on, whether it be applied hot or cold, the efficacy of the heat can avail but little in ſo ſhort a time: and as doſſils dipt in hot ointments are not cleanly, and even grow ſtiff and painful, I think it rather preferable to apply them cold; or perhaps, in winter, a little warmed before the fire after they are ſpread; obſerving, if the ulcer be uneven, to make the doſſils ſmall, in order that they may lie cloſe. Over the doſſils of lint may be laid a large pledgit of tow ſpread with baſilicon, which will lie ſoft on the part. In this manner the dreſſings may be continued till the cavity is incarned; and then it may be cicatriſed with dry lint, obſerving to keep the fungus down as before directed.

In the courſe of dreſſing, it will be proper to have regard to the ſituation of the abſceſs, ſo as to favour the diſcharge as much as poſſible; and to this end the diſcharge muſt be aſſiſted by compreſs and bandage. The frequency of dreſſing will depend on the quantity of diſcharge: once in twenty-four hours is generally ſufficient. I have already mentioned not to be ſcrupulouſly nice in cleaning a wound; but it is worth remarking, that a ſore ſhould never be wiped by drawing a piece of tow or rag over it, but only by dabbing it with lint. The parts about it may be wiped clean in a rougher manner, without any prejudice. Another caution neceſſary in the treatment of abſceſſes is, that we ſhould not on all occaſions ſearch into their cavities with the probe or finger, becauſe this often tears them and indiſpoſes them for a cure.

SECT. V.

Of Ulcers.

AS Horſes have been more cruelly treated in complaints which come under this denomination, than perhaps in any other diſorder, I cannot act with greater humanity towards that valuable part of the creation, nor with more juſtice to their owners, than

than by still continuing to be guided by Mr. Sharp, who has with so much judgment, and a praise-worthy contempt of mystery, thrown off the trappings of surgery, and reduced it to plain and just principles, in which he had the ease and welfare of the patient constantly in view.

When a wound or an abscess, says he, (*a*) degenerates into so bad a state as to resist the methods of cure before laid down, and loses that complexion which belongs to a healing wound, it is called an ulcer; and as the name is generally borrowed from the ill habit of the sore, it is a custom to apply it to all sores that have any degree of malignity, though they are immediately formed without any previous wound or abscess.

Ulcers are distinguished by their particular disorders, though it seldom happens that the affections are not complicated; and when we lay down rules for the management of one species of ulcer, it is generally requisite to apply them to almost all others. However, their most distinguished characters are, the callous ulcer, the sinuous ulcer, and the ulcer with caries of the adjacent bone; though there be abundance more known to surgeons, such as the putrid, the corrosive, the varicous, &c. but as they have all acquired their names from some particular affection, I shall speak of the treatment of them under the general head of ulcers.

It will often be in vain to pursue the best means of cure by topical applications, unless we are assisted by internal remedies: for as many ulcers are the effects of a particular indisposition of the body, it will be difficult to bring them into order while the cause of them remains with any violence, though they are sometimes, in a great degree, the discharge of the indisposition itself; as in contagious diseases, and also in other disorders which proceed from some gene-

(*a*) *Treatise of the Operations of Surgery; Introduction, chap. iii.*

ral indiſpoſition of the blood. Theſe general or chronical indiſpoſitions will be conſidered when I come to treat of the uſe of alteratives.

When an ulcer becomes foul, and diſcharges an acrid thin ichor, the edges of it, in proceſs of time, tuck in, and growing ſkinned and hard, give it the name of a *callous ulcer*, which, ſo long as the edges continue in that ſtate, muſt neceſſarily be thereby prevented from healing: but we are not immediately to deſtroy the lips of it, in expectation of a ſudden cure; for while the malignity of the ulcer remains, which was the occaſion of the calloſity, ſo long will the new lips be ſubject to a relapſe of the ſame kind, however often the external ſurface of them be deſtroyed; ſo that when we have to deal with this circumſtance, we are to indeavour to bring the body of the ulcer into a diſpoſition to recover by other methods. Reſt, with the aſſiſtance of powerful internal medicines, or even a rowel near the part affected, may give ſuch a diverſion to the humour, as ſhall diſpoſe an ulcer to heal; yet when the ſurface of the ulcer begins to yield thick matter, and little granulations of red fleſh ſhoot up, it will be proper to quicken nature by deſtroying the edges of it, if they remain hard. The manner of doing this, is by touching them for a few days with the lunar cauſtic, or infernal ſtone. If the part will bear the application of a compreſs and bandage, the preſſure ſoon reduces the callus. Some chooſe to cut them off with a knife; but this is very painful, and not, as I can perceive, more efficacious; though when the lips do not tuck down cloſe to the ulcer, but hang looſe over it, the eaſieſt method is cutting them off with the ſciſſars.

To digeſt the ulcer, and to procure good matter from it when in a putrid ſtate, an infinity of ointments have been invented; but the yellow baſilicon alone, or ſoftened down ſometimes with turpentines or balſam capivi, and ſometimes mixed up with different

ferent proportions of red precipitate, ſeems to ſerve the purpoſes of bringing an ulcer on to cicatriſation, as well as any of the others. When the ulcer is incarned, the cure may be finiſhed as in other wounds; or if it does not cicatriſe kindly, it may be waſhed with lime-water, or with the ſame water in a pint of which half a dram of corroſive ſublimate mercury has been diſſolved, or dreſſed with a pledgit dipt in tincture of myrrh.

The red precipitate has of late years acquired the credit it deſerves for the cure of ulcers. When mixed up with baſilicon, it is moſt certainly a digeſtive; ſince it hardly ever fails to make the ulcer yield a thick matter in twenty-four hours, which diſcharged a thin one before the application of it. As greater proportions of it are added to the ointment, it approaches to an eſcharotic; but while it is mixed with the ointment, it is much leſs painful and corroſive, than when ſprinkled on a ſore in powder: in which laſt form it is a ſtrong eſcharotic, and much of it can never be uſed without making a ſlough. On that account, when the nature of the ulcer requires ſo ſtrong an eſcharotic, the powder ſhould not be renewed till the former ſlough is caſt off; which it will generally be the next day, or at fartheſt the day after.

If the ulcer ſhould be of ſuch a nature as to produce a ſpongy fleſh, ſprouting very high above the ſurface, it will be neceſſary to deſtroy that fleſh by ſome eſcharotics, or the knife. This *fungus* differs very much from that which belongs to healing wounds, being more prominent and lax, and generally in one maſs; whereas the other is in little protuberances. It approaches often towards a cancerous complexion; and when it riſes from ſome glands, does ſometimes actually degenerate into a cancer. The lunar cauſtic, or infernal ſtone, is here the beſt eſcharotic; and the precipitate, or what I think better,

better, the angelic powder (a compoſition of precipitate and burnt allum), may be alſo uſed.

In ulcers alſo, when the ſubjacent bone is carious, great quantities of looſe flabby fleſh will grow up above the level of the ſkin; but as the caries is the cauſe of the diſorder, it will be in vain to expect a cure of the excreſcence, till the rotten part of the bone is removed; and every attempt with eſcharotics will be only a repetition of pain to the diſeaſed, without any advantage.

In ulcers of the glands, and indeed of almoſt every part, this diſorder is very common: but before trial of the ſevere eſcharotics, I would recommend the uſe of the ſtrong precipitate medicine, with compreſs as tight as can be borne without pain; which I think generally keeps it under.

Mr. Sharp informs us, that he had the pleaſure of ſeeing an eminent ſurgeon bring an ulcer ſoon to diſcharge good matter, and put on as kindly an appearance as he ever beheld in a ſore, by the uſe of pledgits dipt in balſam capivi with an equal quantity of oil of olives, applied as hot as the patient can poſſibly bear. What ſeemed ſurprizing to him was, that a heat, which he was perſuaded would have bliſtered the ſkin, mended the appearance of the ſore. The ſurgeon declared, that he had found this manner of application to be not only the beſt and moſt effectual eſcharotic, the pain of which is but of a ſhort duration, but alſo that it fills the ſore with the beſt fleſh. If the aſpect of an ulcer is white and ſmooth, as happens in ulcers accompanied with a dropſy, external applications will anſwer no purpoſe, till the conſtitution is repaired.

When ulcers or abſceſſes are accompanied with inflammation and pain, they are to be aſſiſted with fomentations made of ſome of the drying herbs, ſuch as wormwood, bay-leaves, and roſemary; and when they are putrid and corroſive, which circumſtances give them the name of *phagædenic* ulcers, ſome ſpirit

of

of wine ſhould be added to the fomentation, and the bandage be alſo dipped in brandy or ſpirit of wine; obſerving in theſe caſes where there is much pain, always to apply gentle medicines till the pain is removed. If a *varix* attends an ulcer, the moſt certain cure is to dilate it, and tie it below with a waxed thread.

As to the frequency of dreſſing and fomenting, I think it may be laid down as a general rule in all ſores, that where the diſcharge is ſanious and corroſive, twice a day is not too much; and if the matter be not very putrid and thin, once will ſuffice. When the pain and inflammation are exceſſive, bleeding and other evacuations will often be ſerviceable. In horſes, we are deprived of the horizontal poſition, which in man is found to be of ſo great importance to the cure of ulcers in the legs, that without it the ſkill of the ſurgeon will often avail nothing: but the horſes in this caſe ſhould certainly have all the reſt that can poſſibly be given them.

As old ulcers are very apt to break out again, it is proper to put a rowel as near the part as can conveniently be, in order to continue a diſcharge which the conſtitution has been habituated to, and to prevent it's falling on the cicatrix; and in the legs, a bandage ſhould be continued for ſome time after the cure. The neateſt is the ſtrait ſtocking, which may be made to fit a horſe, as well as a man. If the leg is œdematous after the healing of the ulcer, it may be worn with ſafety and advantage.

When an ulcer or abſceſs has any ſinuſes or channels opening and diſcharging themſelves into the ſore, they are called *ſinuous* ulcers. If theſe ſinuſes continue to drain a great while, they grow hard in the ſurface of their cavities, and then are termed *fiſtulæ*, and the ulcer a *fiſtulous* ulcer; alſo if matter be diſcharged from any cavity, as thoſe of the joints, the abdomen, &c. the opening is called a *ſinuous ulcer*, or a *fiſtula*.

The

The treatment of theſe ulcers depends on a variety of circumſtances. If the matter in the ſinus be thick, ſtrict compreſs and bandage will ſometimes bring the oppoſite ſides of the ſinus to a re-union: if the ſinus grow turgid in any part, and the ſkin thinner, ſhewing a diſpoſition to break, the matter muſt be made to puſh againſt that part, by plugging it up with a tent; and then a counter-opening muſt be made, which often proves ſufficient for the whole abſceſs, if it be not afterwards too much tented, for this locks up the matter, and prevents the healing; or too little, which will have the ſame effect; for dreſſing quite ſuperficially ſuffers the external wound to contract into a narrow orifice before the internal one is incarned, which does almoſt as effectually lock up the matter, as a tent. To obſerve then a medium in theſe caſes, a hollow tent of lead or ſilver may be kept in the orifice, which at the ſame time that it keeps it open, gives vent to the matter. When, after ſome trial, the matter does not leſſen in quantity, and the ſides do not grow thinner, the ſinus muſt be dilated the whole length, if practicable; for there is then no expectation of a cure without dilation. When abſceſſes of the joints diſcharge themſelves, there is no other method of treating the fiſtula, but by keeping it open with the cautions before laid down, till the cartilages of the extremities of the bones being corroded, the two bones ſhoot into one another, and form of the joint an *anchyloſis*, or ſtiff joint.

When an ulcer with looſe rotten fleſh diſcharges more than the ſize of it ſhould yield, and the diſcharge is oily and ſtinking, in all probability the bone is carious; which may eaſily be known by running the probe through the fleſh. If it be ſo, it is called a *carious* ulcer. The cure of theſe ulcers depends principally upon the removal of the rotten part of the bone, without which it will be impoſſible to heal. Thoſe caries which happen from the matter of the abſceſſes lying too long upon the bone, are moſt likely to recover.

The

The method of treating an ulcer with a caries, is by applying a caustic of the size of the scale of the bone that is to be exfoliated, and after having laid the bone bare, to wait till such time as the carious part can, without violence, be separated, and then to heal the wound. I caution against violence, because the little jagged bits of bone that would be left, if we attempted exfoliation before the piece was quite loose and disengaged from the sound bone, would form little ulcerations, and very much retard the cure. Several applications have been devised, in order to quicken the exfoliation; but that which has been most used in all ages, is the actual cautery, with which the naked bone is burnt every day, or every other day, to dry up, as is said, the moisture, and by that means procure the separation. Now, if we consider the appearance of a wound when a scale of a bone is taken out of it, there is hardly any question to be made, but that burning retards, rather than hastens, the separation: for as every scale of a carious bone is flung off by new flesh generated between it and the sound bone, whatever prevents the growth of these granulations, will also in a degree prevent the exfoliation; and this must certainly be the effect of a red-hot iron applied so close to it, that it may even damage parts of the bone which are sound, and thereby add to the number of scales to be exfoliated. With or without the actual cautery, it is very uncertain how soon the exfoliation may happen, it taking sometimes many months, and at other times not so many weeks: nay, Mr. Sharp says that he has, upon cutting out the eschar made by a caustic, taken away at the same time a large exfoliation. If it be only uncertain whether the actual cautery is beneficial or not, the cruelty that attends the use of it should intirely banish it out of practice. It is likewise often employed to keep down the fungous lips that spread upon the bone: but it is much more painful than the eschoratic medicines: though there

will

will be no need of either, if a regular compreſs be kept on the dreſſings; or if a flat piece of the prepared ſponge before-mentioned, of the ſize of the ulcer, be rolled on with a tight bandage, it will ſwell on every ſide, and dilate the ulcer without any pain.

Some caries of bones are ſo very ſhallow, that they crumble inſenſibly away, and the wound fills up: but when the bone will neither exfoliate, nor admit of granulations, it will be proper to ſcrape it with a rugine, or perforate it in many points with a ſuitable inſtrument down to the quick. The dreſſing of carious bones, if they are ſtinking, may be doſſils dipt in the tincture of myrrh; otherwiſe thoſe of dry lint are eaſieſt, and keep down the edges of the ulcer better than any other gentle application. Very good ſucceſs has attended the uſe of the balſam capivi and oil, as recommended by Mr. Sanxay, in ſuch caſes.

That noble animal, the horſe, is, as well as his rider, liable to gun-ſhot wounds, particularly in battle. What renders theſe wounds ſo alarming, is the contuſion and laceration of the parts, and the admiſſion of extraneous bodies into them. The treatment of theſe wounds conſiſts in removing the extraneous bodies as ſoon as poſſible; to which end the horſe muſt be put into the ſame poſture, as near as may be, as when he received the wound. If the bullet cannot be extracted this way, nor by cutting upon it, which ſhould be practiſed when the ſituation of the blood-veſſels, &c. does not forbid, it muſt be left to nature to work out, and the wound be dreſſed ſuperficially; for we muſt not expect that if it be kept open with tents, the bullet, &c. will return that way: and there is hardly any caſe where tents are more pernicious than here, becauſe of the violent tenſion and diſpoſition to gangrene which preſently enſue. To guard againſt mortification in this and all other violent contuſed wounds, it will be proper to bleed immediately, and ſoon after to give a glyſter.

glyster. The part should be dressed with soft digestives, and the compress and roller applied very loose, being first dipt in brandy or spirit of wine. The next time the wound is opened, if the appearance threaten danger, the spirituous fomentation may be employed, and continued till the danger is over. In gun-shot wounds, it seldom happens that there is any effusion of blood, unless a large vessel is torn; for the bullet makes an eschar, which usually separates in a few days, and is followed with a plentiful discharge. When the wound is come to this period, it is manageable by the rules already laid down.

When burns are superficial, not raising suddenly any vescication, spirits of wine give the speediest relief; for by their quick evaportion, they render the part so cool that inflammation is prevented, much more effectually than by the application of any other less volatile, and therefore less cooling substance. Though this reason was not known till within these few years, yet the practice was very frequent among persons whose trade subjects them often to this misfortune. If the burn excoriates, the spirit would turn the sore to a slough, and therefore must not then be made use of; but, instead of it, a mild application, such as oil, or a mixture of oil and ointment of elder. When the excoriations are very tender, flannels wrung out of warm milk and applied hot, are very comfortable. If the burn has formed eschars, they must be dressed with a soft digestive, till they cast off, and then cured as before directed. Great care is necessary to keep down the fungus, to which end, the edges may be dressed with lint dipt in a weak solution of vitriol, and afterwards dried; or they may be touched with the vitriol-stone. There is also greater danger of contractions from burns after the cure, than from any other wounds: to obviate which, embrocations of neat's-foot oil, and keeping the part extended, are absolutely necessary.

SECT.

SECT VIII.

Of Tumours.

ENCYSTED Tumours, being eſſentially different from thoſe which tend to ſuppuration, claim to be treated of ſeparately. Under this head, I ſhall not only conſider ſuch tumours as do not uſually terminate in ſuppuration, and are properly called *encyſted* tumours, but alſo, with Vegetius, include a *ganglion*, a *varix*, and an *exoſtoſis*.

The *encyſted* tumours are diſtinguiſhed by the appellations of *atheroma*, *ſteatoma*, and *meliceris*; names given to denote the different conſiſtence of the matter contained in them (*b*), as alſo their being contained in a ſurrounding coat; and to them may here be added a *ganglion*, becauſe the method of cure is the ſame for all. The coat which ſurrounds them ſometimes adheres, but generally does not, to the parts underneath it. They are without pain, and preſage no great danger, unleſs they grow very large. If they are near a joint, or ſo ſituated as to incommode the motion of it, they ſhould be cut out; otherwiſe they may continue long without much inconvenience.

The thickneſs of a horſe's ſkin renders every other means of cure beſides extirpation ineffectual. To this purpoſe Vegetius adviſes, (*c*) "That the horſe be laid down and bound, and that on the part affected an inciſion be made lengthways, with a knife, on the right and left ſides, in proportion to the largeneſs of the tumour, leaving in the middle a ſmall

(*b*) The matter contained in the *atheroma* reſembles milk-curds; that in the *ſteatoma* is compoſed of fat, or a ſuety ſubſtance; and the contents of the *meliceris* look like honey.

(*c*) *Lib. ii. c. xxx.*

ſwarth

ſwarth of the ſkin which is above the tumour untouched: the tumour being then cut out, the part is healed without leaving a ſcar." If the tumour is too large to admit of a ſwarth being left in this manner, a longitudinal inciſion muſt be made upon the tumour, and if this does not appear ſufficient, let another inciſion be made acroſs the former, till the tumour is laid ſufficiently bare. The tumour is then to be diſſected out, without wounding it's coat, if poſſible, or any veſſel or membrane that may be contiguous. The tumour being extracted, if the hæmorrage be ſmall, the lips of the wound may be brought together, and being retained by proper compreſs and bandage, the wound is generally cured in a few days. If the hæmorrhage is profuſe, it muſt be ſtopped as before directed; but if by accident or neceſſity, any part of the including cyſt or coat ſhould be left, it muſt be taken away by the uſe of eſcharotics, ſuch as the lunar cauſtic, or, if milder will do, red precipitate may be uſed, and the ſlough be brought away by mild digeſtives: for if the leaſt part be left, there is danger of a relapſe.

Hard ſwellings in the glands in any part of the body, but eſpecially in the neck and about the head, which have not a tendency to a kindly ſuppuration, ſhould alſo be cut out in the ſame manner as ſoon as they are obſerved; for the longer they remain, the larger, and therefore the more troubleſome they become. Of this kind is, in particular, that which, for want of proper care in bleeding in the neck, or afterwards, frequently falls on the part, is attended with many bad ſymptoms, and does not digeſt kindly.

Mr. Oſmer (*d*) here very properly adviſes to the following effect, " Warm fomentations, cooling ointment, and a poultice of bread and milk, applied as ſoon as the evil is perceived, will very probably remove it. But if that method ſhould fail, a rowel

(*d*) *Page* 104.

is to be put into the ſkin, in the middle of the horſe's boſom, and with a tobacco-pipe, or any other tube, the ſkin to be blown up quite to the part affected; in order that an immediate derivation may be made therefrom as ſoon as the rowel runs. If, after this, any ſwelling or induration ſhould ſtill remain on the neck, it will now be removed by poultice and fomentations, or by the following mixture:

"Take of ſprit of wine four ounces, camphor and bole powdered, each one drachm, aqua fortis twenty drops; dip ſome lint or tow in ſome of this, apply it to the part, and bind over it ſome warm thick cloaths, without which this application does no good on any occaſion."

Alſo ſwellings on any part of the back or withers, occaſioned by bruiſes from the ſaddle, he declares this medicine more efficacious than any other he is acquainted with; for that it will in a few days either intirely diſperſe ſuch ſwelling, or bring it to a head: and what is particular, adds he, when matter is produced, the ſwelling itſelf is of much leſs magnitude than it would be by any other application productive of matter. It may be uſed twice a day, rubbing ſome of it upon the ſwelling, and wetting with it ſome lint or tow to be bound on the part. As ſoon as the matter is formed, and perceived to fluctuate under the finger, it ſhould be let out with a knife, and ſome lint dipped in this mixture, and applied to the part once or twice a day, will cure it without any digeſtive or other means. Mr. Oſmer farther obſerves, that it will cure a rawneſs on the back, or other part, if the fungus fleſh be not grown too high.

When an extraordinary dilatation happens in the coats of the veins it is called a *varix*, or bloodſpavin, and is ſeldom attended with pain or much inconvenience. A compreſs and proper bandage ſometimes give an opportunity to the coat of the vein to recover itſelf. If this does not ſuffice, and if the ſwelling is at all troubleſome, the effectual way of curing of it

is,

is by laying it open the whole length with a lancet, discharging the grumous blood, and healing it up as a common wound. If an hæmorrhage ensues, a ligature may be made on the vein above and below the incision.

When an acute eminence, or excrescence, which is properly called an *exostosis*, pushes preternaturally above the bone, creating no pain or inconvenience, and unaccompanied with a *caries*, the best way is to let it alone; but if, on the other hand, it impedes any action, or produces great pain or other mischief, it will be adviseable to take it away. For this purpose an incision mmst be made in the skin, large enough to lay the whole tumour bare; the next day holes must be bored in the tumour to the depth of the natural surface of the bone, and so near to each other that it may be pierced like a sieve; then the whole surface so pierced must be taken off with a chissel and mallet, and the wound be afterwards treated as already directed when an exfoliation is waited for.

Mr. Osmer says, (e) that the most proper method of curing *ring-bones*, *bone-spavins*, and *splints*, which are exostoses, is as follows. "First, clip the hair from the diseased part; make several punctures on that part through the skin with a sharp-pointed instrument, make a longitudinal incision through the skin above the diseased part, about the middle thereof; there introduce a cornet, and dilate the skin with it as far as the swelling reaches. Make another smaller longitudinal incision through the skin below the swelled part, directly opposite to the wound above, in doing which, your probe introduced at top will direct you. At the superior wound a caustic, wrapped up in a piece of lint, is to be introduced, and there left. The caustic dissolved, is carried off by the inferior wound. The whole is directly to be covered with a warm adhesive charge; and this is the

(e) *Page* 88.

whole of the operation. The cauſtic thus introduced under the ſkin acts both ways, namely, on the membrane underneath it, and on the outer tegument upon it: thus the membrane, the outer tegument, and the charge, throw themſelves off together, and the diſeaſed or ſwelled part becomes fair and ſmooth. The horſe ſhould be turned out, or kept in an airy ſtable; and if the charge comes off before the wound is well, another ſhould be immediately applied. But in ſpite of this, and all other methods uſed for theſe diſorders, the horſe will very frequently remain full as lame as he was before, although the appearance of the diſeaſe is removed; the reaſon of which is, that the perioſtium only is ſometimes diſeaſed, at other times the bone itſelf, and it's cellular part."

Excreſcences, which may alſo be included under this head, are in general eaſily got rid of. If they grow from a ſmall neck, a ligature is the eaſieſt cure. This is performed by tying very tight, ſo as to interrupt the circulation, round the root of the excreſcence a well-waxed thread. The knot ſhould be a running one, that it may be tightened if neceſſary. In a few days, the neck of the excreſcence will mortify, and the whole will fall off. If the neck is too large to admit of a ligature, the excreſcence muſt be cut off: and as a branch of an artery ſupplies it with blood, and often brings on a troubleſome hæmorrhage, it is beſt at once to tie up the artery, in the uſual way.

By a violent effort, or other accident, the guts or caul of a horſe may be forced out at the navel, or through the ring of the muſcle in the groin into the ſcrotum or cod. The ſwellings occaſioned by theſe ruptures are of different ſizes, according to the quantity of caul or gut contained in them.

On their firſt appearance, endeavours ſhould be uſed to return them, which is ſometimes eaſily done, if they are ſoft and yield to the preſſure of the hand; and in this caſe their return is attended with a noiſe. If the ſwelling is hard and painful, a large quantity of of blood ſhould be immediately taken away, to remove the tendency into inflammation, and leſſen the ſtricture of the parts. The part ruptured ſhould be fomented with water as cold as can be procured; and it's natural cold may be increaſed by throwing into it ſome ſalt, or rather ſal ammoniac, which adds much to the chillineſs of water. This is done to leſſen the diſtenſion of the gut from rarefied air or vapour contained in it, and to prevent inflammation in the teguments. In the mean time it is proper to throw up ſtimulating glyſters, the effect of which often is, that the gut is reduced as ſoon as the glyſter operates. If the rupture has been of ſo long a ſtanding that the parts adhere, or cannot be reduced, a ſuſpenſary bandage is the only remaining relief; and a proper ſteel truſs, together with care to guard againſt any violent exertion of ſtrength, the only means of preventing it's return.

SECT. VII.

Of Cutaneous Diſeaſes.

CUtaneous diſeaſes, for the moſt part, take their riſe from a general diſtemperature of the juices, in the writings of farriers called *humours*. And indeed, though the ſtrict meaning of this word has not yet been very accurately aſcertained, their uſe of it is in ſome meaſure countenanced by certain general expreſſions in the writings even of phyſicians, ſuch as *nervous*, *ſcorbutic*, &c. This laſt word, perhaps, expreſſes nearly what *humours* are in horſes. However, ſuch as it is, I ſhall, with Mr. Oſmer (*a*), " For the ſake of peace, diſtinction, and cuſtom, " be well content that this good old phraſe ſtand it's " ground unmoleſted;" meaning by it, that there

(*a*) *Page* 61.

is,

is, either in the blood and juices, or in the veſſels, ſome diſtemper which renders the circulation imperfect in the capillary veſſels, ſo that eruptions, ſwellings, &c. happen in different parts of the body. This imperfection being general, the cure is uſually attempted by the uſe of medicines which, having a general effect on the conſtitution, are called *alteratives*; becauſe they, for the moſt part, produce no immediate ſenſible operation, but imperceptibly reſtore a proper tone to the veſſels, and due conſiſtence to the blood and juices. I ſhall give a ſhort account of the medicines uſually comprehended under this denomination, before I treat of the cutaneous diſeaſes for which they are uſed.

Of Alterative Medicines.

Nature affords us in the ſpring, and during the beginning of ſummer, one of the moſt efficacious, as well as moſt univerſal *alteratives*, in the juice of ſucculent plants then in vigorous vegetation. Plants at that time abound in a watery juice, in which is contained much of the native ſalt of the plant. This ſalt renders them at that ſeaſon more peculiarly purgative than when they are farther advanced towards ripeneſs, in which laſt ſtage their juices become thicker, tending more to an oily nature, and therefore are more nouriſhing. The ſalt in the ſpring juices renders them more active in removing obſtructions every where in the courſe of the circulation. So powerful reſolvents are they then, that Dr. Boerhaave has recorded an obſervation made by butchers, purporting, that though ſtall-fed cattle generally have gall-ſtones, yet no ſuch are found in cattle fed on graſs, and killed in the latter end of the ſummer.

The fine coat which ſoiling ſoon gives to horſes is an evident proof of its utility; and every prudent man will, in order to preſerve the health of his hor-

ſes,

ses, cultivate such plants as are observed to abound in this so salutary juice. In the opinion of the antients, no plant exceeds lucerne in this respect, and the experience of the moderns has amply confirmed their judgment. I have instanced several proofs of it in my system of husbandry, and many more might be adduced if necessary. So peculiarly excellent is lucerne for this purpose, that if it was of no other use, it would highly deserve all the care we could bestow upon it: but when we reflect, that, added to this, it is the most profitable of any plant in the quantity as well quality of the fodder it yields, we have the strongest motives to cultivate it with all possible attention. The use of carrots in the winter must also be of great advantage, both as food and as physick; for, containing a rich saponaceous juice, they are deobstruent as well as nourishing. Even turnips, given with their hay, have been found to be beneficial to horses.

Before the horse is put to grass (*b*) (as many do their young ones till they are seven or eight years old) he must be bled, and not put to grass till three days after, choosing the time when it is high enough for him to crop it by whole mouthfuls. He should then be left day and night in the pasture, for at least a month, without currying, dressing, or bleeding; for the coolness of the grass will purge him sufficiently, restore his legs, purify his blood, and cure him of all itchings in the skin. Only care must be taken to make him drink at noon and evening. He should be taken from pasture when the heat of the weather begins to harden the grass, because it then has no longer the same virtue as when fresh and tender; and the flies would also then be too troublesome. The after-math, or second growth after mowing, is not at all good for horses either green or dry.

When the horse has fattened at grass, before he is

(*b*) *Maison Rustique, tom.* 1. *p.* 244.

put

put to work, he muſt be fed with hay and oats for twelve days, be bled, and not made to labour hard at firſt; and in order to kill or force out the worms which the graſs may have engendered in him, he ſhould be made to take a pound of freſh butter, and half an ounce of mild ſublimate in powder mixed, made into balls, and given in a pint of red wine. Or, inſtead of ſublimate, four ounces of cinnabar in powder may be mixed with the butter.

Salt-marſhes are found to be of ſingular benefit to horſes, probably on account of the ſea-ſalt which enters into the plants that grow in ſuch marſhes, from the ſalt water's overflowing them at times: for it appears, that the fixed ſalt obtained by burning ſuch plants, is of the nature of that ſalt which is yielded by the plant kali, commonly called barilla.

The author of nature has been remarkably kind to the brute creation, in beſtowing upon them an inſtinct which directs them in the choice of their food, with a ſeeming judgment ſuperior, perhaps, to what our boaſted reaſon gives us. Their love of ſalt, when at a great diſtance from the ſea, is an evident inſtance of this: for, as we before obſerved, wherever they find an earth in which ſalt abounds, they at times flock thither, and lick up the earth. This is alſo a convincing proof of the propriety of frequently giving ſalt to horſes, as well as to other cattle, as an alternative medicine.

Mr. Oſmer (*c*) very rightly recommends the uſe of ſalt for horſes, from the ſalutary effect it is obſerved to have on the human ſpecies, when purſued for a due courſe of time; and as horſes are fond of it, it may be given mixed with their corn or hay, to the quantity of two or three ounces a day, or ſuch quantity as ſhall keep them gently open.

M. Bourgelat, in his Hiſtory of Drugs (*d*), judi-

(*c*) *Page* 189. (*d*) *Page* 48.

ciouſly

ciously wishes that all duty was taken off sea-salt used as a medicine for cattle, and especially for sheep. Now, as in this kingdom, salt employed in the manure of land is already exempt from duty, it is scarcely to be doubted but that, if a proper representation of it's great utility in this respect was made to Parliament, the tax would also be remitted for what should be used for this purpose.

Nitre, or salt-petre, has nearly the same qualities as sea-salt; and as it has been so often and so justly recommended in all disorders attended with heat, little need be said of it here. Mr. Osmer gives a remarkable instance of the large quantity of this salt which a horse may take without being hurt by it. "A horse, says he (*e*), mad with the staggers, broke out of the stable belonging to a powder-mill, and got to a large cistern of water, in which so much salt-petre had been dissolved, that it was barely in a state of fluidity. He drank, or rather swallowed, several gallons. This soon promoted a very copious secretion by the urinary passages, after which he became immediately well, without any farther assistance. Yet others, he observes, from a difference of constitution, more particularly when they eat grass, shall not be able to take the smallest quantity of it without being affected with the gripes or colic: therefore it is always best to begin with a small quantity, but not less than an ounce, which should be mixed and made into a ball with some mucilage of gum Arabic; and if the horse be not affected with colicky pains, the dose may by degrees be encreased to a greater quantity, according to the different age and circumstances." An advantage attending the use of salt-petre is, that it requires no regimen, and gentle exercise will be an advantage.

General practice has so well established the use of antimony as an alterative, that the bare naming of it

(*e*) *Page* 126.

is sufficient. The liver of antimony is thought to be most efficacious; and in fact it soon brings a shining lustre on the coat, if given to horses in the quantity of from half an ounce to two or three ounces a day, mixed with their corn or other food, or in a ball. Both ways it should be finely powdered.

Mr. Osmer observes (*f*), that nitre added to antimony will make the mixture a powerful deobstruent, and an efficacious medicine in all diseases befalling horses. If we take two parts of nitre, and one of antimony, first rubbed together, and deflagrate them over a fire, in a crucible, by putting in a little at a time, we shall have a medicine nearly analogous to Dr. James's powder; and one or two ounces of it may be given once or twice a day, as occasion may require.

This will be found a very potent remedy in the farcy, in cutaneous diseases, in local swellings, in cases where the circulation is become languid, in a loss of appetite, and many chronical disorders, in which the secretions and excretions stand in need of being promoted.

It is of late become a very frequent practice to add quicksilver to antimony; and perhaps the antimonial æthiops before recommended for the glanders, is the best preparation of them, when intended as an alterative. The other preparations of mercury are too acrid to be given for this purpose, and therefore are judiciously used only a few times in particular disorders, as before directed. Care should be taken that the horse be not exposed to cold when he takes the æthiops, and that it do not affect his mouth. As soon as it is perceived so to do, the use of it should be intermitted for some days, till the horse's mouth gets well, and he can again chew his oats or other food. If this does not happen speedily, flower of sulphur may be given to the quantity of two or three ounces daily, till the mouth becomes as dry as usual.

(*f*) *Page* 268.

A rowel

A rowel may be conſidered as an alterative medicine, ſince is intended to make a gradual diſcharge of ſome noxious humour. The utility of ſuch drains being fully evinced by the experience of ages, I ſhall not ſpend time in attempting to account for the effects they produce.

Horſes of groſs habits, or on whoſe body, eſpecially limbs, any humour has been depoſited by nature, or a humour falls on any part in conſequence of a hurt received, are in the caſe in which moſt benefit is received by rowels. They are alſo of ſervice in chronical internal diſeaſes, eſpecially in thoſe of the breaſt. It is a general rule to make them as near the part affected as may be. They are uſually made in the depending part of the horſe's belly, that ſo the matter may have a free diſcharge. The forepart of the breaſt, and the neck, are alſo proper places for them. It is a general rule never to make them where there is the action or ſwell of a muſcle underneath, leſt the irritation on the muſcles ſhould bring on an inflammation and its conſequences.

Of Hide-bound.

A horſe that is hide-bound grows lean, has a feveriſh heat, his ſkin ſticks to his ribs, the ſpine becomes harder than uſual, ſmall boils break out on his back, and yet his appetite ſometimes continues good. As this diſorder ſeldom is an original complaint, but generally ariſes from ſome former cauſe, regard muſt be had to that cauſe in the method of cure: though I ſhall here treat it only as an ill in itſelf.

Vegetius (*g*) here directs anointing the whole body with wine and oil well mixed together, rubbing them ſtrongly againſt the hair, in a warm ſun, in order that the ſkin may be relaxed, and a ſweat break out; after which the horſe ſhould be well covered, and placed in a warm ſtable, with plenty of litter.

(*g*) *Lib. III. c. liv.*

The

The authors of the *Maison Rustique* advises (*b*), that the next day after bleeding the horse, a fomentation be made of emollient and aromatic strengthening plants boiled in lees of wine, or beer, and that the whole body of the horse be rubbed with these plants, whilst they are warm, till it is thoroughly wet; and that the loins, belly, and neck, as well as the rest of the body, be anointed with a mixture of one part of honey and three parts of ointment of elder, or populion; rubbing it strongly in with the hand, that it may penetrate the skin. This done, the horse should be covered with a cloth dipt in the warm fomentation, and doubled, and another covering should be put over this, tying it on with one or two surcingles. The horse should remain in this condition twenty-four hours, and then be fomented, rubbed, &c. again, twice. These fomentations being finished, a warm covering must be continued, lest the horse catch cold, and he should then have an opening glyster, and the next morning a purging medicine; continuing to wash his head and neck, and also to rince his mouth, with the decoction.

" For food, put into a pail of water about half a bushel of barley-meal coarsly ground, stir it well about, and then let it settle. When the heaviest parts have subsided to the bottom of the pail, pour the thin part off into another pail, for the horse to drink, and give him what remained at the bottom of the first pail, at three different times in the day, mixing with it a due quantity of crude antimony. If he refuses to eat it alone, some oats may be mixed with it, in order to accustom him to it; lessening daily the quantity of the oats, till he eats the barley by itself. This should be repeated daily. He must have rest for some time, and be fed with the best hay, or grass, according to the season of the year. In spring, there there is nothing better than new grass, especially lu-

(*b*) *Tome I. p.* 238.

cerne;

cerne; and the quantity ſhould be proportioned to his degree of thriving. In about three weeks, he will begin to mend remarkably; and then he may be returned to his former food. In winter, when there is nothing but hay, it may be ſprinkled with water in which honey has been diſſolved, in ſuch proportion that he may take from half a pound to a pound of honey each day; and he ſhould likewiſe take daily at the ſame time one of the proportions of antimony before directed. Some add ſliced liquorice to the hay inſtead of honey. When the horſe begins to drink freely, it is a ſign that he is on the recovery."

Of the Surfeit and Mange.

The diſeaſe very improperly termed by us a *ſurfeit*, is a leſſer degree of what Vegetius *(i)* calls the *elephantiaſis*, from the reſemblance which the horſe's ſkin then bears to the hide of an elephant. The ſigns of it are, " a burning itch over the whole body, eſpecially in the back; it falls off in ſcales; inflamed pimples break out in the noſtrils, head, and feet; or rough and rugged ſores frequently ariſe. Theſe ſymptoms are preceded by a looſeneſs; the horſe grows lean, has a hard cough, and the mouth and tongue are rough and dry; yet his appetite does not fail him. This diſorder generally proves deſtructive to foals when they are weaned."

Quite ſimilar to the above is alſo Mr. Bartlet's deſcription of this diſeaſe. " A horſe, ſays he (*k*), is ſaid to be ſurfeited, when his coat ſtares and looks ruſty and dirty, though proper means have not been wanting to keep him clean: the ſkin is full of ſcales and dander, that lays thick and mealy among the hair, and is conſtantly ſupplied with a freſh ſucceſſion of the ſame. Some horſes have hurtles of various ſizes, like peas or tares: ſome have dry fixed ſcabs

(*i*) *Lib. I. c. ix.* (*k*) *Gentleman's Farriery, p.* 170.

all

all over their limbs and bodies; others a moiſture, attended with heat and inflammation; the humours being ſo ſharp, and violently itching, that the horſes rub ſo inceſſantly, as to make themſelves raw. Some have no eruptions at all, but an unwholeſome look, and are dull, ſluggiſh, and lazy; ſome appear only hide-bound; others have flying pains and lameneſs, reſembling a rheumatiſm: ſo that in the ſurfeits of horſes, we have almoſt all the different ſpecies of the ſcurvy, and other chronical diſtempers.

"The wet ſurfeit (*l*), which is no more than a moiſt running ſcurvy, appears on different parts of the body of a horſe, attended ſometimes with great heat and inflammation; the neck often ſwells ſo in one night's time, that great quantities of a hot briny humour iſſue forth, which, if not allayed, will be apt to collect on the poll or withers, and produce the poll-evil or fiſtula. This diſeaſe alſo frequently attacks the limbs, where it proves obſtinate, and hard to cure; and in ſome horſes it ſhews itſelf ſpring and fall."

Of this laſt kind ſeems alſo to be the diſeaſe which Vegetius, or at leaſt his tranſlator (*m*), terms the *farciminous diſtemper*. In this, the horſe's ſides and hips, his genitals and eſpecially his joints, together with, frequently his whole body, are ſubject to gatherings and ſwellings, and as faſt as they are aſſuaged or removed, others ſucceed. The horſe takes his meat and drink as uſual, but yet grows lean.

He remarks (*n*), that unſkilful artiſts are here in a hurry to take away blood; but that this method is repugnant to the diſtemper, becauſe it leſſens what ſtrength the horſe has left. He allows, indeed, that it may be of ſome ſervice in the beginning, to prevent an increaſe of the diſorder; or in the end, when the horſe's ſtrength begins to return; and he directs, that the blood taken away be mixed with vinegar, and the body rubbed with it.

(*l*) *Gent. Farr. p.* 173. (*m*) *Book I. c. vii.* (*n*) *Id. ib.*

The

The common practice however is to begin with bleeding, and then to open the body with a purging medicine.—From what has been said of sea-salt, sea-water appears to be here a very proper purge, and should therefore be made use of by those who are within reach of it. They who are not, may dissolve that salt in water, by boiling them together. If it is given warm, the water may then suspend a sufficient quantity, viz. two ounces; but if it is suffered to cool, the salt will subside. Glauber salt may be given for the same purpose, with the addition of two drams of jalap to quicken it, and repeated once a week, or as often as necessary. The horse should take daily, either the antimony prepared with nitre, or the æthiops mineral; and his food should be green grass, especially lucerne, if the season permits.

If the disorder does not give way to this method, recourse may be had to some mercurial application externally. The most effectual in all cutaneous eruptions is a solution of corrosive sublimate in brandy, a pint of which will suspend half an ounce of the sublimate; and the solution may be weakened by the addition of water, to any degree found necessary; though this will seldom be required. The skin should be quite cleared of scurf and scales before the solution is rubbed on the parts affected. In order to soften scabs or scales which adhere, they should be well anointed with any ointment mixed with flower of brimstone; for this is found to be of singular efficacy in all eruptions.

In a *mangy* horse, the skin is generally thick and full of wrinkles, especially about the mane, the loins, and the tail; and the little hair that remains in those parts stands almost always strait out, or is bristly: the ears are commonly naked and without hair; the eye and eye-brows are the same; and when it affects the limbs, it gives them the same aspect: yet the skin is not raw, nor does it peel off, as in the hot inflamed surfeit (*o*).

(*o*) *Bartlet*, *p.* 174.

Where

Where this distemper has been caught by infection, it is very easily cured, if taken in time; and I would recommend the sulphur ointment as most effectual for that purpose, rubbed in every day. The way of making it is thus: Take live sulphur, or flowers of the same, half a pond, crude sal ammoniac one ounce, and hogs-lard a sufficient quantity to form into an ointment. To purify the blood, give antimony finely powdered and sulphur, before rubbing, and for some time after; or, in place of that, the æthiops mineral.

When this disorder is owing to poverty of blood, the diet must be mended, and the horse properly indulged with hay and corn.

Nearly a-kin to the foregoing disorders are *mallanders*, *grease*, *scratches*, *crown-scab*, and such like complaints. The remedy for these, says Mr. Osmer (p), is warm fomentations applied to the parts; good rubbing of the limbs is also necessary; and a poultice made of rye-meal and milk is a proper application to sore heels. Sometimes, the habit of body requires being altered; in which case, such of the alterative medicines before directed (*q*) as are suited to the disorders, or general temperament of the body, will be found serviceable. In superficial sores discharging an acrid thin ichor, the solution of sublimate applied to the part, at the removal of the poultices, has sometimes very good effects: and if the fungus has risen high, the knife, or a caustic, is much easier and better than the acid spirits used by farriers.

Mr. Osmer (*r*) instances a very strong proof of the great efficacy of sea-water in cases of this kind, when, speaking from his own observation and inquiry, he assures us, that the horses which are constantly used at Margate, in Kent, to draw people who want to bathe, a little way out into the sea, in a machine contrived for that purpose, and which are accustomed

(*p*) *Page* 185. (*q*) *See p.* (*r*) *Page* 186.

to

to ſtand in the ſalt water almoſt every day, for four, five, or ſix hours together, are ſure to be cured of whatſoever ulcers or cutaneous diſorders they might have when they firſt ſat about this work; at leaſt in all ſuch parts as the water can reach.

Of the Farcy.

The diſtinguiſhing mark of the *Farcy* is a cording of the veins, and the appearance of ſmall tumours in ſeveral parts of the body.

Mr. Bartlet (*s*) deems this diſtemper eaſy of cure when it appears on the head only, and eſpecially when it is ſeated in the cheeks and forehead; becauſe the blood veſſels there are ſmall: but he holds it to be more difficult when it affects the lips, the noſtrils, the eyes, and the kernels under the jaws, and other ſoft and looſe parts, eſpecially if the neck-vein becomes corded. When the farcy begins on the outſide of the ſhoulder or hip, the cure is ſeldom difficult: but when it riſes on the plate-vein, and that vein ſwells much and becomes corded, and when the glands or kernels under the arm-pit are affected, it is hard to cure; but ſtill more ſo when the crural veins in the inſide of the thigh are corded, and beſet with buds, as they are here called, meaning ſmall tumours, which affect the kernels of the groin, and the cavernous body of the yard. When the farcy begins on the paſterns or lower limbs, it often becomes very uncertain of cure, unleſs a ſtop be put to it in time; for the ſwelling in thoſe dependent parts grows ſo exceſſively large in ſome conſtitutions, and the limbs are ſo much disfigured thereby with foul ſores and callous ulcerations, that ſuch a horſe is ſeldom afterwards fit for any thing but the meaneſt drudgery: but it is always a promiſing ſign, whereever the farcy happens to be ſituated, if it ſpreads no

(*s*) *Page* 179.

farther. It uſually affects only one ſide at a time; but when it paſſes over to the other, it ſhews great malignity: when it ariſes on the ſpines, it is for the moſt part dangerous, and is always more ſo to horſes that are fat and full of blood, than to thoſe that are in a moderate caſe. When the farcy is epidemical, as ſometimes happens, it riſes on ſeveral parts of the body at once, forms naſty foul ulcers, and makes a profuſe running of greeniſh bloody matter from both noſtrils; and ſoon ends in a miſerable rot." Mr. Oſmer thinks it contagious.

M. Bourgelat ſays (t), that a decoction of the woods, *viz.* guaiacum and ſaſſafras, antimony, powder of vipers, with ſome mercurial preparations, are looked upon as ſo many ſpecifics in this diſeaſe. He alſo confirms a fact related in the Philoſophical Tranſactions, that hemlock, when green, or in powder in the winter, will cure it, even when its bad appearance outwardly ſeems not to leave any proſpect of ſucceſs. Mr. Markham recommends the roots of the cotton broad white leaved thiſtle cut in ſhives, and given with oats, as a remedy that will heal without all fail, if it be given conſtantly for three weeks.

Mr. Oſmer (u) adviſes, that "when ſwellings fall on any part, which is no uncommon ſymptom in this diſorder, a poultice made with an emollient fomentation, thickened with oatmeal, be applied twice a day; and when the ſkin breaks, or buds of ſprouting fleſh appear on any part, ſuch are to be touched with a rag dipt in corroſive ſpirit of ſalt, ſtrong ſpirit of nitre, aqua fortis, or any ſuch kind of medicine."—I cannot help thinking, that a dry cauſtic, which is more eaſily kept within bounds, is a better application.

Whatever method of cure is followed, it is adviſeable to begin with bleeding, and ſome cooling

(t) *'Ecole, Vétérinaire, Matiére Médicale, p.* 135.

(u) *Page* 185.

physic,

physic, giving the alterative medicine on the intermediate days. Long practice has given antimony the preference to almost every other medicine: but perhaps the æthiops mineral is rather more efficacious, as appears by the cases mentioned in the article of Glanders. Sulphur is also recommended to be added to the antimony. Whatever mercurial preparation is administered here, it should be given only as an alterative. Turbith, which Mr. Gibson recommends, is sometimes very violent in it's operations, and what is very remarkable, the dose given makes very little difference in the operation, as six grains will operate on a man as violently as thirty. A physical gentleman, worthy of credit, assures me, that the larger dose is sometimes the mildest in it's operation, especially if given in a bolus with balsam Tolu; and yet though mild in it's operation, is sometimes very efficacious in the cure of venereal eruptions or ulcers. Whether the same may happen in the farcy, may be a matter of future experiment. Soap, or any alkali, decomposes it, and reduces it to the state of quicksilver.

When, by improper applications, or through neglect, a farcy has spread, increased, and long resisted the medicines above recommended; if fresh buds are continually sprouting forth, while the old ones remain foul and ill-conditioned; if they rise on the spines of the back and loins; if the horse grows hide-bound, and runs at the nose; if abscesses are formed in the fleshy parts between the interstices of the large muscles; if his eyes look dead and lifeless; if he forsakes his food, and scours often, and his excrements appear thin and of a blackish colour; if the plate or thigh-vein continues large and corded after firing, and other proper applications; these symtoms, as Mr. Bartlet very properly remarks (*x*), denote the distemper to have penetrated internally,

(*x*) *Page* 197.

and that it will degenerate into an incurable consumption: it is alſo moſt probable, that the whole maſs of fluids is ſo vitiated, as to be beyond the power of art to remedy.—Cuſtom has improperly given the name of *water-farcy* to dropſical complaints. Theſe may be either an *aſcites*, or other water contained in the belly; an *anaſarca*, or water contained in the adipoſe membrane all over the body; or diſtinct watry tumours in particular parts of the body. In caſe the water is contained in the belly, Vegetius(y) adviſes to tap the horſe, as is practiſed on man, and let the water out by a pipe. After the water is drawn off, he directs that ſome grains of ſalt be put into the wound, to prevents it's healing up; and that on the ſecond or third day the pipe be again introduced, to draw off the remaining water, till the parts are dry. In the anaſarca, the back, the ſides, and often the whole body, are inflated, as well as the belly. In this caſe, ſlight ſcarifications on the inſide of the legs and thighs, and in the ſkin of the belly, on each ſide of the ſheath, will often carry off that load of water in a ſpeedy and ſurpriſing manner. Similar ſcarifications will alſo relieve the œdematous ſwellings in particular parts of the body.

While theſe operations are performed externally, internal medicines are alſo neceſſary, to carry off any remains of the diſorder, both by urine and ſtool. For this purpoſe, half an ounce of jalap well rubbed with an ounce of nitre, and given in a ball, is very proper, and on the intermediate days the following decoction: Take one ounce of nitre, two drams of ſquills in powder, inner bark of elder and chamomile flowers, of each a handful, and two ounces of juniper-berries; boil them in a quart of water, and give a pint of this night and morning. Vegetius recommends radiſhes with their leaves to be given as food, becauſe they will both purge and warm the

(y) *Lib. II. c. xxv.*

blood.

blood. The cure may be completed by giving ſuch things as the following ball and decoction to ſtrengthen the body. Take an ounce of Jeſuits bark, and half an ounce of filings of iron, and make them into two balls, to be taken night and morning, drinking after each a pint of the following decoction. Take gentian and zedoary of each half an ounce, chamomile flowers and centuary, of each an handful, of juniper-berries pounded, a handful; boil them in a quantity of water ſufficient to yield a quart of ſtrained liquor.

Vegetius (z) ſpeaks of the *Tympany* as a diſeaſe incident to horſes. The belly of the animal ſwells like that of one affected with the dropſy, and his neck becomes ſtiffer than uſual; but neither his teſticles nor his legs ſwell. He adviſes, to anoint the belly with hot aſhes and melted ſuet, to ſwathe the horſe with bandages, and to give him warm drinks in wine and oil.

SECT. VIII.

Of Diſorders of the Feet.

LAMENESS is often brought on horſes by a falſe ſtep, which, when neglected, renders the ligaments of the nut-bone uſeleſs, and the cartilages become oſſified. An inflammation from this cauſe is diſtinguiſhed by a ſwelling on the coronet, and a great pain when the finger is puſhed againſt it.

In this caſe, the beſt way is to pare the outer ſide till it becomes thin and flexible, to pare alſo the cruſt or the hoof down as low as poſſible, ſo that every part be thin, even until the foot bleeds, and then

(z) *Lib. III. c. xxvii.*

to uſe emollient fomentations and poultices round the foot and coronet, by which means the inflamed parts will be relieved, when the thickneſs and ſtricture of the cruſt has been taken away.

This ſhews how rightly ſportſmen act, when, to prevent the inflammation, and guard againſt the induration and enlargement of the ligamentous parts, and of the integuments of the fetlock joint, the conſequence of repeating violence, they cauſe the joints of the horſe, after hard riding, to be well fomented with flannels dipt in warm water, or a decoction of emollient herbs, and then ſome warm flannel cloths or rollers to be moderately bound thereon for the enſuing night, and afterwards to be treated as directed for ſtrains.

When any extraneous body, ſuch as a nail, thorn gravel, &c. has paſſed into a horſe's foot, it ſhould be got out as ſoon as poſſible, and the foot ſhould then be covered with a poultice or other mild application: but if it be ſuſpected, from the degree of pain, or diſcharge of matter, that any thing remains behind, the ſole ſhould be pared as thin as poſſible, and the hole ſhould be enlarged, that it may be drawn out with a pair of pincers, or be diſcharged by digeſtion. If this ſhould not ſucceed, but the lameneſs continues, with a diſcharge of thin, bloody, or ſtinking matter, the wound muſt be opened to the bottom, and then dreſſed with a warm digeſtive. The ſame directions ſhould be followed when the foot has been pricked in ſhoeing.

If the nail penetrats to the joint of the foot, where matter may be formed, and by it's long continuance putrify, ſo as to erode the cartilages of the joint, the caſe is incurable: and ſo it likewiſe is if the nail has paſſed up to the nut-bone, becauſe this little bone cannot exfoliate, and the cartilaginous part of it is deſtroyed the moment it is injured.

If any extraneous body has brought on great inflammation, ſo that a ſuppuration muſt enſue, the ſole ſhould

ſhould be ſo far opened as to give free vent to the matter; or, if the pain increaſes, the ſole muſt be drawn; but this ſhould never be without manifeſt neceſſity.

A *ſand-crack*, as it is called, is a cleft on the outſide of the hoof. If it remains a ſtraight line downwards, and penetrates through the boney part of the hoof, it is difficult to cure; but if it paſſes through the ligament that unites the hoof with the coronet, it is apt to cauſe a ſuppuration under the hoof, which is very dangerous. When the crack only penetrates the hoof, without touching the ligament, it may eaſily be cured, by raſping the edges ſmooth, and then applying a mild digeſtive: but if there is a hollow under the hoof, the hoof muſt be raſped away as far as the hollow reaches on all ſides.

A *quittor* is an abſceſs formed between the hair and the hoof, uſually on the inſide quarter of a horſe's foot. It often ariſes from treads or bruiſes, or from gravel lodged about the coronet. If it is ſuperficial, it is eaſily cured: but if the matter forms itſelf a lodgment under the hoof, part of the hoof muſt be taken away. If the quarter of the hoof is taken away, the foot ſeldom gets quite ſound again. If, by the lodgment of the matter, the coffin or footbone is injured, the opening muſt be enlarged, and the fleſh deſtroyed, ſo that the bone may exfoliate, as before directed in the cure of ulcers with caries. During the cure, the foot ſhould be kept very eaſy by ſoft applications; and care ſhould be taken not to ſuffer the riſing of proud fleſh, becauſe this would prevent a firm and ſound healing.

Mr. Oſmer (*a*) directs, as a proper method of proceeding when the criſis of a fever falls on the feet, on this or any other occaſion, to cut them off round and ſhort at the toe, till the blood appears, and with a drawing-knife to ſcore the hoof all round longitu-

(*a*) *Page* 160.

dinally, at proper diſtances, quite to the quick, beginning a little below the coronary ring, and continuing on to the end of the foot or toe; becauſe by this means the new hoof will be the more at liberty to puſh itſelf out, and the matter to be diſcharged. The parts ſhould be dreſſed with ſome unctuous medicine, and the whole foot wrapped up with an emollient poultice. By theſe means, he ſays, the feet will often become as good and as ſound as ever.

He remarks farther on this method of ſcoring the foot longitudinally, that it is of late come much into practice, with an intent to cure lameneſs ariſing from the contracted form of the foot; and that this, together with the horſe's being turned to graſs, does in fact expand the foot for a time; but that when theſe ſcorings are quite grown out, and the horſe is taken to houſe, the foot ſo treated ſoon returns again to its primitive natural contracted ſtate, and he becomes as lame as he was before.

When, in conſequence of great inflammation, tending to ſuppuration, it is abſolutely neceſſary to draw the ſole, as is ſometimes the caſe, the foot ſhould be ſuffered to bleed: or if the ſole be ſo looſened by an impoſthumation as to fall off from the bone, in either of theſe caſes, on the removal of the hoof, a boot of leather, with a ſtrong ſole, ſhould be laced about the paſtern, bolſtering the foot with ſoft flax, that the tread may be eaſy. The fungus is to be kept down, and the cure to be compleated as already directed.

SECT. IX.

Of Venomous Bites.

I CANNOT here do better than quote what may relate to this ſubject, from the learned Dr. Mead's Treatiſe on the bite of a mad dog (*a*).

" I am of opinion, ſays that great phyſician, that the wound ſhould be enlarged, and dreſſed with black baſilicon, adding thereto a ſmall quantity of red precipitate as a digeſtive; for it may be of advantage to have a drain continued from the part.

" There are two or three internal remedies recommended I think upon rational grounds. The firſt is, the aſhes of the river craw-fiſh. Theſe were prepared by burning the fiſh alive upon a copper-plate, with a fire made of the cuttings of twigs of the white briony. A large ſpoonful or two of the calcined powder was given every day for forty days together, either alone, or mixed with a ſmall portion of gentian root and frankincenſe.

" Another medicine is the ſponge of the dog-roſe, which is celebrated as an antidote againſt this and other animal poiſons. The plant alyſſum, or madwort, had its name given it by the antients, from its great efficacy againſt this madneſs. To them may be added garlic, agrimony, and oxylapathum.

" Now it is remarkable that all theſe remedies are powerful diuretics, and the ſureſt remedies in all ages againſt this venom have been ſuch as provoke a great diſcharge by urine. Reflecting upon this, I thought it might be right to give to the public a courſe eaſily to be purſued, which, by preventing the fever for a long

(*a*) *The Medical Works of Dr. Richard Mead,* 4*to edit.* 1762, *p.* 86.

long time after the bite, and constantly provoking this evacuation, might secure the patient from danger. The method is this:

" Let the patient [we will here suppose the horse] be blooded plentifully. Take of the herb ash-coloured ground liverwort *(lichen cinereus terrestris)* cleaned, dried, and powdered, two ounces (half an ounce for a man), and of black pepper powdered an ounce; mix these well together, and divide the powder into four doses, one of which must be taken every morning fasting, for four mornings successively, in half a pint of cow's milk warm. After these four doses are taken, the horse must be plunged into cold water every morning fasting for a month. After this he must be put in three times a week for a fortnight longer. Salt-water, where it can be conveniently come at, is preferred for the purpose of bathing."

The following mercurial method having been found successful both in dogs and men, Mr. Bartlet, with very great propriety, recommends it for horses, and indeed thinks it more to be depended on than most others. Dr. James's account of it to the Royal Society, from which Mr. Bartlet's is borrowed, is to the following effect *(a)*.

" About Michaelmas 1731, Mr. Floyer, of Hampshire, complained to Dr. James, that he was afraid of a madness among his fox-hounds; for that morning one had run mad in his kennel: upon which the Doctor told him, he had believed that mercury would, if tried, prove the best remedy against this infection. Mr. Floyer neglected this advice till the February following; and in the mean time tried the medicine in Bates's Dispensary, commonly known by the name of the pewter-medicine, as also every thing else that was recommended to him by other sportsmen, but to no purpose; for some of his hounds ran mad almost every day after hunting.

(a) Bartlet, p. 318, and Philosophical Transactions, No.

Upon

Upon this he took his hounds to the sea, and had every one of them dipt into the salt water; and at his return he carried his dogs to another gentleman's kennel, six miles distant from his own. Yet notwithstanding this precaution, he lost six or seven couple of dogs in a fortnight's time. At length, in February, Mr. Floyer tried the experiment which the Doctor had recommended, upon two hounds that were mad, and both very far gone. They refused food of all sorts, particularly fluids, slavered much, and had all the symptoms of a hydrophobia to a great degree: that night he gave to each of the two dogs twelve grains of turpeth mineral, which vomited and purged them gently: twenty-four hours after this, he gave to each of them twenty-four grains, and after the same interval, he gave forty-eight more to each: the dogs salivated very much, and soon after lapped warm milk: at the end of twenty-four hours more, he repeated to one dog twenty-four grains more, and omitted it to the other; the dog that took this last dose, lay upon the ground, salivated extremely, was in great agonies, and had all the symptoms of a salivation raised too high; but got through it: the other relapsed and died.

"To all the rest of the pack he gave seven grains of turpeth for the first dose, twelve for the second dose, at twenty-four hours distance, which was repeated every other day for some little time. The method was repeated, at the two or three succeeding fulls and changes of the moon: from this time he lost not another hound; and though several afterwards were bit by strange dogs, the turpeth always prevented any ill consequences.

"The Doctor and his friends tried the same thing upon a great many dogs, and it never failed in any one instance; though dogs bit at the same time, and by the same dogs, ran mad, after most other medicines had been tried." The same me-

thod

thod may very properly, as Mr. Bartlet obſerves, be practiſed in giving this medicine to a horſe, only increaſing the quantity to two ſcruples, or half a drachm each doſe.

The following recipe has long been in great eſteem, and is thought by ſome to be an infalliable cure for the bite of a mad dog. Indeed it cannot but be of ſervice in all venomous bites.

" Take ſix ounces of rue; Venice treacle, garlic, and tin ſcraped, of each four ounces; boil them in two quarts of ale over a gentle fire to the conſumption of half; ſtrain the liquor off from the ingredients, and give the horſe four or five ounces of it every morning faſting."

The ingredients may be beaten together in a mortar, and applied daily to the wound as a poultice.

Horſes, when feeding or lying down, may offend poiſonous creatures, and are therefore liable to be bit or ſtung by them. Of theſe the viper is the moſt frequent in this country, and that whoſe bite is the moſt dangerous. Whatever will cure it's bite will therefore cure any leſs venomous one. For this reaſon, I ſhall here again take Dr. Mead for my guide. That excellent phyſician lays great ſtreſs on ſucking the wound; but that cannot well be done in a horſe. The cupping-glaſs ſeems the next ſuccedaneum; though the Doctor ſeems to hint that the ſpittle has ſome ſhare in the cure; and remarks, that whoever ſucks the wound, ought to was his mouth well before-hand with warm oil, and hold ſome of this in his mouth while the ſuction is performing, to prevent any inflammation of the lips and tongue by the heat of the poiſon.

" To confirm this practice," continues the Doctor, " I have been aſſured by an ingenious ſurgeon, who lived in Virginia, that the Indians there cure the bite of the rattle-ſnake by ſucking the wound, and taking immediately a large quantity of a decoction

tion of Seneca rattle-snake root, which vomits plentifully, and laying to the part the same root chewed.

"As to any other external management, I think it can avail but little; since it cannot prevent the sudden communication of the poison to the nerves.

Burning the part with a hot iron is of no use. Dry salt upon the wound, recommended by Celsus, promises somewhat more; and not much more is to be said of the remedy of our viper-catchers, in which they place so much confidence, as to be no more afraid of a bite than of a common puncture. This is no other than the *expungia viperina* (fat of vipers) rubbed into the wound;"—of the good effects of which he, however, then gives some instances. ——Some writers conclude, that the efficacy of this application arises only from it's unctuous quality, and that therefore oil will have the effect. I do not know that this has yet been sufficiently ascertained: but when there is no viper's fat at hand, it is surely worth trial.

Dr. Mead adds (*c*), that if the patient [read here the horse] be faint and otherwise disordered, he should be wrapped up warm, and made to take some cordial medicines, particularly about an ounce of Raleigh's confection, and a drachm of salt of vipers, or for want of this, of salt of hartshorn, given in warm wine. A very good remedy in this case likewise is, as Mr. Bartlet advises (*d*), where it can be afforded for a horse, half an ounce of musk, and as much cinnabar, so strongly recommended in bites of poisonons animals.

Vegetius (*e*) gives the following signs of a horse's having been wounded by a poisonous animal. He loaths his food, drags his feet, and when brought forth, he lies or falls down at every step, a corrupted matter flows from his nostrils, there is a weight and heaviness in his head, so that he hangs it down

(*c*) *Page* 46. (*d*) *Page* 317. (*e*) *Lib.* III. *c. lxxvii.*

to

to the ground, and the ſtrength of his whole body fails, corrupted matter iſſues out of the wound, and if the viper be pregnant, the horſe's whole body breaks out, and ſwells ſo as to be like to burſt.

The uſe of oil externally, in caſes of this kind, was well known to the antients, and certainly is very right.

Horſes, in drinking, ſometimes ſwallow leeches, which may faſten on the fauces, or in the æſophagus, ſo as to be out of reach; and in this caſe it is adviſed to pour warm oil down the throat, as a means of making them quit their hold. They may alſo ſwallow ſpiders in their hay, or other venomous creatures, hen's dung, &c. which, Vegetius ſays (*f*), will ſoon occaſion great pain in the inward parts, an inflammation of the belly, a tumbling with violent gripes, and a harſh cough. To remedy this, he directs, to bruiſe two ounces of parſley-ſeed, and mix it with a pint of old wine and half a pint of honey, to be poured down the horſe's throat; afterwards walking him gently about till this moves his belly. If the violence of the pain ſhould occaſion a ſwelling in any part of the body, or a ſtiffneſs of the joints and limbs, take a pound of bay-berries, half a pound of nitre, a quart of vinegar, and apint of oil, mix and warm them upon the fire, and anoint him with it in a warm place, rubbing him heartily againſt the hair. This repeated for three days, will, by making him ſweat, certainly cure him, ſays Vegetius.

(*f*) *Lib. III. c. lxxvi.*

SECT.

SECT. X.

Of the Arthritis.

VEGETIUS (*a*) gives the following description of a disease in horses similar to the *rheumatism* in men. The horse will be lame in his joints, as if he had received some injury on them, with this difference, that a hurt is fixed to a place, but in this ailment he will be lame sometimes in his fore, and sometimes in his hind-feet, the coronets and knees will be sometimes swelled, or the skin be bound fast to the bones, the spine becomes stiff, his hair stands on end, and he grows careless of his food.

He orders, "that blood be taken away from the neck, then thoroughly mixed with very sharp vinegar, and the horse's body, especially where the pain is, to be well rubbed therewith. Blood should also be taken from the veins nearest to the parts affected, and this, after being mixed with vinegar, cummin-seed, salt, &c. is also to be rubbed wherever there appears a tumour. Then take centuary, wormwood, sow-fennel, mother of thyme, betony, saxifrage, round birthwort, and saggapen, of each equal quantities, which reduce to powder. Give a large spoonful of the powder every day in a draught of warm water, if the horse is feverish, or in a pint of wine if he is free from a fever."

He likewise describes a distemper which he thinks analagous to the *gout* in man (*b*). "The horse, in this case, can neither stand nor walk, and if he is compelled to move, he hobbles, and often throws himself down. By reason of this pain he does not digest his food, and therefore becomes ill-favoured;

(*a*) *Lib. I. c. vi. b. xiii.* (*b*) *Lib. II. c. viii.*

his

his body will be hot, his veins ſwelled, his yard hanging down, and his dung will ſtick to his feet, becauſe of his too great heat.——He orders repeated bleedings in ſmall quantities, and gentle exerciſe in a dry place till the horſe ſweats, and rubbing. Let his drink be warm water mixed with powdered nitre and wheat-meal: let him be purged, to carry off the noxious humours; and give him green graſs for his food, or, if this be wanting, hay ſprinkled with nitre. Give him alſo an infuſion of the flower of frankincenſe in wine, half a pint for three mornings running. If none of theſe things are of benefit to him, let him be gelded, and he will be free from his diſtemper, for the gout ſeldom afflicts eunuchs."

S E C T. XI.

Of Gelding.

I Place this operation here, becauſe the performing of it generally falls to the lot of the farrier or horſe-doctor. It is attended with very little danger whilſt horſes are young. The legs of the creature intended to be caſtrated are tied with ropes, he is then thrown on his back, and the ſcrotum, or purſe, is opened lengthwiſe with an inciſion-knife, ſo that the ſpermatic cord or veſſels are laid bare. The teſticles being then turned out, a thread well waxed, and preſſed a little flattiſh, that it may not cut through, is tied round the ſpermatic cord, and the teſticle is cut off, leaving about a quarter of an inch of the cord below the ligature. The whole is then dreſſed up with dry lint, and over all is put a large pledget of tow covered with any ointment, that the ſcrotum may remain in a ſoft and eaſy ſituation. If no accident happens, it need not be looked at till the third

third or fourth day, when the ſore will be digeſted, and it ſhould then be dreſſed every day till the ligature falls off, after which it is to be cured as a common wound. In old ſtallions this operation is ſometimes attended with inflammation, &c. in which caſe it is to be treated as before directed for an inflammatory wound. 'Twere needleſs to obſerve, that the horſe ſhould be kept on a cooling diet during the whole of this time.

The moſt proper ſeaſons for performing this operation are ſpring and autumn; great heat and great cold being equally unfavourable: and with regard to age, in ſome countries horſes are caſtrated when they are not above a year, or eighteen months old, or as ſoon as the teſticles are clearly diſcernible on the outſide; but the moſt general practice is, not to caſtrate them till they are two, or even three years old, and this ſome think the moſt judicious way, becauſe the later they are caſtrated, the more they retain of the maſculine qualities; for it is certain that this operation diminiſhes conſiderably their ſtrength, ſpirit, and courage: but on the other hand they derive from it mildneſs, docility, and tractableneſs.

The Perſians, Arabians, and ſeveral other nations of the Eaſt, never caſtrate their horſes: but geldings are as common in China as they are in Europe.

SECT. XII.

Of Shoeing.

THIS being alſo a part of the farrier's buſineſs, it may not be improper to obſerve here, that, as the only intention in ſhoeing horſes is to add ſtrength to the hoof, and to prevent its being worn away by ſtones, grit, &c. eſpecially upon hard roads, it is ſufficient that the ſhoe be wide enough to defend the horny part, or rim of the hoof, beyond which it ſhould not project, and to admit of being faſtened on firmly with proper nails. By this means there being no hollow between the ſhoe and the hoof, the horſe will be leſs apt to pick up ſtones than he is with the broad ſhoes generally uſed. Care ſhould alſo be taken not to pare away any more of the hoof than what is ragged and damaged, and conſequently always to leave a ſufficient breadth for the nails to go into without pricking the quick; an accident by which numbers of horſes are lamed, and ſometimes inflammations are brought on, which ſeparate the whole hoof from the foot, juſt as a whitlow will take the nail off from a finger or toe. For theſe inſtructions I am indebted to an eminent officer of our cavalry, all the horſes of whoſe regiment are ſhod upon the above principles.

BOOK II.

OF ASSES.

FAR from deſerving the contempt in which he is generally held, the *Aſs* is, in fact, one of the moſt neceſſary animals about a farm-houſe: he coſts hardly any thing to keep, and does a great deal of work, ſuch as carrying corn to the mill, proviſions to the market, or to labourers in the field, with numberleſs other uſeful offices; for, in proportion to his ſize, he will carry a heavier load than perhaps any other animal. In ſome countries too he is made to till the ground where the ſoil is light, to draw a cart, and even to ſerve inſtead of a horſe for riding poſt: nor

nor is there any more easy going, or surer-footed creature. The milk of the female is an excellent medicine to man, particularly in consumptive and gouty cases; and the skin of these animals is rendered serviceable and profitable, after they are dead; for of it, being very hard and very elastic, are made drums, sieves, &c. The merit of the ass's-skin pocket-books is well known; and in many parts the peasants make good strong shoes of the tanned skin of the ass's back. It it also with the hinder part of the ass's skin that the Orientals make the *Sagri* (*a*), which we call Shagreen †. The dung of asses is an excellent manure for strong or moist lands.

Is it then, as M. de Buffon compassionately asks on this occasion (*c*), that men extend their contempt of those who serve them too well and too cheaply, even to animals? The horse, continues he, is trained up, great care is taken of him, he is instructed and exercised; whilst the poor ass, left to the brutality of the meanest servant and the wantonness of children, instead of improving, cannot but be a loser by his education. Most certainly, if he had not a large fund of good qualities, the manner in which he is treated would be sufficient to exhaust them all. He is the sport, the butt, the drudge of clowns, who, without the least thought or concern, drive him along with a cudgel, beating, over-loading, and tiring him. It is not remembered, that the ass would be, both in himself and for us, the most useful, the most beautiful, and most distinguished of animals, if there were no horse in the world: he is the second, instead of being the first, and for that alone he is looked upon as nothing: it is the comparison that degrades him: he is considered, he is judged of, not in him-

(*a*) See *Thevenot's Travels, Tom. II. p.* 64.

† The best is made with the skin that covers the rump and buttocks of the wild ass. It is prepared in Syria, and comes to us from Constantinople.

(*c*) *Histoire Naturelle de l'Asne.*

 self,

ſelf, but relatively to the horſe: we forget that he is an aſs; that he has all the qualities of his nature, all the gifts annexed to his ſpecies, and think only on the figure and qualities of the horſe, which are wanting in him, and which he could not have without ceaſing to be an aſs.

By his natural temper he is as humble, as patient, and as quiet, as the horſe is proud, fiery, and impetuous: he bears with firmneſs, and perhaps with courage, blows and chaſtiſements: he is ſober both with regard to the quantity, and the quality of his food, contenting himſelf with the harſheſt and moſt diſagreeable herbs, which the horſe and other animals diſdain to touch. In water, indeed, he is very nice, drinking only of that which is perfectly clear, and at brooks he is acquainted with: he is as temperate in his drinking as in his eating, and does not plunge his noſe into the water, from a fear, as is ſaid (*d*), of ſeeing the ſhadow of his ears; and to this alſo ſome, with great ſeeming reaſon, impute his being leſs ſubject to the glanders than the horſe, as was before obſerved in treating of that animal *. As no one beſtows

(*d*) *Cardanus, de Subtilitate, l. x.*

* Quadrupeds do not all drink in the ſame manner, though all are under the like neceſſity of ſtooping their heads to the water, becauſe they cannot otherwiſe reach it; the monkey and ſome few others excepted, which, having hands, can drink like a man out of a veſſel given them; for they put it to their mouth, and, inclining the veſſel, pour out the liquor, which they ſwallow merely by the motion of deglutition. The dog, the aperture of whoſe mouth is very large, and furniſhed with a long and ſlender tongue, drinks by lapping; that is, licking up the water, and forming with his tongue a cup, which being filled every time, brings up a pretty large quantity of liquor: this method he prefers to that of wetting his noſe: whereas the horſe, having a leſs mouth, and his tongue too thick and ſhort to form a large cup, and which, beſides, drinks eagerly, thruſts his noſe to ſome depth into the water, which he thus ſwallows plentifully by the ſimple motion of deglutition. But this very circumſtance obliges him to drink all at a breath; whereas the dog breathes freely all the time he drinks; and ſo does likewiſe the aſs, who only juſt touches the water with his lips.

ſtows upon him the pains of currying, he often rolls himſelf on the graſs, on thiſtles, or on fern; and, without minding his load, he lies down to roll as often as he has an opportunity, as if to reproach his maſter with the little care taken of him; for he does not welter like the horſe in mud and water, but is cautious even of wetting his feet, and turns aſide to avoid any dirt: accordingly, his legs are dryer and more cleanly than thoſe of the horſe. He is ſuſceptible of education †, and ſome have been trained in ſuch a manner as to be ſhewn for a curioſity (g). Regular currying and rubbing down would undoubtedly much improve the look of the aſs, and be of ſervice to its health.

In his early youth he is ſprightly, and not void of prettineſs, agility, and good humour; but he ſoon loſes theſe good qualities, either through age or ill treatment, and becomes ſluggiſh, untractable, and obſtinate; eager only for pleaſure, or rather ſo mad after it, that nothing can reſtrain him; nay, ſome have been known to be ſo violent, as to die within a few minutes after copulation; and as his love is a kind of frenzy, ſo he has alſo the ſtrongeſt affection for his iſſue. Pliny aſſures us, that if the dam be ſeparated from her foal, ſhe will ruſh through flames of fire to rejoin it. The aſs is alſo fond of his maſter, though generally ill-treated by him; he ſmells him at a great diſtance, and diſtinguiſhes him from every other man: he likewiſe knows again the places where he has been uſed to live, and the roads which

† In Perſia they are taught to amble; to which purpoſe the fore and hind legs of the ſame ſide are tied together with cotton lines, at a greater or leſs diſtance aſunder, according to the ſtep the creature is to make in ambling. Theſe lines are faſtened to the girth at the place of the ſtirrup: a ſort of grooms ride them morning and evening, and habituate them to this pace. Their noſtrils are ſlit to give them the more wind, and they go at ſuch a rate that there is no keeping up with them but on a gallop. *Voyages des Chev. Chardin, Tom. II. p.* 26, 27.

(g) *Aldrovand, de Quadruped. ſoliped. lib. I. p.* 308.

he has travelled. His ſight is ſtrong, and his ſmell is ſurprizingly quick, eſpecially with regard to the effluiva of the ſhe-aſs: he is very quick of hearing, which has contributed to his having been ranked among the timid animals, who are all ſaid to be very quick of hearing, and to have long ears. When over-loaded he hangs down his head and drops his ears; when too much vexed, he opens his mouth and draws back his lips in a very diſagreeable manner, which gives him a ſneering and deriſory aſpect. If his eyes are covered, he ſtands motionleſs; and when lying on his ſide, if his head is placed in ſuch a manner that one eye reſts on the ground, and the other eye be covered with a ſtone, or piece of wood, he will continue in that poſture without ſhaking himſelf, or attempting to riſe. Like the horſe, he walks, trots, and gallops; but all his motions are ſhort and and much ſlower: though he may run at firſt with ſome ſwiftneſs, he can do ſo but for a little way and a ſhort time; and whatever pace he takes, he ſoon gives over, if hurried.

The horſe neighs, and the aſs brays, which laſt is done by a very long and highly diſagreeable and diſcordant cry through alternate diſſonances, from the grave to the acute, and from the acute to the grave. He hardly ever makes this noiſe but when ſtimulated by luſt or by hunger. The voice of the ſhe-aſs is clearer and ſhriller than that of the male. A caſtrated aſs brays but weakly; and though he ſeems to make the ſame efforts, and has the ſame motions with the throat, his cry does not reach to any great diſtance *. Of all hairy animals, the aſs is the leaſt ſubject

* That judicious inveſtigator of the works of nature, M. de Buffon, thinks it a rule without exception, that in all quadruped animals, the voice of the male is ſtronger and deeper than that of the female; though ſome of the antients tell us, that that the cow, the ox, and even the calf, have a deeper voice than the bull. Certain it is, that the bull has a far ſtronger

ſubject to vermin: he is never troubled witih lice, propably owing to the hardneſs and dryneſs of his ſkin, which is indeed harder than that of moſt other quadrupeds; and this alſo renders him leſs ſenſible than the horſe, to the whip, and the ſtinging of flies.

At the end of two years and a half the aſs ſheds his foal-teeth, and next the other inciſories, which dropt out, and are renewed in the ſame order as thoſe of the horſe. The age of an aſs is alſo known by the teeth; and the third of the inciſories, on each ſide, is denoted as in the horſe.

The aſs is capable of generating ſo early as at the age of two years: the female is even ſooner ripe than the male, and full as laſcivious; for which reaſon ſhe is a bad breeder, ejecting again the ſeminal fluid ſhe had juſt received in coition, unleſs the ſenſation of pleaſure be immediately removed by loading her with blows; the only method of preventing the conſequences of her amorous convulſions. This is a precaution without which they would very ſeldom retain. The moſt uſual times of her heat are in the months of May and June. After pregnancy, her heat is ſoon over, and in the tenth month the milk appears in her teats. In the twelfth month ſhe foals; and ſeven days after parturition the heat returns, and ſhe is again fit to receive the male; ſo that ſhe may, as it were, be kept continually engendering and nouriſhing her young. There is hardly an inſtance of her having two foals at a time. At

ſtronger voice, as being heard to a much greater diſtance than either of them; and what gave riſe to a belief of his voice being leſs deep probably was his manner of lowing, which is not a ſimple ſound, but compoſed of two or three octaves, the laſt of which moſt affects the ear; and if we liſten to it, we ſhall perceive a ſound more hollow than that of the ox, the cow, or the calf, whoſe lowings are alſo much ſhorter. It is love only that cauſes the bull to low; the cow oftener lows from fear than love; and when the calf lows, it is from grief, hunger, or a deſire to be with it's mother.

the end of five or ſix months the foal may be wained; and 'tis even neceſſary that it ſhould, if the dam be pregnant, in order that the fœtus may have proper nouriſhment. At the age of three years he ſhould be accuſtomed to work, and it will be right then to ſhoe him with a light ſhoe, particularly to guard the fore part of his hoof.

To have good aſs's milk for medicinal uſes, the ſhe-aſs muſt be ſound, in good caſe, and one that has foaled lately, and not been covered ſince. The foal that ſhe then ſuckles muſt be taken from her; ſhe muſt be kept clean, and fed with hay, oats, barley, and herbs whoſe ſalubrious qualities are adapted to the diſeaſe. This milk muſt not be ſuffered to grow cold, nor ſhould it even be expoſed to the open air, becauſe in either of theſe caſes it ſoon ſpoils.

A ſtallion-aſs ſhould be choſen from among the largeſt and ſtrongeſt of his ſpecies. He ſhould be at leaſt three years old, and not exceed ten. His legs ſhould be long, his body full, his head erect and airy, his eye lively, his noſtrils large, his neck longiſh, his breaſt broad, his back fleſhy, his ribs broad, his rump flat, his tail ſhort, and his pile gloſſy, ſoft, and of a dark grey. The moſt common colour in aſſes is the mouſe grey; but there are alſo gloſſy greys, and grey mixed with dark ſpots, as well as ſome of a dun colour, ſome brown, and others black.

There are different breeds amongſt aſſes, as well as amongſt horſes; but the former are leſs known, becauſe they have been leaſt attended to. That they all came originally from hot climates, is a fact ſcarcely to be doubted. Ariſtotle (*i*) aſſures us, that in his time there were no aſſes in Scythia, nor even in Gaul, where, he ſays, the climate is ſomewhat cold to which he adds, that a cold climate diſables them from propagating their ſpecies, or cauſes them to

(*i*) *De Generat. Animal. Lib. II.*

degenerate:

degenerate: and we have Linnæus's testimony(*k*) that they have not been long known in Sweden*. In fact, they seem originally to have come from Arabia, and thence to have passed into Egypt, from Egypt into Greece, from Greece into Italy, from Italy into Spain and France, and afterwards into Germany, England, and lastly into Sweden, &c. in all which countries it is to be observed, that the colder the climate is, the weaker and smaller the asses are.

The Spanish asses are by far the finest of any now in Europe. The climate, and the care that is taken of them, render them such: for, undoubtedly on account of the badness of their roads and the surefootedness of these creatures, the Spaniards, who make great use of them and of mules for travelling, feed and treat them well, and thereby render them beyond compare more gentle, active, and docile than they are with us. So great is the estimation in which they hold these animals, that a large stout he-ass frequently sells for sixty guineas on the spot; and if it be suspected that he is to be carried out of the country, he will not be parted with less than an hundred. In Auvergne too, where indeed the cold is felt as much as in any province of France, they have large and high-priced asses; and as they thrive as well, work as hard, and live as long in all parts of this island as they do in any other country whatever, it cannot be doubted that they would likewise do as well here in all respects, with proper management. The present goodness of our

(*k*) *Fauna Suæca.*

* Neither asses nor horses were found in America when the Spaniards first discovered that country, though the climate, especially that of the southern parts, agrees with them as well as any other. Those carried over thither by the Spaniards, and turned loose in the large islands, and on the continent, have increased so considerably, that in several places wild asses are seen in troops, and they are taken in toils, like wild horses.

roads

roads in general, and the great plenty we have of all ſorts of horſes, may indeed, in ſome meaſure account for our neglect of aſſes: but do we not carry that neglect too far? A little attention might perhaps diſcover purpoſes for which theſe animals are peculiarly proper; ſuch as their travelling ſafely over high and ſtony mountains, paſſing ſecurely through narrow winding paths in mines, and in the working of machines, for which they ſeem perfectly qualified by their natural ſteadineſs.

The aſs, which like the horſe, requires three or four years to attain its full growth, lives alſo, like that animal, twenty-five or thirty years: but the females are generally ſaid to be longer lived than the males: a conſequence, perhaps, of their being a little more tenderly uſed, on account of their being often pregnant; whereas the males are worked and beaten without intermiſſion.

Aſſes ſleep leſs than horſes; and if ever they lie down to ſleep, it is only when they are quite ſpent with labour. The ſtallion aſs alſo laſts longer than the ſtallion horſe: his eagerneſs ſeem to increaſe with his age; and in general the health of this animal is much more ſteady and confirmed than that of the horſe. He is far more hardy, and ſubject to a much leſs number of diſeaſes. Even the antients mention few, except the glanders, and this is very rare. As to the reſt, the diſeaſes of theſe animals are to be treated in the ſame manner as thoſe of horſes.

BOOK III.

OF MULES.

THE Mule is a beaſt of burden, begot by a male aſs and a mare, or by a ſtallion horſe and a female aſs. There are both male and female mules, and both of them are very eager for copulation; but they do not breed, at leaſt, in climates like this. Some think it is becauſe they proceed from two different ſpecies of animals: but others ſay poſitively that they do breed in hot countries*. In France, where many mules are bred, they are not ſuffered to couple, becauſe that renders them vicious and ſpiteful.

Mules

* All animals which owe their origin to creatures of different ſpecies are generally termed *mules*, and accounted barren: but, though it does not appear that mules proceeding from the aſs and mare, or from a ſtallion-horſe with a ſhe-aſs, produce any thing either among themſelves, or with thoſe from whom they are derived; yet, as M. de Buffon obſerves, in his Natural Hiſtory of the Goat, this opinion is perhaps ill-founded: for the antients poſitively aſſert that the mule is able to procreate at ſeven years, and that he does actually procreate with the mare *(a)*. They alſo tell us, that a mule is capable of conception, though it never brings it's fruit to maturity *(b)*. Theſe things, which throw a veil of darkneſs over the real diſtinction between animals and the theory of generation, ſhould therefore either be confuted or confirmed. Beſides, had we ever ſo clear a knowledge of all the ſpecies of animals around us, yet we know not what a mixture between themſelves, or with

(a) *Mulus ſeptennis implere poteſt, et jam cum equa conjunctus binnum procreavit.* Ariſt. Hiſt. Animal. Lib. VI. cap. xxiv.

(b) *Itaque concipere quidem aliquando mula poteſt, quod jam factum eſt: ſed enutrire atque in finem perducere non poteſt. Mas generare interdum poteſt.* Ariſt. de Generat. Animal. Lib. II. cap. vi.

foreign

Mules live a long while, often above thirty years: they are very healthy, and partake of the qualities of the animals from which they proceed; that is to say, they have the strength of the horse and the hardiness of the ass. They seem born for carrying heavy burthens, for carrying them gently, and for lasting a long time. They hardly ever stumble: their sense of smelling is uncommonly quick: they are very fantastical, and apt to kick, and their obstinacy is become proverbial. We know not of any wild ones.

In Spain, almost all the carriages are drawn by mules; they carry the baggage and equipages of princes and officers, and are of excellent service particularly in mountainous places. Traders and millers use them there to carry their merchandize and their corn; they are even made to plow the ground, and to thrash the corn by treading it out.

They are also much used in Italy; and in Auvergne they are employed for every thing that is usually done elswhere by horses and oxen, of which there are but few in that province of France. They form a part of the parade of great personages abroad when they make their public entries; and it is not long since

foreign animals would produce. We are, continues this judicious writer, but little acquainted with the *jumar*, that is, the prouce of the cow and the ass, or the mare and the bull. We know not whether the zebra would not copulate with the horse or the ass: whether the thick-tailed creature known by the name of the Barbary ram would not produce with our ewe: whether the chamois be not a species of wild goat; whether it would not with our goat form some intermediate breed: whether monkies differ in real species, or whether, like dogs, they are all of one and the same species, but varied by a number of different breeds; whether the dog can produce with the fox and the wolf; whether the stag produces with the cow, the hind with the buck, &c. Our ignorance, with regard to all these facts, is almost invincible; the experiments by which alone they can be decided, requiring more time, and more attention and expence, than the life and fortune of a common person will admit of.

the magiſtrates in France rode upon mules to their courts of juſtice, and phyſicians to viſit their patients. The Flemings uſed formerly to breed from their large ſized mares conſiderable numbers of very ſtately mules, ſome of them ſixteen and ſome ſeventeen hands high, and they were very ſerviceable as ſumpter-mules in the army: but ſince the Low-Countries have ceaſed to bear the Spaniſh yoke, they breed fewer mules. They were alſo much more common in this country in former times than they are at preſent, being often brought over hither in the days of popery by the Italian prelates. They continued longeſt here in the ſervice of millers, and are yet in uſe among them in ſome places, on account of the great loads they are able to carry. We alſo ſend ſome to our American colonies, where they are much uſed and eſteemed, particularly in the iſlands. Poitou, and the Mirebalais in France ſtill continue to breed great numbers of mules, but Auvergne yet more, and theſe laſt are moſt eſteemed *.

To have handſome and good mules, the ſtallion-aſs ſhould be in his full vigour, and therefore above three years old, and not more than ten; he ſhould be of a good breed; for in the ſtuds of mules, which are not uncommon in foreign countries, a ſtallion-aſs of a good breed is worth ſixty or ſeventy pounds, whereas a middling one will fetch above eleven or twelve: he ſhould be well made, that is to ſay, large ſized, with a ſtout thick neck, ſtrong and

* The Spaniards have long had ſuch a predilection for mules, that it raiſed the price of ſhe-aſſes to the high degree before mentiond (p. 274), and produced an abſolute prohibition and exportation. It has alſo leſſened their regard and attention to horſes; inſomuch that the ſtuds in Audaluſia, formerly eſteemed the fineſt in Europe, have loſt their credit, and future ages will hardly believe what has been truely ſaid of the Spaniſh horſes. To remedy this, the government have more than once thought of reſtricting the uſe of mules to eccleſiaſtics and women.

broad

broad ribs, an open and mufcular cheft, flefhy thighs, tight-made legs, and above all well provided in his genitals, as thofe of the Mirebalais are remarkably. As to the colour, the plain black or black fpeckled with a rather lively red, or the filver-grey or grey intermixed with dark fpots, are the moft efteemed: the moufe-grey, which is the moft common colour of affes, fhould be rejected.

The mares fhould be under ten years of age, and as near as can be of the fame colour as the ftallion, efpecially when one defires to have black mules, which are the moft efteemed. In the year 1689, it was enacted in France, that no ftallion-afs fhould be given to a mare under fourteen hands high, which is tall enough to produce the fineft mules; and the large full bodied mares in that country are referved for the multiplication of this breed.

The ftallion-afs becomes fo furious at the fight of the mare intended for him, that he muft always be kept muzzled at that time, left he fhould maim the grooms who lead her to him.

It generally is from the middle of March to the middle of June that the afs is given to the mares, in order that, as they go eleven or twelve months, the mules may be born at a time when there is plenty of good fucculent grafs, fit for the dam and her young one. The afs fhould be refted for a week before he covers the mare, and during that time he fhould have oats once a day, and be fed with good hay. As to the reft, what was before faid concerning ftuds for horfes, is equally applicable to the breeding of mules; with this only difference, that mares which have been covered by a ftallion-afs go a whole year, and that they cannot fuckle their young ones above fix months, on account of a pain they have in their teats after that time. Thefe mule-colts muft therefore be weaned at that time, or made to fuck another mare.

The mules begot by an afs and a mare are better and

and handsomer than those which come from a she-ass covered by a stone-horse; they are even two different kinds. Also, the male-mules are stronger than the female, and therefore preferred for labour and long journeys.

A good male mule should have round and thickish legs, little belly, the body firm, and the rump hanging down towards the tail. The female should also be full bodied, but with small feet and dry legs, well-spread buttocks, a wide chest, a long and arched neck, and a small lean head.

The age of mules, both male and female, is known by their teeth, in the same manner as that of horses. Many judge of the height they will be of by the length of their legs: at three months the legs have attained their full growth, and they are then half the height of the mule.

When three years old, they are broken and trained like colts; but much greater patience is required here, because they are much more headstrong and fantastical. Wine is said to familiarize them; and one of their feet is tied up to their thigh to prevent the kicking, and at the same time render them docile. They kick only with their hind legs. Many do not use them for work till they are five years old.

They are fed and managed in the same manner as horses, and are subject to the same diseases; consequently the methods of cure before pointed out for the latter, are likewise to be recurred to for these animals. The *Maison Rustique*, from whence I have borrowed the greatest part of this article, M. de Buffon not having any where professedly spoken of the mule, says, (*c*) in addition to the treatment of their diseases, that a pint of red wine, in which half an ounce of flour of brimstone, a raw egg, and a dram of myrrh have been mixed, will, if given repeatedly

(*c*) *Tom. I. Part I. Liv. III. chap. iii.*

for ſome time, in caſe of their growing lean, reſtore them to their fleſh and good appearance; and alſo, that the ſame remedy will cure them of gripes and coughs.

BOOK IV.

OF HORNED CATTLE.

CHAP. I.

Of the general Properties and Uſes of Horned Cattle.

THE Ox is the moſt valuable of horned cattle: he coſts but little to keep, and yields a conſiderable profit; is very good for draught, and for the plough; ſubject to few diſeaſes, and thoſe eaſily cured: he lives to a good age, and requires but a trifle to harneſs him, though no creature turns up the earth ſo well; and when he is worn out with ſervice, he is fattened, and becomes excellent food; or, if he breaks a limb he is killed, and his fleſh is eaten. His ſkin and his ſuet ſell for a good price: even his horns and his gall fetch ſomewhat, and his dung is a good manure: in ſhort, he may juſtly be ſtiled, by way of excellence, *the animal*; for, beſides the great ſervices which he renders to man, he returns to the earth full as much as he takes from it, even meliorates the ſoil on which he lives, and fattens his paſtures; whereas the horſe, and moſt other animals, exhauſt the richeſt meadows in a few years. Without the ox, both rich and poor would find it difficult to ſubſiſt; the earth would lie uncultivated; our fields,

fields, and even our gardens, would be dry and barren. He is a principal inſtrument in all works of huſbandry, the moſt uſeful ſervant in a farm, and the ſupport of rural œconomics; for on him depends the moſt laborious part of agriculture.

Formerly the wealth of man conſiſted chiefly in his herds of black cattle, and they ſtill continue to be the baſis of national opulence; for it is only by the cultivation of lands, and the abundance of cattle, that a ſtate can be maintained in a flouriſhing condition. Theſe are, alone, real goods: all others, gold and ſilver not excepted, are only arbitrary; money and credit having no other value than what they derive from the products of the earth.

That the ox is not ſo proper for carrying burdens as the horſe, the aſs, the mule, the camel, and ſome other beaſts, is evident, from the form of his back and reins: but his thick neck and broad ſhoulders declare him to be perfectly fit for draught; and accordingly it is with them that he draws to the greateſt advantage, though ſuch is the abſurdity of ſome men, and ſuch their blind attachment even to the moſt ridiculous cuſtoms, that he ſtill is, in many parts, and particularly in ſeveral of the provinces of France, made to draw by his horns, on the ſhallow pretence of his being then moſt eaſily guided:—A cuſtom almoſt as prepoſterous as was that of the Iriſh, who, till lately, uſed to make their horſes draw the plough by their tails. It may indeed be true, that the ſtrength of the ox's head is ſufficient to enable him to bear tolerably well this method of labouring: but certainly he performs his work much leſs eaſily, and leſs well, than when he draws by the ſhoulders, which nature ſeems to have formed purpoſely for the plough. The unwieldy magnitude of his body, the ſlowneſs of his paces, the ſhortneſs of his legs, every thing, even his quietneſs and patience in toil, evidently concur to fit him for tillage, and enable him, beyond any other animal, to ſurmount the conſtant resistance of the earth against his efforts. The horse, though perhaps equally strong, is less proper for this use; his legs are too long, his paces too quick and impetuous, and he soon frets and tires. Besides, by putting him to the plough, we deprive him of all the agility and suppleness of his motions; of all the beauty of his attitude and carriage: for this heavy work requires rather perseverance than hard labour; rather strength than swiftness, and weight rather than elasticity: and accordingly, wherever the comparison had been made with any degree of accuracy between horses and oxen for the labours of the field, and especially for ploughing, the difference has been found to be considerably in favour of the latter, in every respect but that of speed; and even in this article their inferiority amounts to nothing more than being two hours in a day longer at work than horses: for they perform the same quantity of work every day, and that too in a better manner. It is universally allowed that they are cheaper in every sense; for they cost less when bought, are less expensive in their food, their harness, and their shoeing, are subject to much fewer disorders, require far less attendance, and at last remain fit for fatting when their labours are over, as was before observed. Yet, strange fatuity! notwithstanding all these advantages, they are so little used at present for the works of husbandry in this kingdom, that, if we may trust to the report of the author of the *Six Months Tour through the North of England* (a), and surely we may confide in what that gentleman says from his own personal inquiries and observations on the spot, whole counties in England, which, not many years ago, scarcely possessed a plough-horse, now have not a single ploughing-ox.

To account for this very extraordinary and every way highly detrimental change, and at the same

(a) *Vol. IV. Letter xxxii.*

time

time to refute the groundless opinion of those who look upon it as a kind of proof that horses are really preferable, the author here referred to, Arth. Young, Esq; F. R. S. very judiciously attributes it to the great price which live cattle have yielded of late years. "It is well known," says he, "that the regular course of business in the ox-counties used to "be, to keep three sets of beasts; one of young "cattle that were coming into work; the teams; "and fattening cattle, that had been worked three "years But when cattle came to be so very dear, "as to cost when lean near as much as they sold for "when fat, the ox-farmers were tempted to sell "their young stock before they ploughed them; or "at least to throw them directly to fattening, that "their high value might come in the sooner. And "as horses, once bought, required no annual addi-"tion, they by degrees increased with all poor farm-"ers, to enable them to sell their oxen at high pri-"ces. The great decrease of the use of oxen dur-"ing the period of live cattle selling so very high, "gives some reason to suppose this the cause of it. "I need not, surely, add, that this, or indeed any "other reason that can be offered, is and must be "false and incomplete; and that the use of them "in tillage is much superior to that of horses. The "avarice of the farmers has alone driven them out "of use, not for the sake of profit, but for raising "money at a future expence. The great farmers "in Northumberland, who, we are certain, are not "*poor*, still continue to make much use of oxen, "*viz.* half and half."

If the above arguments are not sufficient, the following indisputable fact, attested by the same observant writer, who relates what he himself saw, must surely silence for ever the most prejudiced advocates for ploughing with horses. (*b*)

(*b*) In *the Farmer's Tour through the East of England, vol. I. letter iv.*

Wenman Cooke, Eſq; of Longford in Derbyſhire, executes all his ploughing and home-carting, which are very conſiderable, with oxen harneſſed nearly in the ſame manner as is practiſed for horſes, excepting that the collars open to be buckled on, and are worn with the narrow end, which is the part that opens, downward. The chains are faſtened to them in the ſame direction as in a horſe-harneſs, but much above the cheſt, and in a line almoſt even with their backs. The beaſts of courſe draw thus much higher than horſes. He likewiſe finds that they draw with much greater power in this manner than in yokes, that they move much faſter, are more handy and convenient, and that they perform their work at much leſs expence, than could be done by horſes, as well as even more expeditiouſly, as appears from Mr. Cooke's ploughing as much land in a day with three oxen, as the farmers do with four or five horſes. A Diſproportion ſo amazingly great, that, as Mr. Young very properly remarks, it decides at once, and in the cleareſt manner, the long-conteſted point, whether horſes or oxen are the fitteſt for the plough. Mr. Cooke feeds them in ſummer on graſs alone, and in winter on ſtraw; on which laſt indeed, he works them only moderately; but if hard, they then have hay, or ſome turneps. Mr. young declares that he ſaw a a team of oxen thus harneſſed drawing a heavy load of bricks, and obſerved that not one horſe-team in ten could have out-walked them. The drivers aſſured him, that they worked much better thus than when yoaked, that they were able to draw a greater weight, and were far more eaſily managed. When oxen are yoaked, they move aukwardly, and often with ſuch inequality between the couples, that, as is well known to all ox-drivers, it is common for one beaſt to make its companion bear the whole ſtreſs of the draught. This inconvenience, as well as the objection that oxen trample the land too much when they are yoaked together in ploughing, is totally removed in Mr. Cooke's method, which ſeems in fact to be an improvement of M. de Chateauvieux's; mentioned in the ſecond volume of my Syſtem of Huſbandry (*c*). The making of the oxen go in a ſingle line inſtead of a double one, is alſo extremely uſeful in ſome ſorts of ploughing; and it has been proved by repeated experience, that they may eaſily be rendered ſo tractable as to be guided by a line like horſes.

The cow may alſo be rendered fit for the labours of the field, and, though not ſo ſtrong as the ox, be made to ſupply his place: but when ſhe is employed in this ſervice, care ſhould be taken to match her as nearly as poſſible with an ox of equal ſtrength and ſize, in order to preſerve an equality of draught between them; for the leſs unequal they are, the more eaſily and readily the tillage is performed. Stiff lands, eſpecially ſuch as turn up in large long clods, often require ſix or eight oxen to plough them; whereas a ſandy and looſe ſoil may be tilled with only two cows: and beſides, in this laſt, the furrows may be continued to a greater length than in the former. Among the antients, an hundred and twenty paces was the greateſt length of a furrow which the ox was to make by one continued effort, after which, ſay they, he is not to be goaded farther, but allowed to breathe a while, before the ſame furrow is continued, or another begun.—But, among the antients, agriculture was a favourite ſtudy: They did not diſdain to put their own hands to the plough; at leaſt, they countenanced the huſbandman, and conſulted both his eaſe and that of the ox: whereas amongſt us, they who enjoy the moſt of the products of the earth are, in general, the laſt to eſteem, encourage, and ſupport the art of cultivation. There are few STUART MACKENZIES, ſenſible, like the immor-

(*c*) *Page* 92—94: where is alſo a drawing of the ox-harneſs invented by that illuſtrious cultivator.

tal SULLY, that tillage and pastures are the only real foundation of the lasting prosperity of states.

The barren cow, which the country people call a *free martin*, has almost as much strength, and is nearly as fit for the works of husbandry as the ox. Its flesh too is said to be very nearly as good to eat *.

The principal use of the bull is to propagate the species; and though he also may be subjected to the yoke, yet one cannot be sure that he will work quietly, and the use which he may make of his prodigious strength is constantly to be guarded against. He is naturally untractable, stubborn and fierce, and, in the bulling season, absolutely uncontroulable, and often furious: but castration destroys the source of these violent impulses, without diminishing his strength. He also grows larger, heavier, and more unwieldy when castrated, and thereby becomes the better adapted to the labour for which he is intended. This operation likewise renders him more tractable, patient, docile, and less troublesome to others. A herd of bulls could not be either teamed or managed by all the skill and power of man.

Most country people know how to perform this operation: but the different effects which will result from the various times of performing it have not perhaps yet been sufficiently attended to. In general, the most proper age for castration is that immediately preceding puberty, which, in horned cattle, is eighteen months or two years; few of those that undergo the operation sooner long surviving it. It is true, indeed, that calves, whose testicles have been taken

* We are told, but may perhaps desire leave to doubt it, that when a cow brings a bull and a cow-calf together, the latter is always a *free martin*, and never bears. The Romans were not unacquainted with the sterile cow, and call her *taura*. According to Mr. Lisle's information, the head of the free martin is coarser made than that of a heifer, her horns are wider spread, and her udder is smaller. He adds, that the flesh of a fatted free martin will fetch a halfpenny a pound more than any cow beef.

out

ont ſoon after their birth, become, if they ſurvive the operation, which is very dangerous at that early age, larger, fleſhier, and fatter, than thoſe which are not caſtrated till their ſecond, third, or fourth year: but in return, theſe laſt ſeem to retain more ſpirit and activity; and thoſe which are not caſtrated till their ſixth, ſeventh, or eighth year, loſe little or nothing of their other maſculine qualities, being more impetuous and difficult to manage than other oxen; nay, in their bulling ſeaſon, they endeavour to get at the cows, which muſt be carefully guarded againſt, becauſe the copulation, or even the bare touch of ſuch an ox, produces in the vulva of the cow a kind of carnoſities or warts, which nothing but the actual cautery can deſtroy.

The horned cattle, of which we now ſpeak, afford a proof that the heavieſt and moſt ſluggiſh animals are not always thoſe which ſleep the longeſt, nor the moſt ſoundly; for the ſleep of theſe is ſhort, and ſo unſound, that the leaſt noiſe awakes them. They uſually lie on the left ſide, and the kidney on that ſide is always larger, and has more fat about it than that on the right ſide.

CHAP. II.

Of the Choice of Cattle, and of fitting them for Tillage.

OXEN, like other domeſtic animals, are of various colours. The dun is the moſt common, and the redder it is, the more the creature is eſteemed: the black are alſo valued; and bay oxen are ſaid to be vigorous and long-lived; whereas the brown ſoon decay. The grey, the pied, and the white, are commonly deemed fit only for ſlaughter; it being the general opinion, which by the bye I doubt, that no pains can render them fit for labour. However, be that as it may, whatever is the colour of an ox's coat, it ſhould be gloſſy, thick, and ſmooth to the touch; for if it be harſh, rough, or thin, there is room to ſuſpect that the animal is out of order, or at leaſt not of a ſtrong conſtitution.

The age of the ox is known by his teeth and horns. The firſt fore-teeth, which he ſheds at the end of ten months, are re-placed by others, larger, but not ſo white: at ſix months after this, the teeth, next to thoſe in the middle, fall out, and are alſo replaced by others; and in three years all the inciſory teeth are renewed. They are then even, long, and pretty white; but as the creature advances in years they wear, and become unequal and black. It is the ſame with the bull and the cow; ſo that, conſequently, the growth and ſhedding of teeth are not affected by caſtration, nor by the difference of ſexes. Neither is the ſhedding of their horns affected by either; for the ox, the bull, and the cow, loſe them alike at the end of three years, and they are alike replaced by other horns, which, like the ſecond teeth, remain; only the horns of the ox and cow are thicker and longer

longer than thoſe of the bull. The manner in which theſe ſecond horns grow is not uniform, nor is their ſhooting equal. In the firſt year of their appearance, which is the fourth of the ox's age, two ſmall pointed horns bud forth, neatly formed, ſmooth, and terminated by a kind of button towards the head of the animal. The next year this button moves from the head, being impelled by a corneus cylinder, which, alſo lengthening, is terminated by another button, and ſo on; for the horns continue to grow as long as the creature lives. Theſe buttons become rings, or annular joints, which are eaſily diſtinguiſhed in the horn, and by which the age of the animal may at once be known; reckoning three years for the point of the horn down to the firſt joint, and one year for each of the other intervals.

A good ox for the plough muſt be neither too fat nor too lean; his head ſhould be ſhort and thick; his ears large and ſhaggy; his horns ſtrong, gloſſy, and of a middling ſize; his forehead broad; his eyes full and black; his muzzle thick, ſhort, and flat; his noſtrils wide and open; his teeth white and even; his lips black; his neck fleſhy; his ſhoulders large and heavy; his breaſt broad; his dew-lap hanging down to his knees; his reins very broad; his ribs broad, and not cloſe; his belly ſpacious and ſloping downwards; his flanks firm; his haunches large; his rump thick and very round; his thighs and legs large, fleſhy, and nervous; his back ſtrait and full; his tail reaching to the ground, and well covered with thick and fine hair; his feet firm; his hide thick and pliable; his muſcles raiſed; and his hoof ſhort and broad: he muſt alſo anſwer to the goad; be obedient to the voice of his driver, and eaſy to govern: but it is only gradually, and by beginning early, that he is brought willing to bear the yoke, and be eaſily managed.

At the age of two years and a half, or at fartheſt three, it is time to begin to tame him, and bring him

under

under ſubjection; for if this is delayed longer, he becomes headſtrong, and often ungovernable. The only method of ſucceeding herein is, by patience, mildneſs, and even careſſes; for violence and rough uſage will only diſguſt him beyond the power of recovery: ſtroaking him gently along the back, clapping him with the hand, giving him occaſionally boiled barley, ground beans, and ſuch other aliments as pleaſe him moſt, all of them mixed with ſalt, of which he is very fond, will prove of the greateſt uſe. At the ſame time a rope ſhould be frequently tied about his horns, and ſome time after the yoke ſhould be put about his neck, and faſtened, firſt to a pair of wheels only, and then to a plough, with another ox of the ſame ſize ready trained: after this, they ſhould be tied together at the ſame manger, and be led together to paſture, that they may become acquainted, and accuſtomed to ſtep alike. The goad ſhould never be made uſe of at firſt, becauſe it then would only render him more untractable: he muſt alſo be indulged, and labour only at ſhort intervals; for till he has been thoroughly trained, he tires himſelf very much; for which reaſon alſo he ſhould then be fed more plentifully than at other times. Alſo, when he is to work, eſpecially if it be in ſtiff or ſtony ground, and likewiſe when he is to go upon the road, he ſhould be ſhod, or, as the country people and farriers term it, cued. He ſhould draw the plough only from his third to his tenth year; for after this it will be adviſeable to fatten and ſell him, his fleſh being then better than if he was kept longer.

It is ſaid, that oxen which feed ſlowly bear labour better than thoſe which eat faſter; that ſuch as have been bred in dry and high countries are handſomer, more vigorous, and more ſprightly than thoſe of low and moiſt countries; that dry hay ſtrengthens them more than ſoft graſs; that they cannot bear a change of climate ſo well as horſes; and that, for this reaſon, oxen for labour ſhould always be purchaſed in the

the neighbourhood of the place where they are to work.

In general, countries ſomewhat colder than our own ſeem to agree better with black cattle than thoſe which are hotter; and they are larger and more fleſhy, in proportion as the climate is moiſter, and abounds in paſture.

The largeſt black cattle that we know of are thoſe of Denmark, Podolia, the Ukraine, and Calmuck Tartary. The Engliſh, Iriſh, Dutch, and Hungarian cattle are alſo larger than thoſe of Perſia, Turkey, Greece, Italy, France, and Spain; and the ſmalleſt we know of are thoſe of Barbary, and our own Iſlands of Alderney and Man. The Dutch import yearly from Denmark numbers of large lean cows, which, when improved by living in the rich paſtures of Holland, yield a great deal more milk and butter than our common breed of cows: their calves are alſo much larger and ſtronger; and except four or five days before their calving, they may be milked during the whole year. Theſe cows, commonly called Flanders cows, require excellent paſtures, though they eat little more than the common ſort; but as they are always lean, the ſuperabundance of their food turns wholly to milk; whereas our common cows, after living ſome time in luxuriant paſtures, become fat, and yield little or no milk. From a bull of this kind and a common cow, is produced another breed, called *baſtard*, which is both more prolific, and abounds more in milk than the common breed. Theſe baſtard cows often bring two calves at once, and alſo yield milk all the year round. They conſtitute a large part of the wealth of Holland, which exports every year butter and cheeſe to a very conſiderable amount. Theſe cows give much more milk than our common ones, as was before ſaid, twice as much as thoſe of France, and ſix times as much as thoſe of Barbary.

The

The beſt Engliſh oxen and cows, for largeneſs and neatneſs of ſhape, are bred in the counties of York, Derby, Lancaſter, Stafford, Lincoln, Gloucester, and Somerſet. Thoſe bred in Yorkſhire, Derbyſhire, Lancaſhire, and Staffordſhire, are generally black, with large well-ſpread horns: thoſe of Lincolnſhire are, for the moſt part, pied, very tall and large, and fitteſt for labour: thoſe bred in Somerſetſhire and Glouceſterſhire are generally red, and for ſhape much like thoſe of Lincolnſhire. Wiltſhire breeds large cattle, but with ill-ſhaped heads and horns. Surry is famed for a breed of white cows, which are ſaid to yield an uncommonly rich milk; and it is added, that their fleſh takes ſalt more readily than that of any other breed. The black ſort is commonly the ſmalleſt, but at the ſame time very ſtrong, and conſequently fit for labour. The cows of this colour ſeldom yield more than a gallon of milk at a meal, as it is called; but continue to bear being milked till within a very few days of calving. The white and red ſorts give, in general near three times as much milk as the black, but grow dry much ſooner; eſpecially the white. The red kind is generally the largeſt of any ſort we have in England, and is commonly thought to give more and richer milk than thoſe of other colours: ſome likewiſe ſay that they bring better calves, and therefore adviſe keeping this breed ſree from mixture with any other.—It may certainly be looked upon as a general rule, that the cow which gives milk longeſt is beſt both for the dairy and for breeding; and that the younger the cow is, the better will be the breed, provided ſhe be paſt her ſecond year.

A gentleman will chooſe the cow that gives the beſt milk, in preference to one which yields a larger quantity of leſs good; whereas the latter will anſwer beſt to the farmer, for fattening calves, lambs, and his whole breed of ſwine. The bullock of a

moderate

moderate ſize will alſo be preferred by the gentleman, for beef for his table, becauſe its fleſh is better reliſhed, and finer grained; and the larger ſize may be more prized by the farmer, becauſe they fetch more money at market, their fleſh being moſt eſteemed for ſalting, eſpecially for naval uſe; for it is found to ſhrink leſs, and to be leſs preyed on by the ſalt, than the beef of ſmaller cattle.

CHAP.

C H A P. III.

Of Feeding, Fattening and Tending of Cattle.

THE ox eats faſt, and takes in a ſhort time all the nouriſhment he wants, after which he ceaſes to eat, and lies down to chew the cud; whereas the horſe feeds both day and night, ſlowly, but almoſt inceſſantly. This difference in their manner of feeding proceeds from the different make of their ſtomachs: for the ox, whoſe two firſt ſtomachs form but one very capacious bag, can eaſily ſwallow ſo large a quantity of herbage as ſoon to fill his maw, and that done, he chews the cud afterwards, and digeſts it at leiſure; whilſt the horſe, having but a ſmall ſtomach, can put into it only a ſmall quantity of graſs, and continue to repleniſh it as the food ſinks and paſſes into the inteſtines, where the decompoſition of the aliments is chiefly performed: and accordingly, upon inſpection of theſe parts both in the ox and the horſe, and the ſucceſſive effect of digeſtion, particularly the decompoſition of hay, M. de Buffon ſaw, (*a*) that, in the ox, on it's leaving that part of the maw which forms the ſecond ſtomach, it is reduced to a kind of green paſte, like ſpinage minced and boiled; that it retains this appearance in the folds of the third ſtomach; that the decompoſition is completed in the fourth ſtomach; and that what paſſes into the inteſtines is only the huſks and recrements: whereas in the horſe, he obſerved, that this decompoſition is hardly viſible, either in the ſtomach or firſt inteſtines, where it be-

(*a*) *Hiſtoire Naturelle du Boeuf.*

comes

comes only more ſupple and flexible, having been macerated and penetrated by the active liquor with which it is ſurrounded; and that it reaches the cœcum and colon without any great alteration; that it is in theſe two inteſtines, whoſe enormous capacity anſwers to the maw in ruminating animals, that the decompoſition of a horſe's aliment is chiefly performed; and that this decompoſition is never ſo perfect as that in the fourth ſtomach of the ox.

From theſe obſervations, and the bare inſpection of the parts, it is eaſy to conceive, how rumination is performed, and why the horſe neither ruminates nor vomits; whereas the ox, and all the horned cattle, with other animals which have ſeveral ſtomachs, ſeem to digeſt the graſs only by rumination, which is nothing more than vomiting without effort, occaſioned by the re-action of the firſt ſtomach on the aliments it contains. The ox fills his two firſt ſtomachs (the ſecond being only a part of the firſt), and the membrane thus extended re-acts on the graſs within it, which has been but very little chewed, and it's bulk increaſed by fermentation. Were the aliment liquid, this contracted force would make it paſs into the third ſtomach, which communicates with the other only by a narrow duct, the orifice of which is ſituated at the upper part of the firſt, and but little below the æſophagus; ſo that no dry aliment can paſs through this duct, or at leaſt none but the more fluid part of it. Thus the drier parts neceſſarily aſcend through the æſophagus, whoſe orifice is larger than that of the duct into the mouth. Here the animal chews them again, macerates, and once more impregnates them with it's ſaliva; and thus by degrees renders the aliment more fluid, till it is reduced to a paſte of a proper liquidity to paſs through the duct which communicates with the third ſtomach: and here again it undergoes another maceration, before it paſſes into the fourth ſtomach,

where

where the decompofition of the food is compleated, by being reduced to a perfect mucilage.

What confirms the truth of this explanation is, that while thefe animals fuck, or are fed with milk and other fluid aliments, they do not chew the cud; and that they chew the cud much more in winter, and when fed with dry food, than in fummer, when the grafs is fucculent and tender. In the horfe, on the contrary, the ftomach is very fmall, the orifice of the æfophagus very narrow, and the paffage from the ftomach to the inteftines, or pylorus, very wide, which alone would render rumination impracticable; for the food contained in this fmall ftomach, though perhaps more ftrongly compreffed than in the large ftomach of the ox, cannot re-afcend, becaufe it may fo eafily defcend through the capacious orifice of the pylorus. It is therefore owing to this general difference in the conformation of the parts, that the ox ruminates and the horfe cannot: but there is another particular formation in the horfe, which renders him not only unable to ruminate, that is, to vomit without effort, but even hinders him from vomiting at all, though he fhould make the ftrongeft efforts fo to do; and this is, that the duct of the æfophagus enters fo obliquely into the horfe's ftomach, that inftead of opening by the convulfive motions of the ftomach, it becomes contracted. Though this difference, like all the other differences of conformation obfervable in the bodies of animals, depends on nature when conftant and unvaried; yet, in the growth, and efpecially in the foft parts, there are differences apparently conftant, which however may, and actually do, vary by circumftances: for inftance, the capacity of the ox's maw is not wholly derived from nature; it is not fuch by it's primitive conformation, but is gradually rendered fo by the large bulk of the aliments put into it; for in a young calf, or even in one that is older, if the animal has fed only on milk, and never on herbage, the

maw

maw is much ſmaller in proportion than in the ox. The very great capacity of the maw therefore proceeds from the extenſion occaſioned by the large bulk of aliments put into it at one time; as M. de Buffon has clearly proved by the following experiment (*b*). He cauſed two calves of the ſame age, and weaned at the ſame time, to be fed, one with bread, and the other with graſs; and at the expiration of a year, on opening them, the maw of the calf which had lived on graſs and herbage was become much larger than the maw of that which had been fed with bread.——I have been the more particular in the above account of the manner in which ruminating animals are nouriſhed, and of the cauſes why the horſe can neither ruminate nor vomit, becauſe it may afford ſome ſatisfaction to thoſe who might not, perhaps, otherwiſe be able readily to aſign a reaſon for their different ways of feeding.

A general caution proper to be attended to on this occaſion, is, that great care ſhould be taken not to over-ſtock a paſture with cattle; becauſe the greateſt profit really ariſes from their being conſtantly kept in good condition; eſpecially thoſe that give milk, and thoſe that are big with young. The ſtinted breed of cattle which we often meet with, and uſually impute to the poorneſs of the paſture, badneſs of the climate, &c. is in fact generally owing to the miſmanagement of their owners, who, through a very ill-judged greedineſs, over-ſtock their paſtures, and thereby diſable the mothers from giving ſufficient nouriſhment to their young, either before or after they are born: and this original ſtinting ſticks by them through life, unleſs they chance to get very early into a rich paſture; for then, indeed, they ſometimes ſoon outſtrip their original breed; a circumſtance which proves, that if they were at all times equally well kept, the breed would be much mended.

(*b*) See ibid.

As oxen are not worked much in the winter, good straw, and a little hay will then nourish them sufficiently; but during the time that they do labour, they should have a great deal more hay than straw, and even a little bran or oats before they go to work. In summer, if hay be scarce, they may have grass fresh cut from the field, or the young succulent boughs and shoots of ash, elm, oak, and other trees; but these last should be given sparingly, because an excess of this aliment, of which they are very fond, sometimes causes them to make bloody urine. Clover, lucerne, sainfoin, burnet, when these can be had, vetches, boiled barley, turnips, carrots, parsnips, cabbages, &c. are also excellent food for these animals. There is no need to measure out the quantity of their food, because they never eat more than they want; and it is therefore proper always to give them more than they do eat*. They should never be turned into the pastures till about the middle of May; because the first growth of the grass and other herbs is too crude, and though they eat them greedily, they disagree with them. After they have spent the summer in the pastures, they should be housed about the middle of October; taking care that these transitions from green food to dry, and from dry to green, be not done at once, but by degrees.

The custom of giving salt among the fodder is of an old date, for Columella mentions it (c) as the practice of his time, and very properly recommends it much, as well calculated to promote their appetite, and consequently to assist their fattening.—I have

* Cattle, and all other animals which chew the cud, have the singular advantage that they never eat more at once than is sufficient for them; for they then lie down and chew the cud: whereas horses, and many other animals, continue to eat as long as they are able to swallow.

(c) *Lib. VI. c. iv.*

heard

heard it observed by a gentleman from America, that the desire for salt is much greater in cattle and horses at a distance from the sea, than in the countries near it; owing perhaps to a greater freshness of the water. Even in Switzerland, the native horses of that country are very fond of salt, and it is a constant custom to give it them. There are in several parts of America, distant from the sea, spots discovered by the wild beasts, such as deer and buffaloes, where the earth is of a saline nature, to which these creatures resort regularly, and lick the earth with their tongues. They are called *salt-licks*, and are sometimes an hundred or an hundred and fifty feet wide.

Salt mixed with hay which has not been well got in, seems to act as an enemy to that fermentation in the juices which raises the heat in the hay: for where it is mixed with paste or other soft substances, it prevents putrefaction; probably by hindering the necessary preceding ferment.—Thus it becomes useful in hay on a double account.

Though violent cold is very hurtful to these creatures, great heat is perhaps still more so. For this reason, in the summer-time they should be led to their work by break of day, and when it grows very hot, be either sent home, or left to feed under the shade of trees, and not returned to work again till three or four o'clock in the afternoon. In autumn, winter, and spring, they may be at plough from eight or nine in the morning till five or six in the evening without intermission. But I cannot, by any means, approve of keeping them continually out of doors; especially for cows that give milk, or are with calf. It is surely inhuman to expose a creature to a degree of cold which it is not naturally fenced against.

Though oxen do not require so much attendance as horses, yet to keep them brisk and healthy, it will be proper, especially when they work, to curry them every day, to rub them down, wash them, clear their feet of gravel and dirt, greafe their hoofs, &c. They muft alfo have drink twice a day, morning and evening. The horfe likes a thick and warmifh water; but for the ox it muft be clear and cool. The pavement of their ftables fhould be a little inclined, that wet may not reft on it, and they fhould alfo have dry litter laid under them.

The age at which oxen are generally fattened is their tenth year, becaufe there is no certainty of fucceeding therein afterwards, nor is their flefh fo good when they are older. They may be fattened in any feafon of the year; but fummer is commonly chofen, becaufe it is done then at leaft expence. If it is begun in May or June, they are generally compleatly fattened before the end of October. From the very beginning to fatten them, they muft be taken from all work, drink often, and have plenty of fucculent food, fometimes mingled with a little falt as before faid; or, when a beaft falls off his ftomach, grafs dipped in vinegar will alfo reftore his appetite, and confequently help to make him fatten the fooner. They muft not be difturbed while they are chewing the cud; and during the great heats, they fhould fleep in a cow-houfe, or fome other fhady place. By this means they will become fo fat in four or five months, as to be fcarce able to walk; fo that if they are to be fent to any diftant place, it muft be by very flow journies that they are removed. Cows, and even bulls whofe tefticles have been knit, may alfo be fattened: but the flefh of cows is drier, and that of the knit-bull redder and tougher, than the flefh of oxen; and that of the bull has always a ftrong difagreeable tafte.

Turnips are made to yield a great profit in feeding and fattening of cattle, particularly in Norfolk, and, of late years, in feveral other counties in England. When large, they fhould be fliced, as well to enable the beafts to eat the quicker, as to prevent their choaking themfelves, which they would

otherwife

otherwise be apt to do. Carrots are yet wholesomer, much more substantial, and consequently more profitable food: besides which, they render the flesh of the cattle that are fed with them firmer and better tasted, as the Flemings have long experienced: but a yet more nourishing food is parsnips, especially for milch-cows, which, when fed with them, give more milk than with any other winter-fodder, and that milk yields better butter than the milk of cows nourished with any other substance. Cattle eat these roots raw at first, sliced lengthwise; and when they begin not to relish them, they are cut in pieces, put into a large copper, pressed down there, and boiled with only so much water as fills up the chasms between them. Our neighbours in Brittany reckon one crop of parsnips, used for feeding cattle, equal in value to more than three crops of wheat (*b*). Potatoes are another good and very heartening food, and may, as was before said of parsnips, be parboiled when cattle like them best that way.—Buckwheat makes very good fodder for cattle; and so does, in particular, the yellow-flowered vetch. In Germany and Flanders, spurrey is preferred before any other fodder, not excepting even corn, and is found to produce the richest milk and best butter. Cabbages, especially the Scotch kale and the great American cabbage, are reckoned preferable to turnips, in point of health as well as speed in fattening, and it is said, that one acre of them will go as far as three of turnips: but it is to be observed, that in using them, especially for milch-cows, the withered or decayed leaves should be thrown away, because they are thought to give a bad taste to the milk.

Clover is undoubtedly an excellent food for cattle, and we are told that one acre of it will feed as many of them as four or five acres of common grass: but

(*b*) *Observations de la Societé d'Agriculture, de Commerce, et des Arts, établie par les Etats de Bretagne. Années* 1757, *et* 1758. *p.* 88.

they ſhould never be turned into it in wet weather, nor whilſt the dew is yet upon the plant, leſt it ſhould burſt them. It ſhould be given them ſparingly at firſt, till it purges them: for when it has produced this effect, the danger is generally over. But of all the plants that are given to cattle for their food, none is equal to lucerne, either for early, ſpeedy, or good fatting; for with this the grazier may begin fattening towards the end of April, and finiſh about the middle of harveſt, when meat generally bears an high price. A large fatting ox may be allowed forty pounds, or perhaps more, of green lucerne each day*. All cattle are remarkably fond of lucerne, and always prefer that which has been cut a day or two, and ſtood twenty-four or forty-eight hours in a dry ſhady place. By this precaution too all danger of it's ſwelling them, which it might otherwiſe be apt to do, like clover and trefoil, is removed: only it is to be obſerved, that more caution ſhould be uſed in giving it to cows, than to bullocks. When oxen or heifers are fed for the butcher with lucerne, the fat will ſpread itſelf through the lean, like veins in marble; and the fleſh will be remarkably well-flavoured.

Oil-cakes, meaning the reſidue of the ſeeds of lin, rape, or coleſeed, after their oil has been expreſſed from them, are well known to be great fatteners of cattle, eſpecially if theſe drink plentifully with them: but they are apt to render the fat yellow and rank. To remedy this, the cattle ſhould be fed with dry fodder, for a fortnight or three weeks before they are killed.

A beaſt is well-fed outwardly, that is to ſay, well covered with fleſh, when his huckle-bones appear round and plump, his ribs ſmooth, his flanks full, his neck thick, his cod round, and, on feeling him upon

* The antient Romans allowed twenty pounds of lucerne-hay at night to a large labouring ox, that was not fatting.

the

the nethermost ribs, the skin feels soft and loose; and if, besides the above marks, the setting on of the tail feels thick, full and soft, and the navel round, soft, large and plump, it is a sure sign that he is also well tallowed, that is, well fatted inwardly.

All these creatures are very apt to lick themselves, when at rest, and this is thought to be an impediment to their fattening. To prevent it, all the parts of their bodies within their reach are rubbed over with their dung; without this precaution, their tongues, which are very rough, abrade, or take of their hair, which they swallow; and as this cannot be digested, it remains in the stomach, gathers together there, and forms by degrees round balls, called *ægagropiles*, which always hinder digestion, and sometimes grow so large as to be very troublesome, and even to indanger the life of the animal. They are, in time, covered with a brown crust proceeding from an inspissated mucilage, which, by continual friction and coction in the stomach, becomes hard and glossy. These balls are found only in the maw: for if any hair gets into the other stomachs, it does not remain either there or in the intestines, but probably goes off with the excrements. However, this subject, and the disorders occasioned by these balls will be treated of more fully in the fifth chapter of this book, where I shall speak of the distempers to which these animals are subject.

I cannot conclude this subject of the feeding of oxen, without adding M. de Buffon's just remark, that animals which have incisory teeth in both jaws, such as the horse and the ass, nip short herbage more easily than those whose upper jaw is without incisories; and if sheep and goats cut the grass very close, it is owing to the smallness and thinness of their lips; but the thick-lipped ox can only crop the long herbage; and this is the true reason why he never injures the pastures in which he lives. As he crops only the extremity of the long herbage, he does not affect the

 root,

root, and retards it's growth but very little; whereas the ſheep and the goat, by biting the herbage very cloſe, both deſtroy the ſtem, and injure the crown of the root. The horſe chooſes the moſt ſlender herbage, and leaves the larger, whoſe ſtems are hard, to ſeed and multiply; whereas the ox crops thoſe thick ſtems, and thereby deſtroys by degrees the coarſer herbage. Hence it is, that, after ſome years, the herbage where a horſe has lived becomes coarſe; whereas that where the ox has fed becomes a fine paſture.

CHAP.

CHAP. IV.

Of the Propagation of Cattle; Care of the Cow whilst pregnant, and Management of the Calf till fit for Slaughter, or for Work.

SPRING is the ufual feafon for cows to be in heat. In this country, moft of them admit the bull, and become pregnant, between the middle of April and the middle of July. Some indeed are more forward, and other more back-ward in their heat. They go nine months, and calve at the beginning of the tenth; confequently the regular feafon for calves is from the middle of January to the middle of April: but there is no fcarcity of them during the whole fummer, autumn being the time when they are leaft abundant. The tokens of the cow's heat are not at all equivocal: it is known by her frequent lowings, which are alfo more violent than at other times: fhe leaps on cows, oxen, and even bulls; and the vulva is inflated fo as to project outward. The time of this ftrong heat fhould be particularly noticed, and the bull fhould be brought to her then; for if fhe be fuffered to cool, fhe will not fo certainly retain afterwards.

The bull, like the ftallion among horfes, fhould be chofen from among the moft beautiful of the fpecies, and between the age of three years and ten, as before obferved; but the nearer he is to three, the greater will be his vigour. He fhould be large, well-made, and in good plight; his eyes fhould be black, his look proud, his forehead broad and curled, his head fhort, his horns thick, fhort, and black, his ears

ears long and ſhaggy, his muzzel large, his noſe ſhort and ſtrait, his neck thick and fleſhy, his ſhoulders and breaſt broad, his reins firm, his back ſtrait, his buttocks ſquare, his tail high-placed, long, and full of hair, his thighs round and well truſſed, his legs thick, ſhort-jointed, and full of ſinews, his knees round, big, and ſtrait, his feet far aſunder, not broad, nor turning in, but ſpreading eaſily, his hoofs long and hollow, his hide pliable, the hair of all his body thick, ſhort, and ſoft as velvet, and his walk firm and ſteady.

The cow ſhould be high of ſtature, her horns well ſpread, fair and ſmooth, her fore-head broad and ſmooth, her body long, her belly round and large, and her udder white, not fleſhy, but large and lank, with only four teats; theſe having been experienced to yield the moſt milk. She ſhould alſo be young; and ſome hold it to be moſt adviſeable for her to be of the ſame country as the bull, and as near as can be of the ſame colour.

The cow reaches the age of puberty at eighteen months, and the bull at two years; but though they are at that age capable of generating, it is adviſeable not to ſuffer them to copulate under three years. The time of their greateſt ſtrength is from three to nine years, after which the beſt way of diſpoſing of them is by fattening them for ſlaughter. As they acquire the greateſt part of their growth in two years, the duration of life with them, as with moſt other ſpecies of animals, is nearly ſeven times two years; and accordingly we ſeldom find them live above fourteen or fifteen.

Cows often retain at the firſt, ſecond, or third time of covering; and when they are pregnant, the bull refuſes to cover them again, whatever appearance of heat there may be in them. Indeed, their heat generally ceaſes almoſt immediately after they have conceived, and they themſelves will not then ſuffer the bull to approach them.

Cows

Cows require greater care when pregnant than at other times; particularly, they ſhould not then be ſuffered to leap over hedges, ditches, &c. or to do any other thing by which they may ſtrain themſelves; for they are ſubject to abortion: conſequently they muſt not by any means be uſed for draught whilſt in that condition; but they ſhould then be put into the richeſt paſtures, provided they be not too moiſt or fenny, and for ſix weeks or two months before they calve, they ſhould be fed more plentifully than uſual; giving them in the ſummer-time graſs in the cow-houſe, and in the winter bran, lucerne, ſainfoin, burnet, &c. During this time they muſt not be milked, that fluid being then abſolutely neceſſary to the nouriſhment of the fœtus. Some cows, indeed, do not yield any milk for a month or ſix weeks before they calve; but thoſe which have milk to the time of claving are both the beſt mothers and the beſt nurſes; though it is generally bad and in ſmall quantity. The ſame care and cautions muſt be obſerved at the delivery of the cow, as at that of the mare; or rather more, the former ſeeming to be on this occaſion more ſpent and weakened than the latter. One indiſpenſable point is, to put her in a ſeparate ſtall, where ſhe muſt be kept warm, at her eaſe, and on good litter. She muſt be well fed for ten or twelve days after ſhe has brought forth, with ground beans, corn, or oatmeal, diluted with water in which ſalt has been diſſolved, and with lucerne, burnet, ſainfoin, or good graſs, thoroughly ripe. By this time ſhe is uſually recovered, and may therefore by degrees be put to her common way of living, and turned into the paſture; obſerving not to take any milk from her during the two firſt months, that the calf may thrive the better; and beſides, the milk is not then of a good quality *.

As

* Good milk is neither too thick nor too thin; it's proper conſiſtence is, when a ſmall drop preſerves it's ſpherical form without

As ſoon as the young calf is born, whilſt the mother licks it, or to excite her ſo to do, it is right to ſhrew over it a couple of handfuls of ſalt and crumbs of bread mixed together. This licking ſtrengthens the calf or at leaſt clears it of all filth, which could not be removed by any other means, becauſe the young creature is then too tender to be handled without danger; and at the ſame time it ſhould be made to ſwallow the yolk of a raw egg, likewiſe to give it ſtrength.

The young half ſhould be left with it's dam during the firſt five or ſix days, eſpecially if it be in winter, in order that it may be kept conſtantly warm, and ſuck whenever it pleaſes; and at the end of this time, by which it will have gathered ſtrength and have grown viſibly, it muſt be tied up in a ſeparate pen at a little diſtance from her, that it may ſuck only when the keeper thinks proper; for it would exhauſt the cow if left continually with her. Two or three times a day will now be often enough for it to ſuck; and when it has done ſucking, it muſt be led back to it's pen and tied up as before. After the mother is returned to paſture with the other cows, the calf ſhould ſtill be kept in the cow-houſe, and there made to ſuck twice a day before it's dam goes out.

without ſpreading: it muſt alſo be of a delicate white; that with a yellow or blue caſt being of little value. The taſte of it muſt be ſoft, without any bitterneſs or acridity; it muſt have a good ſmell, or none at all. It is better in the month of May, and in ſummer, than in winter; and for it to be perfectly good, the cow muſt be of a proper age, and in good health. The milk of heifers is too thin; and that of old cows too oily, and in winter-time too thick. Theſe different quallities of milk have relation to the butyrous, caſeous, and ſerous parts of which it conſiſts. Milk too thin abounds too much with ſerous particles; that which is too thick has few or none of theſe particles; and the too oily has not a proper portion of butyrous and ſerous particles. The milk of a cow when bulling is not good; nor that when the creature is near, or juſt paſt, the time of her calving. *Buffon, Hiſt. Nat. du Bœuf.*

If

If it be intended to fatten the calf ſpeedily, and at the ſame time render his fleſh fine and delicate, he ſhould have every day about half a dozen raw eggs, and crumb of bread boiled in milk. This, in four or five weeks time, will render his fleſh excellent. Calves intended for the butcher ſhould therefore not ſuck above thirty or forty days; but thoſedeſigned for keeping ſhould be left with the dam two months at leaſt, becauſe, the more they ſuck, the ſtronger and larger they will be. The beſt for bringing up are thoſe that have been calved in the months of April, May, and June; for thoſe which come later ſeldom acquire vigour enough to enable them to bear the inclemencies of the enſuing winter; cold making them droop, and often killing them. Thus, calves deſigned for keeping ſhould be weaned at two, three, or four months: but before they are taken wholly from ſucking, a little fine graſs, or chopt hay, ſhould be given them from time to time, to accuſtom them to this new aliment; after being uſed to which, they muſt be never ſuffered to come near their dam, either in the ſtall or paſture. They themſelves ſhould be ſent to paſture every day, and remain there from morning to evening during the ſummer: but when the cold of autumn begins to ſet in, they muſt not be let out till late in the morning, and ſhould be brought back early in the evening; and during the winter, the cold of that ſeaſon being extremely detrimental to them, they muſt be kept very warm in a cloſe cow-houſe, be well ſupplied with water, have ſainfoin, lucerne, burnet, &c. mixed with their common graſs, given them in a cow-houſe, and be let out only when the weather is very fine. A great deal of care is neceſſary to bring them through the firſt winter, which is the moſt dangerous period of their lives: for if they ſurvive this, the following ſummer will ſtrengthen them ſo that they will have nothing to fear from the cold of a ſecond winter.

It ſometimes happens that a calf is troubleſome to rear, becauſe it will not readily take the teat, but muſt have it held a conſiderable time in it's mouth before it will ſuck; and likewiſe ſome ſhew for a long while a reluctance to ſuck at all, which is a ſign of their having pimples under the tongue; a diſorder to which young calves are ſubject, and which is eaſily cured by cutting them off with a pair of ſciſſars, and waſhing the wound with vinegar and ſalt: others rub them with hog's lard and ſalt pounded very fine.

In Spain, and ſome other countries, they place near a young calf in a cow-houſe one of thoſe ſtones called *ſalegres*, which are found in the mines of rock-ſalt: by licking this ſalt-ſtone whilſt it's dam is at the paſture, it becomes ſo hungry and thirſty, that when the cow returns, the calf eagerly ſeizes the teat and ſucks his fill; and by this means he fattens and thrives much faſter than thoſe to which no ſalt is given.

The clods of curdled milk which are found in the third and fourth ſtomach of a ſucking calf, are, after being dried in the air, the rennet made uſe of for curdling milk. The longer it is kept the better it is: and a very little of it is ſufficient to turn a large quantity of milk, as is well known to all who keep dairies.

As to the reſt, the management of milk and dairies is a ſubject ſo generally and ſo well underſtood in this country, that it might be needleſs for me to enlarge upon it here, any farther, perhaps, than juſt to obſerve in general, that the dairy ſhould be kept extremely clean and well aired, at a diſtance from all diſagreeable ſmells of any kind whatever, and that it ſhould be ſo ſituated as to be of as equal a temperature as poſſible during the whole year, and therefore open to the north in ſummer, and to the ſouth in winter. The dairy-maids ſhould not only be clean in their perſons, but alſo ſuch whoſe per-

iration

ſpiration is not rank.—The veſſels in which milk is now kept are generally lined with lead, becauſe it is a ſubſtance that cleans eaſily: but great care ſhould be taken that the milk do not remain in any leaden veſſel till it contracts the leaſt degree of acidity; for if it does, it ſoon diſſolves part of the lead, a very little of which will be of extremely bad conſequences to health, by occaſioning the moſt dangerous diſorders in the ſtomach and bowels, and often depriving people of the uſe of their limbs, as is daily ſeen in painters, and in thoſe employed in making white-lead.

CHAP-

CHAPTER V.

Of the Diseases of Horned Cattle.

THE treatment before directed in the several diseases of horses is, in general, in similiar cases, so applicable to the whole species of animals commonly distinguished by the appellation of Horned Cattle, that little remains to be added here, unless it perhaps be, to point out some few particulars more peculiarly relative to the management of these last. The Romans paid very great attention to them, as sharing with man the labours of the field; and as the climate of Italy is more kindly than that of England, surely whatever care was necessary there, cannot be less requisite here. The writers of that country may therefore properly become our guides again on this occasion.

Nature has cloathed with thick furs, or warm covering, such creatures as she intended to be exposed to the severity of the cold: but as cattle are not sheltered with such defence, I really think it cruel to expose them too much to the inclemencies of the winter, as many among us are apt to do *. Such was

* For, notwithstanding the very strong arguments used by M. de Buffon, in support of his opinion, that these creatures are original natives of these climates; such as, in particular, that they are not found beyond Armenia and Persia in Asia, and Egypt and Barbary in Africa, (for he looks upon the buffalo, the aurock, and the bisonet, as creatures of a different species); I cannot but incline here to think somewhat differently from that great man, and that principally for this obvious reason: Nature, as is evident throughout the whole creation, gives to every animal a covering suited to the climate she intends it for; and that of the ox is plainly calculated for a warm region. It therefore seems to me not improbable, that our black cattle came originally from some more southern part.

not

not the practice of the Romans, who very expreſsly enjoin, that the ox, in particular, be defended from the cold by a warm ſtable, and if it can be done, that there be a fire in it, which both Vegetius and Columella (*a*) declare to be of great advantage to this animal, as he thereby breathes a dry air, which carries off not only the exhalations from his own body, but alſo other noxious vapours. According to them, the manger ſhould be ſo contrived that their food be not loſt among their feet; and their ſtalls ſhould be placed on dry ground, with a gentle ſlope to carry off their urine, and kept conſtantly clean with dry litter, eſpecially for the labouring ox. How different from theſe directions is the condition of too many of our farmers yards where the cattle often ſtand knee-deep in dirt!

When the ox returns from labour, his neck ſhould be waſhed, and rubbed for a long time; his whole body too ſhould be freed from clay or dirt, eſpecially his feet, which ſhould be well waſhed.

In ſummer, it is proper that cattle ſhould ſtand in cool ſhades during the heat of the day, and in the night in the open air; for they contract as many diſeaſes by ſuffering too great heat, as by being expoſed to too much cold.

It is of great benefit to them to give to each, about once a week, a raw egg, and ſome ſalt in a pint of wine or ale; and to this may likewiſe be added bruiſed garlic, vervain, and rue.

Cattle do not require the cleareſt water, nor are they very much hurt by it if it is dirty; nevertheleſs, it is the duty of the perſon who attends them, to ſee that they drink the beſt water, and ſuch as is clean, and that they be well fed. There is no danger of their over-feeding themſelves; for when nature is ſatisfied, they lie down and chew the cud. Labour breaks, heat vexes, and cold penetrates an animal

(*a*) *Lib. III. c. i.*

that is empty and exhausted, sooner than one that has been well fed: and surely no man will grudge them a sufficient plentiful allowance of food, who considers how far the price of oxen which perish through want, exceeds the expence of that food.

If oxen are put upon running at their full speed, or if they are otherwise over-fatigued, at any time of the year, but especially in the summer, either they contract thereby a looseness, which proves pernicious to them, or slight fevers: for this animal, being naturally slow, and rather adapted to easy labour than to swift motion, is grievously hurt, if forced to go beyond his strength.

Neither swine nor hens should come near their cribs; for when an ox has swallowed hen's dung with his food, he is presently tormented with violent pains in his belly; and when he swells with it he dies. In case of his having swallowed any, the best way is to give him three ounces of parsley-seed, half a pound of cummin-seed, and two pounds of honey, mixed together, and poured warm down his throat, to force him to walk, and to rub him heartily till the draught moves his belly. The ashes of any wood well sifted boiled in a sufficient quantity of oil to render them liquid, and then poured down the ox's throat, will also be of great benefit against the bad effects of this sort of dung.

But if an ox swallows hog's dung, or more especially the filth which a sick sow has vomited, he is presently seized with so contagious a disease, that it speedily affects a whole herd. When therefore there is the least suspicion of this distemper, the cattle must be removed and separated to pastures where none such have been fed, that so they may not hurt one another; for by feeding they infect the grass, and the water by drinking of it. An ox, though otherwise in perfect health, may perish by the smell and breath of the diseased blowing upon him. When this happens, the dead carcase must be carried to a distance, a diſtance, and buried deep, leſt the ſound be infected by it, and the negligence of the owner be imputed (as is uſually done by fools, ſays Vegetius) to the divine diſpleaſure. In the caſe here ſpoken of, he recommends half an ounce of ſquills ſliced thin, infuſed in a pint of wine, with about two ounces of ſalt, to be given every morning to each creature thus infected.—But as infectious diſeaſes will be the profeſſed ſubject of the laſt part of this work, I ſhall not enlarge upon them here, any farther than juſt to mention the ſimilitude which Mr. Oſmer thinks there is between the diſtemper in horſes before deſcribed, and that amongſt oxen.

"To the beſt of my obſervation," ſays he, "what is called the diſtemper amongſt the horned "cattle, is exactly correſpondent to the diſtemper "amongſt the horſes; the ſymptoms in each animal "being ſimilar in all reſpects.—The diſcharge from "the noſtrils, &c. of the cow in theſe fevers, about "the nature of which, and of this diſtemper, there "has been abundance of fine writing, is nothing "elſe but an extravaſation of the ſerous particles of "the blood, the effect of inflammation; and there-"fore in obedience to the attempts of nature, our "buſineſs is to invent all the methods we can to car-"ry off this extravaſated ſerum; and the inciſions, "as before directed for the horſe, made in the ſkin "of the cow, will, as it does in horſes with the "ſame ſort of fever, produce in twenty-four hours "a naſty fœtid purulent matter. By a number of "theſe drains the parts will be unloaded, and the "animal relieved, and they do in all inflammatory "fevers amongſt horſes, and I dare ſay will too "amongſt the cows, anſwer nearly the ſame end "and purpoſe as a critical abſceſs. But when no "critical abſceſs happens, or no artificial drains are "made uſe of, the natural ones not being ſufficient "to carry off the extravaſated ſerum, the viſcera and "more noble parts are, in time, affected, the blood "and juices deviate by degrees into a ſtate of pu-"trefaction and corruption, and the animal dies a "moſt wretched death.

"If any man object and ſay, this diſtemper of "the cows is infectious, and therefore it is of the "putrid, and not of the inflammatory kind :—I an-"ſwer, that it does not appear to be infectious, be-"cauſe ſome cows amongſt a number of infected "ones have eſcaped it. But allowing it to be of "the putrid or peſtilential kind, and to ariſe from "air, infection, or both, theſe artificial drains made "in the ſkin will be very proper, becauſe they will "anſwer in ſome meaſure the ſame end, as the bu-"bo or critical impoſthume befalling the human ſpe-"cies in peſtilential diſorders, if they are properly "managed.—And here it may be obſerved, that "when diſtempered cows have eſcaped death, it has "been generally owing to ſome critical abſceſs ; va-"rious inſtances of which I have ſeen.

"To theſe artificial drains ſhould be added the "uſe of cooling ſalts, and laxative glyſters, if "needful.

"It is neceſſary ever to remember, that bleeding "the horſe or cow will be wrong, and muſt do harm, "when a diſcharge from the noſtrils, &c. is begun, "becauſe it is contrary to the effort of nature ; and "ſo it is when there is any ſwelling that is tend-"ing to matter, which kinds of ſwellings can be "diſtinguiſhed by the ſkilful only."

Indigeſtion is very hurtful to oxen, and is known by the following ſigns : frequently belching, loathing of their food, noiſe in their belly, heavy eyes : the creature neither chews his cud, nor licks himſelf as uſual.—In this caſe, pour down his throat two gallons of water as warm as he can bear it, and ſoon after give him about thirty leaves of colewort boiled in water, and afterwards ſoaked in vinegar ; and he muſt abſtain from food for one day.

Neglected indigeſtion brings on colics: but theſe having already been fully treated of in the diſeaſes of horſes, I ſhall here mention *boving*, a diſorder which is almoſt peculiar to the horned cattle.

This diſorder proceeds from a too-ſudden ferment in their green ſucculent food, whereby the elaſtic air let looſe by the fermentation, but confined by the hard fæces which do not ſpeedily enough give way to it, becomes highly acrid, like the gaſs ariſing from fermented liquors, which often proves mortal to thoſe who breathe it. The method of cure ſhould therefore be, clearing the great gut of hard excrement, injecting a ſtimulating glyſter, and giving cooling things internally. This agrees with what M. Bourgelat propoſes, when he ſays (*b*), "Thus "it is, for example, that with nitre given in half a "glaſs of brandy, and often even with emollient glyſ-"ters only, we have ſaved conſiderable numbers of "oxen ready to expire in their paſtures, after vain "endeavours had been uſed to eaſe them, accord-"ing to the common practice, by many inciſions "made in the ſkin, doubtleſs with an intention to "diſengage the cellular membrane from the air that "filled it, and of which carminatives would inevi-"tably have increaſed the diſorder, and haſtened "the death of the beaſt."

Farmers are apt to fall into a great error when their cattle have got the better of this diſorder; and that is, by letting them become coſtive again, and conſequently liable to a return of the ſame danger when they next feed on ſucculent plants; whereas were they to continue to give them green food after a purging has been once brought on, no farther inconvenience could enſue. Immerging them in cold water when thus diſtended brings on an immediate purging, and thereby ſaves their lives.

The mouths and tongues of horned cattle are ſub-

(*b*) *Ecole vétérinaire; Matiere Médicale, p.* 112.

ject to the ſame ſorts of ſwellings as thoſe of horſes, and a like productive of an inability to eat.

Theſe ſhould alſo be cut off with a knife or ſciſſars, and then rubbed with ſalt and let heal. If they have no appetite to their food, and yet no ſigns of indiſpoſition appear, it will be proper to rub their chops with ſalt and garlic beaten together, or with ſome other ſtimulating ſubſtance.

The cure of internal diſeaſes in cattle is ſo nearly the ſame as for horſes, and the doſes of their medicines ſo much alike, that a repetition of them here ſeems needleſs. The cauſes of their lameneſſes, and the methods of curing them, are alſo ſimilar; and the feet of both require ſo nearly the ſame cutting and care of the hoof, that the leaſt degree of intelligence will ſuffice to vary them properly.

The caſtration of calves is likewiſe performed in the ſame manner as that of horſes.

BOOK V.

OF SHEEP.

CHAP. I.

Of the Qualities and different Kinds of Sheep.

"SHEEP have golden feet, and wherever they set them the earth becomes gold," say the Swedes, by way of expreſſing their high eſtimation of this animal. In effect, there is not any one domeſtic creature which yields greater profit to man than ſheep do. Their fleſh, their milk, their ſkin, their inteſtines, their dung, in ſhort, every part of them, is neceſſary for ſome uſe or other, and turns to good account.

Though their fleſh and milk furniſh us with variety of excellent food, yet their wool is the chief object, eſpecially to a commercial nation like this; for of it is formed in Britain the ſtaple-commodity to which we owe the wealth and grandeur that render us the arbiters of power in Europe.

At the ſame time that this creature is the moſt uſeful, it is alſo, in itſelf, one of the moſt defenceleſs againſt enemies: Providence intending, as it would ſeem, that it ſhould owe its very exiſtence to our care, and be entitled to our protection, in return for the means of enjoyment and wealth which it affords us: for it not only wants protection but care alſo, more than any other domeſtic animal.—Sheep are of a very weakly conſtitution; much fatigue exhauſts them;

they can ill bear extremes of heat or cold; their diseases are many, and most of them contagious; and their yeaning is attended with difficulty and danger.

They are said to be sensible to the charms of music, so as to feed more assiduously, to be in better health, and to fatten sooner by the sound of a pipe: but perhaps it may be more rightly thought, that music serves to amuse the shepherd's tedious hours, and even that the origin of that art was owing to this solitary life.

Sheep love their keepers and those who take care of them; they follow them, and obey their voice. It must however be observed, that if the shepherd has not a watchful eye over them, one or other of his sheep may easily stray from the rest of the flock, wander into places it is unacquainted with, and there fall down a precipice, or tumble into a hole or ditch, especially, if the creature has been frightened, which sheep very easily are; for when they have once lost their way, they run strait on, without stopping, and always directly against the wind, particularly if it blows hard, and they chance to be in an open place, a wide road, or on the borders of the sea. They are very fond of light, and never thrive well in dark places; and such is their fondness for society, that frequently a sheep left alone will pine away, become emaciated, and quite lose his strength.

The re-establishment of the best kinds of sheep in England, and greater care of their fleeces, are objects well deserving the attention of government: for, notwithstanding all our boasted improvements, it is certain that the quality of our wool in general has been on the decline for some time past *. These

* Mr. Lisle, whose judgment and veracity in matters of this kind stand unimpeached, tells us, in his *Observations on Husbandry*, article *Sheep*, that, even so late as his time, and he has not been dead many years, the clothiers complained that our Herefordshire wool, and particularly that of our great staple, was no longer so fine as formerly.

useful

useful creatures, which were the chief wealth of former ages, become of still greater value as art and industry increase among us. One cannot, therefore, but be astonished at the indifference into which this nation has fallen with regard to her sheep, and especially too at a time when every other country is exerting it's utmost endeavours to improve it's breed, and the manner of managing it's flocks. At this very instant, we are strongly called upon to be particularly attentive to this great object, by the measures which the French are indefatigably pursuing to mprove the breed of their sheep, by introducing those of every country where they excel.

We have no particular accounts of what our sheep were in antient times; though we may presume that our wool was always sought for by foreign manufacturers, because our History informs us, that the duty paid on the exportation of it was a considerable article of the royal revenue *.

If we take a general view of the whole of England, we shall find, that the temperature of our climate, and the quality and almost perpetual verdure of our pastures, render it one of the best situated countries in the world for raising flocks of sheep. We are free from every discouraging circumstance with regard to them. We have no armies of insects or reptiles that are enemies to them; no wolves, nor any other animal whose nature is to prey upon them, if we except foxes, of which again the numbers are scarcely more than suffice to give

* In former times, "the wealth of the nobility, gentry, and "monasteries consisted chiefly in wool, which also then made "the bulk of private property at home. It was at the same "time the prime article in commerce. Aids to the crown was "granted therein.. It supplied the demands for the support of "armies, the payment of subsidies, and all other expences incurred on the account of the public in foreign parts," says the learned Dr. Campbell, in *vol. II. p.* 152, of his excellent *Political Survey of Great Britain.*

proper

proper healthy exercife to men, who might otherwife indulge themfelves in too much eafe. Our froft and fnow are generally of fhort continuance. Our extenfive downs, our hills, the fides of our mountains, and even our fteep rocks, abound in fine grafs, which feeds a fmaller breed of fheep; whilft our richer paftures of Lincolnfhire and Ely maintain thofe of a larger fize; and we are furrounded with a fea-coaft, the air of which is thought to be particularly favourable to the health and thriving of fheep, as well as to the finenefs of their wool.—The air of the fea is found to be fo wholefome and favourable to fheep, that the hufbandmen who live at a diftance from that element find their advantage in recruiting their flocks with fheep from near the fea.

Columella (*a*) mentions the feveral kinds of fheep moft in repute in his days, and gives an inftance of the judgment of his uncle, M. Columella, an excellent hufbandman, in mending the breed of his own fheep, by coupling with them rams brought from Africa: and indeed it is highly probable, that the excellence of the Spanifh wool, now fo juftly valued, took it's rife from combinations of this kind during the long refidence of the Moors in that kingdom.

Dom Pedro IV, King of Caftile, was the firft Prince who introduced the good kind of fheep which they now have in Spain, by bringing thither the Barbary breed. In two ages, they began to decline; when Cardinal Ximenes reftored the breed, by procuring a frefh fupply of rams from Barbary, that is to fay, of rams bred by the Arabians there; by exciting amongft the people an emulation which continues to this day; and by fixing their attention to this object, which has hitherto preferved the goodnefs of the Spanifh wool *.

The

(*a*) *De re ruftica, Lib. VII. c. ii.*

* The fineft of the Spanifh wools are thofe of Caftile, which are divided, according to the places of their growth, into Segovians,

The memoirs of the Royal Society of Agriculture at Rouen ſay (*b*), that in the fifteenth century, our Edward IV. obtained a number of this race from the king of Caſtile, which throve very well, and laid the foundation of the excellency of our wool. Henry VIII, and Queen Elizabeth, contributed much to it's perfection, by directing the attention of government to this great national concern. Men of diſtinguiſhed judgment and integrity were commiſſioned to ſuperintend the proper diſtribution and future care of the Caſtilian ſheep. How this commiſſion has ſince come to be neglected, I know not. Theſe commiſſioners ſent two Caſtilian ewes and one ram to every pariſh in which the paſture was thought proper for them; and the care of them there was intruſted to the yeomen and moſt conſiderable farmers, to whom peculiar privileges were at the ſame time granted on this account. Farther, in order the ſooner to have a quantity of good wool, the fineſt native ewes were alſo ſingled out, and covered by the Spaniſh rams, from whence proceeded a baſtard race, much ſuperior in quality to thoſe of the country. Shepherds were taught the art of managing ſheep, and written inſtructions were given them, which, I am ſorry to ſay it, are now loſt †. At this time began the cuſtom

vians, Leoniſas, Segovias, Sorias, and Molinas. The wools of Arragon are leſs fine: theſe are Albarazins, fine and middle, the Campos, and the black wool of Saragoſſa. Portugal and Navarre produce alſo fine wools. Our imports of wool from Spain have generally been of the prime of the Caſtilian, uſed in making our fineſt cloths.

(*b*) *Tome II. p.* 58.

† Dr. Campbell, in his very valuable *Political Survey of Great Britain, Vol. II. p.* 151, treats the whole of this account of Edward the Fourth's, or any other of our Kings procuring ſheep from Spain, to renew or improve our breed, as a mere fiction, invented by P. Chomel, in his *Dictionnaire Oeconomique*, to ſhew how eaſily ſuch a ſcheme might be executed in France; and

custom of holding them in the warm kindly weather, and the same practice was afterwards continued during the winter. The abode of the Spanish sheep in England altered by degrees the nature of their wool; it became much longer, but did not continue so fine as before; owing, probably, to the difference of the pasture. Our wool is however whiter and cleaner than that of Spain, through the

and I confess that the Doctor's arguments seem to me next to absolutely conclusive against it: indeed, if it rested solely upon the credit of Father Chomel, I should not hesitate a moment to pronounce him right. But as it comes to me from an infinitely more respectable quarter, from a society justly revered by the whole world, some of whose members are nobles of the first distinction, and others highly eminent for their great knowledge, I cannot suppose them to have taken this upon trust from the Dictionary-writer, or to have advanced it as a fact, without better authority than his for their so doing. The Gascon and Norman Rolles, published by the late Mr. Carte, are a proof, not to mention several more which might be instanced, that there may still be in France, and particularly in those parts of it which once were jubject to us, records relative to our history which we are yet unacquainted with; and it is not impossible that the anecdote here alluded to may be one of them, even though the name of the prince, and the date, may be mistaken. However, I speak here only from surmise.—Let me now use an argument which may possibly be more striking. The Doctor himself, adopting the opinion of those who think that the Northern parts of this island were peopled from Germany, the Southern from Gaul, and the Western and Ireland from Spain, says, p. 150. "it "cannot be doubted, that as the inhabitants of Britain and Ireland, so the sheep also came originally hither from some other "country, and most probably, for many reasons that might be "assigned, from Spain.—This seems to be confirmed by the "breed being the same in both islands, and having a great resemblance unto those of Spain—Now, with submission to the Doctor, to whose opinion I shall ever pay a sincere deference, is it any way unreasonable to suppose, that the breed of sheep imported into this island at the time of it's being first inhabited, might have degenerated, in the course of many centuries, so as to stand in need of a kind of renewal; and, in that case, could there be any more proper way than applying to the country from which the good breed first came? No matter which of our princes did it; or even whether it was not done at all. Some such expedient would be of service now to improve our present race.

great

great care which the Englifh take to keep their flocks free from filth; an attention hitherto neglected by the Spaniards.

To the above mixture of the Spanifh fheep with the natives of this ifland, and the greater or lefs degeneracy of their pofterity, is owing that we now fee in England three forts of fheep; the common, which are very fmall; the baftard, which are of a middle fize; and the ftrong, fine and plentiful breeders.

The Gloucefterfhire, particularly thofe of Cotefwold, the Herefordfhire, Shropfhire, and the ifle of Wight fheep, yield the fineft wool of any in England: they are fhort-legged, and have commonly a black forehead or a black head. The Warwickfhire, Leicefterfhire, Buckingham, and Lincolnfhire fheep are the largeft and beft fhaped, and their wool is the deepeft of any we have, but not fo fine as that of the former. The Yorkfhire fheep are likewife pretty large, but their wool is coarfe; and in general, that of all the Northern counties is long, but hairy. The Welfh fheep are the fmalleft of, all and their wool is by no means the fineft; but in return their flefh is excellently well flavoured. The wool of the Caftilian fheep is undoubtedly much finer than that of even the beft Englifh; but it is lefs in quantity, chiefly becaufe the fheep themfelves are fmaller: though there are in fome parts of Spain fheep larger and covered with more wool than any of the Englifh. For their wool, the Englifh are certainly the next beft to the Spanifh.

The Irifh wool in general, but efpecially in Limerick, Kilkenny, Kerry, Waterford, Cork, and fome other counties, is of the fine long combing kind, fcarcely furpaffed by any of the fort in England. This is the wool that is moft acceptable in foreign parts, where they have fhort wool enough of their own, or may eafily procure it from Spain and Portugal.

In

In the laſt century, the Dutch brought from the Eaſt-Indies a race of tall ſheep, long and thick in the body, with wool proportioned to the ſtature of the animal. This valuable breed has ſucceeded beyond expectation in the iſland of the Texel and in Eaſt-Frieſland. One of theſe ſheep yields a fleece of from ten to ſixteen pounds of a fine ſilky wool, which the Dutch ſell for Engliſh wool.

The Flemings alſo procured ſome of the ſame ſort of ſheep, which they breed about Liſle and Varneton, where they thrive well, and are known by the name of Flemiſh ſheep.

The largeſt of theſe ſheep are ſix feet long from head to tail. In Holland, they give four lambs in the year; whereas in Flanders they bring but two, of which the ſtrongeſt is reared in order to keep up the flock. Each of theſe likewiſe yields as far as ſixteen pounds of wool. They would be preferable to thoſe of the Texel, if the ſame care was taken of them, and if they were more numerous than they are. Moſt of the ſheep about Liſle are a baſtard race proceeding from the Indian rams and the ewes of the country, and yield from ſix to ten pounds of wool, little inferior to that of the true breed. Their fleſh is well-taſted and wholeſome: a carcaſe of it weighs from ninety to a hundred and twenty-five pounds, and yields about thirty pounds of ſuet. They are in themſelves the fineſt, largeſt, and ſtrongeſt of any ſheep. They require, indeed, a larger quantity of food; but on the other hand they are indifferent in regard to it's quality: they are eaſily taken care of, naturally healthy, and if ſick eaſily cured. Their wool differs little from that of England, only it does not ſo eaſily take fine colours. It is not ſo fine as it might be, for ſeveral reaſons, the principal of which are, that they are ſeldom folded; that they are kept too warm in their houſes during the winter; that their litter is not changed often enough, whereby it not only dirts, but alſo gives a bad ſmell to their

wool;

wool; and that sufficient care is not taken to keep them from hedges, bushes, and brambles, which not only tear off their wool, but scratch their skin, which, if not healed in time, degenerates into the scab.

The Swedes, after having tried in vain to mend the breed of their sheep in the reign of queen Christina, sat the same design again on foot in the year 1725. They imported into their country a number of the best kinds of sheep from England and Spain, and put them under the management of skilful shepherds, to be treated according to their several natures. After the example of England, heretofore, they established schools for training up shepherds, who were sent from thence to the different parts of the kingdom; and those schools are continued to this day. They put the foreign rams to their native ewes, and from thence proceeds a valuable bastard race. By this care, Sweden now has, notwithstanding the rigour of it's climate, wool which nearly resembles the English and Spanish. The French have, in several parts of their kingdom, numbers of sheep of the true Spanish breed, and they multiply there exceedingly; so that, as the authors of the *Maison rustique* observes (*c*), it might be easy for them, by following the method formerly practised in England, to establish every where that race, which would yield twice or thrice as much profit as their own common sheep, as well in point of size, of the goodness of their lambs and rams, of fruitfulness, and of milk, as of the quantity and quality of their wool and skins.

The provinces of Berry and Beauvais are those in which the most and best sheep in France are reared. Those of Beauvais, and some other parts of Normandy, are the largest, and the fullest of suet. In Burgandy, they are very good; but the best are

(*c*) *Tom. I. Part I. Liv. iv. c.* 3.

those

thoſe that are feed on the ſandy coaſts of the maritime provinces of France. In Poitou, Provence, the neighbourhood of Bayonne, and ſome other parts of France, there are ſheep which ſeem to be of a foreign breed: they are ſtronger, larger, and have a great deal more wool than thoſe of the common breed. Theſe ſheep are alſo more prolific than the others; it being nothing extraordinary for them to have two lambs at a time, and to yean twice a year. The rams of this breed, engendering with the common ewes of the country, produce an intermediate breed, partaking of the two from which it proceeds.

Some think that the preſent Italian ſheep are the offspring of a mixture of the Aſiatic and the European kinds. But be that as it may, there are in the Breſſan (*d*), towards Mantua, ſheep whoſe wool is indeed coarſe, but of ſo quick growth that they are ſheared three times a year, namely, in March, in July, and in November. It is true, they would not yield ſo great a quantity of wool in cold countries; but in warm ones they will, every where; and yet they are of ſo robuſt a conſtitution, that they fear neither rain, cold, nor even hoar froſts, but will feed at all times in the open field, provided the ground be not covered with ſnow. They yield plenty of milk during four or five months of the year, and excellent cheeſe is made with it. Another kind of Breſcian ſheep, called baſtard ſheep, but for what reaſon I know not, bears ſhearing twice a year, and is much eſteemed, though ſmaller than the former. But the fineſt wool of all Italy proceeds from that kind of ſheep which the Breſcians call *gentili*, and of which numbers are fed in the Trentin, eſpecially about the villages of Ghede and Montechiaro: but as theſe ſheep are extremely difficult to rear and take care of, and as the fineneſs of their wool is owing to the climate and paſture of the country, they probably might not thrive elſewhere.

(*d*) *Ibid. Tom. I. p.* 348.

The

The wool of the Ruſſian, Poliſh, and Tartarian ſheep, is better than that of the common German ſheep; and accordingly the Swedes make uſe of it in their manufactures of cloth, ſtockings, &c.

All the above-mentioned ſorts of ſheep certainly form but one greatly-diverſified ſpecies, which in M. de Buffon's opinion (*e*) hardly extends beyond Europe: for as to thoſe long and broad-tailed creatures ſo common in Africa and Aſia, and to which travellers have given the name of *Barbary ſheep*, they ſeem to him to be of a different ſpecies from our ſheep; as do likewiſe the American vigonia and lama.

Daily experience proves that the European ſheep in ſome degree alter their very nature; for inſtance, in Lincolnſhire they are large, heavy, and ſlow in their gait. On the downs of Suſſex, Wiltſhire, and Dorſetſhire, they are ſmaller, more hardy, and fleeter; and in the mountains of Wales they are ſtill leſs of ſize, and ſo active as ſcarcely to be confined by any incloſures. If we extend our view farther, we ſhall find, that the kind which yields the ſofteſt and fineſt wool in Britain, when ſent to the Weſt Indies becomes hairy like a goat. It is alſo obſerved in North America, that the quality of their wool depends much on the temperature and climate of the country: in ſome of the middle provinces, ſuch as New York, the Jerſeys, &c. their wool is of ſo good a quality, that a ſample of it ſent hither ſome years ago ſold for as high a price as our beſt; although this was only from a common tobacco-plantation, where no care had been taken of it ſince America was firſt ſettled *.

(*e*) *Hiſtoire Naturelle de la Brebis.*

* The fact here alluded to is mentioned in *The Preſent State of America, p.* 142; allowed by Sir J. Dalrymple, in his *Political Eſſays, Sect. I. Colonies, p.* 263; and confirmed by a letter to the writer of this work from an eminent merchant in New York, who ſays poſitively, " our wool in general is *better* than the Eng-
" liſh:

" lish: but how small is the quantity we raise! It is true, some " late oppressive acts, as the sugar-act, stamp-act, and new du- " ty act on glass, paper, &c. raised a spirit in the country for " manufactories, and double the number of sheep; but I affirm, " that our wool was not a quarter part sufficient for our consump- " tion. I have taken pains to get an account of the number of " sheep in New Jersey; and as they were formerly taxed, I be- " lieve it just, and that the whole number does not exceed one " hundred thousand. These, at an average, yield about 2½lb. " each, which is sold for about fifteen pence sterling a pound. " This quantity will be under 3½lb. *per* head, for apparel and " bed-clothes, and not near sufficient for their demand. The " country-people, indeed, mix linen-yarn in their cloth, which " helps out, and makes it very strong; yet, though every pound " is worked up, the towns, villages, and iron-works cannot be " supplied, and depend on English cloth and stuffs. I think " Pennsylvania keeps still fewer sheep. It is true Long-island " and the islands in the Sound greatly exceed: but then the " northern parts of the colony of New-York keep much fewer; " so that, on the whole, they are not equal to Jersey.

" I have found from experience that no farming is more pro- " fitable than sheep, and now keep an hundred and fifty on the " same farm where my predecessor kept but twenty-five. I esti- " mate the profit from eight to ten shillings a head *per annum*, " and this on land that rents at two shillings sterling *per* acre. I " would willingly increase my stock, but find my farm will not " bear it; though, on four hundred acres of arable and mea- " dow land, I only keep besides, eighteen head of cattle, thirty " hogs, eight horses, and plough about eighty acres for sum- " mer and winter grain. I winter, indeed, thirty head more of " young cattle which I summer in the woods. The smallness " of this stock will surprize a British farmer: but our fields do " not yield like those of England; owing to our cold springs " and hot summers, long droughts and heavy rains, bad hus- " bandry and want of manure.

" To what I before said of our not having a sufficient quantity " of wool, I will now add the prices which I actually paid for " manufacturing a piece of cloth, three quarters of a yard " wide.

New York Currency.	£.	s.	d.
" Spinning 23½ lb. of wool, at 3*s*. 6*d*. *per* lb.	4	2	0
" Weaving 34 yards of cloth, at 1*s*. —	1	14	0
" Fulling, pressing, and dyeing 25 yards at 1*s*. 6*d*. — —	1	17	6
" Wool 23½ lb. picked and cleaned, at 2*s*. 6*d*.	2	17	9
£.	10	11	0

" Which

"Which is 8*s*. 5*d*. Currency, or near 5*s*. sterling *per* yard.

"The cloth, after a few days wear, looked very indifferent. "I had it made up for myself, as most of the gentlemen here "pique themselves in setting an example of wearing country-"made cloth; but we were under a necessity of buying Eng-"lish cloth for our negroes. The restrictions being taken off "our trade, we are returned to wearing English cloth, and "hope like causes will not oblige us to recur to the same resolu-"tions.——We are now convinced that we cannot hire to make "cloth under almost double what the English does cost: but at "the same time farmers who have the labour done within them-"selves, and by this means employ the women, who would "otherwise be idle, will always make cloth for themselves with "advantage; especially as it is said to wear better: but we "have not the least prospect of making a yard for exportation." ——This letter was written in December, 1773; the facts related in it may be depended on; and the writer of this work most sincerely wishes, that the long and literal extract of it here given may tend in any sense to rectify the mistaken opinions now, unhappily, too prevalent.——Such is his reason for inserting it here.

CHAP. II.

Of the Management of Sheep.

AS the ſize and welfare of the ſheep, and the goodneſs of their wool, depend much on the nature and quality of their paſture, this becomes an article of the utmoſt importance to the huſbandman, and therefore deſerves a particular enquiry.

In order to their being rightly managed, the owner ſhould be very careful what kind of ſhepherd he entruſts his ſheep to: for the ſhepherd not only accompanies them to the field, but ſhould alſo take care that they do not feed in improper places; improper, on account of the quality of the food and drink, as well as other dangerous circumſtances. He ſhould likewiſe be particularly attentive that no improper rams mix with the flock; to give immediate relief to thoſe that fall ſick, eſpecially in lambing-time, and for this reaſon he ſhould be well acquainted with their diſeaſes. In ſhort, his preſence and care ſhould be ſo conſtant, that the ſheep ſhall obey him out of a kind of love. He ſhould be vigilant and circumſpect, govern them with great clemency, and ſays Columella (*a*), who ſtrictly enjoins the ſame rule to the keepers of all ſorts of cattle, be more like a captain and leader than a lord and maſter. When he threatens them it ſhould be with a loud ſhout and ſhaking his ſtaff at them: but he never ſhould throw any offenſive weapon at them, nor remove to any great diſtance from them; neither ſhould he lie down, or

(*a*) *Lib. VII. c. iii.*

or ſit down, but, unleſs he be going forward, he ſhould ſtand, to be the better able at all times to look around him, to ſee that neither the ſlow and big with young, whilſt they loiter, nor the nimble, whilſt they run before, be ſeparated from the reſt; leſt either a thief or a wild beaſt deceive the heedleſs inattentive guardian.

We find by Columella, that it was an early cuſtom to lead ſheep to far diſtant paſtures at different ſeaſons of the year; and the Spaniards have ſtill retained this practice, as will appear from the following abridgment of a judicious account of their manner of managing the royal flocks, tranſmitted by a gentleman in Spain to the late Mr. Peter Collinſon, F. R. S.

"There are two kinds of ſheep in Spain, namely, "the coarſe-woolled ſheep, which remain all their "lives in their native country, and which are houſed "every night in the winter; and the fine-woolled "ſheep, which are all their lives in the open air, "which travel every ſummer from the cool moun-"tains of the northern parts of Spain, to feed all "the winter on the ſouthern warm plains of Anda-"luſia, Manca, and Eſtremadura. It has appeared "from very accurate calculations, that there are not "fewer than five millions of fine-woolled ſheep in "Spain; and it is reckoned that the wool and fleſh "of a flock of ten thouſand ſheep produce yearly "about twenty-four reals a head, which we may "ſuppoſe to be nearly the value of twelve ſix-pences "ſterling *.

* Of theſe, but one clear a head goes to the owner yearly; three ſix-pences a head go yearly to the king, and the other eight go to the expences of paſture, tythes, ſhepherds, dogs, ſalt, ſheering, &c.——Thus the annual produce of five millions of ſheep amounts to thirty-ſeven millions and a half of ſix-pences, a little more or leſs, of which about three millions and an half are for the owners, above fifteen millions enter into the treaſury, and ſeven millions and a half go to the benefit of the public. Hence it is that the Kings of Spain call theſe flocks, in their ordinances, *The precious Jewel of the Crown.*

"Special ordinances, privileges, and immunities "are issued for the better preservation and government of the sheep, which are under the care of "twenty-five thousand men, who, as the Spaniards "express it, cloath kings in scarlet, and bishops in "purple.

"These sheep pass the summer in the cool mountains of Leo, Old Castile, Cuença, and Arragon. "The first thing the shepherd does when the flock "returns from the south to its summer-downs, is to "give the sheep as much salt as they will eat. Every owner allows his flock of a thousand sheep "twenty-five quintals of salt, which the flock eat "in about five months: they eat none in their journey, nor in their winter-walk. It is believed, "that if they stinted their sheep of this quantity, "it would weaken their constitutions, and degrade "their wool. The shepherd places fifty or sixty flat "stones at about five steps distance from each

Formerly, this jewel was really set in the crown; for a succession of many kings were lords of all the flocks: thence that great number of ordinances, penal laws, privileges, and immunities which issued forth in different reigns for the preservation and special government of the sheep. Hence a royal commission was formed under the title of The Council of the grand royal flock, which exists to this day, though the King has not a single sheep. Various exigencies of state, in different reigns, alienated by degrees the whole grand flock from the crown, together with all its privileges, which were collected and published in the year 1731, under the title of "Laws of the royal Flock;" in a large folio, of above five hundred pages.

The wars and wants of Philip the First's reign, forced that King to sell forty thousand sheep to the Marquis of Iturbieta, which was the last flock of the crown.

Ten thousand sheep compose a flock, which is divided into ten tribes. One man has the conduct of all. He must be the owner of four or five hundred sheep, strong, active, vigilant, intelligent in pasture, in the weather, and in the diseases of sheep. He has absolute dominion over fifty shepherds and fifty dogs, five of each to a tribe. He chooses them, and chastises or discharges them at will. He is the *prepositus*, or chief shepherd of the whole flock.

"other;

"other; he ſtrews ſalt upon each ſtone; he leads "the flock ſlowly through the ſtones, and every "ſheep eats to his liking. What is very remarka-"ble the ſheep never eat nor deſire a grain of ſalt "when they are feeding on land which lies on lime-"ſtone: and as the ſhepherd muſt not ſuffer them "to be too long without ſalt, he leads them to a ſpot "of clayey ſoil, and after a quarter of an hour's "feeding there, they march back to the ſtones and "devour the ſalt. So ſenſible are they of the diffe-"rence, that if they meet with a ſpot of mixed ſoil, "which often happens, they eat ſalt in proportion †.

"Towards the latter end of July, the rams are "turned in among the tribe of ewes, regulated at "ſix or ſeven rams for every hundred ewes; and "when the ſhepherd judges that theſe have been "ſerved, he collects the rams into a ſeparate tribe to "feed apart. There is alſo another tribe of rams "which feed apart, and never ſerve the ewes, but "are kept ſolely for their wool and for the butchery: "for though the wool and fleſh of wethers are finer "and more delicate than thoſe of rams, yet the "fleece of a ram weighs more than the fleece of a "wether, who is likewiſe ſhorter-lived than the "ram: for theſe reaſons there are but few wethers "in the royal flock of Spain. The fleeces of three "rams generally weigh twenty-five pounds; and "there muſt be the wool of four wethers, and that "of five ewes, to make an equal weight. There is "the ſame diſproportion in their lives, which depend "on their teeth: for when theſe fail, they cannot "bite the graſs, and are of courſe condemned to "the knife. The ewe's teeth begin to fail after five "years of age, the wether's after ſix, and thoſe of "the robuſt ram not till towards eight.

† This ſhews how favourable for ſheep thoſe paſtures are which lie on lime-ſtone, or chalk, as moſt in England do; for in the ſouth of this iſland there is chalk almoſt every where, and lime-ſtone abounds in the north-weſt.

"At the latter end of September they put on the "redding or ocre, which is a ponderous irony "earth, common in Spain: the shepherd dissolves "it in water, and dawbs the backs of the sheep with "it from the neck to the rump. It is an old cus-"tom. Some say it mixes with the grease of the "wool, and so becomes a varnish impenetrable to "the rain and cold; others, that it's weight keeps "the wool down, and thereby hinders it from grow-"ing long and coarse; and others again, that it "acts as an absorbent earth, and receives part of the "transpiration, which would foul the wool, and "render it harsh.

"Likewise in the latter end of September the "sheep begin their march towards the low plains. "Their itinerary is marked out by immemorial cus-"tom, and by ordinances. Their journies are of-"ten so long, that the poor creatures go six or se-"ven leagues a day to get into open wilds, where "the shepherd walks slow, to let them feed at their "ease and rest: but they never stop; they have no "day of repose; they march at least two leagues a "day, constantly following the shepherd, till they "get to their journey's end. From the territory "called the Montana, at the extremity of Old Cas-"tile, from whence they set out, to Estremadura, "is an hundred and fifty leagues, which they "march in less than forty days. The chief shep-"herd's first care is to see that each tribe is conduct-"ed to the same district it fed in the year before, "and where the sheep were yeaned, which they "think prevents a variation in the wool; though "this requires but little care; for it is a known "truth, that the sheep would go to that very spot "of their own accord. His next care is to fix the "toils ‡ (in England hurdles) where the sheep pass

‡ The toils are made of Sparto, in meshes a foot wide, and the thickness of a finger. Sparto is a sort of rush which bears twisting into ropes for coasting vessels. It is so light as to swim; whereas hemp sinks. The English sailors call it boss.

"the

" the night, lest they should stray, and fall into the
" jaws of wolves.

" Next comes the time when the ewes begin to
" drop their lambs, which is the most toilsome and
" most solicitous part of the pastoral life. The
" shepherds first cull out the barren from pregnant
" ewes, which last are conducted to the best shelter,
" and the others to the bleakest part of the district.
" As the lambs fall, they are led apart with their
" dams to another comfortable spot. A third divi-
" sion is made of the last-yeaned lambs, for whom
" was allotted from the beginning the most fertile
" part, the best soil, and the sweetest grass of the
" down, in order that they may become as vigor-
" ous as the first-yeaned; for they must all march
" on the same day towards their summer-quarters.
" The shepherds perform four operations upon all
" the lambs about the same time in the month of
" March; *viz.* they cut off their tails five inches
" below the rump, for cleanliness; they mark them
" on the nose with a hot iron; they saw off part of
" their horns, that the rams may neither hurt one
" another nor the ewes; and they emasculate the
" lambs intended for bell-weathers to walk at the
" head of the tribe.

" As soon as April comes, the sheep express, by
" various uneasy motions, a strong desire to return
" to their summer-habitations. The shepherds must
" then exert all their vigilance to prevent their
" escaping; for it has often happened that a tribe
" has stolen a forced march of three or four leagues
" upon a drowsy shepherd; and there are many ex-
" amples of three or four strayed sheep walking a
" hundred leagues to the very place they fed on the
" year before.

" In the summer sheep-walks I learnt that the
" three following opinions should be ranked among
" vulgar errors:

" 1. That salt-springs are not found in the high
" mountains, but in the low hills and plains only.

" —The

" —The whole territory of Molina is full of ſalt-
" ſprings, and there is a copious one riſing out of
" land higher than the ſource of the Tagus, and
" not far from it; which is one of the higheſt lands in
" all the inward parts of Spain.

" 2. That metallic vapours deſtroy vegetation;
" and that no rocks nor mountains pregnant with
" rich veins of ore are covered with rich vegetable
" ſoils.——There are many iron, copper, lead, and
" pure pyritous ores in theſe ſheep-walks, where
" grow the ſame plants, and the ſame ſweet graſs,
" as in the other parts.

" 3. That ſheep eat and love aromatic plants;
" and that the fleſh of thoſe that feed on the hills
" where ſweet herbs abound has a fine taſte.—I
" have obſerved, that when the ſhepherd made a
" pauſe, and let the ſheep feed at their will, they
" ſought only for fine graſs, and never touched any
" aromatic plant, that when the creeping *ſerpillum*
" was interwoven with the graſs, they induſtriouſ-
" ly noſled it aſide to bite a blaid of graſs; and that
" this trouble ſoon made them ſeek out a pure gra-
" mineous ſpot. I obſerved too, when the ſhep-
" herd perceived a threatening cloud, and gave a
" ſignal to the dogs to collect the tribe and then go
" behind it, walking apace himſelf to lead the ſheep
" to ſhelter, that, as they had no time to ſtoop,
" they would take a ſnap of ſtæchas, roſemary, or
" any other ſhrub in their way: for ſheep will eat
" any thing when they are hungry, or when they
" walk faſt. I ſaw them greedily devour henbane,
" hemlock, glaucium, and other nauſeous weeds,
" upon their iſſue out of the ſheering-houſe ‖.

" The

‖ Mr. Collinſon's correſpondent obſerves very juſtly on this occaſion, that if ſheep loved aromatic plants, it would be one of the greateſt misfortunes that could befall the farmers of Spain; for that the number there is incredibly great, and the bees ſuck all their honey, and gather all their wax, from the aromatic flowers which

"The ſhepherd's chief care now is, not to ſuffer the ſheep to go out of their toils till the morning-ſun has exhaled the dew of a white froſt, and never to let them approach a rivulet or pond after a ſhower of hail; for if they ſhould eat the dewy graſs, or drink hail-water, the whole tribe would become melancholy, loſe all appetite, pine away and die; of which there have been frequent inſtances *.

"The ſheep of Andaluſia, which never travel, have coarſe, long, hairy wool. I ſaw ſome in Eſtremadura whoſe wool trailed on the ground. The itinerant ſheep have ſhort, ſilky, white wool; the fineneſs of which is owing to the animal's paſſing its life in the open air, of equal temperature; for it is not colder in Andaluſia or Eſtremadura in the winter, than it is in the Montana or Molina in ſummer. Conſtant heat, or conſtant cold, with houſing, are the cauſes of coarſe, ſpeckled, black wool: and I do believe, from a few experiments and long obſervation, that if the fine-woolled ſheep ſtayed at home in the winter, their wool would become coarſe in a few generations; and on the other hand, that if the coarſe woolled ſheep travelled from climate to climate, and lived

which enamel and perfume two thirds of the ſheep-walks.—He aſſures us, that he himſelf knew a pariſh-prieſt who had five thouſand hives, and whoſe method was cautiouſly to ſeize the queens in a ſmall crape fly-catch, and then clip off their wings. This obliged their majeſties to ſtay at home; and he declared, that he never had loſt a ſwarm from the day of his diſcovery to the time of his relating this, which was five years.—I mention this circumſtance the more readily, becauſe I do not recollect having noticed it in my *Treatiſe on the management of Bees*, where it ought to have been.

* Hail-water is likewiſe ſo pernicious to men in the climate here ſpoken of, that the people of Molina will not drink their river-water after a violent ſhower of hail; experience has taught them the danger: but let it be never ſo muddy, and riſe never ſo high after rain, they drink it without fear.—Perhaps this may be the unheeded cauſe of many epidemics in other cities.

" in the free air, their wool would become fine, " ſhort, and ſilky likewiſe in a few generations.

" All the animals that I know of, who live in the " open air, conſtantly keep up to the colour of their " ſires. There are the moſt beautiful brindled ſheep " in the world among the coarſe-woolled ſheep of " Spain. I never ſaw one among the fine-woolled " flocks: the free but leſs abundant perſpiration in " the open air, is ſwept away as faſt as it flows; " whereas it is greatly increaſed by the exceſſive " heat of numbers of ſheep houſed all night in a " narrow place. It fouls the wool, makes it hairy, " and changes it's colour.—The Swine of Spain, " who paſs their lives in the woods, are all of one " colour, as the wild boars. They have fine, ſil- " ky, curled briſtles. Never did a Spaniſh hog's " briſtle pierce a ſhoe.—What a quantity of dander " is daily ſcoured from the glands of a ſtabled horſe; " the curry-comb and hair-cloth ever in hand! How " clean is the ſkin of a horſe that lives in the open " air!

" The ſhepherds begin to ſheer their ſheep on " the firſt of May, provided the weather be fair: " for if the wool were not quite dry, the fleeces, " which are cloſe piled one upon another, would " rot. It is for this reaſon that their ſheering-houſes " are ſurprizingly ſpacious. I ſaw ſome large enough " to contain twenty thouſand ſheep in bad weather, " and which coſt above five thouſand pounds ſterling. " Beſides, the ewes are creatures of ſuch tender " conſtitutions, that if they were expoſed immedi- " ately after ſheering, they would all periſh.

" An hundred and twenty-five ſheermen are em- " ployed to ſheer a flock of ten thouſand ſheep. " One man ſheers twelve ewes a day, and but eight " rams. The reaſon of this difference is, not only " becauſe the rams have larger bodies, ſtronger, " and more wool; but alſo becauſe the ſheermen " dare not tie their feet as they do thoſe of the un-

" reſiſting

" resisting ewes. Experience having taught, that " the bold rebellious ram will struggle, even to suf- " focation, when held captive under the sheers, they " gently lay him down, stroke his belly, and be- " guile him out of his fleece. A certain number of " sheep are led into the great shelter-house, which " is a parallelogram of four or five hundred feet " long and an hundred wide, where they remain all " night, crowded as close together as the shepherd " can keep them, that they may sweat plentifully, " which, say they, softens the wool for the sheers, " and oils their edges. They are led by degrees, in " the morning, into the spacious sheering-hall, " which joins the sweating-room. The shep- " herd carries them off as fast as they are shorne, to " be marked with tar: and as this operation is ne- " cessarily performed upon only one at a time, it " gives a fair opportunity to the shepherds to " cull out for the butchery all the sheep of the flock " who have outlived their teeth. The sheered sheep " go to the fields to feed a little if it be fine weather, " and they return in the evening to pass the night " in the yard before the house, within the shelter of " the walls; but if it be cold and cloudy, they go " into the house, and are thus brought by degrees " to bear the open air."

The above, or a similar practice, might be followed to advantage by the counties which border on Wales, or on the Grampian hills in Scotland: for in both those countries there is summer-pasture for a much greater number of cattle than they can maintain in the winter. In both, the pasture is not only dry and healthy for sheep, but they would likewise thereby avoid the great summer-heats to which they are at times exposed, even in this moderate climate.

In dry and high grounds, where the herbage is thick and fine, the sheep are much more healthy, and their flesh is of a much finer flavour than that of those which are fed in moist vallies and low plains;

unless

unleſs thoſe vales be ſandy, or very dry, or near the ſea. Theſe laſt are, indeed, the beſt of all, becauſe the herbage there is naturally ſprinkled with ſalt. Alſo the ewes fed on them yield more milk, and of a better taſte.

Sheep ſhould not, if poſſible, be ſuffered to feed on low moiſt grounds, or ſuch as have been lately drained, unleſs theſe are become very dry; and even then it ſhould be only in the middle of the day. Grounds over which mineral or hard waters run are alſo prejudicial to them; as is likewiſe graſs in which the webs or eggs of graſs-hoppers, or other inſects, are found; or in which the dung of rats or field-mice lies. When ſheep are forced to feed on ſuch paſtures, it is adviſeable to rub their mouths frequently with ſalt, and to have ſalt laid for them in veſſels, where they will greedily lick it one after another; for they are remarkably fond of ſalt, and nothing is more healthful when given in moderation.

The world is greatly indebted to the celebrated Linnæus for the enquiry which he has excited in regard to ſuch plants as are agreeable or hurtful to each domeſtic animal. He has obſerved, in a diſſertation intitled *Pan Suecus* (*b*), that ſheep eat 387 ſorts of Swediſh herbs and plants; and that they leave 141 of them untouched, as being hurtful, or leſs nouriſhing, and therefore leſs ſuitable to their nature. —A ſimilar account of our Engliſh plants might be of great ſervice to our huſbandmen and owners of land, eſpecially to ſuch as are concerned in grazing.

Among other intereſting obſervations, Linnæus remarks (*c*), that the milfoil, or yarrow, is a food which ſheep are particularly fond of; and I have been told by a gentleman who had been at much pains to clear his ground of this plant, that having turned ſome ſheep into a field where there yet remained a good deal of it, he was greatly ſurpriſed at

(*b*) *Page* 387. (*c*) *Pan Suecus, page* 95.

finding

finding the next day that the ſheep had ſcarcely left a plant of it, but had eaten it quite down to the ground. He then lamented his former induſtry, and laid down as an eaſy rule, by which every one may judge what plants are moſt agreeable to the dfferent animals, to obſerve which are thoſe that they prefer on being turned into a freſh paſture, or what are the plants in common paſtures which the creatures feeding there never ſuffer to raiſe to ſeed. Thus the milfoil never runs to ſeed but in places where ſheep cannot get at it. It is the ſame with the chamomile, though ſo bitter a plant, and with the narrow-leaved plantain or ribwort. Theſe plants have another advantage attending them with regard to ſheep, which is, that as they ſtrike deep roots they retain their verdure the longer, and therefore deſerve to be carefully cultivated by thoſe who have flocks of ſheep.

Burnet has, on all occaſions, been found to be peculiarly pleaſing and healthful to ſheep. An inſtance of it's being both happened to a gentleman of my acquaintance in the year 1766; the ſummer of which being extremely wet, ſheep in general were much afflicted with the rot. This gentleman, very attentive to rural oeconomy, bought ſome ſheep in the autumn of that year, which he put into a field of burnet, and killed them during the winter, as his family-conſumption required. Every one of them was found to be in a perfectly ſound ſtate; whilſt every ſheep belonging to a neighbouring gentleman, and which had been part of the ſame flock, which was Welſh, was diſeaſed. It was very remarkable too in theſe laſt ſheep, that, though they had plenty of graſs and turnips, they could not be confined; but the moment they were put into the field of burnet belonging to the former gentleman, they became perfectly quiet, and never endeavoured to ſtir from thence, though the gate was left open.

The

The common opinion that ſheep hurt lucerne in the autumn by biting it too cloſe, is without foundation; for the ſpring-ſhoots have no communication with thoſe that remained in the autumn, but are quite freſh ſhoots iſſuing from the crown of the root. Lucerne is an excellent food for all ſheep in the autumn, and particularly ſo for ewes and lambs in the ſpring.

Clover is a very ſucculent food for ſheep, and theſe creatures are extremely fond of it; but if the ſhepherd is not attentive, it may prove dangerous to them. He ſhould always turn them into the clover with their backs to the wind, and not leave them too long in it. It is ſaid by ſome, that the wind mixing with the clover, which they ſwallow greedily, ſwells them, and makes them die in a few hours: others believe that it is the venom of the reptils which this plant attracts, that occaſions theſe pretty frequent accidents: but, in truth, the cauſe of this ſwelling is undoubtedly the ſame as was before aſſigned for the hoving of cattle; and accordingly the remedy directed for it by the Royal Society of Agriculture at Rouen is, as ſoon as this misfortune is perceived to have happened to ſome of the flock, to throw cold water over their bodies, if it be at hand, or to pen them up ſo cloſely as to make them preſs ſtrongly one againſt another. This will reſtore them to their natural ſtate.

Sheep likewiſe readily eat turnips, and thrive upon them, when they have been accuſtomed to them early; but they do not reliſh this food when it has not been offered to them till after they are grown old; however, if they are kept faſting two or three days, moſt of them take to it; and when they have once taſted it, they become fond of it, and feed very kindly upon it. In ſome places people feed their lambs with turnips till the middle of April, though they then begin to run up to ſeed. Some parboil them a little at firſt, till their cattle, and particular-

ly

ly their ſheep, are accuſtomed to them: but a lamb only three weeks old will, after it has once eaten of this food, ſcoop out a raw turnip with great delight. Parſley corrects the inconveniencies which may ariſe from the too-great moiſture and coldneſs of the turnips, and therefore ſhould be given them in plenty when they are fed upon this root. The ſheep alſo are fond of it.

Carrots are another excellent food for ſheep, and theſe creatures are remarkably fond of them. One acre of theſe roots, well planted, will fatten a greater number of ſheep, or bullocks, than three acres of turnips, and their fleſh will be firmer and better taſted. Parſnips are alſo another excellent and profitable food for them.

It is a cuſtom in moſt countries, eſpecially where the verdure of the graſs is not ſo conſtant as in Britain and Ireland, to collect the leaves of trees during the ſummer, or before they turn yellow, for feeding all kinds of cattle, and particularly ſheep; and when theſe are mixed with their hay, they have a good effect. Straw, eſpecially of oats, cut and mixed with their hay, is alſo recommended during the winter. The bark of the branches of the fig-tree, and it's buds, are likewiſe mixed with their hay in countries where that tree abounds.

It is undoubtedly moſt healthy for ſheep to range at large; but as that is not in the power of every one, they ſhould at leaſt be kept as airy as poſſible.

We are ſo happy in the mildneſs of our climate in England, and in our ſafety from wolves, that our ſheep lie out of doors all the year. Yet I cannot help thinking that they would be greatly benefited if there were at leaſt ſheds under which they might retreat in ſtormy weather: for though ſheep are well cloathed by nature, yet when the rain is ſo conſtant and heavy as to ſoak through their fleeces, they become quite chilled, and that damp cold in them is frequently the cauſe of many diſorders. It is ſaid, that when they are enclosed in the narrow compass of a fold, they cherish one another by their mutual warmth: but this cannot give relief to the damp which each of them feels.

In climates less fortunately circumstanced than ours, the sheep are housed in winter, and fed chiefly with dry fodder. They are led out every day, unless the weather be very bad, though this is rather to air and walk than to feed them. In winter it should be near ten in the morning before they are led out, and they should be brought back again early in the evening, after having had an opportunity of drinking. In spring and autumn they are led to pasture as soon as the sun has dispersed the hoar-frost or dew on the grass, and continued there till sun-set. It is sufficient that they drink once a day in these seasons; and when brought back they should find fodder, though in less quantity than in winter. It is only during the summer-months that they can live entirely on the pastures, and they should then have water in their power twice a day. They may in this season be let out early in the morning; and in very warm weather they should be led to cool or shadowy places during the mid-day heat, which is found to be remarkably prejudicial, disordering their heads, and throwing them into vertigoes. In very hot countries, Columella advises, that they be led in the morning so that their backs be turned to the sun, and in the evening so that the head may be shaded by the body.

Many people doubt whether it be more profitable to fold sheep, than it is to let them range a field at large both night and day; on the principle that their dung and urine are in either case pretty equally spread over the surface of the ground. Custom has, however, given it in favour of folding; and I believe it will be found, that if equal numbers of sheep are confined during the same time in two fields, that in which they are folded will be the most effectually

and

and moſt regularly dunged; and therefore I muſt incline to prefer folding.

In the heat of ſummer, the fold ſhould be large enough to admit of the ſheep lying at a moderate diſtance from each other; for, even in the open air, a great heat is generated by the ſheep when forced to be cloſe together; and more than an ordinary degree of warmth ſhould be avoided at all times. As the weather becomes colder, the extent of the fold may be diminiſhed; but ſpecial care ſhould be taken never to pitch it in a damp place, particularly in rainy weather, or winter; for nothing is ſo prejudicial to ſheep as their being laid wet. On this account it is that in Sweden, ſince the late regulations there, they have in ſome provinces a kind of covered fold going upon wheels, ſo that it can be moved from one place to another: and I am perſuaded, that if this practice was introduced into England, eſpecially in rich low paſtures, a conſiderable advantage would attend it, particularly in preventing the rot and purging which ſheep are liable to in wet weather.

Where the great degree of cold, or any other cauſe, renders it neceſſary to houſe ſheep in the winter, their cotes ſhould be built on a dry ſpot; the ſheep ſhould have ſufficient room in them, and openings ſhould be made in the upper parts to carry off the heated air: they ſhould not, on any account, be made too warm, nor ſhould the dung and litter ever be ſuffered to riſe too high in them. The racks for the ſheep ſhould never be fixed to the wall, but hang from the roof, ſo that they may be raiſed or lowered at pleaſure. They ſhould never hang too high; becauſe when the ſheep are obliged to raiſe their heads too much, little bits of their food are apt to fall among their wool, which they intangle, and alſo in their eyes, where they bring on inflammations, and ſometimes blindneſs. The rack ſhould therefore not be higher than the flanks of the ſheep.

The roof of the cote ſhould be covered with laths rather than with ſtraw, or other ſuch material, becauſe the duſt, chaff, or inſects falling from theſe laſt would damage the wool. Spiders eſpecially are very hurtful to ſheep. The Swedes are ſo particularly careful in this reſpect, that they even white-waſh the walls of their ſheep-cotes.

When the winters are very ſevere, or the ſheep are in great danger from ravenous animals, it becomes neceſſary to lodge them in houſes, or cotes, during the winter (*d*). Such cotes ſhould be built in dry and airy places, free from ſprings, and from the coming in of water any other way. Whilſt the ſheep are houſed, great care ſhould be taken that the cotes be not kept ſo cloſe as to render the air in them too warm, and that the ſheep have very ſufficient room to lie down. In order to ſecure them from too much heat, the beſt way of admitting a ſupply of freſh air will perhaps be by windows in each end, near the roof; for it is known that the heated and putrid air aſcends, and therefore it will be diſcharged by theſe windows; for there will be a conſtant current of air from the one to the other, as the wind ſhall happen to ſet. The ſheep will, by this means, be kept cool, without having openings through which the wind would blow upon their bodies partially, and thereby occaſion coughs and colds, as every one can teſtify from his own experience.

The proportion of ſpace which Mr. Haſtfer, an ingenious Swede, adviſes (*e*) as a rule in building theſe ſheep-cotes, is to allow ſix feet ſquare for each ſheep*; the height ſhould be proportioned to the extent of the building, and to the number of ſheep; but there muſt be at leaſt ten feet between the floor

(*d*) *Memoires de la Societé Royale d'Agriculture de Rouen, tom. ii.*

(*e*) *Manierè d'élever les Bêteſà Laine, Part ii. c.* 2. §. 2.

* Three Swediſh ells, ſays he, which make very near ſix of our feet; the Swediſh ell being exactly 23 $\frac{380}{1000}$ inches Engliſh meaſure.

and

and the roof, ſo that when the depth of dung and ſtraw ſhall amount to four feet, there may ſtill remain an height of ſix feet for the heat to aſcend in: for when the hot exhalations of the ſheep have not ſufficient room to aſcend, they return back, and fall upon the lungs of the ſheep, open their pores, and make them ſweat more than ever. Conſequently great care ſhould always be taken to make theſe buildings high enough, and large enough to prevent ſuch immoderate heat. †

A cote twenty feet long ſhould be ten feet high; that is the proportion for ſmall cotes: but to twenty feet more in length there muſt always be added two feet more in height; that is to ſay, that for forty feet of length there muſt be twelve feet of height, and ſo in proportion for larger ſizes.—The breadth is generally half of the length: that is the beſt ſymmetrical proportion, and gives the greateſt ſtrength to the roof: though Mr. Hatsfer would have them rather exceed the above dimenſions in point of height, becauſe that contributes greatly to keep the air purer than it would otherwiſe be, and nearer to the temperature of a cool ſummer's day, or a fine clear day in autumn, which is the degree of warmth moſt to be deſired, and that for the following reaſons in particular:

"1. In the ſpring, when the cold is greater abroad than in the cote, it is wrong to keep the cote too warm, becauſe the ſudden change from heat to cold is too ſenſibly felt by the ſheep, has an influence on their blood, and neceſſarily affects their ſtrength and health.

"2. In winter, the ſheep, by paſſing ſuddenly from hot to cold, and from cold to hot, cannot but get coughs.

† A cote twenty feet ſquare is large enough for thirty ſheep; and a cote ſixty feet long and thirty feet wide is ſufficient for an hundred and fifty ſheep, including rams and lambs. Any one may of courſe form his calculation from hence. HASTFER. *Manière d'éleverles Bêtes à Laine. Part ii.*

" 3. It is plain, that if too great perſpiration is hurtful to ſheep in ſummer, when freſh graſs gives them the moſt ſtrength, it muſt be much more ſo in winter, when they eat only dry hay, or even ſtraw, which affords them leſs ſtrength, and leſs nouriſhment; eſpecially as the heat, which ought to prevent, or at leaſt moderate, the bad effects of the ſuperfluous humours, is at the ſame time evaporated and waſted.

" 4. The heat which penetrates through the pores into the groſs winter's wool, makes it grow too much: now this wool is not only of leſs value than the other good wool which the ſheep is to keep till ſhearing-time; but it falls off of it's own accord as ſoon as the ſheep paſs from the cote into the cold ſpring-air; and then this loſs of their wool cauſes illneſſes in them, and even death.

" The floor of the ſheep-cote ſhould be paved either with ſtones, or with bricks or clinkers, and raiſed a little archwiſe in the middle, in order that the urine of the ſheep may run off eaſily on all ſides through ſmall holes made for that purpoſe at the bottom of the building. Some cover this floor with earth, and others with ſand, to the depth of five or ſix inches, in order that the urine of the ſheep may ſoak into it, and thereby render it fit for manuring of land.—The floor itſelf may indeed be made of ſand, as is the practice of ſome; and in that caſe, inſtead of raiſing it in the middle, it ſhould be ſome-what lower there, in order that the urine may penetrate thoroughly into the ſand; and when it is ſufficiently impregnated, it is covered with new ſand, or thrown out of the cote with the dung of the ſheep, and laid up in a heap for manure.

" It is likewiſe to be obſerved, that of whatever height the cote may be, the dung in it ſhould never be ſuffered to increaſe to more than four feet deep: for which reaſon the ſides of the cote ſhould be lined with wood to that height in the inſide. The cote

ſhould

ſhould be more or leſs high in proportion to the number of ſheep kept in it; for by this means the heat will be more or leſs great, as it will riſe to a greater or leſs height.

" In whatever manner the floor of the cote is made, it ſhould always be covered with freſh ſtraw before the ſheep are put into it; as well for their pleaſure as for their health. By this means too their wool is preſerved from filth; and when the floor is made of wood, as is alſo the way of ſome, the ſtraw preſerves the ſheep from having their ſkin or their fleſh hurt by ſplinters, or their wool by turpentine in the boards, eſpecially if of deal. This ſtraw muſt be removed from time to time, and in ſome caſes pretty often. Care muſt likewiſe be taken that there be neither ſplinters nor turpentine in the ſide-linings towards the bottom; for which reaſon the wood uſed there, and indeed as high as the ſheep could reach from the top of the greateſt quantity of dung that ought to be in the cote, ſhould not be touched with either axe or plane, but left in its natural round form, with only the rough bark thoroughly peeled off it, and the wood then left for ſome time to dry in the ſun, in order that all it's reſinous parts may be exhaled. Such is the method of the Swedes when they build cotes of this kind.

" Beſides the above-mentioned windows at each end of the cote, intended chiefly to purify the air in it, there ſhould likewiſe be other common windows at convenient diſtances in the ſides of this building; becauſe, as was before obſerved, ſheep are fond of much light, and never thrive well in dark places.

" Their fodder ſhould ſtand in ricks near the cotes, and be kept as free as poſſible from duſt and all other impurities.

" The ſheep in the cote ſhould be foddered in cribs made for that purpoſe, as well for the ſake of ſaving, as to prevent the falling of any thing upon their wool; and for this reaſon theſe cribs ſhould be placed in the middle of the cote; for if any hay chances to fall upon the ſheep, they pull off each others wool in trying to eat it.

"The cote thus built, however ſmall it be, muſt be divided into two parts at leaſt, in order to ſeparate the ſick ſheep, or ſuch as are ready to lamb, from thoſe which are not in either of theſe caſes: but they who would have a perfectly complete building to houſe their ſheep in, ſhould divide it into ſeveral compartments, in proportion to the number and kinds of the ſheep, and according to the other circumſtances attending them. Theſe compartments may be made of whatever ſize is thought moſt proper, provided the ſheep have but room enough in them.—Or, which would ſeem to be an improvement on Mr. Haſtfer's plan, the cotes ſhould rather be built ſeparate, becauſe then, beſides the more effectual parting of them in caſe of need, each kind of ſheep will naturally go to the home where they are fed.

"Beſides the above-mentioned compartments, it is neceſſary to have a moveable crib, about four feet high, going upon four wheels of ſeven or eight inches diameter each, to be drawn from one place to another. The uſe of it is to bring the ſheep cloſe up together in a ſmall compaſs, when one would either make them ſweat, or count them over. By this means their rubbing one againſt another, by which they loſe a great deal of wool, is avoided.

"It is likewiſe neceſſary to have a ſmall building ſeparate from the common cote or cotes, to keep apart ſuch ſheep as are attacked with contagious diſeaſes, in order that their breath may not infect the others.

"As to the colour of the ſheep-cote, ſome would have it to be white, or of the colour of the wood it is built of, in order that the ſheep big with young may not ſee in it any thing to ſurprize them.

"The

"The beſt covering, or roof, is that which is made of ſtraw or holly. The roofs made of boards are apt to warp, and let in the air through their crevices.

"Great care muſt be taken to preſerve the cote free from ſpiders and their webs.

"The outſide ſhould be ſmooth, and free from every kind of glutinous ſubſtance, at leaſt as high as the ſheep can reach, leſt they ſhould rub themſelves againſt it, and thereby tear off their wool.

"There ſhould be gutters all along the lower part of the roof to receive and carry off rain.

"As ſoon as the cote is finiſhed, it ſhould be fumigated in the inſide, by burning in it hoofs or horns of cattle raſped, the hair of cattle, woollen rags, brimſtone, and boughs of juniper with their fruit on."

Mr. Haſtfer's above directions appear to be chiefly calculated for a woody country: but where ſtones are plentiful, the walls will be beſt built with them, and tiles or ſlates will make proper cocovering for the cotes.

A certain fixed time of the year cannot be obſerved in all countries for ſhearing of ſheep, becauſe the ſummer does not advance equally in each of them. The beſt way therefore is to be directed by the weather, ſo that the ſheep may neither ſuffer by the cold when ſtripped of their wool, nor be injured through too great heat by being made to wear it too long. After they are ſhorne, they ſhould be anointed with ſomething that will deſtroy any remaining vermin. Columella (*f*) recommends for this purpoſe a ſtrong decoction of lupins, lees of wine, and the dregs of oil, of each equal quantities, mixed together. Some uſe a decoction of tobacco in ſalt water. After the ſkin has been ſoaked with one or other of theſe li-

(*f*) *Lib. VII. c. iv.*

quors

quors for three days, the ſheep ſhould be waſhed in the ſea, if near; otherwiſe in water in which ſalt has been boiled.

The wethers have generally more wool than the ewes, and it is alſo better. That of the neck and the top of the back is the prime; that of the thighs, tail, belly, throat, and head, is not ſo good; and the worſt is that which is taken from dead beaſts, or ſuch as are ſick. White wool is alſo preferred to the grey, brown, and black, becauſe it will take any dye. Strait wool is better than curled; and it is even ſaid that the ſheep whoſe wool is too much curled are not in ſo good a ſtate of health as thoſe whoſe wool is ſtraiter.

The general colour of ſheep is a dirty white, or pale yellow; there are alſo many of a blackiſh brown, and not a few ſpotted with a yellowiſh white and black.

The flock ſhould be examined every year, in order to pick out ſuch as begin to grow old, and are intended for fattening; for as theſe require a different management from the others, they ſhould then be formed into a ſeparate flock. They ſhould be led abroad in ſummer before the riſing of the ſun, that they may feed on the graſs whilſt it is yet moiſtened with dew; for nothing forwards the fattening of wethers more than a great quantity of moiſture: and as, on the other hand, nothing obſtructs it more than too much heat, they ſhould be brought home, or at leaſt driven to a ſhady place, at about eight or nine in the morning, before the ſun begins to be too powerful; and ſalt ſhould then be given them to excite thirſt. About four in the afternoon, they ſhould be led a ſecond time into cool and moiſt places, and be again made to drink as much water as they can before they are either houſed or folded at night. Two or three months of this management will give them all the appearance of being full of fleſh: indeed they will be fattened as much as they can be: but as this fat

fat proceeds only from the great quantity of water which they drink, it may properly be looked upon as no better than an œdema, or bloated humour, which would in a ſhort time turn to the rot; the only means of preventing which is to kill them whilſt in this ſtate of fatneſs: though even then their fleſh, far from being firm and juicy, is extremely inſipid and flabby. To render their fleſh perfectly fine and good, they ſhould, beſides feeding on the dew and drinking a great quantity of water, have at the ſame time more ſolid food than graſs. To this end the ſhepherd ſhould alſo, in the ſeaſon, turn them into the fields, to glean, as ſoon as the corn has been taken off. They may be fattened in any ſeaſon, even the winter not excepted, by only keeping them apart in a ſheep-cote, and feeding them with good hay, meal, or barley, oats, wheat, beans, &c. mixed with ſalt, to make them drink the more copiouſly. But in whatever manner, and in whatever ſeaſon they are fattened, they muſt be diſpoſed of immediately; for they cannot be fattened twice, and if they are not killed by the butcher, they will die by diſeaſes of the liver. Three months are at all times ſufficient to fatten them; but leſs will do near the ſea.

Ewes fatten very faſt near their pregnancy, becauſe they then eat more than at other times: but their fleſh, and eſpecially that of an old ewe, is flabby and inſipid. That of the ram, though he has been knit before fattening, is always rank and ill-flavoured. The fleſh of the wether is by far the moſt ſucculent, and the beſt of all common meats.

The proper time for caſtration is when the lambs are five or ſix months old, and the weather mild. The beſt way of performing this operation is by inciſion. The teſticles, which are eaſily ſeparated from the bag, are then drawn out at the wound, and cut off. The lamb will probably be ſick and dull for a little while after the caſtration, and therefore it will not be improper to give him for two or three days

days a ſmall quantity of ſalt, to prevent a loſs of appetite, which this operation often occaſions.

The antients tell us that all ruminating animals have ſuet; but this is ſtrictly true only of the goat and ſheep, and that of the ſheep is in greater quantity, whiter, drier, firmer, and of a better quality than the other. Fat differs from ſuet, in that it continues always ſoft; whereas ſuet hardens as it grows cold. It is chiefly about the kidneys that the ſuet is found; and, as was before obſerved of the horned cattle, the left has always more of it than the right. There is alſo a great deal of it in the cawl, and about the inteſtines; but this ſuet is far leſs firm and good than that of the kidneys, the tail, and other parts of the body. Wethers have no other fat than ſuet; and ſo predominant is this fat in their conſtitution, that all the extremities of their fleſh are covered with it. Their very blood is not without it; and the ſeminal lymph is ſo ſaturated with it, as to appear of a different conſiſtence from that of other animals.

CHAP. III.

Of the Propagation of Sheep.

THE ram is capable of generating at eighteen months, and a ewe may yean at the end of a year: but it is better to ſtay till the ewe be two, and the ram three years old; for the produce of theſe, if too early, or even the firſt at any time, is always weak, and of a bad conſtitution. One good ram will ſuffice for twenty-five or thirty ewes.

The qualities required in a good ram are, that he be ſtrong and comely: his head muſt be large and thick; his forehead broad, round, and well riſing; his eyes large and black; his noſe ſhort; his neck thick, and arched like that of a fine horſe; his body long and raiſed; his ſhoulders, back, and rump broad; his teſticles large, and his tail long; his legs ſmall, ſhort, and nimble; he muſt alſo have horns; for thoſe which have not any, as is the caſe of ſome, are very indifferent creatures for breeding, at leaſt in climates like our's. The beſt rams are white, with a large quantity of wool on the belly, tail, head and ears, quite down to the eyes; and particular care ſhould be taken that neither the mouth nor tongue be either black or ſpeckled, becauſe the wool of the lambs would moſt probably partake of this defect.

The beſt ewes for propagation are thoſe which have moſt wool, and that cloſe, long, ſilky, and white; eſpecially if they have alſo a large body, a thick neck, and an eaſy, light gait.

The natural ſeaſon of the ewe's heat is from the beginning of November to the end of April; but they

they may be brought to conceive in any ſeaſon, by giving them provocative foods, ſuch as bread made of hemp-ſeed, or oatmeal, oil cakes, &c. and water in which ſalt has been diluted. Each ewe ſhould be covered three or four times, and then ſeparated from the ram, which always prefers the older ſheep, and neglects the younger. In the ſeaſon of copulation, they ſhould not be expoſed to rain or bad weather; wet hindering their retention, and a clap of thunder often producing abortion. In a day or two after they have been covered, they ſhould be returned to their common diet, and not have any more ſalt-water; becauſe the continual uſe of this, as well as that of hemp-ſeed bread, or other hot aliments, would infallibly cauſe abortion: but they may always be given to the ram for ſome time before he is put to the ewe. Ewes go five months, and yean at the beginning of the ſixth. They ſeldom bring more than one lamb at a time. In hot climates they yean twice a year, but in colder countries only once. Thoſe which are rather lean than fat, bring forth moſt eaſily.

Some put the ram to their ewes about the end of July, or the beginning of Auguſt, in order to have lambs at Chriſtmas, or early in January: but then they run a hazard of the lambs being deſtroyed by the cold, for they are extremely tender creatures. However, the ram is given to the much greater number in the months of September, October, and November; and lambs are accordingly to be had in plenty in February, March and April. They are alſo to be had in May, June, July, Auguſt, and September; there being no ſcarcity of them but in October, November, and December.

When a ewe is near yeaning, ſhe muſt be ſeparated from the flock, and carefully watched, in order to her being aſſiſted, if needful; for the lamb often preſents itſelf croſs-wiſe, or with it's feet foremoſt;

moſt, and in either of theſe caſes the ewe's life would be in danger if ſhe were not helped. As ſoon as the lamb is yeaned, it muſt be raiſed on it's feet, and at the ſame time all the milk in the ewe's udder ſhould be drawn out, becauſe it is vitiated, and would be very noxious to the lamb, which muſt therefore be kept from ſucking till the udder is repleniſhed with freſh milk. The lamb muſt be kept warm, and ſhould be ſhut up with it's dam for three or four days, that it may learn to know her. During this time, the ewe ſhould be fed with good hay, barley-meal, or bran mixed with a little ſalt; and her drink ſhould be water, the chill of which has been taken off, mixed with a little flour, bean-meal, or ground millet. At the end of four or five days ſhe may be gradually brought back to the ſame kind of food as the other ſheep, and be returned to the flock; only taking care that ſhe be not driven too faſt, nor too far, leſt her milk ſhould be heated: and ſome time after, when the ſucking lamb ſhall have gathered ſtrength, and begins to play, it may be left to follow it's dam to the paſtures; no farther care being then neceſſary; for it will find it's dam amidſt a very numerous flock, and ſeize her dug, without ever being miſtaken.

Lambs yeaned between the beginning of October and end of February muſt be kept in the houſe, on account of the cold, and be ſuffered to go out only in the morning and evening to ſuck; but in the beginning of April they may be turned into the open fields. Some time before this is done, a little graſs ſhould be given them daily, in order to accuſtom them by degrees to this new food. They may be weaned at the end of one month; but it is better to let them continue to ſuck for ſix weeks or two months.

The largeſt, moſt vigorous, and thickeſt-fleeced lambs, eſpecially if their wool be all white and without ſpots, are the beſt for keeping. Thoſe of a weakly

weakly appearance are generally diſpoſed of to the butcher. Lambs of the firſt yeaning, as was before obſerved, are never ſo good as thoſe of the following: and it is a general rule with all good huſbandmen, rather to bring up the young of their cattle of every kind, than to ſell them off when young; the profits in the former caſe being by much the moſt conſiderable.

The ewe yields, during ſeven or eight months, plenty of milk, which is good food for children and peaſants. It alſo makes good cheeſe, eſpecially if mixed with that of cows. Ewes may be milked twice a day in ſummer, but only once in winter, viz. immediately on their going to paſture, or at their return.

Ewes eat more during their pregnancy than at other times, and accordingly they then fatten very faſt: but they are alſo then very apt to hurt themſelves, ſo as, frequently, to miſcarry, and ſometimes to become barren from that time: nor is it very extraordinary for them to bring forth monſtrous productions. If no accident befalls them, and they are properly tended, they are capable of yeaning during their whole life; that is, to the age of ten or twelve years: but generally they break and become ſickly when they are turned of ſeven or eight. A ram lives to twelve or fourteen years; but is no longer fit for propagation after eight: he ſhould therefore then be knit, and fattened with the old ſheep; though even then his fleſh will be rank and ill-taſted: that of an old ewe is at beſt flabby and inſipid: the fleſh of the wether is moſt ſucculent, and the wholeſomeſt of all common meats.

CHAP.

CHAP. IV.

Of the Diseases of Sheep.

A Shepherd well versed in feeding his flock properly during the different seasons of the year, and skilled in the methods of curing the several disorders to which sheep are subject, is a very valuable person, and therefore should be sought for with the utmost diligence; for on his care and abilities the welfare of the flock greatly depends. How injudiciously then do they act, who resign the care of their sheep to boys, or to the least deserving of their servants!

Mr. F. W. Hastfer, the Swedish gentleman before quoted, and to whom the world in general, and his own country in particular, is much indebted for a well-methodized set of *Instructions concerning the manner of rearing and improving sheep*, reduces the general causes of their diseases to the five following heads, *viz.* 1. Too great heat; 2. Severe cold; 3. Water; 4. Fright; and 5. Unhealthy pasture.—If due care is taken to prevent the inconveniencies which arise from these causes, there will not be much room to fear a general sickness or mortality amongst men.

It is generally thought that the brain of a sheep is more affected by heat than that of any other creature: hence the inconveniencies which arise to them from the burning heat of the summer; and as their wool forms a warm covering around them, the least additional heat greatly increases that which they have naturally. Even in the winter, sheep, particularly in foreign countries, often suffer from the too-great heat of their cotes, which their shepherds shut up very close, and can scarcely be persuaded that they are doing them an injury. In this very wrong practice, which prevails in the northern parts of Europe, and in France, the heat becomes prejudical on a double account; first, from the heat itself, which, in crowded cotes, sometimes rises to the dog-day heat; but chiefly by the perspiration of the sheep, which not only makes the air less fit for breathing, but by degrees renders it so putrid as to give rise to fevers of the worst kind.

Though sheep can bear cold much better than heat, yet they should not on any account be exposed to a too-severe degree of it; and above all, particular care should be taken that the pregnant ewes do not drop their lambs in the open air when the weather is very frosty, because that might cripple the the lamb for life.

Too rainy a season is very prejudical to sheep, as was remarkably experienced all over England in the summer of 1766, when whole flocks perished with the rot. They who had luckily sown burnet before were then made thoroughly sensible of it's good effect, not only in preventing this fatal disease, but also in curing sheep that were then in almost a dying condition. Paisley would have the same effect, as it is probable that both of these plants carry off the too great humidity by urine. Where neither of them can be had, the sheep should be housed during violent falls of rain, be fed with dry hay, and, as much as possible, sheltered from the wet.

Mr. Hastfer, (a) recommends the following powders as efficacious preservatives in such seasons. He calls the first of them *ant-powders*, and the two others *drying-powders*. The ant-powder is made thus:

"In autumn, when the ants have done working, take the whole of an ant-hill, ants and all, scooping it out quite to the bottom, in order to have the more

(a) *Part II. p.* 139. 141.

of

of the mastic or resinous substance which they provide for winter. Dry it well in an oven, till the ants and earth can easily be crumbled into dust betwixt one's fingers; then pound and sift it very fine, and keep it in a vessel that has been used for salted meat or pickled herrings; first drying the vessel well before the powder is put into it.—Give to each sheep a quarter of a pint of this powder mixed with twice as much oats, in their cribs, or otherwise, after having sprinkled it with pounded salt, very salt water, or human urine. It will make the sheep sweat, and experience will prove it's good effect."

Mr. Hastfer adds, that this ant-powder is much used in Germany, as the writings of Colerus, Bayer, and others testify; that he has seen it given in some places in Sweden, though not many; and that he himself has used it on several different occasions, and found that nature frequently affords in simple remedies as much real utility as in the most costly. In the year 1746, which was a very wet year in Sweden, he gave this powder, by way of trial, to four sheep, once a week, and when they were killed the next autumn, their gall and liver were perfectly sound, whilst other sheep, which had not taken it, where full of gall, and their livers covered with hydatides, or watery tumours, in great numbers and of all sizes.

Of his *drying powders*, as he terms them, one is composed of two ounces of crude antimony, four ounces of bay-berries, four ounces of sulphur, two ounces of nitre, pounded together, and mixed with ten pounds of salt. This is then to be put into the cribs for the sheep to lick of it, and into their drink especially in autumn after they are housed, and after a rainy summer, when there is room to fear they may have suffered by the wet.

The other of these powders is made thus: Take a pound of crude antimony, half a pound of nitre, and a quarter of a pound of red tartar; pound them well ſeparately, and mix them together. A good ſpoonful is enough for ſix or eight ſheep. Mix it with a little meal and dry wormwood, make it into a paſte, and give the bigneſs of a walnut of it once or twice a week to each ſheep, in autumn and ſpring, when a general mortality prevails. This caſe excepted, it is uſed only as a preſervative once in three weeks or a month; and then not till after the ewes have lambed, and the lambs are ſomewhat biggiſh. The ſheep muſt not be ſuffered to drink the ſame day that they have taken this remedy; but on the contrary, they ſhould be driven about a little backwards and forwards. This powder purges them by urine and ſweat, drives out their too-abundant humours, and is a very ſalutary medicine.

The ſame ingenious writer gives us alſo, from Van Aken's *Pharmacopœia* for ſheep, the following recipe for making the *Pomeranian powder*, famed for it's efficacy in curing many diſorders in ſheep.

"Take a pound of the grey powder of compound ſalt-petre; of gentian and bay-berries, each four ounces; juniper-berries, common ſalt, roots of angelica, elder, pimpernelle, ariſtotolochia, monks-hood, cyclamen, black hellebore, root of fern, betony, millepertuis, carduus benedictus, rhue, millefoil, fumetory, and hyſop, an ounce and a quarter of each, with two ounces of tops of worm-wood, two drams and an half of aſſa-fœtida, ſix balls of caſtor prepared. Pound all this into a groſs coarſe powder, and give to each ſheep half an ounce of it two or three times a week in the morning, mixing it with paſte, or making it up into pellets. They are very fond of it. When contagious diſtempers prevail amongſt ſheep, and there runs from their mouths a thick and glutinous ſlaver, it is a good ſign; but people who have large flocks, as the ſhepherds of Pomerania, who have ſometimes five or ſix thouſand ſheep to take care of, may give this powder to a dozen or more ſheep at a time in the water, a little thickened with flour;

taking

taking care that each ſheep has, as nearly as poſſible, it's portion of half an ounce of it. When this powder is given them they muſt not have drank water for two days before.

After they have taken this remedy they ſhould be driven about a little, and not ſuffered to drink till the next day, when juniper and worm-wood ſhould be put into the water that is given them. If they are dropſical, they ſhould not be let drink oftener than every third day. There are extraordinary proofs of the excellent effect of this powder in caſes where other celebrated remedies have not done any ſervice; and experience will convince thoſe who uſe it properly; for it not only expels the noxious humours, and dries gently the ſcab and ſmall-pox, but likewiſe eaſes the breaſt, ſo that the ſheep that it has been given to twice a week have recovered their health, and in a fortnight after, the dropſy being come on, and their heads ſwelled again as big as ever, they have been perfectly reſtored by the uſe of this powder given two days together. Care muſt therefore be taken to uſe this powder in time, in caſe of a relapſe.

A little ſalt ſhould be ſprinkled over almoſt all the medicines that are given to ſheep: it will make them reliſh what might otherwiſe be be loathſome; and ſo far as can conveniently be, they ſhould be phyſicked when the weather is fine: however, this muſt neceſſarily admit of many exceptions.

Peſtilential diſeaſes will be ſo fully treated of in the latter part of this volume, that I ſhall only mention here Mr. Haſtfer's having experienced the efficacy of the above *powder of antimony*, in preſerving ſheep from peſtilential infections, even when thoſe which had taken it chanced to be mixed with ſheep that were infected. He likewiſe recommends the uſe of rhue in their food, and ſuſpended round the neck, when there is a fear of ſuch diſorders: and alſo to prevent their being bitten by ſnakes, theſe reptiles having an averſion to that plant.

SECT. I.

Of cutaneous Diseases in Sheep.

THE *Scab*, or *Itch*, in ſheep is contagious, and therefore carefully to be guarded againſt. It ariſes from various cauſes, ſuch as unkindly ſeaſons, the ſkin's being wounded in ſhearing, or torn by thorns, brambles, &c. Lice alſo, by breaking the ſkin in queſt of food, or perhaps for neſts to lay their young ones in, bring on the itch, as does alſo the ſheep's being reduced by hunger.

As ſoon therefore as the ſheep are obſerved to ſcratch or rub themſelves againſt any thing, or to bite their ſkin, the ſhepherd ſhould examine their ſkin with great attention, to ſee whether they have not the itch. If they have it, the wool muſt be cut off wherever that diſorder is perceived, in order that the part may be the more conveniently rubbed with ointment, in which there is brimſtone; for that ſeems to be the certain antidote, though many forms are boaſted of, in almoſt all of which ſulpher is an ingredient. Quick-ſilver is ſometimes added, on a ſuppoſition of it's being more efficacious to deſtroy the lice. The ſmall lice, commonly called ticks, which are little hairy worms ſhaped like buggs, and which pierce the ſkin, are eaſily deſtroyed by a ſtrong decoction of tobacco-ſtalks poured all along the back of the ſheep, ſo as to run down on both ſides: ſome add brandy, to render it the more penetrating. Others again put half a pound of tobacco and a handful of ſalt into five or ſix quarts of water, boil it well, and after the ſheep is ſhorn rub it in with a bruſh, not over-hard. At the ſame time they may likewiſe take the antimony powder as an alterative, or the æthiops mineral, if the diſorder is come to a great height.

The

The writers of the *Maison Rustique* recommend strongly the following, as an excellent general remedy for all sores of animals, sheep, goats, dogs, cows, horses, &c. "Take an ounce of liver of antimony, wrap it up in linen, then put it to steep in a quart of wine, (white wine is best) and mix therewith eight drams of senna: you may, if you please, add sugar, nutmeg, and other warm spices; for almost all the diseases of grazing animals proceed from cold and damp. The remedy is not the less good for not having any spice. It has been tried every way. Let the drugs steep twenty-four hours, or boil them with the wine for six or eight minutes, and give a gill of it to each sheep, the same dose to other small animals, and to large ones, such as cows and horses, a quart. The creature must be kept in a warm place all the day, be well covered, and not have any thing to eat till the evening. He will purge both upwards and downwards. The scab and itch will, by this means, be driven out, and the cure will be compleated by beathing the sores with the wine in which the liver of antimony has been steeped, after setting fire to it. No itch will resist this remedy."

Whatever composition is made use of, it should be rubbed upon the parts affected for at least three or four successive nights; and when the scabs begin to heal and peel off, the sheep should be washed in a river, if in summer, or in a tub of water made a little warm in winter, and be kept within doors till the wool is quite dry. Special care must be taken that the sheep be perfectly cured before they join the flock.

Another cutaneous disorder (*a*), to which sheep are liable, sometimes attacks the face in particular, in such manner that the skin and flesh fall off, the eyes drop out, the ears and horns fall off, and the skull is left bare. Sometimes too it spreads itself over half

(*a*) *Hastfer, P. II. p.* 179. calls it an *Erisipelas*, or *St. Anthony's fire.*

the body before the ſheep dies. This is thought to be incurable, but not contagious. The following application has here been attended with the greateſt ſucceſs. Take oil of tobacco and ſulphur, with quenched mercury, mix, and rub the ſore with them, and waſh it once a day with a very ſtrong decoction of rhue boiled in water. A peaſant, who had a ſheep ſo ill of this diſorder, that its head was eaten all round, freed it from the diſtemper in five weeks, by treating it as above. Mr. Haſtfer (*b*), who relates this caſe, adds, indeed, the creature's eyes fell out of it's head, and that it's wool became ſo intangled and confuſed as to be all over full of knots.

S E C T. II.

Of Diſeaſes of the Head and Throat.

WHEN ſheep are expoſed to a great heat of the ſun, they are frequently ſeen to become giddy, and turn round. Too much heat of any kind, feeding too long on a dry paſture without drink, or other ſuch cauſes, may have the ſame effect. This is remedied by bleeding, either in the jugular, or in the vein under the eye, or by cutting off the tip of the ear, and by keeping them in a cool place, with plenty of cooling drink, till the ſymptoms quite diſappear. But if the complaint ariſes from water contained in the head, as is ſometimes the caſe, it is incurable; and therefore, when it does not readily yield to eaſy remedies, the beſt way is to kill the ſheep before the diſorder has reduced it.

Sheep are alſo frequently ſeized with an apoplexy, in which they fall dead at once. If ſigns of life re-

(*b*) *Part II. p.* 180.

main after they are fallen down, ſuch things as will hereafter be pointed out as antidotes againſt poiſon may be given, and blood be drawn from every place that will afford any. Some are very fond of cutting off the end of the tail, and leaving it to bleed as long as it will.

Sheep are liable to tumours in the throat, which ſhould, if poſſible, be brought to ſuppurate, leſt the matter be tranſlated to ſome other part. When ſuppurated, the ſwelling ſhould be opened, and a free diſcharge given to the matter: but ſome caution ſhould be uſed at firſt in the opening, to avoid a worm that is ſometimes found in ſuch tumours, which being of a poiſonous nature, would, if cut, envenom the ſore, and endanger the life of the animal. After the worm has been extracted, the abſceſs is to be cured as before directed for horſes.

SECT. III.

Of Coughs and Shortneſs of Breath.

THE diſeaſes of the breaſt, ſuch as cough and difficulty of breathing, are to be treated nearly in the ſame manner as before directed for horſes *(a)*. In caſe of a fever, which is known by the frequency of breathing, heat, dry mouth and tongue, diſreliſh of food, *&c.* blood ſhould be taken from the neck, and repeated occaſionally. Frequent bleeding becomes therefore neceſſary in ſheep, becauſe it is ſeldom that much blood can be got at a time. In other reſpects, they are to be treated as before directed for horſes in ſimilar caſes, and the diſcharge from the noſe ſhould be encouraged, as is likewiſe there adviſed *(b)*.

(*a*) See *Sect. II. p.* 100. (*b*) See *Sect. III. p.* 107.

When

When a cough arises to such a degree as to occasion a discharge from the nose, it is adviseable to separate the sick from the sound, because there is reason to fear that, in this state, the cough may be contagious. Mr. Hastfer says (c), that knot-grass is so very prejudicial to sheep, as to occasion violent coughs, in which they dart forth a thin stinking matter.

SECT. IV.

Of Diseases of the Belly.

DISEASES of the belly may also be cured in the manner before directed for horses, only altering the quantities of the doses in proportion to the strength of the sheep. Their having the colic, or any other disorder in their bowels, may be discovered by their directing their head to their belly, and being otherwise disordered.

SECT. V.

Of Diseases of the Liver.

THE livers of sheep are subject to several disorders. In the rot, the liver is constantly distempered: hydatides, or small watery tumours, are often found in it, and frequently worms; concerning which last M. de Buffon (a) gives us the following curious extract of a Letter written by a doc

(c) *Part I. p.* 105.
(a) *Histoire Naturelle de la Brebis.*

tor of physic at Montiers, in the duchy of Tarantaise in Savoy, communicated to him by M. Rouillé, secretary of state in France for foreign affairs. "It "has for a long time been observed, that the sheep "of our Alps, which are the best in all Europe, "sometimes fall away surprizingly. Their eyes become white, sunk, and bleared; their blood serous, with scarce any redness to be seen in it; "their tongue dry and shrivelled; their nose stuffed with a yellow viscid and putrid mucus; an extreme debility, though they eat a great deal; and, "in fine, the whole animal system visibly decaying. "After several close inquiries, these animals were "found to have in their liver white *papillons* (moths), "with proper wings, their heads of a semi-oval "form, and of the brightness of those belonging "to the silk-worm. I have been convinced of the "reality of this fact, by squeezing about seventy "out of the two lobes; and, at the same time, all "the convex part of the liver became lacerated. "They have been found in the veins only, without "a single instance of their being in the arteries. "In the cystic duct, small ones have been found, "together with maggots. The vena porta, and "the capsula of Douglass, which are visible there as "in man, yielded to the softest touch. The lungs "and other viscera were sound."—Here M. de Buffon very justly remarks, that it were to be wished the doctor had given us a more circumstantial description of these *papillons*, as he calls them, lest it should be doubted that the animals which he saw were in truth no other than the common worms found in the liver of a sheep, which are indeed very flat and broad, and of so singular a figure, that they might rather be taken for leaves than worms.

The chief reliance for a cure of this disease should, I think, be in antimony and mercurials; perhaps of choice in the æthiops mineral. Mr. Hastfer recommends here rhue mixed with antimony.

Christopher

Chriſtopher Baldwin, Eſq; of Clapham, in Surry, has found burnet to be remarkably efficacious for the cure of the rot, as appears from a letter of his publiſhed in a well-intended and very uſeful work, called *The Repoſitory for ſelect Papers on Agriculture, Arts, and Manufactures*, begun in 1768, but unfortunately dropt at the end of only a ſecond volume; and a farmer in the North, in the autumn of the year 1766, when all his ſheep were ſo far gone in the rot that he did not expect one of them to live the winter over, ſent them into a field of burnet, which, in a month's time, reſtored them to perfect health.

The Memoirs of the Royal Society of Agriculture at Rouen inform us (*b*), that one of their members had recommended parſley as a good remedy for ſeveral of the diſeaſes to which ſheep are ſubject, ſuch as pimples, the ſmall-pox, running at the noſe, the itch, &c. and that it had been found to anſwer, when tried by a dealer in ſheep, whom they name. The way of uſing it is, to turn the diſeaſed ſheep faſting into a field of parſley, and leave them there for a quarter of an hour a day during eight days. The parſley will grow again, ſo as to yield ſeed, or may be cut and dried for ſheep that are ill in the winter.

When ſheep have ſwallowed any live creature, ſuch as ſpiders, caterpillars, leeches, &c. the beſt way of treating them is as before directed for horſes in a ſimilar caſe.

(*b*) *Page* 28.

SECT.

SECT. VI.

Of the Dropſy.

SHEEP are ſubject to a watery ſwelling, which frequently affects the whole body; and is at firſt diſcovered by the head's becoming larger, particularly under the lower-jaw, where the water is collected into a kind of bag, and by the body's being ſwelled.

The cure ſhould begin with antimonial purges, keeping the ſheep at the ſame time on dry food.—A full pint of ſtrong decoction of the leſſer ſpecies of ſedum (*ſedum minus*) given to a ſheep as ſoon as this diſeaſe is perceived, is ſaid to be an excellent remedy in caſes of this kind. It purges ſtrongly.

Likewiſe the following is recommended by Mr. Haſtfer (*a*), as very efficacious for ſheep that have the dropſy.—After purging them, which ſhould always be the firſt thing done in this diſeaſe, take of dried wormwood, either powdered or cropt ſmall, of parſley picked clean and ſhred ſmall, of bark of elder pounded or ground, a quart each; alſo a gallon of ſtrong ſea-ſalt well pounded, and a full quart of oat-meal, or as much as may be wanted to make the whole into a paſte. Put all theſe ingredients into a kneading-trough, mix them well together, and knead them into a paſte with good river-water. Make this paſte into pellets about the bigneſs of a walnut, and give to each ſheep faſting two or three of them, according to its ſize and age. The ſheep muſt re-

(*a*) *Part II. p.* 213.

main

main housed for three or four hours after they have taken this remedy, and then they may be walked out, if the weather is fair and dry, but with great care to keep them from water all that day. If the weather be bad, the best way is to feed them that day and the following night in their cote, with straw or other dry food.

The way to make them take this remedy, at least till they become accustomed to it, is, to thrust the pellets down their throat with one's fingers: but they will soon eat them of their own accord, if they are only laid in the crib.

These balls are used every year in the sheep-cotes of Hojentorp and Berga, in Sweden, and have been found to be a certain cure for the dropsy in sheep. The above-mentioned quantity of ingredients will make from 170 to 180 balls, which are sufficient for sixty old sheep, or eighty or ninety young ones, or lambs.

In case the necessary ingredients cannot be had in the country, take for ten or twelve sheep the value of five or six quarts of oatmeal, and dry it well in an oven, or over the fire, in a pot or pan, then mix with it salt and bay berries dried and pounded, of each a good pint, half a pint of powdered wormwood, an ounce of laurel-berries pounded, and a pint of nettles with their seed dried and pounded. All this being well mixed together, it may be given to the sheep in a trough or crib made on purpose for that end, or it may be divided into portions of a pint for each sheep, and given in the morning fasting, with care not to let them eat any thing else till two or three hours after, at the end of which they may have hay or dry straw; but they should not be suffered to drink that day. This should be continued twice a week so long as is necessary, and in proportion as the distemper is more or less obstinate. One may likewise from time to time, offer them wormwood water to drink.

If

If the ſheep refuſe to take the medicine thus prepared, let ſome oats be ground, and a paſte made of their meal, with the other ingredients, to which may be added for each ſheep three or four drops of oil of ſoot, and of bark of the birch-tree. Let the ſame number of balls be made of it as was before ſaid, and given to the ſheep in the ſame manner.

Another remedy is made thus: Take four pounds of rhue, ſhred it fine, put it into a tub, pour upon it ſix or eight gallons of boiling water, cover the tub, and let it remain to infuſe ſix hours: then ſtrain the water off through linen, and put in as much ſugar as will make an egg ſwim upon it.

When ſheep are dropſical, two ſpoonfuls of this are given them evening and morning, till they are cured: but as a preſervative, only one ſpoonful is given them, evening and morning, twice a week. Five ſpoonfuls of it are given, evening and morning, to large cattle, in the ſame manner as it is given to the ſmall. Alſo, a mole may be taken, cleaned, and dried, then pounded, and when a ſheep or other animal is ſeized with the hydrophobia, let the bigneſs of a pea, or of a ſmall bean, be given to it in a ſpoonful of beer. This remedy has been repeatedly tried, and found ſucceſsful (*b*).

(*b*) *Haſſer, Part II. p.* 218.

BOOK VI.

OF GOATS.

THE Goat is naturally more ſagacious and beter able to ſhift for itſelf than the ſheep: it comes readily to man, ſoon grows familiar, is ſenſible to careſſes, and capable of attachment; it is alſo ſtronger, and leſs timorous than the ſheep. It is quick in its motions, capricious, more lively, nimble, obſtinate, and ſo fond of roving, that the ſtrongeſt and moſt active man cannot drive above fifty goats at a time; conſequently it is difficult to keep them in herds. They are fond of ſtraying in ſolitary places, of climbing up craggy mountains, of ſtanding and even ſleeping on the ſummits of rocks and the brinks of precipices. The moſt ſcorching rays of the ſun never incommode them; they are not frightened by ſtorms, and they bear rain quietly, but they ſeem to be affected by great cold. There is ſcarcely a ſpot ſo barren as not to afford them ſufficient ſuſtenance, for they will browſe even upon thorny ſhrubs; and very few ſorts of herbs diſagree with them, even hemlock not excepted, which is poiſon to other animals.

Goats are naturally ſo fond of man, that they never become wild near inhabited places. As a proof

proof of this; in the year 1698, an English ship having put in at the island of Bona Vista, two Negroes came on board, and after some intercourse told the English that they should be welcome to as many he-goats as they pleased. The captain expressing some surprize at this offer, the negroes answered, that they were only twelve persons on the whole island, and that the goats had increased so prodigiously as to be even troublesome; and that they were so far from being difficult to catch, that they would follow a man like tame animals.

The most usual colours of goats are white and black; some are entirely white, and others wholly black; but generally white and black, and often with a mixture of brown and fallow. The hair is of an unequal length on different parts of the body; every where stronger than that of horses, but less harsh than that of the horse's mane; and there have been instances of it's being intermixed with tufts of a whitish wool, as long as the hair, on the back and upper parts of the sides. The beard of a he-goat, which M. de Buffon measured, was nine inches long, and it's mane, towards the withers, was six inches in length. On the rest of the body, the hair was in general about three inches long, but somewhat more on the pasterns and coronet.

The male goat is capable of engendering at a year old, and the female at seven months; but the kids of this forward commerce are weak and defective; for which reason they are generally both restrained from copulation till eighteen months, or two years. The he-goat, besides being no despicable animal, is so very vigorous and sallacious, that one will be sufficient for above an hundred and fifty she-goats, during two or three months; but this ardour consumes him, and never lasts above three or four years; so that he becomes enervated, and even old, before he has reached his sixth or seventh year.

Such is the disposition of the she-goat, that the fickleness of her temper is plainly seen from the irregularity of her actions. She walks, stops, runs, skips, leaps, draws near, flies off, appears in sight, hides herself, or flies away, as by caprice, and without any other determining cause than the unaccountable vivacity of her internal sentiments; and all the suppleness of her limbs, and vigour of her body, can hardly answer the wantonness and rapidity of these motions, which are purely natural.

For propagation, the he-goat should be young, and of a good figure; that is, about two years old, and of a large size; his neck short and fleshy, his head slender, his ears long and lapping, his thighs large, his legs firm, his hair black, thick, and soft, and his beard long and bushy. The she-goat should have a large body, full rump, large thighs, light head, capacious udder, long teats, and soft and thick hair. Their usual season of heat is during the months of September, October and November; but at any other time, if they happen to be near the male, they are soon disposed to admit him; for they can copulate and yean at any time of the year. They however, retain best in autumn; and the months of October and November are preferred, in order that the young kids may find a soft succulent herbage when they first begin to feed: for the she-goat goes five months, yeans at the beginning of the sixth, and suckles her kids about a month or five weeks. Generally, indeed, she brings only one kid; though sometimes she has two, very seldom three, but never above four. These creatures sometimes suffer greatly in yeaning; and therefore they should be watched, in order to be assisted in case of need.

Goats are turned out to feed very early in the morning, before the dew is off the grass; because this, though pernicious to sheep that are not fattening, is extremely palatable, and even wholesome, to these animals.

animals. In ſnowy and wet weather, they are kept under cover, and fed with herbage, ſmall boughs of trees gathered in autumn, cabbages, turnips, and the like. Plentiful feeding increaſes their milk; and to keep up, or ſtill augment its quantity, they ſhould be made frequently to drink water mixed with nitre and ſalt. They may be milked in a fortnight after yeaning, and during four or five months they yield plenty of milk morning and evening.

When goats are driven with ſheep, as ſometimes happens, they always take the lead of the flock: but it is better to feed them ſeparately on high grounds, hills, mountains, and ſuch like places, in which they take moſt delight. Heaths, fallows, commons, and barren grounds will afford them as much food as they want: but they muſt never be ſuffered to feed in cultivated lands, corn-fields, vine-yards, or woods, becauſe they would browſe greedily on the young ſhoots, or the bark of the trees, and thereby do great damage.

The he goat readily copulates with the ewe, as the aſs does with the mare; and the ram joins himſelf with the ſhe-goat, as the ſtallion does with the ſhe-aſs. But, though theſe copulations are ſufficiently frequent, and ſometimes prolific, no intermediate ſpecies has been formed between the goat and the ſheep: they are abſolutely diſtinct, continue always ſeparated, and always at the ſame diſtance, without having been the leaſt altered by ſuch mixtures.

Goats cannot endure damp places, marſhes, or rich paſtures: few of them are bred in flat and open coutries, becauſe they generally are ſickly there, and their fleſh is of a bad quality: but in moſt hot climates they are bred in great abundance, without any ſhelter over them; whereas in colder regions, the winters would kill them if they were not houſed. In ſummer they do well without litter, but in winter they require it; and as all wet is very hurtful to them, they ſhould not be ſuffered to lie in thier dung, but have freſh litter as often as needful.

The ſhe-goat is prolific to the age of ſeven years, and the he-goat might certainly retain his generative faculty to that, or even a greater age, if he was ſuffered to be with the females only at proper times: but he ſeldom ſerves longer than five years, which bring him to about the ſame age: he is then caſtrated, and ſent to fatten with old ſhe-goats, and young he-goats caſtrated at ſix months, for that is the uſual time, in order to render their fleſh more tender and juicy. They are fattened in the ſame manner as ſheep: but neither care nor aliment, of any kind whatever, can poſſibly render their fleſh equal to that of the ſheep, unleſs, perhaps, it be in hot climates, where mutton is always flabby and ill-taſted. However, the ſtrong ſmell of the he-goat does not proceed from his fleſh, but from his ſkin; and the older he is, the ranker that will be.

M. de Buffon ſays *(a)* that theſe animals might live to the age of ten or twelve years if they were not killed when fattened after being paſt engendering; and I cannot but be of the opinion of that very judicious and experienced Naturaliſt; conſequently, the Chaplain to the Centurion's telling us in his account of Lord Anſon's voyage, that they found upon the iſland of Juan Fernandez a he-goat, which, from the ſlits in his ears, appeared to have been formerly under the power of one Selkirk, who lived ſeveral years on that iſland, and had quitted it above two and thirty years before their arrival, appears to me, ſuppoſing it to be literally true, nothing more than one of thoſe exceptions to a general rule, which M. de Buffon himſelf apprizes us will ſometimes happen.

(a) Hiſtoire Naturelle de la Chévre.

The

The age of a goat may be known by it's teeth, and by the knots in it's horns, when it has any: for though both he and ſhe-goats generally have horns, there are many exceptions to the contrary; and as to their teeth, they have not any of the inciſory ones in their upper jaw, but thoſe of the under jaw are ſhed and recruited at the ſame times, and in the ſame order, as thoſe of ſheep. In the ſhe-goats, indeed the number of teeth is not always the ſame, but uſually leſs than in he-goats, whoſe hair is alſo harſher, and their beards and horns longer. Like the ox and ſheep, they have four ſtomachs, and chew the cud. They alſo differ greatly in the colour of their coats. Thoſe that are white and without horns are ſaid to yield the moſt milk, but the black are the ſtrongeſt and moſt robuſt.

Theſe creatures coſt little or nothing to bring up, as we have ſeen, and their value is by no means inconſiderable, if properly attended to; for their fleſh will always fetch ſomething, and their ſuet, hair, and ſkin, ſell at a good price, eſpecially the ſkins of kids, of which the fineſt gloves are made. The ſkin of the goat is preferred to that of the ſheep, and the fleſh of the kid is nearly equal to that of the lamb. They are leſs affected with the diſeaſes of any climate than ſheep are, and ſtand leſs in need of the aſſiſtance of man. Goat's milk is a part of the *materia medica*, frequently preſcribed in caſes of decay, and wholeſomer than that of the ewe: it curdles eaſily and makes excellent cheeſe; but as it contains only a ſmall proportion of butyrous particles, the cream ſhould not be ſeparated from it.

She-goats ſeem pleaſed with being ſucked, as they often are by children, to whom their milk is an excellent aliment. Like cows and ewes, they are apt to be ſucked by ſnakes, hedge-hogs, and a bird called the Goat-ſucker. They yield a greater quantity of milk than the ewe.

The

The ſpecies of goats extends much farther than that of the ſheep; ſeveral parts of the world affording goats like ours, with this exception only, that in very hot countries they are ſmaller, and in cold ones larger.

The Angora, or Syria goats, with their long pendulous ears, and ſpiral horns, are of the ſame ſpecies with ours, engendering and producing even in our climates. The ſhe-goats in particular, of this breed, like moſt other animals of Syria, have a very long, thick, wiry hair, ſo fine, that the ſtuffs made of it are not inferior to our ſilks, and full as gloſſy; witneſs in particular, the beautiful Bruſſel's camblets.

BOOK

BOOK VII.

OF SWINE.

CHAP. I.

Of the Character, Properties, and Uses of Swine.

OF all the quadrupeds that we know, or at least, certainly of all those that come under the husbandman's care, the Hog appears to be the foulest, the most brutish, and the most apt to commit waste wherever it goes. The defects of its figure seem to influence its dispositions: all its ways are gross, all its inclinations are filthy, and all its sensations concentrate in a furious lust, and so eager a gluttony, that it devours indiscriminately whatever comes in its way, not excepting, frequently, its own young immediately after they are born, and too often infants in the cradle; for whenever these creatures meet with any thing fat, moist, or unctuous, they begin with licking, and soon after devour it. They are consequently fond of blood, and bloody flesh, which they will sometimes eat even when putrid, to the great detriment of their health, though they do not, like the wolf, attack other animals on purpose to kill and devour them. So unbounded is their ravenous desire to fill the vast capacity of their stomachs, and so undistinguishing is their taste, that M. de Buffon, *(a)* declares he has several times seen a whole herd of these creatures, at their return from

(a) Histoire Naturelle du Cochon.

the fields, ſtop and gather round a heap of clay newly dug up, all of them licking this earth, though none of the moſt unctuous, and ſome of them ſwallowing a pretty large quantity of it. This demonſtrates their gluttony to be of a piece with their brutal nature: nor is their ſenſe of feeling leſs ſluggiſh than their taſte; for, not only the harſhneſs of their hair, the hardneſs of their ſkin, and the thikneſs of their fat, render them little ſenſible of blows, but even mice have been known to form lodgments in their backs, and to eat their very ſkin and fat, without their ſhewing any ſigns of feeling them. Their other ſenſes are indeed quick and acute enough: though ſtill they ſeem not to have any one clear ſentiment; for the young hardly know their own dam, or at leaſt are very apt to miſtake, and readily ſuck the firſt ſow that will let them.—Fear and neceſſity probably impart a little more inſtinct and ſentiment to the wild race of hogs; for the young of theſe are ſtrongly attached to their mother, and ſhe, on her ſide, ſhews herſelf more careful to provide for their wants, than the tame ſow does: and as to the very great quickneſs of ſight, hearing, and ſmell in hogs, eſpecially of the wild breed, it is ſo well known to the huntſmen who go in queſt of theſe creatures, and particularly of wild boars, that they find it neceſſary to watch for them in the night, to obſerve a profound ſilence, and to keep themſelves to the leeward, that the hogs may not ſcent the effluvia of their bodies, which affect the organs of ſmelling in theſe animals ſo ſtrongly at a conſiderable diſtance, that they immediately betake themſelves to flight, as if aware of ſome impending danger *.

The

* The reader who is not acquainted with the method of hunting the wild boar, may not be diſpleaſed at the following addition, from M. de Buffon's Natural Hiſtory of the Hog. " The wild boar is, moſt commonly, either hunted openly with " dogs,

The natural defect in the senses of taste and feeling in swine, is also farther increased by a disease which renders them even absolutely insensible, and which is not perhaps so much owing to the texture of their skin, as to their filthiness, particularly in feeding, and especially to their often eating putrid aliments: for neither the wild hog, which does not eat such ordure, nor delight in mire as the tame one does, but generally subsists on acorns, mast, and roots, and lives in dry places, nor a sucking pig, is subject to this disease; whence it follows, that the way to preserve the common hog from it is, to keep him in a clean stye, and to give him plenty of wholesome food.

With all its defects, however, this animal is one of the most profitable that an inhabitant of the country can rear; for, besides its young, which generally are very numerous, and always fetch a good price, its flesh sells for rather more than that of the ox or sheep, and its lard for near twice as much as their

" dogs, or surprized and killed by moon light. As he is not re-
" markably swift of foot, he leaves a very strong scent, and
" often wounds the dogs dangerously in defending himself. For
" this reason, and because it spoils their scent, and breaks them
" to a slow pace, the good hounds used for the stag and roe-buck,
" (or for the fox.) should not be employed in this hunting.
" Mastifs, after a little training, will be fit for this purpose:
" but only the oldest of these animals are to be thus attacked,
" and they are easily known by their tracks. A wild boar of
" three years is not easily run down; he paces over a great deal
" of ground before he stops: whereas an old boar does not run
" far, but suffers the dogs to come near him, and often stops to
" keep them at a bay. In the day-time he generally keeps in
" his soil, which is almost always situated in the thickest part of
" the wood, and when night approaches he goes out in quest of
" food. In summer, when the grain is ripe, it is easy to sur-
" prize him among the corn and oats, which he is sure to visit
" every night. As soon as he is killed, the huntsmen cut out
" his testicles; the smell of which is so strong, that if they were
" left only five or six hours in the dead body, all the flesh would
" be infected by it."

suet

fuet †. Likewife, the flefh of this animal takes falt better than that of any other, and keeps longer in this ftate. Its blood, all parts of its bowels, its feet, and its tongue, are dreffed and eaten. The fat of the inteftines and cawl, which is very different from the lard, makes what is called the hog's greafe: nor is the fkin without its ufes, both faddles and fieves being made of it; and of the briftles are made various kinds of brufhes, fhoe-makers ends, &c. and lapidaries ufe them in polifhing of diamonds. The dung of this animal is accounted a fine manure for fruit-trees.

CHAP. II.

Of Feeding and Fattening of Hogs.

THESE creatures are fo very ftubborn and untractable, that even an active man cannot well take care of more than fifty of them at a time. In autumn and winter, where it can be done, they are driven to fuch woods as afford plenty of wild fruits: in fummer, they feed beft in moift and marfny places, where they find worms and roots; and in fpring they range the fallow fields. From the month of March to October, they are turned out twice a day to feed; in the morning from the time that the dew is exhaled till ten o'clock, and from two in the afternoon till the dew begins to return in the evening. In winter, they are driven abroad but once a day, and then only when the weather is fine; becaufe the dew, fnow, and rain are hurtful to them. Indeed, fuch is their averfion to bad weather, that if a fudden

† The lard of the hog is the fuet of other animals.

ftorm

ſtorm comes on, or only a heavy ſhower of rain, away they run, full ſpeed, each endeavouring to be foremoſt, and all continually crying out, till they reach their ſtye, or ſome other place of ſhelter. The youngeſt cry moſt and loudeſt. This cry is very different from their uſual grunting: it is a cry of grief, reſembling that which they ſend forth when they are bound in order to be killed. The boar cries leſs than the ſow; and the wild boar is ſeldom heard to cry at all, unleſs when wounded in fighting with another. The wild ſow cries more frequently; and both, when ſurprized and terrified, ſnort with ſuch vehemence as to be heard at a conſiderable diſtance.

Theſe animals are very fond of worms, and particularly ſo of ſome roots, eſpecially thoſe of the wild carrot; and to come at theſe they turn up the earth with their ſnouts. The wild boar, whoſe head is longer and ſtronger that of the common hog, delves deeper, and generally continues the furrow in a ſtrait line; whereas the tame hog digs only here and there, and at the ſame time more ſlightly: but as a great deal of damage is frequently done by this means, all hogs ſhould be carefully kept from cultivated lands, and ſuffered only to run in woods and fallows.

The common way of fattening hogs is, to give them plenty of barley, maſt, cabbage, and other greens boiled, and a great deal of water mixed with bran. By this means they acquire a thick ſtratum of ſeam, and are rendered ſufficiently fat, in two months: but this fat is neither very firm nor very white; and the fleſh, though good, is flabby. They may alſo be fattened at ſtill leſs expence in countries which abound in maſt, by driving them into the foreſts in autumn, when the acorns, wild cheſnuts, and beech maſts are ripe. They there eat all kinds of wild fruits, and grow fat in a ſhort time; eſpecially if, at their return in the evening, plenty of luke warm water be given them mixed with a

little

little bran and the meal of tares; for this makes them sleep; and increases their flesh to such a degree that they are sometimes scarce able to move; but the fat thus acquired is disagreeably oily. They likewise fatten soonest in autumn, when the weather begins to grow cold, because they then perspire much less than in summer, and have greater plenty of food. But the best way of all to fatten them for their flesh to acquire a fine flavour, and their fat to be firm and palatable, is, to shut them up for a fortnight or three weeks before they are to be killed, in a clean paved stye, without litter, and to feed them only with pure dry wheat, allowing them at the same time but very little drink. The hog thus treated should be about a year old, full of flesh, and previously half fattened; for the older the hog is, the longer time it requires to fatten, and its flesh is also proportionably worse.

Castration, which must always precede the fattening of any animal, is usually performed on hogs at the age of six months, and either in spring or autumn; but never in very hot or very cold weather, because each of these is equally dangerous to the wound, and renders its healing difficult; this operation, which every tinker knows how to do, is most commonly performed by incision, though sometimes by a ligature only, as in the ram. Those which have been castrated in the spring are generally fattened the next autumn, and commonly killed before they are two years old; though they grow very considerably in the second year, and would continue so to do for several years longer; those which are particularly remarkable for their height and corpulence, being only creatures of a greater age, which have been turned out several years to feed on mast. Their time of growth does not seem confined to four or even five years; for the boars which are kept for propagation continue to grow in their sixth year, and the older a wild boar

boar is, the larger and heavier he becomes. It is true, that the head of an old wild boar is the only part worth eating; whereas all the flesh of the wild boar and sow not a year old, is delicate, and of a fine grain; but the flesh of the tame boar is still worse than that of the old wild boar, and can be rendered eatable only by castration and fattening, unless it be when made into brawn.

The ancients used to castrate such wild pigs as they could at any time find means to steal away from their mother, and afterwards carried them back into the woods: the castrated wild hogs not only exceeding the tame in bigness, but their flesh being also better.

CHAP. III.

Of the Propagation of Swine.

BOTH the male and female of this species of animals are able to copulate when only nine months or a year old: but it is better to let them double that age before they are put together; for the first litter of a sow, when she is not a year old, consists of only a few, and those weak and even defective pigs. She may be said to be in heat at all times; and even when she is pregnant she seeks the boar, which, among animals, may be deemed an excess; the female in almost every species refusing the male after she has conceived. The heat of the sow, which is almost continual, declares itself more particularly at intervals, by her emitting no small quantity of a thick whitish liquid, and by uncommonly-violent motions which always end with her weltering in the mire. She goes four months, and farrows at the beginning of the fifth; soon after which she again grows eager for the male, becomes pregnant a second time; and thus farrows twice a year. The wild sow, which resembles the tame one in all other respects, farrows but once a year; probably because of the scarcity of food, and the necessity she is under of suckling and feeding all her litter for a considerable time: whereas the tame sow is never suffered to suckle all her pigs above a fortnight or three weeks; after which eight or nine only are left with her, and the rest are carried to market. They are fit for eating in a fortnight; and as few sows are wanted, the castrated pigs being more profitable to rear, and their flesh the best to eat, most of the sow pigs are disposed of, only two of these, and seven or eight boar pigs, being generally left with the sow. She should never be permitted to suckle any of her pigs above two months; and even at the end of three weeks it is best to drive them to the field with her, that they may by degrees accustom themselves to feed as she does. In about five weeks after this, they are weaned, and whey mixed with bran, or at least warm water boiled with greens, is then given them morning and evening.

The boar for propagating should be short and thick of body, rather square than long, with a large head, a flat short snout, large flagging ears, small fiery eyes, a large thick neck, a smagging belly, broad buttocks, short thick legs, and thick and black bristles, white hogs being never so strong as black. In the sow, the body should be long, the belly broad and capacious, and the teats long. She should also be of a quiet disposition, and taken from a fruitful breed. When pregnant, she must be kept apart from the boar, or he would probably do her some mischief; and when she has farrowed, she must be fed plentifully, and also watched, lest she should devour some of her pigs: the boar especially must be re-

moved,

moved, for he would ſhew them ſtill leſs mercy. The ſow is commonly put to the boar in the beginning of ſpring, in order that, by farrowing in ſummer, her pigs may have time to grow and gather ſtrength and fleſh before winter: but when it is intended that ſhe ſhould farrow twice a year, ſhe is had to the boar in November, that ſhe may farrow in March, and be again put to him in May. Some ſows farrow regularly every five months. The wild ſow, which, as was before obſerved, farrows but once a year, admits the boar in the months of January or February, and farrows in May or June. She ſuckles her young three or four months, leads them abroad, follows them, and keeps them from ſtraying, till they are three or four years old; ſo that it is not uncommon to ſee wild ſows with their young of the preſent and preceding year about them.

Wild boars are called *ſounders* during their firſt year, and *beaſts of company* till they are three years old, becauſe they keep together till that age, and never go alone till they are ſtrong enough to encounter the wolf: by this means theſe animals compoſe among themſelves a kind of ſquadron, and in this their ſafety conſiſts; for when they are attacked, the largeſt form themſelves into a cloſe circle around the leſſer, to keep off the enemy. The ſame method of defence is alſo practiſed by tame hogs; ſo that there is no occaſion to make uſe of dogs to ſecure them from beaſts of prey.

It is not uncommon for boars to live twenty-five or thirty years. Ariſtotle ſays, that hogs in general live twenty-years; and adds, that the boars engender, and the ſows bring forth, till the age of fifteen.

I cannot conclude this laſt chapter of my work, without continuing to obſerve with M. de Buffon, that this ſpecies of animals, though known, and even found in great plenty all over Europe, Aſia, and Africa,

Africa, had never been ſeen in America till it was carried thither by the Spaniards, who turned great numbers of black pigs looſe on the continent, and alſo on its larger Iſlands, where they have increaſed prodigiouſly, and in ſeveral places become wild. They reſemble the European wild boars; but their body is ſhorter, their head larger, and their ſkin thicker than in other hogs, which in hot climates are totally black, like the wild boar.

A ridiculous prejudice, which owes its continuance to ſuperſtition, deprives the Mahometans of this animal: they are taught to look upon it as unclean, and are ſo far from eating, that they dare not even touch it. The Chineſe, on the contrary, are very fond of hogs fleſh: it is their moſt common food, and is ſaid to have animated them to refuſe the doctrine of Mahomet. The Chineſe hogs, which are the ſame with thoſe of Siam and India, differ from thoſe of Europe, in that they are ſmaller, their legs conſiderably ſhorter, and their fleſh much whiter and more tender. Some perſons breed them here, and they copulate and engender with our common ſwine. The Negroes alſo breed vaſt numbers of hogs; and though they are very ſcarce among the Moors, and in all Mahometan countries, wild boars abound as much in Aſia and Africa as in Europe.

CHAP.

CHAP. IV.

Of the Diseases of Swine.

THE only diseafe that I know of which feems to be peculiar to fwine, is a kind of leprofy, commonly called *meafles*. When it feizes them, they become dull and fleepy. If the tongue is pulled out, the palate, throat, and it, will be found full of blackifh fpots, which appear alfo on the head, neck, and the whole body; the creature is fcarce able to ftand on its legs, and the roots of its briftles are bloody.

As this diforder proceeds chiefly from their gluttony and filth, the only way of preventing it is, as was faid before, to keep them clean; and the moft probable way to remedy it is, to put the difeafed hogs into a feparate clean fty, and there give them wholefome food; to wafh them carefully, and let them have plenty of water to wallow in: antimony, and its preparations, will alfo be of fervice to them.

BOOK VIII.

OF THE CONTAGIOUS DISEASES OF CATTLE*.

THE contagious diſeaſes which have attacked cattle at different times are not all of the ſame nature. The authors who have noticed them, have given different deſcriptions of them. I ſhall firſt deſcribe thoſe of which they have ſpoken, and then proceed to thoſe which have appeared in our days. It muſt be from a knowledge of what was obſerved in former epidemics, that we can learn to guard againſt the dire effects of future ones; for it is but too certain, that thoſe which have already appeared will appear again, as there will hereafter be occaſion to remark: and the proper treatment of diſeaſes which may hereafter attack cattle, can be learnt only by conſidering what was done for them before: for, as in the cure of diſeaſes incident to men, ſo in thoſe of animals, experience is all in all. Experience makes us acquainted with each ſpecies of malady, its genus, the different cauſes which have contributed to its production, the remedies which have been applied, and their effects. "Be always "mindful," ſays Hippocrates *(a)*, "of whatever

* Abridged from *Mémoire ſur les Maladies épidémique des Beſtiaux, par M. Barberet, M. D.* to which the Royal Society of Agriculture at Paris adjudged their premium for the year 1765, and of which they were pleaſed to tranſmit a copy to the writer of this work.

(a) Lib. de decent. Ornat. §. 8.

"has

" has cured diseases, of the appearances under which " those diseases have shewn themselves, of the " changes they have undergone, and of the diffe- " rent manners in which they have affected different " creatures; for this is, in physic, the beginning, " the middle, and the end."

The antients afford us but little instruction concerning the contagious diseases of cattle, a scourge which so often sweeps away whole herds; for they scarcely enter into any description of them. Virgil, at the end of his third Georgic, describes, indeed, a mortality amongst cattle; but what he says is rather the flight of a poet's imagination, painting the ravages of any epidemic disorder, than the description of a particular one: and though we find in Celsus prescriptions for many maladies of horses, oxen, and sheep; yet he has not given us a description of any epidemic disorder: nor is Columella at all accurate in his description of the contagious diseases of cattle.

We must therefore come so far down as Ramazzini, who, in his account of the epidemical constitution of the year 1690, at Modena, says, that the season was cold and moist, and that the reigning distempers of that year attacked all the people who lived in the country, and spread itself indiscriminately amongst all kinds of animals, of which great numbers died after a few days illness. Nature made strong efforts to disengage herself from the disease by a critical discharge on the thighs, neck, and head, resembling the pustules of the small-pox. Most of the animals which had this appearance lost their eyesight. Those creatures which were not carried off by this disease, but resisted its violence, lost their flesh by degrees, and fell into a marasmus. Ramazzini did not scruple to declare these pustules to be the small-pox; for they differed not from it in form, in colour, or in the matter which they contained, nor in size, nor in the manner in which they went off:

 when

when they had dried off after the ſuppuration, they left a black ſcar, like to that which remains after the ſmall-pox.

This epidemic contagion continued in 1691, and attacked chiefly the ſheep, ſo violently that the breed was almoſt deſtroyed: (*Ita ut ovilus grex pene deletus fuerit.* Ramaz. p. 42.) It has been conſtantly obſerved, that, of all animals, ſheep are the moſt ſubject to the ſmall-pox. The French call it, in them, *clavin*, or *claveaux*, and I ſhall ſpeak more fully of it hereafter. It was therefore to be expected that they ſhould be particularly affected by it, ſince they are more diſpoſed to it than other cattle.

In 1693, Heſſe ſaw her herds carried off by a pulmonary phthiſis. (Conſt. epid. Haſſiac. ann. 1691.) The winter of that year began with rain, and ended with very ſevere cold: an extraordinary warmth which commenced in the ſpring, and continued during the whole ſummer, took place all at once of the former cold. Such ſudden changes always occaſion unuſual motion in the fluids, and frequently obſtructions in the capillary veſſels; and hence it ſeldom happens but that a ſudden change from cold to heat brings on epidemical diſeaſes: yet the diſorder which then reigned in Heſſe was alſo attributed to a blight, or corroſive dew, which fell on the paſtures in 1693, in the ſame manner as the paſtures in Italy had been infected in 1690. Beſides theſe cauſes, the above-quoted obſerver imputes the diſorders to the coldneſs of the water, which, the animals drinking greedily of it whilſt they were very hot, contributed much to the pulmonary phthiſis: for if a man in a great ſweat drinks a draught of ice-water, it is to be feared that he will be ſeized with a pleuriſy or peripneumony. The caſe is the ſame with animals.

The ſpring of the year we are ſpeaking of being very warm, the bullocks and cows, heated both by the warmth of the ſeaſon, and by the devouring fire which raged in their bowels, through the infected quality of the plants they had fed on, ran to the coldeſt water they could find. One of the firſt effects of cold is to condenſe fluids, and to leſſen the diameters of veſſels. The fibres of the capillary veſſels, being contracted by the action of the cold, ſtopped and returned the blood which before flowed freely in thoſe veſſels, and from thence proceeded an inflammation. When this happens to a conſiderable number of veſſels, they burſt, and their coats with their contents turn to pus, or that matter which we ſee in boils. This is what happened in Heſſe: the inflammation, at firſt neglected, ſuppurated, and the cattle ſunk under a pulmonary phthiſis.

In the year 1712, they were attacked in Lower Hungary with a moſt dangerous diſtemper, (*Conſt. epid. inter Hungar, ann.* 1712.) The winter had been extremely cold, and the ſpring rainy, with great changes in the temperature of the atmoſphere; for on the ſame day the morning was cold, the middle of the day very warm, the cold began again about three o'clock, and the evening became warm. Theſe changes occaſioned amongſt men many fevers, which were as irregular as the ſeaſon. In the months of June and July, during which the weather continued conſtantly warm, there appeared a prodigious number of inſects, reptiles, and particularly ſerpents which killed many perſons in the country. Their bite brought on a ſwelling which ſpread very faſt all over the body, and particularly to the tongue, ſo that the ſick could not utter a word. The cattle were not leſs ſubject to the bite of theſe ſerpents, than the men; and accordingly the mortality among them was very great.

In Auguſt, which was very rainy, the mortality increaſed, but by a new kind of diſorder, which ſhewed itſelf by white puſtules filled with matter inſufferably infufferably ftinking. A liquor of a cadaverous fmell flowed from the mouths of the fick cattle; it was with the utmoft difficulty that they breathed: the bullocks and cows feized with this diforder bellowed conftantly, and without intermiffion, as death approached. A noife was then heard in their bowels, as if the coats of their inteftines, diftended too much, burft. Though the obferver does not mention it, yet every circumftance, efpecially the puftules, declare this diftemper to have been the fmall-pox complicated with fome other diforder. The liquor which flowed from the mouth greatly refembled the fpitting which comes on in men in the fmall-pox. The difficulty of breathing, the ftench of the breath, and the infectious fmell of the puftules, are fymptoms which conftantly attend the *clavin* or fmall-pox in fheep, when the difeafe is violent or accompanied with putrefaction.

In the ftomach of the animals which were opened were found balls of the fize of a wallnut, filled with hair, and covered with a membranous tunic, fo hard that it could fcarcely be cut with a knife. This membranous tunic is uncommon; for the egagropiles are not organized bodies.

This mortality fpread even to the wild beafts, feveral of which were found dead in the forefts. The dogs which ate of their flefh, or that of any of the animals that died of the contagion, became mad; and the men who were bitten by them were feized with the hydrophobia.

The changeablenefs of the feafon had a great fhare in the epidemic here fpoken of, and the multitude of reptiles contributed to render it ftill more dangerous to cattle: for the great number of infects which adhered to the grafs they fed upon, might caufe as many diforders as the blight before-mentioned; becaufe all animal fubftances are of a more feptic quality than grafs, which is the natural food of cattle.

The

The epidemic diſeaſe of 1711 (*b*), which made ſuch havock in Italy and Germany, came originally from Hungary, by means of bullocks brought from that country: for there appeared nothing in the conſtitution of the air, nor in the food, that could give riſe to it; nor did it affect cattle which had no communication with thoſe that came from Hungary. The infection ſeemed to be communicated by their ſaliva dropped on the graſs; ſo that ſound cattle which afterwards fed on the ſame paſture contracted the diſorder with which the others were infected.

The virus, which was communicated by the ſaliva, was ſo extremely acrid, that it acted as a cauſtic on the gullet, ſtomach, and inteſtines, affected the nervous ſyſtem, occaſioned ſpaſms, contracted the fibres, and cauſed obſtructions in the capillary veſſels: the fluids conſequently became putrid, and the bowels were ſeized with gangrenous inflammations. The diſeaſe was attended with a burning heat, a total loſs of appetite, a difficulty of breathing: in ſome bullocks the tongue was inflamed and covered with many red bliſters; the ſtomach, the epiploon, and eſpecially the inteſtines, were alſo inflamed; the parts near the liver were of the colour of the bile; the excrements were purulent, tinged with blood, and of an inſufferable ſtench, ſo that, ſays the obſerver who has left us this account, the diſorder aſſumed the appearance of a malignant dyſentery: and yet the dyſentery here certainly was only ſymptomatic.

The mortality amongſt the cattle ceaſed but very little during the winter, and began again the next year: the cauſe, however, did not ſeem to be the ſame; for the epidemic diſorder in 1712 appeared with different ſymptoms. It firſt attacked the horſes, eſpecially thoſe which were in the neighbourhood of Augſburgh; yet almoſt all that were in the town eſcaped. It af-

(*b*) *Conſt. Epidem. Auguſt. ann.* 1711, 1712.

terwards

terwards ſpread to the bullocks and cows, and to many other animals of different kinds. On the breaſt, groin, and many other parts, there aroſe hard tumours, which extended greatly, and ſoon carried off the cattle affected with them. This diſorder ſeems to have been the conſequence of that of the former year; the hard tumours and the ſymptoms attending them being imputed to the ſting of hornets, of which there was an incredible number in 1712, of an uncommonly large ſize. It was ſaid that they fed on the bodies of the cattle which died the year before, and had not been buried ſufficiently deep. That the ſting of theſe hornets bred in and fed on infection, could not but be dangerous, will appear from the following event, which ſhews to how great a degree the juices were altered.

A man intending to chop off the foot of a horſe which had died of the ſting of a hornet, and had not been buried deep enough, the foot appearing above ground, ſome drops of the juices ſplaſhed about by the hatchet he made uſe of flew into one of his eyes, and cauſed there an inflammation and ſwelling, which ſoon extended to the other eye, afterwards over the whole head and finally killed him.

Lanciſi informs us, that the wiſe precautions of Pope Clement XI. preſerved for two years the ſtates ſubject to him, from the contagious diſeaſe which a bullock had brought from Hungary into the diſtrict of Padua, from whence it had ſpread all over the Venetian territories and the Milaneſe, and at length penetrated into the kingdom of Naples. In the middle of the ſummer of 1713, information was received, that ſome drovers were conducting a great number of cattle to the fair of Fruſino, a town in the Eccleſiaſtical State, but bordering on the kingdom of Naples. To prevent all danger, orders were immediately given, that the fair ſhould not be held. The drovers ſeeing the impoſſibility of ſelling their

cattle

cattle as they had intended, led them through bye-ways to Rome. They were ſold at a low price; and being ſold again to the inhabitants of the towns and villages throughout that province, the infection was ſoon ſpread over the whole Campania of Rome. An exact regiſter was kept of all the cattle that died from the month of October 1713, to the month of April 1714, when the infection ceaſed in the Eccleſiaſtical State, and preſents us a ſhocking detail of the effects of that peſtilence, by which were deſtroyed 8466 oxen uſed for ploughing, 10125 white cows, 2816 red cows, 108 breeding bulls, 427 young bulls, 451 heifers, 2362 calves, 862 buffaloes male and female, 635 young buffaloes, in all 26252 cattle in the ſpace of nine months. Lanciſi thinks, that if the computation had been begun from the 2d of Auguſt, the number of cattle which periſhed would have amounted to 30000.

That author does great juſtice to the truly paternal care and ſolitude ſhewn by the holy Father on this melancholy and fatal conjuncture. We may ſee by his account, that the ſpeedy extinction of a ſcourge which continued long to ravage other ſtates Italy, was owing more to the Pope's prudent meaſures, than to medicines, which were found to be ineffectual. This evinces, that good laws and active magiſtrates are frequently the moſt effectual ſafe-guards againſt peſtilential diſeaſes.

This diſtemper ſhewed itſelf in ſome animals by lowings, by a kind of terror with which they were ſeized, by a thouſand different motions which ſeemed to ariſe from that terror, and by a ſudden and precipitate flight. Others, chiefly the weak, dropt down dead at once, as if they had been thunder-ſtruck. In almoſt all the reſt was obſerved a great dejection; they could hardly hold up their heads; their eyes were dull and full of tears; a ſurprizing quantity of mucus flowed from the noſe, and of ſaliva from the

mouth;

mouth; the fever in them was very high; they were ſo dejected that they could not ſtand up; their hair ſtood on end; their tongue, mouth, and gullet were inflamed, ulcerated, and more or leſs covered with bliſters: at firſt they ſhewed a great thirſt, but ſoon refuſed every kind of drink and food: many had a conſiderable purging; what they diſcharged was of different colours, always very fœtid, and ſometimes bloody. Moſt of them ſunk under the diſtemper in a week, being ſeized with the moſt violent oppreſſion. Their breath was inſufferably ſtinking, a ſtrong cough was frequently joined to all theſe ſymptoms, &c.

It was ſeldom that the appearances in the viſcera were alike in the creatures which died of this plague. The contagion fell ſometimes on one part, and ſometimes on another, ſeemingly according to the weakneſs of that particular part. This Lanciſi ſays he was convinced of by opening three bodies. Except the ſmall ulcers obſerved in the mouth, throat, æſophagus and paunch of each of them, and likewiſe the gangrenous ſpots obſerved in their lungs, all the other effects were totally different. In the paunch of the firſt, which died on the third day of the diſeaſe, he found a maſs of the creature's laſt food, extremely hard, and what Pliny calls *juvencarum tophum*, that is, an ægagropile. The liver, inteſtines, and lungs of the ſecond, which died on the ſixth day, were intirely ſphacelated; the heart and brain of the third were become putrid maſſes, with ſcarcely any vaſcular appearance. He obſerved nothing particularly remarkable in the fluids.

The young and fat cattle, which had worked little and been well fed, were more eaſily affected by the diſtemper, and died ſooner, than the cattle which had been made lean by hard labour, and were come to a certain age.

Lanciſi

Lancisi thinks that the greater or less abundance of the fluids, and their flowing more or less freely through the vessels, was the true cause of this difference; for the pestilential ferment, says he, insinuates itself more easily into the blood and spirits, and falls more severely on the bowels, when it meets with a greater plenty of fluids liable to be corrupted, and with obstacles which prevent its finding a passage out of the body.

Though the lean cattle did not escape the contagion, and though they generally died of it, yet some of them recovered; probably owing to the less interruption which the pestilential ferment met with in them, than in those that were fat.

What was very remarkable is, that most of the female buffaloes, which were seized with the plague when they suckled their young, did not die. Their teats were ulcerated all over, and none of their young escaped. Lancisi is of opinion that the acrid venom taken in by the nose of the mother, and with her food, flowed with the chyle into the blood, and by that means into the minutest vessels of the udder. There it happily deposited; and as part of the venom was taken off by their young, and the rest of it remained stopped at the extremity of the lactiferous vessels ulcerated and corroded by that same ferment, the mothers, by means of these salutary sores, frequently escaped death; perhaps as happens to men seized with the plague, who are often cured by a lucky suppuration of buboes.

In the year 1730, a great number of cattle died in Bohemia, Lithuania, Saxony, the Marche of Brandenburgh, and the Dutchy of Magdeburgh (*Hist. Feb. Catarrh. ann.* 1730;) but we have no account of the distemper which carried them off. Perhaps it might be like that which destroyed so many in some of the provinces of France in 1731, the first symptom of which was a white blister that appeared on the tongue.

This

This bliſter afterwards became red, and ended with turning black and degenerating into a cancerous ulcer, which ate away, and, in a ſhort time, conſumed the whole tongue. It was very like an anthrax. This diſtemper was the more dangerous, becauſe there was no ſymptom which declared its approach; for the creature which was ſeized with it ate and drank as uſual, till the ulcer had made a conſiderable progreſs, and often nothing was perceived till it was too late to aſſiſt.

From the year 1740 to 1750, the horned cattle, not only in France, but all over Europe, died in vaſt numbers of a putrid, malignant, inflammatory fever, like that which made ſuch havock in Germany and Italy in 1711, and which was called a malignant dyſentery. Of all the diſeaſes that have at any time attacked cattle, this ſeems to be the moſt dangerous, the moſt complicated, and the moſt difficult to cure. Its approach was indicated by a languor and general dejection: the beating of the heart was as quick again as in a natural ſtate, which denotes a very briſk fever. The ſick animal, hanging down its head, could hardly ſtand upon its feet; it tottered; its loins panted; its eyes were red and full of tears; its horns and ears were cold; a thick glutinous ſlaver ran from its noſe and mouth; and a convulſive motion was apparent from the head all along the back. The other ſymptoms were ſimilar to thoſe before mentioned in ſpeaking of the epidemical diſeaſe of of Augſburgh.

In 1756, the French loſt a great number of cattle in Minorca. Theſe animals, tranſported thither from Auvergne, were little accuſtomed to the heat of a climate where they were expoſed all day long to the burning rays of the ſun: for, excepting the middle of the iſland, ſcarce any ſhade to be found in it. This became the more grievous to them as they naturally delight in a cold climate, and in ſuch it is that they

they thrive beſt. In fact, the cattle of Denmark, Podolia, and Ukraine are the largeſt, and next to them thoſe of Ireland and England, whilſt thoſe of Spain and Barbary are the ſmalleſt. They found not in Minorca any thing that could allay in their bowels a heat which they had not felt elſewhere. They had no cooling graſs, for all is burnt up in that iſland by the month of May. The water, being every where warm and in many places brackiſh, afforded but little refreſhment to creatures which love it cool and pure. They languiſhed, and loſt their fleſh viſibly from day to day: their breath was hot, and they ended with piſſing blood.

We were terrified in 1762 with accounts of an epidemic diſeaſe which made great havock in Denmark and had advanced to the frontiers of Germany. The following is an account of it, ſent to one of the members of the Royal Society of Agriculture at Paris.

" The contagion ſpread with great rapidity; the " youngeſt, the moſt robuſt, and the moſt healthy " cattle were the firſt ſeized with it, and died the " ſooneſt. In moſt of them a cough was the ſymp- " tom of the diſeaſe. Their eyes became dull, wa- " tery, and bleared; and even tears trickled from " them. In a day or two after the cows were thus " ſeized, their milk dried up, and this was a ſure " ſign that the contagion had reached them. In the " beginning, the creatures were cold even to ſhiver- " ing, nearly as men are on the firſt attack of a fe- " ver. A heat ſucceeded, and continued for ſeveral " days: it was moſt perceptible at the nape of the " neck, either by the heat itſelf, or by the beating " of the pulſe. The ſick animal loſt its appetite for " eating, but continued to drink freely till the inflam- " mation deprived it of the power of ſwallowing. " A great quantity of inſufferably-ſtinking ſnotty " matter flowed from the noſe, and the teeth became

looſe

" loofe in moft of them. Some became coftive; " but in much the greater number a diarrhæa came " on in the beginning, with a difcharge of fcarce " any thing except water, with very little excrement. " Towards the end of the difeafe, the two laft joints " of the tail became foft and rotten: if the fkin " which covered them was opened, there came out " a fœtid purulent matter. The gangrene proceed- " ed by degrees even to the horns, which became " cold and empty. When the ears and nofe became " cold, the difeafe was in the laft ftage; and then it " was that the animal generally died on the fixth or " feventh day from its being taken ill.

" On opening the dead bodies, the gall-bladder " was found greatly enlarged, and full of a " liquor more like urine than bile. In fome of them " there was even three pounds weight of this liquor " in the bladder; in many, the ftomach and intef- " tines were full of worms yet alive at the opening " of the body. There were likewife in the blood- " veffels certain infects called *plaice*, becaufe of the " refemblance of their fhape to that of the fifh fo " named. Sometimes the brain appeared diffolved " into a purulent water. In many, the veins were " full of black blood. Numbers had the neck in- " flamed. In others, the inflammation fell on the " bowels, and fometimes another part of them was " found gangrened. The ftomachs were full of " food not digefted; and that food was fo dry, and " fo much compacted together, that it could not be " feparated without great difficulty. Livid and black " fpots on the ftomachs and inteftines fhewed evi- " dently a gangrene. In fome animals, the liver and " fpleen were covered with fmall tumours fo hard " that they could not be broken, and they felt like " grains of fmall fand under the fingers; while the " reft of the fubftance of thefe vifcera was, on the " contrary, fo foft, that it could fcarcely be touched without

"without piercing into it. Some dead bodies afforded no ſign of any diſtemper. The blood that was taken from the animals was of a clear red, and diſcovered ſigns of great inflammation by its frothing and ſmoaking, and not having any liquid in it after it had cooled: the whole was one coagulated maſs, which might be cut like a jelly."

In the years 1746, 1754, 1761, and 1762, there appeared among the ſheep in the neighbourhood of Beauvais (in Picardy) a contagious diſeaſe which the French commonly call *clavin* or *claveau*, and which is in fact no other than the ſmall-pox, as was before obſerved. It is, of all the contagious diſtempers which affect ſheep, the moſt eaſily communicated, and that to which they are the moſt liable. Like the ſmall-pox too it is diſtinguiſhed into the diſtinct or mild, and the confluent or malignant.

The Royal Society of Agriculture at Paris having received the following very particular account of this diſeaſe, as it appeared in 1762, from M. Borel, Lieutenant General of Beauvais, and Member of the Society of Agriculture of that city, gladly pay him the tribute of praiſe juſtly due to the zeal and diligence which he manifeſted on this occaſion. He himſelf examined the condition of the ſheep in many villages and hamlets, in order to become perfectly acquainted with the ſymptoms of the diſorder, which he has deſcribed with a preciſion that ſhews he judged and ſaw with his own eyes.

The diſorder manifeſted itſelf by a want of appetite and a dejection in the animal. Some perceived it twenty-four hours before the eruption; the moſt attentive perceived it two or three days ſooner; but the greateſt part did not notice it till after the eruption had begun. The diſguſt was proportioned to the degree of the malady; for the ſheep that were affected continued to eat, thoſe that were moſt ſeverely attacked took no food of their own accord, people

people ſupported them as well as they could; they were very thirſty and water was given to them all. As ſoon as they were ſeized with the diſorder, they ceaſed to chew the cud; their eyes were heavy, ſwell-ed, and watery, they became very dim, and frequently the eye-lids were ſo glued together, that the creatures could not ſee. Many of thoſe which had been cured had loſt one eye, and others were quite blind: a depoſite or tranſlation of the pocky matter being made, brought on a ſuppuration which deſtroy-ed the whole ſubſtance of one or both eyes; but theſe depoſites contributed much to a recovery. There flowed from the noſe a thick tough matter, of the colour of pus, generally white, ſeldom yellow. Their ſtrength failing them to follow the flock, they laid down, and remained in the place where it may be ſaid they fell. Their ears were very cold; though this was not always the caſe. They were quite motionleſs, and collected into the ſmalleſt compaſs poſſible with the head inclining as much as could be to the ground, the tail drawn in between the legs, and the hinder parts brought near to the fore ones without ſeeming to be griped. The oppreſſion they laboured under was in proportion to the violence of the diſorder. When the attack was mortal, they groaned during the laſt twenty-four hours of life, and their loins palpitated ſtrongly. If they recovered, their wool fell off from the places where there had been an eruption. Their excrements were nearly the ſame as in a ſtate of health, but rather dryer, and blacker than in the natural ſtate. The pimples reſembled exactly thoſe of the ſmall-pox. They were of different forms and different colours. Some were perfectly round and diſtinct; others confluent and of an eliptical ſhape. All of them were at firſt red and hard. The diſtinct ſort became afterwards white and ſoft, ſuppurated,

dried

dried up, and fell off in ſcales. In the confluent kind the pimples were ſo near together that they touched each other; they became of a purple colour, and inſtead of riſing and turning white, they appeared flat and became black. The fever, heat, thirſt, and dejection continued, attended with a difficulty of breathing, and working in the loins. Some died ſo early as the third day after the eruption. The more the head was affected, the greater was the danger, and the ſpeedier the death. Thoſe that outlived the diſorder, were long in recovering. Some did not recover in leſs than two months, others at the end of ſix weeks, or a month: in the diſtinct kind, they generally recovered in a fortnight: but in both ſorts, ſeveral died at the end of theſe periods. People were at firſt of opinion, that the ſheep fed in moiſt paſtures were more liable to be ſeized with this diſorder than thoſe fed in dry paſtures: but it was afterwards obſerved that there was not any difference between them. The ſheep were ſeized in the winter as well as in the ſummer. In ſeveral places the infection ſpread without any immediate communication with the ſick ſheep: in others, it ſeemed to be the effect of their coming near to one another. The eruption appeared chiefly on the head, on the inſide of the fore and hind legs, on the belly, and around the anus. Some ſheep had but very few pimples. Theſe the country people called the flying ſmall-pox. Some had pimples only on their legs, others on their ears only, and ſome again had only one cluſter of the breadth of a crown-piece. A ſheep had ſuch a cluſter on one ear, which it treated ſo roughly that the ear remained curled up, and diſplaced from its natural poſition. Another had one on its foot; the hoof fell off, and the creature remained lame ever after. The eruption was generally complete

 by

by the fourth or fifth day. The inſide of the mouth was full of pimples, which would have prevented the ſheep's eating even if it had not had a diſguſt to food. The breath was exceſſively ſtinking. M. Borel obſerves, that when a flock of ſheep was ſeized with this diſtemper, at leaſt one half or two thirds of them was very ſick. In moſt places, no attempt had been made to cure it, the country people being perſuaded that there was no cure for it, becauſe they had never ſeen their fathers adminiſter any; only ſome of them aſſured him, that the open air was better for the ſick ſheep, than houſing them.

This gentleman, not contented with examining the ſymptoms of the diſeaſe in the living, endeavoured to diſcover its effects in the dead bodies. A ſheep which was firſt obſerved to be ſick on a Thurſday, continued in the field all Friday, and on Saturday morning was found dead in the ſheep-fold: it was brought to M. Borel in the afternoon of the ſame day; ſigns of putrefaction appeared already in it by an offenſive ſmell, by a livid greeniſh colour upon its neck and under its fore and hind legs, and by the largeneſs of its lower belly, which incloſed a great deal of infected air. This ſheep had not any pimples on the head, nor was that part of it at all ſwelled; only two pimples were found on the upper, and two on the lower part of the tongue; and in thoſe places the ſkin peeled off as it does from a tongue put into boiling water. On raiſing the eye-lids, it was ſeen that the eyes had loſt their brightneſs and tranſparency, and that more in one than the other. The pimples were numerous on the belly, under the fore and hind legs, and on the neck and throat. —They appeared like tumours or white puſtules, round, flat, and of a ſixth, a fourth, or a third part of an inch in diameter. They did not

pierce

pierce deeper than the ſkin, and moved with it. The matter of which they were formed had not yet made pits, as in the white puſtules of the ſmall-pox. On opening them, they appeared like a pinguous tumour; ſome were excoriated in the middle. It was preſumed that they had not become white till after the death of the creature, and that they were red before, as in the other ſheep during the firſt days of the eruption. The remains of a ſanious humour, of the colour of coffee, were found in the noſtrils; but no judgment could be formed of its mucoſity at the end of twelve or eighteen hours after death, when a putrefaction had begun. The lower belly being opened, the cawl appeared of a dead blackiſh red, and the fat of it had not that coheſian and conſiſtence which it has in ſheep killed when in health. The liver was of a dark-green colour; which colour penetrated about a twelfth part into the ſubſtance of it, in ſome places more, in ſome leſs, and the part ſo coloured was brittle, as if boiled. The gall bladder was flabby, and ſeemed to have contained more bile, and that thinner, than in its natural ſtate. The inner coat of the firſt ſtomach was looſe and wrinkled, of a green colour, and prodigiouſly full of white lenticular puſtules, of the ſame nature as thoſe on the ſkin, but ſmaller in diameter. The ſtomach contained a greeniſh liquor in ſmall quantity. The ſecond ſtomach contained alſo but little. The third was very full of food pretty well chewed, and as green as the graſs of which it was the produce. It was alſo much extended with a very rarefied and fetid air. The ſmall guts were almoſt empty. In the colon and cæcum were excrements of a middling conſiſtence. The kidneys were like the liver, green and dry on the outſide. The bladder had little urine in it. The lungs were flabby, and of a dark

 livid

livid red. Some ſmall tumours were obſerved in them, like thoſe on the ſkin, but round and thick. The heart appeared larger than in its natural ſtate. The right ventricle contained a very black blood: a clod of blood taken out of the inferior vena cava was black in its upper part next the heart; but in its lower part next the liver it was yellow, and reſembled that coat which covers the blood in pleuriſies. The head of this ſheep was not opened, as well on account of the putrefaction, as becauſe the diſeaſe did not ſeem to have fallen on that part. M. Borel adds, that if a child had died at the ſame period of a diſeaſe, and with the ſame ſymptoms, it would be thought to have died of the ſmall-pox ſtriken in. The reſemblance between the *claveau* in ſheep, and the ſmall-pox in men is very ſtriking, whether we examine it in its beginning and progreſs, or in its effects and conſequences in the ſheep that were cured. In many of theſe the ſkin of the head, eſpecially about the lips, was ſeamed as the ſkin of a human face is by the confluent ſmall-pox.

It were to have been wiſhed that M. Borel's occupations had permitted him to notice with the ſame care and exactneſs the effects of ſome medicines, which were pointed out to him at the time by one of the members of the Royal Society at Paris, and to purſue the experiments then propoſed to him. The queſtions which that ſociety put to him may, however, help to direct others on a ſimilar occaſion; and I ſhall therefore tranſcribe them here.

1ſt. Are old ſheep more ſubject to the *claveau* than young ones? Is the *claveau* apter to be of the confluent or malignant kind, and conſequently more dangerous in the former than in the latter? M. Borel anſwered, that no difference had yet been obſerved between the old ſheep and the young, with

with regard to the height to which the malignity or other ſymptoms aroſe. The ſociety, however, wiſh that this important point may be aſcertained by more accurate obſervations.

2d. Are the lambs ſubject to this diſorder? Is the diſtinct or mild kind the moſt common amongſt them? Are they ſubject to a looſeneſs in either kind of this diſtemper? Have they the diſcharge by the noſe in the confluent kind? Does this diſcharge precede or does it accompany the eruption?

3d. At what time preciſely does the eruption appear, and how long alſo does it laſt, in the one and in the other kind of this diſeaſe? Does it vary according to the kinds of the diſeaſe, and according to the age of the animal?

4th. After the eruption, are the ſymptoms leſſened in the diſtinct kind? Do they become more alarming and ſeem to increaſe in the confluent kind?

5th. Is a ſheep which has recovered of either the one or the other kind of this diſtemper, ever attacked with it a ſecond time, or oftner?—The country people aſſured M. Borel, that they never knew a ſheep attacked a ſecond time by it.

6th. Could not inoculation be tried on a ſound ſheep, or on an uninfected lamb, which has been prepared before-hand? What would be the iſſue of ſuch an experiment, made with all poſſible precaution to guard againſt the ſpreading of the contagion.

7th. If a ſheep cured of the *claveau* in the natural way is inoculated, will it be infected?

8th. What would be the conſequence of inſerting ſome of the variolous matter into an aſs, a mule, a horſe, a bullock, a dog, or, in ſhort, into any animal of a different kind? What would be the effects of inoculating a ſheep, or other animal, with

with the variolous matter taken from the human body?

9th. Prepare ſome ſheep as for inoculation, and expoſe them afterwards to be infected in the natural way; will they be infected, and of what kind will the infection be?

10th. Inoculation not having had any effect, expoſe the ſheep to the *claveau* in the natural way, will they be infected?

Plenciz, a celebrated phyſician at Vienna, in a treatiſe on contagious diſeaſes, printed by Trattner, in 1762, has taken into conſideration, in p. 142, &c. the havock made by the diſtemper among cattle for thirty years paſt, in almoſt every country in Europe. He aſcribes the cauſe of it to ſmall worms, and founds his opinion on what he obſerved by the help of a microſcope in the ſeveral ulcers which extend from the mouth and throat to the ſtomach and lungs of the diſtempered animals. He cites the teſtimony of Rodius, *Cent.* 3, *Obſervat.* 61, & 62. that of Bidloo, and that of Bono in his letters to Valiſnieri.

The progreſs of this cruel diſeaſe having been ſuch towards the end of the year 1761, that the ſymptoms of it became daily more and more ſevere, this zealous author determined to ſearch firſt into the cauſe of its ſpreading ſo rapidly, and next into the means of getting the better of it. Theſe two points are the ſubject of a ſmall work ſerving as a ſupplement to that we have been ſpeaking of, viz. *Additamentum ad Tractatum de contagione, p.* 142, 143, 144, *&c. ſeu de lue bovina ad finem vergente anno* 1761, *epidemia graſſante, &c.*

Michael Sagar, Phyſician in the Circle of Iglaw in Moravia, has given us the hiſtory of a diſtemper which reigned among the cattle in 1764. It was printed in 1765, by Kraus at Vienna, under the title of, *Libellus de aptbis pecorinis anni* 1764, *cum*

cum appendice de morbis pecorum in hac Provincia tam frequentibus, corundemque causis et medelis preservatoriis.

These two works contain excellent observations, and cast a great light on the subject; as does also the work of M. Ens, intituled, *Disquisitio Anatomico pathologica de Morbo Boum Ostervicensium.*

We find in the second volume of Sydenham's works printed at Geneva in 1736, by the brothers Detourne, not only all that Bernard Ramazzini has said of the constitutional epidemics of 1690, 1691, 1692, 1693, and 1694, but likewise a collection of what Schroeck, Harder, Valentinus, Garhliep, Behrens, Rayger, Stegmann, Schelhamer, Hoyer, Gerbezius, &c. have written on the epidemical constitutions of different countries at different times. They have all been sufficiently attentive, whenever the contagion extended to any kind of cattle, not to neglect this circumstance, though it was not, so much as might have been wished, the principal object of their writing. We are, however, obliged to Physicians who, whilst they search into the causes of diseases fatal to men, at the same time cast an eye on those of cattle. *Sunt enim animalia post hominem, ita ars veterinaria post medicinam secunda est.* Veget.

Of

Of the Causes of the contagious Diseases of Cattle.

THE constitution of the air, and the quality of their food, are the original causes of all the epidemic diseases of cattle. They breathe the same air as we do, and consequently must be affected by its various temperature, its changes, its gravity, its lightness, its greater or less elasticity. The vapours, the exhalations, and whatever it carries with it must make on them at least as much impression as on us, and even more, since, not being cloathed, as we are, they are more exposed to the immediate contact of the air; so that what is contained in the atmosphere finds an easy admission by the mouth and nose, and being lodged in their hair, may insinuate itself into the body, and so occasion many disorders.

It appears that whatever in the air is hurtful to animals, affects them chiefly by the mouth and nose: for these effects generally shew themselves first in the head or stomach, and frequently in both at once. Hoffman is clearly of opinion that morbific ferments are mixed with the blood by means of the saliva, more than by any other means. That liquor, whether it be swallowed constantly, or only when it accompanies the food, carries the ferment with it into the stomach and intestines, where, mixing with liquors easily susceptible of putrefaction, or of being affected by any particular ferment, the liquors are in this depraved state carried with the chyle into the body, and produce effects similar to their different qualities, either on the body in general, as in a fever, or on some particular part: whereas if the venom entered by the pores, it would meet with liquors in continual motion, and therefore not so susceptible of putrefaction,

trefaction, or of being affected by any peculiar ferment.

That the air is the great ſource of contagious diſtempers, was an opinion of the moſt ancient writers. Hippocrates *(Sect. 4. de Flatibus)* looks upon the air as the ſource of all diſorders. Virgil *(Georg. Lib. 3.)* promiſes to teach us the cauſes of all the diſeaſes of cattle; *Morborum quoque te cauſas et ſigna docebo.*

"The cauſes and the ſigns ſhall next be told,
"Of ev'ry ſickneſs that infects the fold."

Yet he mentions only the air as if that was the ſole cauſe.

Hic quondam morbo cœli miſeranda coorta eſt,
Tempeſtas, totoque autumni incanduit æſtu,
Et genus omne neci pecudum dedit, omne ferarum,
Corrupitque lacus, infecit pabula tabo.

"Here from the vicious air, and ſickly ſkies,
"A plague did on the dumb creation riſe:
"During th' autumnal heats th' infection grew,
"Tame cattle and the beaſts of nature ſlew;
"Pois'ning the ſtanding lakes, and pools impure:
"Nor was the foodful graſs in fields ſecure."

Livy too *(Lib. V. Decad. 1.)* ſeems to impute to the air a peſtilential diſeaſe which carried off both men and animals in his time.*

Though the air is unqueſtionably a moſt powerful agent in communicating contagious diſeaſes, yet it is not the only one; for if it were, how comes it that the peſtilential diſeaſes which at different times have deſtroyed mankind, have ſpared the beaſts of the field? Thucydides, in his deſcription of the plague of Athens *(de Bell. Pelo-*

* *Tryſtem hyemen ſive ex intemperie cœli raptim mutatione in contrarium factâ, ſive aliâ de cauſâ gravis peſtilenſque omnibus animalibus æſtus excipit.*

pon.

pon. Lib. 2.) does not ſay that it extended to beaſts: he only relates, that the carnivorous animals would not touch the bodies of thoſe which died of the plague, and that thoſe which were ſo voracious as to eat of them died; which is a tacit proof that the other animals did not die of it. The plague ravaged the Roman Empire during fifteen years under the Emperors Gallus & Voluſian (*Zonar. Tom.* 2.): in the year 263, it killed five thouſand people in one day in Rome only (*Baronius, Annal. Tom.* 2.) Under the Emperor Juſtinian, there died of the plague at Conſtantinople, from five thouſand to ten thouſand people likewiſe in one day (*Procop. de Bello Pers. Lib.* 2.) Guy de Chauliac ſpeaks of a plague which appeared in his time, viz. in 1348, ſo extremely ſevere, that it ſwept away three fourths of mankind from off the face of the earth. According to Rondelet, it made dreadful havock in France, Germany, Italy, and Spain, in 1450. Valeriola ſays that, in 1553, men dropt down dead of the plague in Narboneſe Gaul, whilſt they were talking together or walking, as if they had been ſtruck with thunder. Jerom Mercurialis relates the ſame thing of that which appeared at the ſame time at Padua and at Venice. Zacutus ſpeaks of a moſt dreadful plague which happened at Liſbon in 1601. In fine, it appeared in Muſcovy in 1655, in England in 1665 and 1666, in Poland in 1708 and 1709, at Marſeilles in 1720; and yet the authors who have ſpoken of theſe terrible ſcourges make no mention of their having affected any other creatures than mankind. Can it be ſuppoſed that all of them neglected or forgot a circumſtance of ſo great conſequence? Their ſilence is a convincing proof that all epidemical diſeaſes do not ariſe ſolely from the conſtitution of the air.

It

It may be objected, that as the air acts differently on different bodies, so the diseases which the air communicates to men may not affect other animals, nor those which are peculiar to any one species of animals affect any other species: for what proves mortal to one species does not to another; and that there is a plague for men, another for horses, another for cattle, and another for sheep. A sound bullock put into the same stable with a glandered horse does not catch the glanders. A bullock put into a house with sheep ill of the small-pox, does not catch that disease, nor do horses; and sound sheep do not catch the glanders or farcy from horses, when confined with them in the same stable: and yet one should be cautious not to mix sound animals of any species with diseased ones of any other: for men who had not so much as a scratch on their hands have been seized with a true anthrax by opening the bodies of cattle dead of a contagious distemper; and almost all the cow-herds who were appointed to watch an infected herd, have been seen to fall into malignant fevers accompanied with a gangrene.

Independant of the air, it is certain that many epidemic diseases take their rise from the bad qualities of food. If the bread-corn is any way distempered, it never fails to bring on disorders among the country people; of which a remarkable instance is recorded in the History of the Royal Academy of Sciences for the year 1710; viz. that the peasants of Sologne who lived on rye which had the spur were seized with a dry black gangrene, which began in the toes, acended insensibly, and made their limbs drop off, in such manner that some of them were alive in the Hotel-Dieu at Or-

leans

leans with nothing left but the trunk of the body *. Grafs equally diftempered becomes equally pernicious to the cattle which are fed with it. The diftemper in grafs called ruft (*ærugo & rubigo,*) has always been looked upon as very dangerous. The holy fcriptures fpeak of it as an effect of the wrath of God. Pliny reckons it more hurtful than hail; and therefore it was, fays he, that Numa Pompilius inftituted feftivals, called *Rubigalia Fefta*, to avert the effects of it. They were celebrated in the month of April, becaufe this diftemper ufually begun in that month. The nature of it is not yet well underftood. It generally begins when, in hot weather, there has fallen a plentiful dew, which was fuppofed to break the veffels of the leaves and ftems of plants, from whence iffued a thick extravafated juice, which being dried by the fun, was turned into a red powder which adhered to the plants, and did them great injury; for they foon after appeared gangrened, if we may apply this word to plants. Count Francefco Ginnani, in his work intituled *Delle Mallatie del Grano in Herba, C. 5. Part. II.* attributes this diftemper in vegetables, not to the extravafation of their juices, but to the hatching of the eggs of infects. He has feen them, he fays, between the outward and the inward covering of the leaves. Plenciz, in the work before-mentioned, quotes the microfcopical difcoveries of Needham, the Obfervations of Mercurialis, and the Acta Eruditorum of Leipzick for the year 1718, in order to demonftrate that what is properly called *the Ruft*, depends on

* Several other fatal effects which arife to men and beafts from their feeding on diftempered corn, or diftempered grafs, are frequently noticed in Mills's *Syftem of Hufbandry*. The above fact in particular is related in Vol. II. p. 407. of that work, with the addition of fome farther obfervations thereon made by our illuftrious Royal Society.

the

the eggs of certain vermin, which, being laid on vegetables, penetrate the outer ſkin, hatch, and afterwards multiply there. Calm and temperate weather, rather warm, and in which there are dripping rains without a cloudy ſky, favours their production. This, ſays he, is what was experienced in Auſtria in the year 1751, and what was obſerved on the 31ſt of March and 30th of June 1759, on both which days it did not ceaſe to rain, though the ſky was clear. In the former of theſe caſes, almoſt all the vegetables in the country were covered with ruſt; and in 1759 the wheat was greatly damaged by it. This opinion of the cauſe of this diſtemper is adopted by M. Tillet, by Loewenhoeck in his 109th letter to Van Leeween, and by M. Duhamel. Whatever be the caſe as to this opinion, all agree that damaged or corrupted food muſt be as hurtful to other animals as to men. Clover, ſainfoin, and lucerne are certainly wholeſome plants; but let them be attacked with this diſtemper, they become as hurtful as the crow-foot (ranunculus,) tithymal (ſpurge,) or hellebore; and theſe too, dangerous in themſelves, become more ſo when thus affected. This ruſt, ſays Ramazzini in his Obſervations on the Epidemic Diſtemper at Modena, ſeems as corroſive as ſpirit of nitre. The paſtures corrupted by it were ſo fatal to cattle, that whole herds were carried off. In 1693, the graſs was infected by it in Heſſe, and accordingly, ſays Bernard Valentine, the cattle died there by whole droves. The ſame happened in Carniola in 1712, and in the Ferrareſe in 1715; and the ſame conſequences enſued. Rye which has the ſpur is not only fatal to men, but occaſions internal and external ulcers in hogs and geeſe.

In the months of July and Auguſt, 1756, there was a mortality among the cattle in Minorca, which having been tranſported thither, could not bear the

the heat of the climate, as was mentioned before. The herdsmen who attended them fell sick; but the disease was much more severe in those who had been so imprudent as to eat of the flesh of the sick cattle; for all of them was seized with a malignant fever, accompanied with a gangrene which shewed itself on the second day, especially at the elbow and heel.

The rust is to grass, what a corrupted state is to flesh: If flesh in this state occasions fevers amongst men, why should not vitiated plants have a similar effect on cattle? Independent of this, there are plants which are in themselves prejudicial to cattle. We see them frequently die in marshy ground, whilst those fed on the neighbouring heights are healthy. In our pastures, hurtful plants grow among the good, and the care of selecting the latter is left to the cattle. It is true that the Creator has indued them with an instinct to distinguish the hurtful from the good; but the former often grow so close to the latter, that it is almost impossible for them to crop the one without eating of the other. We see the crow-foot growing every where: All the species of it contain an acrid juice, especially the parsley-leafed marsh crowfoot, *ranunculus palustris apii folio*, otherwise called *herba scelerata*, a name which sufficiently indicates its noxious quality. This grows by the sides of rivers, and is indeed not so often met with as the acrid upright meadow crowfoot, *ranunculus pratensis erectus acris foliis*, and the creeping hairy meadow crowfoot, *ranunculus pratensis repens hirsutus*, which are very common in our meadows, and though less dangerous to cattle, yet are injurious to such as eat them. The *ptarmica vulgaris, dracunculis pratensis*, which some likewise call the sneezing-plant, is not less common nor less acrid than the *ranunculus*. We also find in them the spurge (*tithymalus*,)

a very

a very acrid plant, and the ſmall kind of hemlock, which ought to be baniſhed from them. A careful obſerver will remark other plants perhaps equally prejudicial; and the huſbandman who ſuffers ſuch plants to grow in his paſtures is inexcuſable: for when one or two of the creatures fed on them become ſick, the diſeaſe ſoon communicates itſelf to many, already pre-diſpoſed, by the effects of their food, to receive the infection; and thus it is inſenſibly ſpread.

Water, which ſhould be accounted an aliment, may, by bad qualities communicated to it, contribute greatly to the production of epidemic diſeaſes; and ſtill more ſo, when aſſiſted by diſtempered or acrid food.

We read in the philoſophical Tranſactions, that, during the plague in London, there was collected from off the ſurface of water, expoſed in a veſſel to the air, a blue pellicle, which having been mixed with bread, and given to a dog, killed him in twenty-four hours. But without being infected by theſe peſtilential particles which drop upon it from the atmoſphere in a peſtilential conſtitution of the air, the water may be charged with other ſubſtances pernicious to animals, taken up whilſt paſſing through mines of lead, copper, &c. It ſometimes carries with it gypſous matters and ſelenites, which may form concretes or obſtructions, and cauſe many diſeaſes. The waters in Minorca are of this kind: having too ſhort a run to drop the earthy particles with which they are loaded, they conſtantly form ſtrong concretions adhering to the ſides of the veſſels in which they are contained. Standing, heavy, ſlimy water, loaded with many inſects and their eggs, as well as with many particles from the animals and vegetables which die and rot in them, is the cauſe of many diſeaſes to cattle which are often obliged to drink of it. Water is both

the

the moſt univerſal diſſolvent, and the apteſt vehicle for carrying noxious particles into the blood.

Standing putrid water is not more pernicious by reaſon of its viſcidity, than it perhaps is on account of vaſt numbers of ſmall worms which are ſwallowed along with it, and live and grow in the ſtomachs of cattle; as do alſo their young brood. Theſe by their motion irritate, and by pricking inflame the ſtomach and inteſtines, from whence proceed ſpaſms and convulſions, ſomewhat ſimilar to what ariſes from the uſe of acrid or diſtempered food: for theſe too irritate the ſtomach and inteſtines; and the ill effect that will follow is an acceleration of the periſtaltic motion of the inteſtines; whence more frequent diſcharges, and even bloody flux. The acrimony, being ſometimes ſo ſtrong as to erode the coats of the ſtomach and inteſtines, occaſions inflammations and intolerable pain, convulſions, &c. and the inſpection of the dead bodies ſhews us, that in contagious diſeaſes, the ſtomach has been inflamed, and that the internal coats, by the livid ſpots in them, which are ſometimes continued down the whole length of the inteſtines, had a tendency to a mortification or gangrene.

Of the Cure of the contagious Diſeaſes of Cattle.

IT has been already ſaid, that the conſtitution of the air is one of the general cauſes of contagious diſeaſes among cattle. M. Le Clerc, treating of the epidemic diſeaſes which deſolated Ruſſia, lays down the following rules for judging of the nature of contagious diſeaſes, and of the method by which they may moſt probably be cured. "An unexpected diſtemper," ſays he, ſuppoſing the caſe, "breaks out at once with alarming "ſymptoms and terrible effects, and communi-

"cates

"cates itſelf from creature to creature. The ef-
"fects of this diſtemper, howſoever complicated
"they may be, teach me the time, the order, and
"the means of correcting an evil ariſing from a
"cauſe unknown. Nature alſo ſhews me, by the
"criſis ſhe brings on, the manner in which the diſ-
"order ſhould be expelled. Moreover, I attentive-
"ly conſider the qualities of the air we breathe, the
"ſituation of the place, the qualities of the ſoil, the
"kind of life which the inhabitants lead, the diſor-
"ders which at the ſame time affect cattle or
"plants, the neighbourhood of mines, marſhes,
"ſtanding water; and if I do not trace the cauſe in
"any of theſe, I look back, and ſearch for it in
"things already paſt. I reflect on the ſeaſons an-
"terior to the diſorders: I examine the time, the
"courſe, the duration, the anticipation, the chan-
"ges, the temperature, and finally the mixt or
"extraordinary qualities of the ſeaſons, and the
"winds which have been moſt frequent during that
"time. I then reflect on the nature of the diſeaſes
"which theſe variations have given riſe to; nor do
"I loſe ſight of the changes theſe diſeaſes have un-
"dergone. If in my reſearches I at length find
"one or more cauſes capable of producing the diſ-
"order which I was unacquainted with, I compare
"the effects of the diſtemper with the power of the
"cauſe, and then draw my concluſion from their
"reſemblance, or analogy. Have ſoutherly winds
"reigned long? I anſwer, that theſe winds are na-
"turally peſtilential: they may therefore produce
"peſtilential fevers. Do the mixed or extraordina-
"ry qualities of the ſeaſons, their heat and moiſture
"united, occaſion the diſtemper? The effects, be-
"ing truly diſcovered, make known the ſtate of the
"fluids and ſolids during and even after, ſuch a
"conſtitution of the air. The diſorder being known,
"(as far as our limited knowledge can reach) I
"form my indication of cure. I guard the infected

"body against the effect of the present venom, by "giving of choice, such medicines as have been "employed with the greatest success in such diseases "as have been particularly marked by similar ef-"fects. These are the means of coming at the "knowledge of venom; a knowledge which is not "otherwise sufficiently manifested to our senses. "Does the intemperature of a season give me room "to think that it is the efficient cause of any disor-"der? I have immediate recourse to the hydro-"scope and engyscope. The first informs of the "real state of the air; the second gives me an in-"sight into the nature of the particular salts then "diffused in the atmosphere (*a*). I then expose to "the air every substance which the salts of the air "can alter, as silks died of such particular colours "as are tarnished by the nitrous or sulpherous acid, "and are turned black by the vitriolic acid. I "moreover observe the alterations which the va-"pours of dew have produced on white linen be-"fore it has been washed with ley or soap."

In all the cattle which have died of contagious diseases, and have been opened, there have been evident marks of inflammation and putrefaction. These distempers may therefore be reduced to the putrid and the inflammatory kinds. Putrid diseases differ among themselves, as do likewise the inflammatory: but that difference consists only in the greater or less degree. The epidemic distemper of 1690 shewed itself with pustules. Whenever eruptions appear on the skin, it is a certain proof that the cutaneous vessels are obstructed with a matter that cannot circulate in so minute vessels, and therefore an inflammation arises. In almost every creature that was opened in 1693, there was found in the lungs a suppuration, which must have been preceded

(*a*) The curious may likewise consult on this subject, *Les Experiences Phys. de Poliniere*, Tom. II. p. 306, *& seq.*

ceded by an inflammation. The distemper which proved so fatal to the cattle in Lower Hungary in the year 1712, appeared with pustules which contained an extremely fœtid matter. The stench of that matter, and of the humour which flowed from the mouth and nose, proved that a putrefaction was joined to the inflammation in that disease. The author who has described the epidemical constitution at Augsburg, declares the distemper of the cattle was putrid and inflammatory. In the contagious distemper which prevailed in 1740 and the following years, the fever appeared to be inflammatory, malignant, and putrid. The contents of the first stomach were very putrid, and the air which proceeded from it was extremely fœtid; those of the second looked as if they had been dried: it's membranes were black, gangrened, and easily torn to pieces; as were also the membranes of the third stomach and of the intestines, which likewise contained sometimes purulent matter. Black spots and hydatides were observed on the liver, the lungs, and on the meninges of the brain. In the cattle which were opened in Minorca in 1756, traces of inflammation, terminating in mortification, were observed in almost all the bowels. The appearance of the sheep which died of the small-pox in the neighbourhood of Beauvais, likewise confirms that the disorder was highly inflammatory and putrid.

As it has constantly appeared upon opening the bodies of cattle which died of contagious distempers, that the diseases were either inflammatory or putrid, the method in which these disorders should be treated is hereby pointed out. When they are inflammatory, the first intention should be to cool the too-great heat of the blood, to lessen it's rarefaction, the velocity and force of it's motion, in order to take off or lessen the obstructions in the capillary vessels. These purposes are answered by plentiful bleedings, by so much the more necessary

 in

in cattle, as the action of their vessels is stronger than in men. The heat and strong action of the vessels soon dissipate the thinnest watery part of the blood, whence farther obstructions ensue; and hence it is that inflammatory diseases are most dangerous in the most healthy constitutions, and in the most robust animals. Evacuations become therefore the more necessary, lest suppurations or mortifications should be the consequence. Plenty of cooling and diluting liquors should be given at the same time.

If, on the contrary, signs of putrefaction appear, the first passages should be immediately cleared of whatever putrid substance they contain, or of any substances that may become so; for if they were to remain there, they would communicate their putrid taint to the blood. This end is obtained by glysters and purging medicines. The first passages being thus cleared, digestion is better performed, and room is made for antiseptic medicines, which may destroy the remaining infectious venom.

Comparative anatomy teaches us, that the structure of other animals differs but little from ours. The animal and vital functions are the same; the secretions are made in the same manner. Why then should not the same medicines be used in their disorders as are used in ours?

In case a contagious epidemic distemper amongst cattle is attended with a cutaneous eruption, it will be first of all necessary to examine what kind of eruption it is: for cutaneous eruptions proceed sometimes from the violence of the fever, from acrid and stimulating substances taken down into the stomach, or from medicines of too warm and cordial a nature. In this case, no good is to be expected from the eruption. But sometimes it is an effect of nature to relieve herself by throwing the peccant matter out upon the skin and in this case the eruption is favourable, and should be encouraged.

In

In the firſt caſe, the fever is high, the heat conſiderable, and all the ſigns of inflammation appear. Recourſe muſt therefore be immediately had to bleeding, and to cooling and diluting liquors, ſuch as water in which ſalt petre or ſal-prunel has been diſſolved; an ounce in about fifteen pounds (or pints) of water. In lieu of ſalt-petre, vinegar or ſpirit of vitriol may be mixed with water in quantity ſufficient to give it a grateful acidity. The food ſhould be light; ſuch as freſh graſs or other plants, and bran boiled in water. By theſe means the progreſs of the inflammation may be ſtopped, or a reſolution may be obtained of the veſſels already obſtructed.

In the latter caſe, the above method muſt be avoided: evacuations might ſtrike in the eruption, and thereby prove mortal. The eruption muſt, on the contrary, be encouraged, by giving an ounce of theriac to a bullock or a horſe. The eruption will likewiſe be kept up by giving them daily a ſpoonful of the flower of ſulphur with bran. Their drink ſhould be water in which ſea-ſalt has been diſſolved. That ſalt is a diuretic which helps to depurate the blood by urine. The depuration ſhould be aided by a ſeton made in the dew-lap of a bullock, by piercing it thro' with a biſtory, and drawing through the inciſion a rag of linen or a ſkein of thread, daubed with baſilicon. Care muſt be taken to draw the rag or ſkein through the wound daily, ſo as to leave a freſh piece of it in the inciſion, in order to keep it clean. If, notwithſtanding theſe means, the eruption does not keep out, the doſe of theriac muſt be repeated, and a decoction of ſarſaparilla and ſaſſafras, or of contrayerva, muſt be given for drink.

The contagious diſtemper which appeared in Heſſe in 1693 terminated in a pulmonary phthiſis, which might have been prevented, or rendered milder, by bleeding in the beginning, and by cooling and nitrous or acidulated drinks. If it could not be entirely prevented, it might have been very proper to have given to the ſick animals half an ounce of ſulphur, and the ſame quantity of cinnabar of antimony mixed with bran; at the ſame time rubbing them heartily and often, in order to determine to the pores of the ſkin the matter which would have produced an abſceſs in the lungs. When the ſmall-pox does not ſuppurate kindly, the diſeaſe often falls on the lungs; and by the rule of contraries, a cutaneous eruption, a determination of the humours towards the ſkin, often draws the humour from the lungs, as is frequently ſeen. An ulcer, an iſſue, make drains which often relieve the lungs. The phthiſis might therefore have been thus prevented, ſeeing it proceeded from the ſame cauſe which three years before brought on the ſmall-pox. This is making nature our guide.

The contagious diſtemper which reigned in France and over all Europe from 1740 to 1750, and which had appeared before in Hungary, Germany, and Italy in 1711 and 1712, ſhewed itſelf with evident ſymptoms of an inflammatory, malignant, putrid fever. As the throat, ſtomach, and inteſtines were greatly irritated by an extremely acrid humour, the firſt care, in ſuch a caſe, ſhould be to allay the acrimony by mild drinks which reſiſt putrefaction, and to prevent the inflammation it may cauſe, by bleeding. With this view, a glaſs of oil of olives, or of linſeed oil, with half as much vinegar, ſhould be given morning and evening in a pint of warm water. During the two firſt days, a decoction of ſorrel rendered gratefully acid with vinegar, or ſpirit of vitriol, ſhould be given, and for food only bran boiled in water, in order to give time to the ſtomachs to free themſelves of the food lodged in them, as was before obſerved; after which it will be right to give them an ounce of crocus metallorum in powder, or, which is yet better, the

the ounce of crocus may be infused for twenty-four hours in a quart of white wine, and the whole be given at once through a horn. A quart is the dose for horses, bullocks, and cows, and half a pint for sheep. The creatures which take this remedy should be kept all the day warm in a stable, and not be suffered to eat till the evening; the effect of this medicine being as much by the skin as by purging. The efficacy of this medicine has been often experienced; yet the violence of the distemper requires that we do not stop here. The seton before recommended is here of the greatest utility. If people in the country cannot procure the crocus metallorum, they may substitute in it's place two ounces of dry briony roots, or one ounce and a half of those of asarabacca. The crocus metallorum is however by much the best. In order to cause a freer discharge from the mouth and nose, powder of hellebore, or of horse-chesnut, may be blown up the nose, and the mouth may be washed with a mixture of vinegar and theriac: or if the nose is dry, it may be proper to throw up into it, with a syringe, some barley-water and honey; and if a stimulant is wanted, some flower of mustard may be added.

If, notwithstanding this treatment, the symptoms do not abate, recourse must be had to the Peruvian bark, half an ounce of which, mixed with two drams of sal-prunel and twenty grains of camphire, should be given night and morning. These medicines are powerful preservatives from putrefaction, especially the bark, the virtue of which in gangrenes is well known. Country people, who cannot afford the expence of these medicines, may substitute in their place half an ounce of gentian-root with half an ounce of kitchen soot, this abounding most in sal-ammoniac. The sal-prunel and camphire, may be added to them, because these medicines powerfully promote the secretions by the skin and kidnies. Instead of the theriacated vinegar, one

may

may uſe ſtrong vinegar, in which a handful of ſalt has been diſſolved, and a few heads of garlic bruiſed. It is proper to obſerve that, if the animal has not been bled in the beginning of the diſorder, bleeding ſhould not be attempted now; for it will do much hurt.

When hard tumours or buboes appear on the breaſt, or groin, as happened in the contagious diſtemper in Germany which ſucceeded to that in Hungary, cupping-glaſſes are thought to be of great uſe, to draw the humours the more to theſe parts. They ſhould alſo be ſcarrified, and brought to ſuppuration as ſoon as poſſible by applying warm ointments and poultices; and to determine the remaining peccant matter to the pores of the ſkin, half an ounce of ſoot ſhould be given daily in a glaſs of theriacated vinegar. A bubo in the glands about the throat and neck has often proved a happy criſis, and carried off peſtilential fevers. The theriacated vinegar conſiſts of two ounces of theriac diſſolved in a quart of common ſtrong vinegar. The ſtrongeſt is the beſt.

If a red bliſter, turning black at the bottom, is perceived on the tongue of an animal, ſuch as was obſerved in the years 1731 and 1765, that bliſter is much to be feared. It is a peſtilential puſtule which may carry the creature off in twenty-four hours; and therefore the cure muſt be very ſpeedy. The whole of this bliſter ſhould be immediately cut out and carefully ſeparated from the live fleſh. The ſkin and every part which appears black ſhould be taken away, and the wound be afterwards waſhed three times a day, at leaſt, with ſtrong vinegar in which ſome ſalt has been diſſolved; and this ſhould be continued till the wound is cicatriſed.

The Royal Society of Agriculture at Paris have publiſhed the following method, which was found ſucceſsful in the generality of Moulins, where it was tried on three hundred and thirty horned cattle, all of which were cured.

"The

"The first care was to administer preservatives to the sound cattle. To this end they were bled in the jugular, their mouths were washed frequently, acidulated nitrous drinks were given them, and their habitations were fumigated.

"The lotion was made of vinegar, pepper, salt, and assa-fœtida bruised. The whole was mixed together, and steeped, shaking it at different times. The tongue and all the parts of the mouth and jaws were then strongly rubbed with this liquor. Every part of the tongue was in an especial manner rubbed with a cloth wet in the liquor. Sometimes half an ounce of sal-ammoniac was added to this lotion.

"The drink was barley-water, with an ounce of salt-petre, and vinegar enough to render it gratefully acid.

"The fumigation consisted either of vinegar thrown upon live coals in the stable or cow-house; or of four handfuls of juniper-berries, two of worm-wood, two of elecampane-root, and two of leaves of sabine, with an ounce of myrrh; the whole powdered and burnt on a chafing-dish.

"Likewise, juniper-berries were steeped in vinegar, and a handful of them mixed with bran was given twice a day.

"In places where the contagion had been extremely violent, the drink prescribed consisted of two handfuls of rhue infused in a pint of red wine; to which were added a few cloves of garlic, some juniper-berries, and two drams of camphire. A hornful of this was given every morning to each creature fasting; and by the use of all these means, two hundred and twenty-five bullocks and cows were preserved from all taint, though several of them had communication with the sick animals.

"With regard to the treatment of these last, all bleeding was forbid; the fumigations were recommended; and as to the tumour which appeared on the

the tongue, it was thought better and ſurer to cut it entirely out with a biſtory or ſciſſars, than only to ſcrape and rub it. Scarifications were ordered to be made in the bottom and ſides of the ulcer, and the whole tongue was afterwards fomented five or ſix times a day with tincture of myrrh and aloes, or with ſpirit of wine in which ſal-ammoniac and camphire had been diſſolved, in the proportion of half an ounce of each to eight ounces of the ſpirit. A waſh of theriacated vinegar, with ſome camphire added to it, is likewiſe very proper in this caſe; and it will not be at all amiſs to make the creature ſwallow a ſpoonful or two of it every time it is uſed: for it cannot be thought that a diſtemper, of which the effects are ſo rapid and ſevere, that the tongue of the animals may be cut aſunder by it and drop off in leſs than twenty-four hours, can be ſufficiently treated by external remedies only. The following alexiteric medicines are therefore adviſed to be given inwardly.

" Take roots of contrayerva and elecampane of each three drams, a dry viper in powder, and one dram of camphire; mix them with a ſufficient quantity of the extract of juniper, make them into a ball, and give it to the animal.

" Or, take of the root of ſwallow-wort, of maſter-wort, of elecampane, and of angelica, of each half an ounce; boil them in two pounds (or pints) of vinegar of roſes till one third of it is evaporated. Strain off the liquor, and then add to it one ounce of orvietan: then divide it into two doſes, and give one of them in the morning faſting, and the other in the evening, taking care to cover the ſick creatures well whilſt they are taking the medicine. This done, there will be no need to fear returns of the diſorder, ſometimes by ſo much the more fatal, as it afterwards appears on other parts, and in a different form; as experience has ſhewn. It is moreover neceſſary that the diſeaſed be perfectly cured, that

both

both ſound and ſick be well curried, and that their mouths be examined ſeveral times a day to be aſſured of the ſituation the beaſt is in; for this gangrene does not ſhew itſelf by any other external ſign."

The ſmall-pox is, next to the plague, the moſt dangerous of all the contagious diſeaſes to which ſheep are liable. I ſhall here diſtinguiſh it only into the diſtinct and the confluent kinds. The diſtinct, or mild, ſtands very little in need of medicines: it may, and indeed ſhould, be left to nature. The confluent, on the other hand, requires the greateſt attention. Whatever the cauſe of this diſeaſe may be, we look upon the expulſion of the matter, and the ſuppuration and drying of the puſtules, as the natural progreſs of it. There muſt then be an eruption: but ſometimes the eruption is imperfect, comes on with difficulty, or is even ſuppreſſed; and at other times it is ſo great as to endanger the life of the animal. It therefore is plain that this diſeaſe ſhould not always be treated in the ſame manner; for ſometimes cordials may be requiſite in order to ſupport a too feeble eruption, and cooling medicines may be neceſſary to check a too-high inflammatory fever. If therefore, the fever appears high, blood muſt be taken from the jugular, and this muſt be repeated, becauſe not above two or three ounces can be got from the jugular of a ſheep at one time. This operation was found to give great relief to the ſheep before ſpoken of at Beauvais. It ſometimes leſſens the number of pimples; but thoſe which remain become larger, and ſuppurate more kindly. Two drams of ſalt-petre mixed with honey are given every day to each ſick animal, and for drink warm water rendered gratefully acid with vinegar or ſpirit of vitriol; nor ſhould the ſeton be forgotten here. If the pimples are of a violet or purple colour, they indicate a gangrene, or at leaſt a diſpoſition towards it. In this

caſe,

caſe, a dram of Peruvian bark, half a dram of ſal-prunel, and eight grains of camphire, mixed up with honey, ſhould be given two or three times a day. Some ſheep thus affected, and which had been given up as loſt, were recovered by the uſe of theſe medicines. They muſt be kept within-doors, eſpecially in the winter.

If the ſheep are weak, and the eruption feeble, not only bleeding ſhould be avoided, but ſuch medicines ſhould be given as will incline the matter to the pores of the ſkin; ſuch, for example, as a dram of vipers in powder in a decoction of contrayerva-root. A bliſter may be put on the neck after clearing it intirely of wool. This bliſter ſhould be made of cantharides and a little vinegar mixed with leaven. It is commonly left on for a long while, becauſe the flies do not eaſily affect the ſkin of ſheep. One might even uſe from time to time a decoction of the ſudorific woods; for the common drink of the ſheep in this condition ſhould be water in which ſea-ſalt has been diſſolved.

When the pimples appear again, the eruption is kept up by giving every day half an ounce of flower of brimſtone with as much laurel-berries in powder, mixed with bran. This ſhould be continued till the pimples begin to ſuppurate; after which the ſulphur and laurel-berries ſhould be ſuppreſſed, but their drink ſhould ſtill continue to be water rendered diuretic by the mixture of ſea-ſalt. The diſcharge from the noſe ſhould be encouraged, by waſhing the noſe with a decoction of tobacco and blowing up the noſtrils hellebore and betony in powder: for though a great diſcharge from the noſe is a bad ſymptom, as it always indicates much putrefaction; yet a free diſcharge from thence is beneficial, juſt as a plentiful ſpitting is to mankind.

As ſoon as the pimples become dry, it is highly proper to purge the ſheep with half an ounce of aſ-ſafœtida in powder mixed with bran, to prevent a

tranſlation

translation of matter on the eyes or breast, which otherwise happens frequently.

In a village called les Echerres, about three leagues from Lyons, one half of a flock of sheep was seized with the small-pox: the sound half was immediately separated from the infected; but though all communication between them was cut off, the disease broke out in some of those which had been deemed sound, and those infected ones were returned back to the sick. Endeavours were used to ward off the infection by properly fumigating the sheep-cotes, and clearing them of every ordure or other thing that could communicate or continue the infection.

Blisters were immediately applied to the inside of the thighs of most of the infected sheep; whether the small-pox was of the distinct or of the confluent kind; and in the others, instead of the blister, a seton was cut. The suppuration was soon established by the one and the other of these means, and the effects which they produced were sensibly advantageous. The former of these creatures were not left wholly to nature; but she was assisted when necessary by decoctions of juniper-berries, or by decoctions of saffron in the proportion of a quarter of an ounce to a pound of water: and these remedies were given through a horn. In the confluent kind, recourse was had to the Peruvian bark, which is known to prevent and even to cure gangrenes. It is a medicine which promotes a favourable suppuration. Half an ounce of roots of swallow-wort was boiled in a pound of water; and in the strained liquor was put a dram of Peruvian bark in powder; it was then boiled up again, and the sediment was given with a horn every morning and evening: by way of precaution, ten grains of salt of wormwood were added to each draught, in order to give the more activity to the bark.

Camphire

Camphire was tried on other ſheep which had the confluent ſmall-pox. Thirty grains of it were rubbed into the yolk of an egg, then mixed with a doſe of the foregoing decoction, and given with a horn morning and evening.

When the diſeaſe fell on the eyes, the following collyrium was uſed.

Take two handfuls of quince-leaves, two drams of rind of pomegranate, one dram of ſeeds of ſumach; infuſe them for ſome hours in a pound of warm water, then give it a ſlight boiling, filtre it, and, after having added to eight ounces of this decoction two grains of camphire and eight grains of ſaffron, foment the eyes of the creature with it.

Emollient glyſters were given occaſionally, and purges towards the cloſe of the diſeaſe. This practice was attended with ſo much ſucceſs, that out of twenty-two ſheep which were ſeized with the diſorder, only one died.

M. Haſtfer treats this diſeaſe in a manner very different from the above related. He attributes it to a too great quantity of humours, and preſcribes only dry, ſweating medicines, ſalt, lovage, rupatorium, ſome grains of civet, and all in a dry form: and, what is ſtill more, he forbids giving any drink to the ſheep whilſt they are ſick. This method may ſucceed in Sweden, a cold country, in which the perſpiration is but little, the plants more watery, and the blood more ſerous: but ſurely ſuch treatment would not anſwer in Languedoc, Provence, or any other warm climate, where the food is drier, and carries leſs moiſture into the blood. Regard ſhould always be had to the country and climate, in the treatment of every diſorder, whether epidemic or other. The ſituation of Naples, bordering on the ſea, in the neighbourhood of a vulcano, in a country which abounds with ſulphur; that of Rome, in a champain country, waſhed by a river whoſe waters having but little deſcent, move ſlowly, are very different

from

from that of Paris or Lyons, cities, more inland, and in a colder climate. This difference in ſituation and climate muſt occaſion a difference in the nature of diſeaſes, and conſequently ſhould do the ſame in the method of treating them.

It is not leſs neceſſary to know how to guard againſt the contagious diſtempers of cattle, than it is to be acquainted with their natures, and a ſucceſsful method of cure. To prevent a contagious diſtemper, the creatures expoſed to it muſt be preſerved from the influence of the cauſe, or the cauſe itſelf ſhould be corrected. When the contagion is the effect of the conſtitution of the atmoſphere, it is very difficult to preſerve animals from it's influence; for being continually expoſed to it's immediate contact, they breathe it, it enters with the food into the ſtomach and inteſtines, it penetrates into the ſubſtance of the lungs, and in each of theſe places it communicates it's noxious quality. It has, however, been found by experiment, that the conſtitution of the air may be changed for the better. We are told of what advantage the fires which Hippocrates ordered to be made were in the plague. Levinus Lemnius (*Lib. II. de occult. Nat. Mirac. cap.* 10.) ſays, that the garriſon of Tournai kept the plague off from that city by firing ſo many cannons, and burning ſo much gun-powder, that the air was totally changed thereby, and the city preſerved from that dreadful ſcourge. In fact, nothing is fitter to correct the bad qualities of a putrid air, than that excellent antiſeptic, the ſulphurous and nitrous acid ſet at liberty by the deflagration of gun-powder. It would therefore be adviſeable to burn ſulphur and nitre in the buildings where the animals are lodged, or to cauſe vinegar to be boiled in them till it is totally evaporated. Juniper-berries, myrrh, olibanum, aſſa-fœtida, may alſo be burnt in them; but theſe laſt fumigations ſhould be uſed only in the winter, nor are they at any time ſo efficacious as the acids.

acids. The habitations of the cattle ſhould be kept as clean as poſſible, their walls ſhould be white waſhed, or waſhed with vinegar, the litter in them ſhould be frequently renewed, their doors or windows on the north-ſide ſhould be opened, and thoſe on the ſide from whence the infectious air proceeds, ſhould be kept ſhut, as adviſed by Varro.

The bad effects of air may alſo be prevented as follows. If the conſtitution of the air tends to produce inflammatory diſeaſes, it is proper to bleed the creatures expoſed to it, to give them from time to time acidulated drinks, to prevent their being expoſed to great heats, not to put them to hard labour, to take care that they do not paſs ſuddenly from a hot to a cold place, and that they do not drink too-cold water when they are heated. If, on the contrary, the conſtitution tends to produce putrid diſeaſes, it would be proper to purge them with crocus metallorum, or aſſa-fœtida, or roots of briony, or with aſſarabacca, to give them acidulated antiſeptic drinks, and to rub them often, as well to free them from infectious particles which may adhere to the hair, and penetrate the ſkin, as to increaſe the perſpiration; for it is not to be conceived how many diſorders ariſe from a ſuppreſſion of perſpiration, and how ſalutary it is to keep the perſpiration clear.

When the contagious diſeaſes of animals ariſe from the bad quality of their food, it is certainly in our power, in a great meaſure, to prevent them. All plants prejudicial to the health of cattle ſhould be rooted out of every paſture; which is eaſily done with a ſpade, when the plants are in bloom; for if they are then cut through beneath the ſurface of the ground, and the clod is again replaced, the remaining root will periſh and thus the whole paſture may in time be cleared of them. Artificial graſſes may be ſown inſtead of the natural. The world is now acquainted with the benefits which ariſe from ſuch

graſſes

graſſes, both in regard to their quantity and their quality. Lucerne, ſainfoin, and clover, are known to be very wholeſome and very nouriſhing. As they grow to a pretty good height, the effects of a mildew or blight may be prevented in them, which cannot be done in plants that creep along the ſurface of the ground. Thus it is a common practice, when corn is mildewed, for two men, holding each of them the end of a rope, and being as far aſunder as the length of the rope will permit, to run along the fields of corn: the rope either ſhakes off the vermin which occaſion the blight, or makes the mildew fall off by the ſhaking of the corn, which afterwards recovers itſelf. If this method does not prove effectual when uſed on artificial graſſes, the owner ſhould not heſitate to cut down the paſture, burn what is infected, and endeavour to procure, a freſh healthy growth. At all events, cattle ſhould not be ſuffered to feed on infected graſs of any kind, nor even in the field where that graſs was, till a new growth has ariſen.

Cattle ſhould not be ſuffered to drink putrid ſtanding water, eſpecially in an infected ſeaſon: for, as was before obſerved, the water which was expoſed to the air during the plague of London, became covered with a blue pellicle, which mixed with bread and given to a dog, made the creature die mad. Such a pellicle may adhere to all ſtanding waters, and will be more or leſs dangerous, according as the air is more or leſs infected, and the water is more or leſs loaded with putrid ſubſtances.

As water is an indiſpenſibly neceſſary article of food, every bad quality in it is the more dangerous, and the means of correcting them are the more requiſite and valuable. In order to attain this deſirable end, a very ſimple eaſy method was tried before the laudable Society for the Encouragement of Arts, &c. at London, with the wiſhed-for ſucceſs. It was found that clay mixed in putrid water, to ſuch a degreee as to take off the tranſparence of the water, ſo that a hand held under it's ſurface could not be ſeen through it, ſoon ſettles to the bottom, if ſuffered to ſtand ſtill, and carries down with it all ſuch vegetable or animal putrid ſubſtances, as are mixed with the water. Theſe ſubſtances, kept aſunder, and buried as it were in the clay, ceaſe to putrify, and the water remains perfectly clear for a long time. It is almoſt needleſs to obſerve, that if there are any living inſects in the water, they ſhould be ſeparated from it, by running the water through ſomething which ſhall keep back thoſe inſects, or their brood, which may be too bulky to be carried down and buried in the clay. If the putrefaction be great before theſe means are uſed, a diſagreeable ſtench may ſtill attend the water, though it appear clear. The reverend Dr. Hales, that friend of mankind, has taught us to get rid of this by ventilating the water, that is, by forcing through it air, which carries off the remaining putrid taint. If any object to the trouble of preparing in this manner a ſufficiency of water for a whole herd of cattle; all the anſwer that ſuch deſerve is, that if they think the health of men and of beaſts not worth this trouble, it is in their power, they and their cattle, to crawl ſlowly, but certainly, to the grave. Even amongſt mankind, many of the uſual autumnal epidemic diſeaſes might be prevented by this eaſy method: for the bad water which is drank at that ſeaſon gives riſe to many diſorders in the bowels, as well as to fevers of various kinds.

If clay cannot be had, it is adviſeable to ſhake the water well, or have it toſſed about by oars, before it is given as drink. Thus it is that people on board of ſhip render their corrupted water leſs unhealthy by beating it; by which means the impurities in it fall to the bottom of the caſks. Mr. Boyle, having taken

taken ſome water which had gone a long voyage beat it frequently; by which means all it's impurities ſubſided, and it became perfectly pure and wholeſome. Where ſweet water is wanting, a well ſhould be dug *.

If a contagious diſeaſe has unhappily ſeized a herd or flock, every means poſſible ſhould be uſed to prevent it's ſpreading. The firſt care to be taken is, to cut off all communication between the ſound and the ſick. Cattle collect the graſs with their tongue before they bite it; by that means ſome of their ſaliva neceſſarily adheres to the graſs which remains, and if they are diſtempered, the graſs is of courſe infected; and other cattle which feed on it catch the contagion. Again, cattle are fond of licking one another; and as their tongues are rough, there ſticks to them a great deal of hair, which afterwards forms in their ſtomachs balls, called *egagropiles*, which incommode them much when they become of a conſiderable ſize: but this is not yet the greateſt evil. The perſpiration is vitiated in infected animals, and their hair falls off eaſily: the infection adhering to the hair thus licked off by a ſound animal, becomes an infection to this laſt, and thus it may be ſpread to many. The herds ſhould therefore be frequently viſited, in order that every creature of which there is the leaſt ſuſpicion may be ſeparated from the ſound, which laſt muſt no longer feed on the ſame paſture, nor drink of the ſame water with the former: even the cribs, trays, tubs, or any other thing made uſe of for the ſick, muſt not be brought near the ſound, at leaſt till they have been well waſhed with lime-water

 or

* The means of knowing where water lies under any ground, how accordingly to come at it, and how beſt to preſerve it in ponds, particularly for the uſe of cattle, are amply pointed out in Vol. III. p. 385—390. of *Mills's Syſtem of Huſbandry*.

or vinegar, and afterwards fumigated. The persons who attend the sick cattle should not approach the sound ones before they have washed themselves, and changed their garments, which, in this case, should be of flax or hemp, and not of woollen; because wool imbibes the contagion, retains it, and readily communicates it.

On the above principle it was that Lancisi proposed to a congregation of Cardinals, during the afore-mentioned plague which made such havock in Italy, to kill not only all the cattle that were manifestly infected, but even all those that there was but the least room to suspect of being infected. This advice was rejected after a long debate, and it was too soon experienced how much wiser and more prudent it would have been to follow it. A proof of this soon resulted from the town of Capravola. Five bullocks there were suddenly seized with the distemper; and after immediate strict inquiry it was found, that a strange bullock had been introduced into the inclosure where all the cattle belonging to the town were kept. The infected bullocks were immediately killed, and the distemper ended there.

All those who took sufficient care to prevent the entrance of any infected creature into their lands, not only about Rome and the Ecclesiastical State, but also in the territories of other princes, preserved their cattle. Such was the effect of the vigilance of the Princes Pamphili and Borghese, that, though at the very gates of Rome, and in the province the most infected, all their cattle escaped unhurt. The same care preserved the fields of Corneto, of the Patrimony of St. Peter, of Umbria, of Picenum, of the Flaminian province, of Tuscany, and of Modena: and it is likewise by the same means that the convents of nuns are generally preserved from the plague, when it unhappily attacks mankind (*a*).

(*a*) See *Lancisi Opera, Tom. II. Gen.* 1713. *Dissert. Hist. de Bovillâ peste.*

By

By a ſimilar care the Temple was preſerved from the plague, when it made ſuch havock in London, in 1666.

Too much care cannot be taken that the bodies of creatures which have died of contagious diſeaſes be buried deep, eſpecially in warm and moiſt countries; not only to prevent carnivorous animals from being infected, which may ſoon ſpread the contagion, but alſo to avoid increaſing the putrid exhalations with which the air is already too much loaded. They were very near being fatal to the French in Minorca. That iſland being a rock covered with very little earth, it was not poſſible to bury the bullocks which died; they were thrown into the harbour, with heavy weights tied to them: but notwithſtanding this precaution, the bodies ſoon roſe up and floated on the ſurface of the water, which is conſtantly the caſe as ſoon as an incipient putrefaction ſets the fixed air in the animals at liberty, and the bodies become ſpecifically lighter than the water. Theſe bullocks infected the air of the port with a horrible ſtench, which rendered ſick many of the ſeamen who remained on board of the ſhips; and though the carcaſes were towed out into the open ſea, yet as the current brought them frequently back, it was found that the only ſafe way was to burn them.

Reflecting men obſerved, with much concern, that, during the contagious diſtemper which prevailed from 1740 to 1750, the country people, in France in particular, took very little care to prevent the ſpreading of the contagion. They ſkinned their dead cattle, and kept the ſkins; an œconomy fatal to the ſurviving cattle, and ruinous to their owners. None ſhould be permitted to keep ſuch ſkins, unleſs they are immediately put into lime-water, and ſteeped in it for ſome time.

The

The dung of diseased cattle does not require less attention, because the infection is quickly communicated by it when it is left exposed to the air. Every particle belonging to infected creatures should therefore be immediately burnt, or buried very deep.

When one is obliged to make use of a building in which creatures infected had formerly been, too much care cannot be taken to clean the floor, walls, roof, and every other thing belonging to it, and also to sweeten the air: for it has been observed, that healthy creatures have been seized with contagious diseases by being put into buildings in which infected animals had been, even though those buildings had not been used for a considerable time. Trincavel relates (*Lib. III. Consil.* 17.) that ropes, which had been made use of to carry out dead bodies in time of a plague, being taken out of a trunk in which they had lain twenty years, by a servant, he and ten thousand more died of the plague. Sennert (*Tom. II. p.* 159.) mentions a plague at Breslau, which was communicated in 1553, by linen that had been locked up ever since 1542. Since then the contagious virus will remain so long dormant, and yet retain all its strength, too much care surely cannot be taken to purify the buildings into which cattle are to be put. It is not enough to clean them and keep the doors and windows open: every part of them should be well washed with lime-water or vinegar, fumigations should be burnt in them, and vinegar, or spirit of nitre, should be boiled in them till totally evaporated.

By strictly attending to the above precautions, we may hope to prevent many contagious distempers, to hinder their spreading, and even to cure, by means of the few medicines here mentioned, considerable numbers of infected cattle.

Additional

Additional Observations on the Diseases of Cattle, and on their Cures; by the Royal Society of Agriculture at Paris.

TOWARDS the end of the year 1762, a formidable disease attacked the cattle in the parish of Mezieux in the province of Dauphiny. The bullocks and cows were chiefly affected by it: but few horses or mules felt it.

During the first twenty-four hours the following symptoms appeared. A refusal of all kinds of food whether solid or even liquid, a heaviness of the head, hanging of the ears, watery eyes, rough and dull-looking hair, a costiveness not to be got the better of, a painful swelling about the lower jaw and along the neck, a pulse rather dull than frequent, a discharge of a frothy humour from the mouth and nose of some. These symptoms continued for two, three, or four days, at the end of which a great beating in the loins, and the feebleness of the sick creature, foretold a speedy and inevitable death.

The farriers and country people bled them in the ears, gave them cordials, and administered drinks with a view to purging, but which contained nothing capable of producing that effect. At length, the progress and ravages made by the disease determined the unhappy husbandman, on the point of being ruined, to apply elsewhere for the help of which he felt how much he stood in need. More intelligent persons sought in the dead bodies of the animals, that which the ignorant and uninformed could not discover in them. A beginning putrefaction shewed itself, by livid spots, in the hind part of the mouth, in all the muscles of the pharynx and larynx (the gullet and windpipe) in the cellular membrane which surrounds them, in the whole passage of the æsophagus, and in the trachea arteria.

In

In ſome bodies the cawl was affected, in others ſome of the inteſtines. In theſe laſt the ſpleen was greatly ſwelled; in the former, neither the liver nor the lungs were in a natural ſtate, and in all, the digeſtion was depraved, as it uſually is in all dangerous diſeaſes; for the paunch was filled with the food they had taken down before the diſorder had openly appeared in them. The red, and ſometimes brown or even black colour, the ſwelling, the ſoft conſiſtence of the parts about the throat in the greateſt number of the dead, were the conſequences of a violent inflammation, not of the eriſipelas or phlegmon-boil kind, for theſe would have excited a greater degree of fever, and would have ſhewed themſelves with a more remarkable pain and hardneſs; but of a latent inflammation, and a ſwelling cauſed by the want of action in the parts, ſuch, in ſhort, as is found in malignant diſeaſes. A ſimilar diſorder happened at the ſame time in the town of Macon, where a gangrenous quinſey carried off rapidly a prodigious number of people. This ſwelling frequently extended itſelf to all the glands of the lower jaw and about the neck and cheſt, thereby forming conſiderable tumours on the outſide, which in many creatures came to ſuppuration either naturally or by the help of art. In ſome, the throat was not ſo dangerouſly affected; but tumours appeared in all parts of the body indiſcriminately. Theſe were not the leſs looked upon as critical depoſits, and accidents which attended a diſeaſe owing to the ſame cauſe, and of the ſame character. In effect, the ſame treatment, except ſo far as the different depoſits required a particular method of cure, preſerved the lives of fifty-three out of ſixty-two; whilſt out of forty-nine which were treated in the common way, not one eſcaped.

The ſummer had been very hot, and the drought very great. The only paſtures to which the cattle could be led were bordering on a pond full

full of muddy ſtanding putrid water. The place neareſt to this was a dry gravel heated by the ſcorching ſun, and conſequently a truly burning abode for the cattle, which were there moſt part of the day. Thus the exceſſive heat of the ſeaſon, the indifference of the paſture, and chiefly the bad qualities of the water, were the firſt cauſes of this diſeaſe: for all the juices being heated and rarefied, there was neceſſarily a great loſs of the moſt fluid and ſubtile parts of the blood, and the corrupted ſtate of their food gave the diſorder a putrid turn. The hind part of the mouth, the larynx and pharynx affording a continual paſſage to very hot air, and the mucus which ſhould naturally moiſten them being leſs, owing to the blood's being deprived of it, or to the excretory ducts being dried up, the whole became very ſuſceptible of inflammation. Add to this the bad qualities of their food, and we ſhall not wonder that the inflammation degenerated into a quinſey truly gangrenous.

What in all ſimilar fatal caſes ſhould be firſt attended to, became here the firſt object of our care. All communication was cut off between the ſound and the ſick: for the ſureſt way to avoid the plague is to fly from it. The cattle which had hitherto eſcaped were therefore taken out of the infected houſes, after having been ſtrongly rubbed with wiſps of ſtraw previouſly fumigated with thyme, roſemary, ſage, and other aromatic plants, on which a ſmall quantity of vinegar was caſt while they were burning. The buildings into which they were put were cleaned of whatever dung was in them, and fumigated with juniper and bay-berries bruiſed and ſteeped in wine-vinegar and burnt on live coals: others were fumigated with only the fumes of vinegar. The diſeaſed cattle were afterwards carefully confined within the limits in which the diſorder unhappily reigned; thereby to prevent its ſpreading. The ſame precautions that were taken with regard to the ſound cattle, were extended to all

in

in general, to the extent of the boundaries of the village: all were bled again in the jugular vein, and by means of that evacuation, by rendering all their drink lightly acidulated, by diminiſhing the quantity of their food, by not ſending them too ſoon to graſs, by not ſuffering them to remain too long in the heat, and not to be out at all in the night; and laſtly, by giving them ſweet water to drink, above three hundred bullocks and cows were entirely preſerved from this infection, which never went beyond the limits firſt ſet to it.

The ſound cattle being thus taken care of, the infected were treated as follow: The buildings were cleaned and fumigated with the ſame care as for the others; the neceſſity of renewing the air became indiſpenſible. The buildings were in general very injudiciouſly conſtructed, low and not airy. The conſtant reſpiration and perſpiration of the animals that were in them ſoon deprived the air of it's vivifying principle, and thoſe animal particles ſoon putrefied. From both theſe cauſes, the original tendency to putrefaction was much accelerated. Lofty buildings were therefore prepared for the ſick, and they were kept well aired by windows which admitted a conſtant ſupply of freſh air at the ſame time that they carried off the bad.

The inexpreſſible advantages ariſing to mankind from that attention which the reverend Dr. Hales excited to the preſerving of the air ſweet, eſpecially where there are ſick, or numbers aſſembled together, calls upon us in this place to pay him that tribute of praiſe which his unbounded beneficence deſerves. A window in each end of ſuch buildings, and as near to the roof as can be, is, in this caſe, very uſeful; becauſe the one admits freſh air, while the other diſcharges the noxious air; and this without cooling or altering the temperature of the air near the ſick.

Many

Many of thefe fick cattle were bled in the jugular; but that was only once, and in the very beginning of the diforder. Care was taken not to perform this operation after the figns of putrefaction had appeared. Water whitened with bran was their only nourifhment. An ounce of cryftal mineral was added to a pailful of this water for fome; and for others the water was acidulated with vinegar, which was preferred to every other acid. Cooling glyfters were not forgotten. Two of them were given daily to each of the fick animals. They were compofed of leaves of mallows, of pellitory of the wall, and of mercury, of each two handfuls, boiled in five pounds of common water to a confumption of one fourth. Two ounces of common honey, as much oil of olives, and one ounce of cryftal mineral were added to this when ftrained off.

Injections were alfo thrown up the mouth and nofe two or three times a day. Thefe were compofed of the leaves of plantain, briar, and agrimony, of each a handful, boiled half an hour in four pounds of common water, to which were added, when ftrained off, two drams of fal ammoniac; and fometimes in place of this falt, two ounces of oxymel fquills were mixed with this liquor. The liquor thrown by a large fyringe into the nofe, defcended into the back part of the mouth, and moiftened and wafhed all it's parts. It was the more neceffary that thefe parts fhould be well cleaned, becaufe they generally were the parts moft affected. The creatures were likewife from time to time made to fnuff up the volatile fpirit of fal ammoniac, and doubtlefs the volatile fumes penetrating into the live parts, ftimulated them, and excited in them a motion, by the help of which the difeafed parts exfoliated or caft off in white filaments.

The tumours which appeared externally were fuppurated as fpeedily as poffible. The ripening poultice

poultice or cataplasm used for this purpose was made of leaven with one third of basilicon. When this was thought insufficient, another was substituted in it's place, made with six bulbs of lilies roasted under the ashes of a wood fire, four ounces of white lily roots, and four handfuls of sorrel boiled in four pounds of common water, and afterwards bruised in a mortar. Two ounces of hog's lard, and a like quantity of common honey, old grease and basilicon were mixed with them; and lastly, according to the circumstances, half an ounce of galbanum dissolved in wine, and an equal quantity of gum ammoniac in powder, were added. As soon as a fluctuation was felt in these tumours, they were opened with a knife or caustic, but most frequently with the actual cautery, to excite a more plentiful suppuration by giving the greater stimulus to the vessels. If it was not possible to open all the tumours externally, one or two glysters were immediately injected, in order to prepare the way for a purging drench, lest the matter being absorbed into the blood, might add to the already too-putrid disposition of the blood. The purging potion was composed of an ounce of the leaves of senna infused for three hours in a pound of boiling water; and in this liquor, when strained off, an ounce of bruised succotrine aloes was infused all night over hot ashes, and given to the animal warm in the morning out of a horn. This was repeated as occasion required, till the symptoms disappeared: and then the creatures were gradually brought back to their usual wholesome food.

One of the diseases which made the greatest havock, was that which, in the year 1763, left scarcely any cattle alive in the district of Brouage in the Election of Marennes, in the Generality of Rochelle. The accurate account given of it by M. Nicolau, M. D. on the eleventh of September

1763,

1763, is ſo full of inſtruction, that it ought not to be omitted here.

"The pariſhes in which the diſtemper among the cattle exerts its greateſt fury, are ſituated on the borders of a low country, in extent about three leagues. It was formerly laid out in ſalt-pits; but the communication with the ſea has been ſince cut off, and the ſea now comes no farther than the town of Brouage. The whole remains in the uneven ſtate it was in when employed for making ſalt; and the hollows and riſings ſtill retain all the appellations then given them. Some of the hollows have been in time imperfectly filled up, and others remain in nearly their former ſtate. They are filled with water in rainy ſeaſons, eſpecially during the winter; and the water, not having any outlet, ſtagnates till the ſun and heat of the ſummer have evaporated it. The deepeſt, which ſeldom dry intirely, form ſo many pools full of aquatic plants, and, notwithſtanding that, are made to ſerve as watering places for the cattle. The whole forms a vaſt ſlimy marſhy meadow, in which are fed numbers of cattle intended for the butcher, and for the farmer's work. It is the loſs of theſe which has in part occaſioned the miſery of the inhabitants of that place.

"Theſe receptacles of mire ſpread far around foetid exhalations which infect the atmoſphere, and render the inhabitants ſubject to intermitting putrid malignant fevers towards the end of the ſummer. The diſagreeable ſmell is particularly felt at ſun riſe in good weather.

"During the ſpring and ſummer of this year, 1763, the rains have been almoſt inceſſant, and the weather conſtantly cool. In the greateſt heat, Reaumur's thermometer, in a room facing the north, did not exceed 18 or 19 degrees (from 64 to 68 of Fahrenheit's). On the 3d of July we had a ſtorm accompanied with hail of an uncommon ſize, which

which in many places destroyed every kind of crop, and did considerable damage to the buildings. Most of the large cattle which the disease has carried off were exposed to this storm, and felt all it's violence; but the sheep and swine, to whom the distemper proves equally fatal, were under shelter. Besides, the mortality had begun before.

"There was great plenty of grass, owing to the constant rains; but these have prevented it's being made into hay. Great part of it perished without being cut, or rotted after it was cut. The cattle were exposed night and day to the inclemency of the season. All the fruits both of the summer and the autumn have failed, and the trees are now [September the 11th] in bloom, as in the spring.

"The grasses which grew in this place did not appear to me to be unwholesome for cattle; and even if there were any such, the principal cause of the contagion ought not to be imputed to them, since the sheep which fed elsewhere, and some horses which lived on dry hay, are equally affected, as well as the swine which did not feed on it.

"The mortality spreads to the other domestic animals, without excepting even the poultry *, which perished in a hamlet of St. Symphorian. Yet, however epidemic the disorder is, there is room

* The Royal Society of Paris observe here, that the distemper of which the poultry died in the above-mention village, may perhaps not have been the same as that which killed the cattle, nor produced by the same causes; for that the mortality amongst fowls was pretty general every where, and seemed to have been the consequence of a great inflammation on the breast, like that which affected the dogs.

room to think it not contagious. Numbers of dogs died in ſeveral pariſhes, which had eaten of the fleſh of the diſeaſed cattle; but others which had not eaten of it died likewiſe, and ſome continued to eat daily of it without being incommoded.

" In the month of May laſt [viz. in 1763] ſome complaints appeared on the tongues of the horned cattle in a few contiguous pariſhes; but that was only a falſe alarm, for the complaints went off without doing any miſchief. In June, and in the beginning of July, the reigning diſtemper ſhewed itſelf among the ſheep, and has committed ſuch havock as not to leave one of them in ſome places; and in others, the few that do remain are abandoned by their ſhepherds and left to die, literally ſpeaking, like rotten ſheep, without any care being taken of them.

" The mortality among the horned cattle, horſes and other animals, has been fatal principally to two pariſhes ſince the end of July. It now ſpreads on all ſides, though with leſs havock in ſome places than in others.

" The firſt ſymptom obſerved in them as their abſtaining from food. I do not mean to ſay, that no other ſymptoms precede this; but the keepers of the herds, little experienced in, and as little attentive to, ſuch objects, do not diſtinguiſh them. This prelude awakens attention. The creatures are obſerved to be melancholy, to hang their heads, to have cold and drooping ears, rough hair without its uſual luſtre, loins fallen and beating, the belly hard and full, the whole body wreathed and ſeeming to be diſpoſed to make efforts to urine. The urine which they void is often as clear as water; it is ſeldom that any thing paſſes by ſtool, and chewing of the cud ceaſes in the horned cattle. In a few a few hours after, if no tumours appear on the ſurface of the body, they are ſeized with a ſhivering, their eyes become dull and watry, a tough ſnivel iſſues from the mouth and noſe, they lie down and die quietly, or are more or leſs convulſed. In this extremity they ſtretch their heads out frequently, pant for breath, fetch long ſighs, and ſometimes too they cough. Theſe ſymptoms often come on ſo rapidly, that the creature dies before they have been ſeen: many bullocks have dropt down dead under the yoke. The quicker the ſucceſſion of theſe ſymptoms is, the greater is the danger. A violent ſhivering is always fatal. When the ſymptoms come on more gradually, there commonly is no ſhivering, but if there be, the danger is in proportion to its violence and duration. It ſometimes happens that tumours appear indifferently in all parts of the ſurface of the body. They ſometimes remain fixed in the part where they firſt appeared; at other times they diſappear, to ſhew themſelves elſewhere; if they vaniſh intirely, the creature dies; if, on the contrary, they increaſe in number, and on the parts leaſt eſſential to life, whilſt the creature ſtill retains its ſtrength, there is room to hope for a recovery. Daily experience begins to prove, that the cure depends eſſentially on the character of theſe tumours as approaching the neareſt to a phlegmon, and on their good iſſue.

" The tumours are not of the inflammatory kind. They ſeem firſt of all to affect the muſcles. The part affected feels hard, without being much ſwelled. Soon after a humour inſinuates itſelf into the cellular membrane around, which relaxes the fibres ſteeped in it, enervates them, and raiſes a lump in the ſkin. If it is not immediately diſcharged by an opening, its ſtay produces

produces a gangrene which soon spreads farther, or if the humour falls on any of the bowels necessary to life, the creature dies before the gangrene has made much progress. These tumours are flabby, and yield only a thin reddish sanies. If a suppuration comes on, all does well; the creature recovers strength, and appetite to eat. If, on the contrary, there is only a thin discharge without suppuration, the cure goes on but slowly, the creature languishes and sinks, till by the falling off of all the gangrened sloughs, the wound appears well coloured, and the cattle themselves lick it with their tongues in order to heal it.

"The gangrene which succeeds this tumour is of a very particular kind. The cellular membrane and the flesh seem to be rather macerated than rotten. They look of a pale colour inclining to livid; and though their fibres seem disunited, they retain a pretty firm consistence: but the slough which casts off before the cure is black, fœtid, and quite mortified. If the tumours continue long in a lax flaccid state, there is great danger of the matter's being reassumed into the blood, and consequently of its falling the more violently on some other part. This happened to several creatures of different kinds. They died, either because the discharge was interrupted, or because it came out but imperfectly. The more sensible the diseased flesh is, the greater is the room to hope for a cure; and the more insensible it is, the greater is the danger.

"When the tumours from being flat, as they are at first, rise higher into a round circumscribed form, becoming at the same time more firm and elastic, it is a sure sign that nature is getting the better of the disease, by changing that thin discharge into a tumour of the inflammatory kind; which being in a convenient place, always ends

 well.

well, The weakneſs and faintneſs ſoon change for the better when theſe favourable ſigns appear. The flies of every kind, which, attracted by the ſmell of the ſickneſs, ſettle on diſeaſed creatures in greater numbers in proportion to their weakneſs and inability to ſhake them off, leave them likewiſe in proportion as their ſtrength returns. A livelineſs and deſire of eating ſucceed their former dull ſtate.

" The humour contained in theſe tumours, ſhews itſelf ſometimes from the very beginning to be of great acrimony, almoſt cauſtic. M. Drouhet, ſurgeon at Point l'Abbé, has obſerved that having opened one of theſe tumours on the inner and upper part of a thigh of a bullock, the humour diſcharged from it ſtripped off the hair in twenty-four hours, as if the part had been ſteeped in boiling water. The bare ſkin appeared very red and inflamed. The tumours which ſhew themſelves on the breaſt of a horſe are the moſt dangerous; and on the contrary thoſe which are formed in the part correſponding to that which is called the dew-lap in a bullock, are the leaſt dangerous. Thoſe which come in the muzzle, mouth, or fundament of any creature, prognoſticate the worſt of events. It is in this laſt caſe in particular, that the creature, either whilſt dying or when dead, bleeds at the mouth, or noſe, or fundament, and ſometimes at all of theſe together.

" One of the ſymptoms moſt commonly met with on the opening of the dead bodies, is a want of digeſtion. The whole inteſtinal canal is generally empty, while the ſtomachs are full, and as it were crammed with graſs which is more or leſs hard in the third ſtomach of animals which chew the cud. This happens though they have ceaſed to eat for ſeveral days before their death; and even when a

ſudden

ſudden death takes them off before they have diſcontinued to eat.

"The blood taken from the ſick creatures coagulates readily, and is ſoon covered with a thick hard cruſt, of a whitiſh colour, a little inclining to yellow. Bleeding, when properly timed, has had ſenſibly good effects; but when done at an improper time, the conſequences have always been fatal. Moſt of the drenches hitherto given have ſeemed to haſten death, according to the report of thoſe who have made the greateſt uſe of them.

"Though the cauſes of epidemic diſeaſes are ſeldom known, yet I think we may impute the diſorder here ſpoken of to the too long continued moiſture of the air, owing to conſtant rains, fogs, and ſtorms, which have not ceaſed during the whole of this year [1763]. To this may be added, that the moiſture, which had penetrated deep into the earth, may, riſing again, have ſpread in the air uncommon exhalations, which may likewiſe have greatly affected the animal oeconomy. But as diſquiſitions of this kind lead little to the cure, I ſhall not dwell any longer on them.

"This epidemic diſeaſe has ſo great a reſemblance with what we call in man, a putrid malignant, purple and peſtilental fever, that I do not ſcruple to give it theſe names in other animals. So much is it of the ſame ſtamp, that I met with three men in the country, on whom the anthrax or true peſtilential bubo had appeared; probably owing to their being ſo much among the infected cattle. Though, for want of judicious obſervers among thoſe who watch over the brute creation, we have not a regular account of the firſt ſymptoms by which the approach of the diſeaſe might be determined; yet, from the ſymptoms abovementioned,

mentioned, there were evident ſigns of an inflammation in the beginning, as will appear to every intelligent reader, from the recapitulation of them here made. The violence of the fever, and the concomitant putrid diſpoſition of the air, and alſo of the infection communicated, ſoon brought on a putrid ſtate of all the fluids, as appears no leſs evidently from the ſymptoms already mentioned.

"During the courſe of my inquiries, I found but one peaſant who could give any account of the pulſe. This man, examining whether any tumour yet remained in a cow, put his hand between the upper part of the fore-leg and the breaſt, and felt a frequent and ſtrong pulſation of the artary, which anſwers to the axillary in men. The animal was then feeding; but it ſoon loſt all deſire to eat, was thereupon judged to be diſtempered, and died ſpeedily after.

"The pulſation of the arteries is eaſily felt in moſt cattle, and particularly that of the temporal, the axillary, and the crural. The carotid artery in a horſe is frequently perceivable by the eye, in that part where the neck joins to the breaſt; and the artery may likewiſe be felt in that part of the leg of a horſe which anſwers to the ankle in man; and the crural artery is eaſily felt in ſheep.

"The excellent Dr. Hales, who let no inquiry eſcape him which he thought might be of uſe, has given, in his Hæmoſtatics, the number of pulſations which the arteries of different animals make in a minute. He counted forty-two in a minute in a horſe full grown and at reſt; ſixty-five in a very young colt; fifty-five in a colt three years old; forty-eight in a horſe five years old, but a native of Limoges, and conſequently of a country where theſe animals are very backward; thirty-two in an old horſe; and fifty-five, ſixty, and even up to an hundred in a horſe whoſe crural artery was cut on purpoſe for inſtruction. The pulſe was more frequent as the horſe approached its end. In full grown mares he counted from thirty-four to thirty-ſix; which proves that the pulſe is leſs frequent in the females than in the males, in brutes *. The arteries of bullocks and cows beat nearly the ſame as thoſe of horſes and mares. In ſheep, they beat about ſixty times in a minute; in dogs, about ninety-ſeven times. It is, however, to be obſerved, that the pulſe is far from being uniformly the ſame in each ſpecies, nor even in the ſame animal, at all times; the frequency of pulſation frequently depending on many circumſtances, ſuch as reſt, food, as well as the degree of health. The frequency of the pulſe in the different ſpecies of animals may be ſaid to be in proportion to their ſize, ſloweſt in the largeſt animals, and quicker as they become leſs.

"In the beginning of the diſeaſes, the advice judiciouſly given by the Royal Veterinarian School at Lyons ſhould be allowed. Bleeding, a ſpare diet, acidulated and nitrous drinks, and emollient looſening glyſters, will be of great ſervice. Theſe means may mitigate the ſymptoms, check the progreſs of the diſorder, and thereby procure time to place proper remedies fit to prevent that feebleneſs and great degree of putrefaction which are ſo much to be feared. The uſe of the former medicines is therefore to be followed, by giving liquors which ſtimulate, and yet are not too acrid; and by adminiſtering cordials and ſuch medicines as prevent the gangrenous diſpoſition. Emetics and purgatives are, in this caſe, given to men; but the ſtructure of the ſtomachs of cattle render the uſe

* This obſervation may be true with regard to brutes, but we think it is otherwiſe in women.

of

of vomits impoſſible with them; and they are ſo hard to move by purgatives, that theſe become dangerous from their ſtimulating too much. Other animals, whoſe ſtomachs will admit of vomiting, ſuch as dogs and ſwine, have been cured with the help of vomits.

"The putrid and acrid quality of the humours which are contained in the tumours, requires their being opened as ſoon and as faſt as they appear, be they ever ſo many. The longer the opening is delayed, the more the humours are corrupted. It is likewiſe right to draw the humour to places the leaſt dangerous, by applying cauteries, or making ſetons in them, though there is not any humour in them. The parts ſhould at the ſame time, be ſtrengthened by fomentations, ſuch as a decoction of ſcordium, made in wine and ſharpened by the addition of ſea-ſalt, or ſal ammoniac. The wound ſhould be dreſſed with a ſuppurating medicine, covered over with ſome plant more or leſs acrid, according as it ſeems neceſſary to promote a greater flow of humours, or only favour the diſcharge of them. Louſewort, black hellebore, root of iris, &c. anſwer this purpoſe. When the wound becomes clear, it requires no other dreſſing than lint and a proper digeſtive or turpentine.

"By means of this eaſy and plain method, people, little accuſtomed to the care of cattle, have preſerved the lives of many; and it is to be lamented, that we have not in our country-places more expert farriers, capable of carrying on a regular method: for by that ſtill more might be ſaved.

"The cattle never appeared fatter nor in better condition than they are this year [1763]; and the diſeaſe has ſeemed chiefly to attack the fineſt and plumpeſt: no wonder that their owners are grieved to ſee them die."

M. Nicolau

M. Nicolau next gives an account of what was obferved in the dead bodies.

"On the 23d of Auguft 1763, a bullock died at about four o'clock in the afternoon, after having been flightly convulfed. His body was not fwelled, nor did the difeafe appear by any external mark. Being opened immediately after death, the flefh appeared found, without any offenfive fmell. After having cut the fternum and pleura, a fmall quantity of wind efcaped, not at all fœtid; and the mediaftinum, pleura, diaphragm, heart and lungs, were in their natural ftate. When thefe vifcera were removed, fome blood was fpilt, which was not coagulated, but in a diffolved ftate. The lungs had fome hydatides on their furface, filled with a thin ferum. Otherwife nothing extraordinary appeared either externally or internally. The tongue, mouth, and æfophagus appeared found. In the abdomen, the cawl was found. The fpleen had fome gangrenous fpots upon the part which touches the ftomach. The bile was thin, and of a fomewhat paler colour than is natural. The ftomach and inteftines having been torn, through the unfkilfulnefs of the farrier, it was not poffible to examine them with fufficient exactnefs. However, the abomafus appeared intirely fphacelated, and the villous membrane fell off fo eafily, that parts of it were mixed with the food, and others lay upon it.

"A cow was obferved to be fick on the 22d of Auguft, and in the evening of the 23d we were informed that fhe was dying. As we were going towards her, in order to examine her, fhe mounted very quickly upon a high heap of dung, where fhe fell, and died in violent convulfions at about feven in the evening, emitting a thick flimy matter from her mouth and nofe. We opened her at eight in the morning of the 24th. Her belly was fwelled, ſwelled, owing partly to her being big with young, and partly to wind contained in the peritoneum. No fœtid ſmell came from her, nor did any thing uncommon appear on the ſurface of her body.

The ſkin being cut off, the cellular membrane appeared ſound. The milk which iſſued from her udder was white, of a due conſiſtence, and clear. The head and breaſt were in their natural ſtate; but the blood, which flowed plentifully from the large veſſels, was in a diſſolved ſtate, no where coagulated. A ſmall quantity, of wind, not ſtinking, iſſued from the breaſt and belly. The ſtomachs were diſtended; and all of them were full of graſs, except the abomaſus, which contained a ſmall quantity of a muddy dark-coloured liquor. In general, the graſs contained in the other ſtomachs was not ſo dry nor ſo much chewed as in the bullock; yet it ſeemed ſufficiently ſo to render the digeſtion extremely difficult. All the ſtomachs were deprived of the wrinkled membrane which covers their inſide. This membrane lay upon the food, and was partly mixed with it. Alſo ſeveral parts of the coat of the third ſtomach were deſtroyed, looked black, and fell in rags on the leaſt touch. The inteſtines were quite empty and inflamed, as was alſo the meſentery. The inteſtines were likewiſe deprived of their inner villous coat, and in many places ſo ſphacelated, that they fell to pieces on the leaſt touch. Part of the cawl was in the ſame ſtate, whilſt the reſt of it appeared ſound. The bladder, the womb, the fœtus and its covering, and all the reſt of the fleſh looked well, and had no bad ſmell; and what is remarkable, the corrupted parts had not a very bad ſmell.

"On the 28th and 29th of Auguſt, a horſe was obſerved to be ſick. The firſt thing that appeared was a tumour on the left ſide of the breaſt, from whence

whence it ſoon extended over all the lower part of the neck. A farrier, in my preſence, deſtroyed the ſkin to the fleſh with a red-hot iron. The horſe ſhewed no ſign of feeling this operation; though he was at the ſame time ſenſible of the bites of flies in other parts of his body. There was no diſcharge from the wound, and he died at about five in the afternoon of the 31ſt. We opened him early the next morning. He ſtunk, and his belly was ſwelled. On the opening, a quantity of very ſtinking air iſſued out: all the bowels were in their natural ſtate, excepting ſome traces of inflammation. The ſtomach only was full of hay, though the creature had not eaten for three days before his death. The inteſtines were empty. The pericardium contained a great quantity of lymph a little bloody, in which the heart ſeemed drowned; its baſis was drenched, looſe, and as if macerated in it. All the fore-part of the neck from the breaſt to the jaw, that is to ſay, all the tumour, appeared under the ſkin to be only a maſs of fibres, ſome white, others livid, all macerated and drenched in a mucilaginous lymph, reſembling a diſcharge from the noſe, a little tinged with blood. The fleſh all around was likewiſe very moiſt and livid; but elſewhere it was ſound.

" A ſheep, yet warm, was found on the 2d of September. The ſkin between the legs, where it is not covered with wool, was ſpeckled with red and purple ſpots. There was under its throat, between the two branches of the lower jaw, a tumour bigger than one's fiſt; and, upon opening it, there iſſued out a great deal of tawny ſerum, with which all the cellular membrane around, under the ſkin and between the muſcles, was filled. It reached as far as the baſe of the brain, which was likewiſe ſteeped in it. There appeared no ſign of gangrene elſewhere. The reſt of the body was ſound, both within and without, excepting that the inteſtines were empty. The three laſt ſtomachs were not too full; but the omaſus, or firſt ſtomach, contained a great deal of graſs. The liver had in it ſome old ſchirruſes, which ſeemed not to have any relation with the diſeaſe of which the creature died. The gall-bladder was of its natural colour, as well as the bile. The ſpleen was ſwelled, and ſtuffed with black blood.

"On the 7th of September, we examined ſix dead ſheep. The five firſt had no other ſymptom on the external parts of their bodies, than purple ſpots on the places free from wool. The ſixth had many more; beſides which, it diſcharged blood from the noſe and fundament; which laſt was ſwelled all round. We opened this ſheep. The head and all the reſt of the body were ſound and free from inflammation. The firſt ſtomach, called *omaſus*, was diſtended, and ſtuffed with graſs; the ſecond ſtomach contained leſs of it in proportion; the third ſtomach had but little in it, and that ſomewhat hardened; the fourth contained a muddy liquor of a dark green colour; its coats were red, and its wrinkles a little gangrened. The inteſtines contained excrements, the cellular membrane around the anus was full of ſerum, and the veins were filled with clotted blood."

Dr. Nicolau's above-recited account of the diſtemper having been preſented to the Veterinarian School, this highly-uſeful ſociety gave accordingly their opinions thereon, to the following effect, and the Royal Society of Paris have publiſhed it, in order to afford every help in their power in ſo great a calamity, in caſe the like ſhould happen again.

In this conſultation, they agree with Dr. Nicolau as to the cauſes of the diſeaſe, and are of opinion, that it conſiſts in a perverſion of all the humours,

mours, and in a relaxation, inaction, and stupor of the solids.

"As to the tumours which appeared externally, they should, say they, with manifest reason, certainly be looked upon as a salutary crisis; especially when there yet remained strength enough in the solids, to throw the vitiated humours on the part where the obstruction had begun, and by that means so far free the rest of the mass of blood.

"Even the sound cattle in so unwholesome a country as the district of Brouage, above described, carry in them the seeds of the disorder, and therefore the first attention should be directed to their preservation. As to correcting the bad qualities of the air and water, enough has been already said on that head, as well as of purifying the places into which the sound cattle are to be put. Particular care should be taken that their food be wholesome; and if it be dear, it may be given in less quantity: for it is better that the cattle become lean, than that they die. Running water should be got for them, if possible: but if they drink standing water, vinegar should be mixed with it, or red-hot irons may be quenched in it. It should, if possible, be boiled; and the following preservative may be given them.

"Take two handfuls of juniper-berries, bruise them, and let them infuse twenty-four hours in a quart of wine-vinegar; give half a pint of this liquor morning and evening. Repeat this remedy once or twice a week, even to the animals which appear perfectly sound. As to those in which the least sign of sickness appears, give them the following medicine:

"Take Peruvian bark in powder, and filings of steel, of each two drams; one dram of sal ammoniac; mix them in half a pint of wine, or in the

the ſame quantity of a ſtrong decoction of juniper-berries in water, and give this with a horn every morning and evening for a week.

"In the cure of the diſeaſed, bleeding ſeems rather a thing to be avoided; for it inevitably increaſes the loſs of ſtrength, the inaction of the ſolids, and thereby haſtens the putrefaction of the fluids. As it is evident, by the opening of dead bodies, that the digeſtion is much vitiated, no ſolid food ſhould be given to the ſick animals: but diſſolve rock-alum in bran and water, in ſuch a quantity that the creature may take half an ounce of it in a day; and give, as ſoon as poſſible, the following medicine.

"Take gum ammoniac and aſſa-fœtida, of each half an ounce, rub them in a pint of vinegar till they are diſſolved; ſtrain the ſolution, if any dirt be mixed with the gums, and give it as warm as the creature can bear it for ſeveral days only once a day.

"In caſe the ſymptoms are ſo urgent, that there is not time to make the foregoing ſolution, give half a table ſpoonful of volatile ſpirit of ſal ammoniac, in half a pint of wine, or of infuſion of juniper-berries, and do this three times a day. If a ſweat breaks out, it ſhould be kept up with an ounce of theriac or orvietan, diſſolved in the ſame kind of vehicle. With this view the animal ſhould be covered, and towards the end of the criſis ſtrongly rubbed down.

"The critical tumours require the utmoſt attention. As ſoon as there is the leaſt appearance of them, every means ſhould be uſed to draw them outward. On thoſe which are hard at the bottom, and ſhew no diſpoſition to ſuppurate, cataplaſms the moſt capable of exciting the action of the ſolids, and of increaſing the inflammation in the part, ſhould be applied. Epiſpaſtic or bliſtering applications anſwer this purpoſe.

"Take

" Take half an ounce of cantharides, two drams of euphorbium, both in powder, mix them with half a pound of leaven, and vinegar enough to make them of the consistence of a cataplasm or poultice, which keep twelve hours on the swelled part, and repeat it, if the tumour is not in a state to be opened.

" As soon as the least fluctuation, or even a softness only, is felt, it should be opened, rather with the actual cautery than with a cutting instrument; and a knife made red-hot is better than a button cautery. The tumour must be laid open from one end to the other, and as deep as the seat of the matter. The wound may be dressed with digestive and unguentum Ægyptiacum, equal parts of weach; and at every dressing, that is, twice a day, the part must be washed with a mixture of one quart of common water, a pint of brandy, and two drams of sea-salt.

" The rotten parts being cast off, and the suppuration become kindly, the wound may be dressed with the common digestive, made of turpentine dissolved in the yolk of an egg, oil of St. John's-wort, and brandy.

" And finally, the bad symptoms being all gone, and the wound being nearly healed, it will be necessary to give some purging medicine, which must be repeated *pro re nata*. This may be done with safety."

The Royal Society of Agriculture at Paris have likewise given an account of a Peripneumony, which constantly attacks the horned cattle every year, in the latter end of autumn, and the beginning of the spring, in several parts of France, and particularly in the Franche-Comte. It is known there by the name of *Murie*; and the following is the account given of its symptoms.

A dry cough, which at first comes but seldom, but

but is afterwards much more frequent; a ſenſible degree of fever; an oppreſſion more or leſs troubleſome, which increaſes when the animal has eaten, and which ſometimes ceaſes, though this is very rare; a diſtaſte to food, which increaſes with the diſeaſe: creatures which chew the cud, ceaſe that chewing; but this ſign is equivocal, becauſe the ſame happens to them in all ſevere illneſſes. A ſtinking breath; a dryneſs of the noſe, mouth, and tongue; and ſometimes a diſcharge of matter by the noſe, different in its degree of thickneſs: but the three laſt of theſe ſymptoms do not always happen.

Thoſe which are obſerved in the dead bodies are, a lividneſs and ſtuffing of the lungs, an echimoſis on their ſurface, ſuppurated puſtules, gangrenous ſpots on the ſurface, as alſo gelatinous cruſts of different colours, which adhere ſlightly to it; purulent abſceſſes, the matter of which inſinuates itſelf into and waſtes the lobes of the lungs, ſometimes of one only, and at other times of both; an adheſion to the pleura, which is ſometimes thick, inflamed, ſuppurated, or gangrened; a conſiderable quantity of reddiſh, purulent, putrid, ſometimes frothy ſanious water is found in the breaſt.

A ſinking, a feebleneſs, a great difficulty of breathing, a continual cough, a redneſs of the eyes, a dryneſs of the tongue, a rattling in the throat, a ſtinking breath, are ſymptoms of an approaching death; as the being free from them affords hope of recovery.

The moſt common cauſes of this diſorder are, the changes in the atmoſphere from heat and drought to cold continued rains, to which the animals

mals are expofed ; or their being fuddenly turned out from warm houfes into wet cold air.

The cure muft begin with bleeding in the jugular, taking a confiderable quantity of blood, and repeating it on the fame day, as alfo on the fecond and third, if the difeafe runs high. When the blood does not coagulate, but remains fluid and without cohefion, it indicates that the lungs are then fo much ftuffed and obftructed, that only the thinneft parts of it can pafs to the heart, and that farther bleeding cannot be of fervice.

Emollient and refrefhing glyfters given and repeated two or three times a day for the firft five or fix days, have very good effects. No folid food fhould be given to the fick cattle, at leaft very little, or but juft enough to fupport them. The beft food that can be given them is wheaten flour, either mixed with warm water, or made into balls with honey, and given from time to time. Their drink fhould be bran and water, with honey diffolved in it ; or an infufion may be made of the flowers of corn-poppies and violets, of each two handfuls, in boiling barley-water, to which may be added three ounces of honey : this mixture fhould be added to the former.

Rolls or pellets put into the creature's mouth two or three times a day will have very good effects. They may be made of fix flat figs fliced and mafhed, with five ounces of common honey and conferve of rofes ; or of four ounces of fyrop of violets, the yolks of fix eggs, five ounces of rofe-water, and as much flour as to form pellets. Making the fick creature breathe from time to time the fumes of warm water in fuch manner that thofe fumes enter with the air into the lungs is found to give great relief.

When the cough is very hard, frequent, and greatly fatigues the animal, the following bolus may be given, besides the addition made to the common drink. Take spermacæti and liquorice in powder of each two grains, pillulæ de cynoglosso one dram, and mix them up with conserve of althæa into a bolus.

If the fever and oppression abate, the following bolus may be given in the morning fasting. Take agarick in powder, flowers of sulphur, Florentine iris in powder, of each two drams, and make it into a bolus with honey.

If the sinking and putridity, the natural consequences of a great inflammation, still continue, give the following bolus; viz. flowers of sulphur six drams, spermacæti two drams, powder of wood-lice, gum ammoniac, of each a dram and an half, myrrh one dram, white honey as much as is necessary to render them of a proper consistence to be made into two boluses, to be given at two different times. The Peruvian bark, camphire and honey may be used to advantage. To this end, take of Peruvian bark three drams, of camphire one dram, and of simple oxymel as much as shall be sufficient to make them into a bolus, to be given in the morning fasting, and in two hours after, one or two hornfuls of a strong decoction of juniper-berries, or of elecampane. In case there be a defluxion from the nose, the following drink may be given; viz. leaves of periwinkle, of lion's foot, of fluellin, of ground-ivy, of each a handful, which boil in common water till one third is evaporated, and to the strained liquor add four ounces of honey, to be given at two different times: and now the first bolus with the flowers of sulphur need be given only in the evening. This last drink is peculiarly useful in that malignant peripneumony which frequently spreads among cattle. This distemper is, however, not contagious, as some have thought it,

and

and is, ſo far as can be judged, that which affected the horſes, poultry, and dogs, in 1764, and again the horſes in particular in 1766.

The cure may be finiſhed by one or two purging glyſters made as follows. Take leaves of ſenna three ounces, pour upon them two pounds and a half of a boiling emollient decoction, let them infuſe for an hour, ſtrain off the liquor, and diſſolve in it three ounces of catholicon, for a glyſter: but this ſhould not be given till the dangerous ſymptoms have diſappeared, and a chewing of the cud ſhews a return of the ſtomach's being able to do its office in animals which chew the cud.

As the influence of the air is greater in this diſeaſe than in almoſt any other, the ſick creatures ſhould not be expoſed to cold or rain. The buildings in which they are kept ſhould be neither too warm nor too cold, but had better of theſe two exceed in coolneſs. The air ſhould be frequently renewed, and if the diſorder is epizonnic, the air ſhould be fumigated by throwing from time to time a ſmall quantity of vinegar upon live coals.

As to the means of preſerving cattle from it, the ſound ſhould be ſeparated from the ſick, and ſheltered as much as poſſible from the cauſes of the diſorder; a ſmall quantity of blood may be taken from them; they ſhould be kept covered, their common drink ſhould be bran and water boiled, and emollient glyſters may be given in caſe the leaſt tendency to the diſorder be perceived.

The Royal Society of Agriculture at Paris cloſe their obſervations on particular diſeaſes omitted by Dr. Barberet, author of the Memoir to which they adjudged their prize for the year 1765, and of which the greateſt part of the foregoing is an abſtract, with an account of the dyſentery, a diſeaſe which frequently attacks only particular

 horſes,

horſes, and which ſometimes becomes general and even contagious among them. In this laſt caſe, it is always malignant, is conſtantly attended with a fever, in the beginning light, but which afterwards becomes ſo high as frequently to be thought the principal diſeaſe. Its ſymptoms are, ſanious, purulent, bloody ſtools; griping, teneſmus, an enormous heat of the entrails, a falling out of the fundament, &c. together with all thoſe which indicate a fever attended with malignity. On opening the dead bodies, the inteſtines are generally found dry, or dilated with wind, containing a purulent matter, and always with ſigns of inflammation, ulcerated or gangrened: the ſpleen is inflamed and putrid, the rectum eſpecially is in the worſt ſtate of any of the bowels, and clots ſometimes of pure blood, ſometimes mixed with ſanies, are found in it.

If the ſick horſe is not too much ſunk with the diſorder, it is adviſeable to bleed him in the jugular. An ounce of oil of olives or of rape, mixed with half a glaſs of wine-vinegar and a glaſs of water, may be given morning and evening. The common drink ſhould be bran-water, with one third of a decoction of burnt hartſhorn: the food ſhould be only barley, oats, or rye, boiled. An ounce of diaſcordium mixed with bran-water acidulated with vinegar, may be given at times.

Glyſters will be peculiarly beneficial. To this end, take of wheat-bran four handfuls, leaves and flowers of mullein of each one handful, ſeeds of fenugreek and of flax of each half an ounce. The bran, leaves, and ſeeds, ſhould be boiled in five pounds of water to a diminution of one third. At the cloſe of the boiling, the flowers ſhould be added, and let ſtand to infuſe. Two candles ſhould be melted in the ſtrained liquor for a glyſter. In caſe the gripings are violent, a glyſter may be made

of

of the ſame decoction, with, inſtead of the candles, three ounces of ſyrop of diacodium, and half an ounce of ipecacuanha in powder. This glyſter has ſurpriſingly good effects. Towards the cloſe of the diſorder, the following deterſive glyſter may be given. Take leaves of millepertius and of periwincle, of each a handful; boil them in the ſame quantity of water as before directed, and to the ſame degree of diminution; and to the ſtrained liquor add two ounces of Venice turpentine diſſolved in the yolks of eggs, for a glyſter.

Nitre and camphire are frequently given with good ſucceſs. Take an ounce of nitre, diſſolve it in two pounds of decoction of ſorrel, and give it at twice with a horn: or, take nitre and camphire, of each two drams, and make them into a bolus with a ſufficient quantity of honey.

THE END.

POSTSCRIPT.

The learned and judicious PETER LAYARD, of Huntington, M. D. and F. R. S. whoſe reſidence in the country, joined to his univerſal humanity, neceſſarily afforded him frequent opportunities to remark the beginning and progreſs of the contagious Diſtemper which prevailed among the Horned-Cattle in this kingdom a few years ago, particularly from about the year 1765 to 1770; being then applied to by Government for his advice, gave the following as the reſult of many carefully repeated obſervations he had made on that melancholy occaſion *.

SYMPTOMS.

"THE firſt appearance of this infection is a decreaſe of appetite; a poking out of the neck, implying ſome difficulty of deglutition; a ſhaking of the head, as if the ears were tickled; a hanging down of the ears, and deafneſs; a dulneſs of the eyes; and a moving to and fro, in a conſtant uneaſineſs. All theſe ſigns except the laſt, increaſe till the fourth day: then enſue a ſtupidity and unwillingneſs to move, great debility, a total loſs of appetite, a running at the eyes and noſe, ſometimes ſickneſs and throwing up of bile, a huſky cough, and ſhivering. The fever which was continual the three firſt days, now riſes, and increaſes towards the evening: the pulſe is all along

* Theſe valuable Inſtructions were ſo *carefully miſlaid*, amongſt other papers relative to quite different ſubjects, that the moſt diligent ſearch for them, in every place but that where they were, proved ineffectual whilſt this Volume was printing. Accident brought them to light, after it was quite finiſhed at the Preſs; and it is hoped this will be admitted as an excuſe for the rather irregular manner of ſubjoining them here.

quick,

quick, contracted, and uneven. A constant diarrhæa, or scouring of fœtid green fæces, a stinking breath, a nauseous steam from the skin, infect the air in which the morbid creatures are placed. Their blood is very florid, hot, and frothy: their urine is high-coloured: the roof of the mouth and the barbs are ulcerated. Tumours, or boils, are to be felt under the fleshy membrane of the skin; and eruptions appear all along their limbs, and about their bags. If a new milch-cow is thus ill, her milk dries up gradually, her purging is more violent, and on the fourth day she is commonly dry. There is such sharpness in the dung of the diseased, that a visible irritation is observed during some time in their fundament. They groan much, are worse in the evening, and mostly when they lie down. These symptoms continue increasing till the seventh day, on which, generally, though sometimes protracted till the ninth, the crisis, or turn, takes place.

"Bulls and oxen are not so violently attacked as cows and calves; and of these, cows with calf, and weakly cow-calves, are in the greatest danger.

"If a cow with calf, at the critical time of this disease, slips her calf, she then takes her fodder, and recovers. Some may only give signs of such abortion, and bear their calf several days, nay even weeks, before they slip it, and yet recover. Calves receive the infection from the cow, by sucking her milk; and may also, if first seized, infect the cow.

"This disease takes place at all times and seasons: but in summer and autumn it will rage most. The fate of the beast is generally determined on the seventh day from the invasion; though it has been sometimes delayed till the ninth.

"If eruptions appear all over the skin, or boils as big as pigeons eggs in different parts of the body, but especially from the head to the tail, along each ſide of the back-bone, and ſo ripe as to diſcharge putrid and ſtinking matter; if large abſceſſes are formed in the horns, or in any part of the body; if the dung is become more conſiſtent and firm; if the urine is thick, and not quite ſo high coloured as before; if the beaſt has had a ſhivering ſucceeded by a general glow of heat, upon which the fever has abated, and the pulſe beats regularly; if the noſe be ſore or ſcabbed; if the eyes look bright and briſk, and if the beaſt pricks up its ears upon a perſon going into the hovel, and will eat a little hay or peas; theſe ſymptoms will determine that the creature is out of danger.

"But if, on the ſeventh day, the eruptions, or boils, are decreaſed in bulk, or have totally diſappeared without having broke or diſcharged outwardly; if the ſcouring continue almoſt conſtantly; if the breath be very hot, while the whole body, limbs, and horns are cold; if the groaning and difficulty of breathing are increaſed; if the running from the noſe and eyes is leſſened; if the eyes are dim, and ſunk into the head, with a perfect ſtupidity; if the urine is dark coloured, the pulſe intermitting, and a cadaverous ſmell is obſerved; we may aſſuredly pronounce the creature to be near its end.

"Ramazzini's emphyſema was met with.

"All the carcaſſes that were opened appeared extenuated by the ſcouring. Upon opening the ſkin much ſtinking air ruſhed out, and ſometimes a purulent and ſanious diſcharge. The veſſels of the brain were turgid, and filled with blood of a very red colour and looſe texture; the ventricles filled with water. The membranes of the noſe, the glands, the whole extent of the frontal ſinus, and the pith of the horns, were highly inflamed, ulcerated, and full of ſmall abſceſſes. There was the ſame appearance in the mouth and about the glands of the throat. The lungs were inflamed

with

with livid ſphacelated ſpots, here and there loaded with hydatides; and the cellular texture was frequently diſtended with air. The heart was large, flabby, and dark coloured, containing in its ventricles clots of black blood, of a very looſe texture, without ſerum; the fat about it was of a bright yellow. The liver was large: its blood and biliary veſſels were fully extended with dark fluid blood, and very deep-coloured bile: the ſubſtance of the liver was ſo rotten, as to ſeparate on the leaſt touch. The gall-bladder was ſtretched to a great ſize, and full of greeniſh bile. The æſophagus was ulcerated in ſome. The paunch was diſtended with air, flabby, and contained a large ſubſtance like a dried turf, conſiſting of fodder hardened to that degree. There were ſeveral appearances of gangrene on all the ſtomachs. The honeycomb had no fluid in it, but ſome pappy fodder. The manyfold contained between its plaits, a great deal of dried fodder, which clung to their ſides. The rennet-bag was empty, but highly inflamed, and gangrened in ſeveral places. All the inteſtines were empty, and were beſet with red and black ſpots. The kidneys and bladder were large, without urine. The kidneys were of a looſe texture, eaſily torn. The fleſh in ſome was livid, in others of a lively red; but it ſoon turned green. The fat that remained was of a bright yellow. In ſuch cows as were with calf, the uterus was gangrened in ſeveral places, and the water included in it ſtunk moſt intolerably. The virulence of the diſeaſe appeared to have ſometimes fixed itſelf on the vital part, and ſometimes on another, and frequently in more places than one.

To CURE.

"The beaſts ſhould be kept in well-aired houſes and be plentifully bled from two quarts to one, according to their age and ſtrength. They ſhould be waſhed with warm water and vinegar, to clear the

the ſkin from filth, and be frequently rubbed, which affords them much pleaſure, as well as benefit. A rowel ſhould be made as ſoon as poſſible in the dewlap, and it ſhould be kept open for ſome time after the cure. If the dung be hard a cooling purge ſhould be given, and plenty of anti-ſeptic drinks, ſuch as bran-water, vinegar, bitters, ſalt; but no hay till they chew the cud. The mouth, barbs, and noſtrils, ſhould be waſhed carefully and frequently. If a purging comes on by the fourth day, it ſhould be checked by warm medicines proper to throw the morbid matter off by the ſkin, ſuch as ſnake-weed, and other warm plants, or Venice-treacle, with which Mr. Montgomery * cured ſix beaſts out of ſeven. If the colour of the mouth becomes dark, the creature cold, the dung black and fœtid, and the diſcharge from the mouth and noſe ſanious, an ounce of Jeſuits-bark, or oak-bark, with ſnake-root, or other warm ingredients, ſhould be given every four hours, to prevent mortification. If matter is formed in the horns, or any other part of the body, an opening ſhould be made there, as alſo in the emphyſema, and digeſted by warm applications. If a purging does not come naturally after the criſis, the bowels ſhould be emptied with a ſmart purge, after which a draught of warm ale may be given at night. On recovery, the beaſts ſhould be gradually expoſed to cold air, and by degrees habituated to their uſual food."

* One of the Doctor's neighbours in the country.

INDEX.

A

C.

D.

E.

F.

G.

H.

I.

K.

L.

M.

N.

Nicolau,

O.

P.

Q.

R.

S.

T.

V.

W.

ERRATUM. *p.* 300. *l.* 1. for *bolding*, read *folding*.

www.ingramcontent.com/pod-product-compliance
Lightning Source LLC
Chambersburg PA
CBHW052336110726
47901CB00005B/1245
9783337330583